Love on the Sunny Side

Love on the Sunny Side

Confession: Book Two

COZY DUBOIS

For anyone who has been personally victimized by the big light.

Author's Note

WELCOME BACK TO THE *Confession* series! Again, unless we're related, in which case: Thanks for the support. but please put down the book!

If you have not yet read *Loving Lee*, I strongly recommend it. Many contemporary romance series feature interconnected stand-alones, where each couple has a book and past/future couples may make cameos but they can be read in any particular order. The *Confession* series is **not** like that. This is an interwoven romance series, so while Lee and Antonio found their Happy Ending together in Book One, that's not the end of their story. Likewise, Sunny, Tara, and Blanche started their character arcs in Lee's book, and while you can probably figure out the key points based on the context, the moments of growth in this book won't hit quite as hard without the full story.

The *Confession* series is the story of Lee and Antonio's chosen families as they come-of-age a little later in life (as many queer people do), growing together and falling in love along the way. A central theme of this series is that queer love is more than just who we love romantically—our relationships don't necessarily follow heteronormative milestones; our family ties are not always bonded through blood or law, and friendships are powerful influences in our lives. Trauma isn't cured through the power of ~~dick~~ love, and people don't remain in stasis while their bestie gets their heart broken. Character arcs don't wait for someone else's happy ending before they begin, nor do they end with an "I love you." Their journeys continue together as their family changes and grows, even after they've found their happily ever after.

This series is an ode to the queer community I love and the people in it. LGBTQ people of color are the heart and soul of what it means to be queer in America and have always driven our community forward. My goal as a writer is to put more books with happy endings for queer people out into the world, but my lived experience as a white, non-binary person is not reflected in this series. Through reading #ownvoices books, many conversations with trans and queer people of color from all backgrounds, and thoughtful reflection about my writing choices, I hope to have represented the spectrum of the LGBTQ+ identities included in the series with dignity, admiration, and respect.

As with Loving Lee, Sunny's book is *not* intended to be an authentic representation of what it is to be queer, trans and Asian-American—though the amazing sensitivity readers I worked with helped shape this into something that (hopefully) isn't horribly offensive and out of touch. I will never be the person who can write that story, so I encourage everyone to read works by LGBTQ+ Asian authors. For recommendations, check out my Bookshop.org storefront: bookshop.org/shop/cozy dubois (note: any and all affiliate earnings will be donated to the ACLU).

CONTENT ADVISORY

As a reminder for those who read *Loving Lee,* this series centers queer joy. That said, the characters in these books haven't had the easiest lives and deal with the lingering impacts of past trauma. Proceed with caution if the below may be uncomfortable. If you see anything that may be a dealbreaker for you, I have a more detailed explanation (with some spoilers) on my website http://cozydubois.com/.

- Transphobia, including deadnaming and trans erasure by unsupportive parents.

- Sexual content between people of all genders to varying intensity.

- Difficulties managing mental health, including depictions of panic attacks, dissociation, flashbacks, and substance use to cope with emotions.

- The main characters come in a wide range of body types and appearances. This book takes a body-neutral approach, however some characters have biases and insecurities.

- References to past traumatic events occur off-page but may be heavy for some readers, including trafficking, child abuse, addiction, self-harm, and assault.

Tuesday, December Thirty-First

Chapter One

Sunny

"I've outdone myself, yet again." Leaning closer to the mirror, Sunny brushed the finishing touch of bronzer over her contoured face. The wings of her eyeliner were not only sisters, they were twins, making her already stunning coal-brown eyes look even bigger. Mauve eyeshadow accentuated the warm undertones in her tan skin and the plum of her crushed velvet dress. "Innocent, yet sexy. I look incredible!"

Sunny dusted the leftover bronzer down the valley of her chest. Not that her tits needed to look bigger with the plunging neckline of her halter dress, but a little cleavage contour never hurt. She fluffed her long, wavy black hair once more, satisfied she was stunning enough to—

A knock pounded on the bathroom door. "Are you almost done in there? You're not the only one who needs to get ready tonight."

With a huff, Sunny opened the door. "Where are *you* going?"

Her little sister Luna pushed past her, sweeping Sunny's makeup aside and plopping her own bag down. She squinted up at Sunny. "Can you do my eyeliner too?"

"If you answer the question. Where are you going tonight?" Her sister was wearing a black sheath dress. Too cute for staying in. Luna was normally more of a Crocs and leggings girlie, even when she went out.

Luna scowled. "A friend's house."

"Is this friend your 'boy who's a friend but not your boyfriend'? The one in a frat?" Luna was younger by six years, and a freshman at the University of Bellamy. Sunny trusted her nerdy sister to make good decisions, but she had no idea who Luna's friends were anymore.

Luna's silence spoke volumes. Eventually, she asked, "You won't tell Mae, will you?"

"No. But be safe, watch your drink, and use protection—"

"Sunny! Stop!"

Sunny did not stop. "And if you want to leave, text me. Lee's boyfriend doesn't drink, so we have a sober person to pick you up. Or you can just come with me to begin with."

Luna rolled her eyes, but she still handed Sunny her eyeliner. "Sure, because hanging out with *you* on New Year's Eve sounds way funner than a party."

"Don't be a snot! Jazz will be there." Sunny angled her sister's face to flick the wing perfectly. "You'll have another little kid to talk to."

Luna shrugged. "Don't get me wrong, Jazz is great, but we're not besties like you and Lee. She's way cooler than me."

"That's because you're basic as hell, even if you are Miss Popular now," Sunny teased. "Stop talking, I don't want to stab you in the eye."

Luna fell silent, tilting her head the other way so Sunny could do her other eye.

"There, still a dork, but your eyes are cute." Sunny patted her cheek. Even if the rest of Luna's makeup looked like a child had done it, at least her eyeliner was perfect. "Maybe one day, you'll be as hot as me."

"Better a dork than delusional." Luna stuck her tongue out.

"I'll take that as a compliment!" Sunny winked and danced her way to the bedroom she shared with Luna, packing everything she'd need for staying overnight. If for some reason Lee wasn't cool with her crashing, she could stay at Blanche's to avoid riding the bus so late. She'd rather *not* sleep on her ex's couch, but their apartment was close to Lee and Antonio's. *Besides, we're still friends. Friends crash on each other's couches platonically.*

As Sunny laced her boots by the front door, her mother walked in, scrubs still on under her unzipped parka. Birdie's black hair, streaked with gray, was pulled into a low bun that poked out between her winter hat and scarf. "Sunny? What on Earth are you wearing?" Birdie pulled her scarf down and cocked her head, eyeing her up and down. "You're dressed like a hooker."

Sunny cheeks burned. "This dress is vintage! And sex work is a historically impactful profession that's been devalued by puritanical colonial morals."

"Does your bosom always hang out so much when you go out?"

"Mae!" Sunny protested, avoiding her mother's question because she wouldn't like the answer. "Why are you home, anyway? Aren't you supposed to be at work?"

On top of her day job as an X-ray tech at the hospital downtown, her mother picked up shifts at a small urgent care clinic in Eastside "for fun." On a busy holiday, there was no way Birdie would pass up the overtime.

"I came to get my badge for the clinic." Birdie plucked her work badge from the key hook on the wall, clipping it to her scrubs. "Where's Luna?"

"Getting ready in the bathroom."

"Is she going out?"

"Yes, she's going to Emma's." Emma was the only friend of Luna's that Birdie liked. Sunny highly doubted Luna's goody-two-shoes friend would be at this frat party, but Birdie wouldn't ask too many questions if Sunny dropped Emma's name. "Don't worry, she's dressed like a nice girl. No bosom in sight. Mostly because she'd need to grow one first."

"Hey!" came a shout from the bathroom. "At least mine are real!"

Sunny grinned and called back, "Silicone is real!"

"You two..." Birdie rubbed her forehead. "Did the Jones boy invite any nice single girls to his party?"

Sunny's grin fell. "Does Tara count as a nice single girl?"

Birdie scowled, giving Sunny the answer she expected. Her mother did not like Sunny's friends; they weren't "a good influence." Sunny strongly disagreed. She didn't have many friends, let alone ones who actually cared about her.

"It doesn't matter, Mae. I'm not going out to hit on the women who would meet your weirdly traditional standards. I'm just going to have fun with my friends."

"My standards are not weird or traditional. I simply want you to find a—"

"'—nice girl to marry who is preferably Thai but at least Buddhist.' Yes, Mae. I know. You'll get your grandbabies one day." Sunny stifled her eye roll as she bid her mother goodbye and closed the apartment door behind her, harder than she intended.

She wasn't opposed to the life her mother wanted for her. It just wasn't exactly what she envisioned for herself. Sunny did want a family, one day.

One where she could be herself—a woman, wife, and mother—not the dutiful son, husband, and father that Birdie needed her to be. But since a future spouse who would love her as her true self wasn't a guarantee, she'd settle for another year or two of being a hot twenty-something woman—free to get her heart broken and fool around—while she saved up for her vagina upgrade. After that was installed, she'd consider settling down.

Sunny ignored the tab that popped open in her brain, reminding her that her last attempt at having fun had been more heartbreaking than expected. In hindsight, letting herself catch feelings for her close friend and mentor may not have been the best idea. But they'd gotten through it, even if things were still awkward. Blanche and Sunny were trying, and that was everything.

Besides, it was New Year's Eve. Antonio was inviting his friends to the party—who he'd overemphasized were really great guys, while Lee had dropped hints that she wouldn't like them that much—so she'd have new people to practice flirting with.

"New Year, new me," Sunny muttered, pushing open the heavy glass door to the busy street outside. The icy winter wind stung her nostrils and eyes as she hurried to the bus stop.

This was going to be her year to have fun before facing her destiny, and she would make the most of it. And maybe in all her fun, she would find someone who met Birdie's exacting requirements *and* love Sunny for who she was.

Sunny slipped on a patch of ice, laughing as she wobbled in her boots. *Like that'll ever happen.*

RICHARD

RICHARD TURNED OFF THE engine of his Range Rover, tapping his fingers on the steering wheel. While he was right on time for Antonio's housewarming party, there'd be no end to the teasing if he arrived within the next fifteen minutes. Gabe's Outback was nowhere to be seen amidst the sedans and SUVs crammed into the building's parking lot, and he knew no one else who would be at the party. He'd asked Antonio several times who exactly would be coming, only to get an infuriating "Lee's friends" in response, which was no help. Not that Richard knew any of Lee's friends, but it would be nice to know what he was walking into.

Just as he'd settled back into the driver's seat to wait—if he had to be the first one there, he refused to go in right when the party started—Richard's phone rang.

"You can just come in," Antonio said before Richard could say hello. "I see your car."

"I was hoping you were about to say the party's canceled," Richard teased, looking up to see Antonio waving through a third-story window.

"No such luck, Dicky. You're socializing tonight, and there's no getting out of it."

With a reluctant sigh, Richard hung up and climbed out of the car to meet his fate. Every step up the stairwell echoed his dread, from the creak of the wood treads, muffled by the worn carpet, to the buzz emanating from the flickering sconces that were too dusty to provide adequate light.

Before he could knock, Antonio's apartment door swung open. Richard flinched as Antonio and Lee, in coordinating sequin outfits, blew noisemakers. "Happy New Year!" Lee pressed a glass of champagne into his hand, and Antonio stuck a noisemaker into his mouth before Richard could protest. Posing like a Black, gay power couple recording a celebrity house tour, instead of a casual gathering with a handful of friends, they looked at him expectantly with matching, manic grins.

Going home sounded like the best option. Mocking Antonio for being ridiculous and extra was a close second.

But...the glass in his hand was engraved with his name. Lee's and Antonio's outfits looked like significant effort and planning had gone into them. The obscene amount of gold and silver decorations (and was that a disco ball?) were far too elaborate for Antonio's easily distracted ass to have achieved on his own.

And Richard didn't know Lee well enough yet to trust he wouldn't take his personality personally.

He sighed heavily, and the noisemaker unraveled with a halfhearted honk.

"That's the spirit, Dicky!" Antonio's grin turned wicked. He'd always been able to read Richard's thoughts too well.

Dropping the noisemaker on the entry table as he toed his shoes off, he followed Antonio and Lee into their living room. A slender woman with short red hair, sitting cross-legged on the couch, made him freeze. They exchanged a mutually suspicious glare. Far worse than being the first one there, he now had to make small talk with a stranger.

"Dicky, this is Tara-Bear," Antonio said by way of introduction, before he disappeared into the kitchen, abandoning Richard with Lee and... Tara, he assumed.

Richard nodded. "Richard, not Dicky."

She nodded back. "Just Tara. No Bear."

He sat stiffly in one of the armchairs. Tara picked at the plate of cheese and crackers in front of her.

"Oh god," Lee muttered as he looked between them. "Uh... Tara is my best friend. And Richard is Gabe's other best friend."

"Oh," Tara said, stiffly. "Cool."

"You met Gabe when you helped us move in," Lee reminded her.

Tara nodded.

Richard narrowed his eyes. He'd known Gabe had helped Antonio and Lee move in, but Gabe had never mentioned another person being there, let alone an attractive person with big green eyes and freckles. The omission led to questions.

Richard looked away as Tara happened to glance up, both sipping their champagne.

"Anyway, drink up!" Lee said, far too cheerfully. "Plenty more where that came from! Get those conversation skills lubed up!"

"Dude," Tara muttered. "You can't force me to make small talk with Antonio's friends."

A kindred spirit, then. Richard had been mentally preparing to meet new people for weeks. He'd even considered skipping Christmas at the Floreses, in case a week wasn't enough time to replenish his social battery. But Antonio's parents would have sent Antonio to Richard's door with a cooler full of food, so he'd sucked it up and went, and had a pleasant if overwhelming time as always. Richard liked living alone, but sometimes his condo was too quiet, especially during holidays.

It'd be nice to just have someone at home who wanted to stay home. Preferably someone quiet and calm. Maybe he should get a cat until he could find someone who enjoyed the peace and silence as much as he did.

That someone would not be this Tara, though. Knowing Gabe, he'd been obsessing over her since they'd met; he would have mentioned her existence otherwise. Maybe Richard was paranoid, but if he needed to dig deeper into who this Tara was before Gabe got hurt again, he'd rather get the background check started.

"So, Tara works in graphic design," Lee tried again as Tara rolled her eyes.

"I'm fine sitting in silence," Richard offered.

"Cheers to that." Tara lifted her glass with a snort.

"Fine." Lee threw his hands up. "Be awkward then. I'll be in the kitchen getting the food ready."

"Would you like help?" Richard asked.

Lee looked at him in confusion. "You're a guest."

"Lee's never gotten to host a party before," Tara explained once Lee was out of the room. "He'll be happier if you let him do his thing."

Richard leaned forward and asked quietly, "Who all is coming tonight? Tonio didn't say."

"Besides...your other friend," Tara glanced away, "Blanche and Sunny will be here. And hopefully Lee's little sister, Jazz."

"Anything I should know about them?" Richard asked. Better to avoid any missteps if he could help it.

"Uh...Blanche uses they them pronouns, and they *will* send you an invoice if you get that wrong. Don't ask about their personal life. Or anything about their childhood. Or anything about their past at all. You *can* ask them about work." A grin broke across her face. "Sunny, she her, is a ditz with a short attention span, but if you don't feel like talking, ask her about video games. She won't shut up if you get her on a roll. Oh, and she's got great tits!"

Heat crept up Richard's cheeks. That was not what he expected.

"Jazz, also she her, is a sweetheart. Don't hit on her. Lee's overprotective."

"Wasn't planning on it." He hadn't come here to hit on anyone. His personality was usually an acquired taste, to put it kindly. It'd take several of these get-togethers for anyone to see him as anything but an aloof asshole, let alone look twice at him. And if Richard had his way, this would be the *only* get-together.

With a quiet exhale of mutual relief, Richard and Tara sipped their champagne and fell back into a comfortable silence.

Chapter Two

Sunny

"Oh, thank God you're here!" Lee greeted Sunny with an unusually warm hug the second she knocked on his apartment door.

"Uh...you're welcome?" Sunny awkwardly patted his back.

Lee stepped back to let her in, muttering, "Tara and Richard are here, and neither of them is talking, and it's so uncomfortable. Tonio and I don't know what to do."

"Aren't you two the extroverts here?" Sunny teased, unzipping her coat and hanging it on a hook. "Antonio talks enough for all of us."

"Wow, rude!" Antonio poked his head out of the kitchen, a plate of cheese and crackers in hand. "The extroverts are hosting this party. We can't sit and chat. We're still getting ready."

"Didn't this start at six?" Sunny checked her phone as she traded her boots for slippers. It was a quarter to seven. "Why are you still getting ready?"

"I didn't think anyone would show up on time. Tara's here because Blanche sexiled her. And Richard is too white to do fashionably late." Antonio handed her the plate. "Here. Bring this to Tara. Please get them to talk. It's painful."

"We can hear you, you know. Your apartment isn't *that* big," a raspy voice that definitely wasn't Tara's drawled from the living area.

Sunny grabbed the plate with a grin.

"Sun?" Lee pointed a warning finger at her. "No arguing."

"Me? Argue? I'm a gem!" Sunny winked and brought the plate of snacks to the living room, where Tara sat cross-legged on the couch. Her red curls hung over her forehead as she fiddled with a hangnail. A slim blond man sat in one of the armchairs, fingers tapping the upholstery.

"Here." Sunny handed Tara the plate. She had attempted to dress up, wearing black silk wrap pants and a green boat neck top that flattered her red hair and freckled skin. Not terrible compared to her usual athleisure. Not *good*, but not terrible.

Tara's eyebrows raised as she took it. "Damn! Hello, titties!"

Sunny beamed. "Thank you for noticing!"

Tara shoved a cracker in her mouth and held her hands up. "May I?"

"Go ahead."

Batting at her chest, Tara grinned as Sunny's tits jiggled. "You should wear this dress more often!"

Sunny looked over at the blond man, whose cheeks were bright red. The flush dipped beneath the collar of his white button-down shirt. "You must be Richard. I'm Sunny."

Richard nodded politely, but avoided looking at her, obviously trying not to stare at Tara groping Sunny's chest.

"Charmed." Sunny scoffed, annoyed at the doubt creeping in. The groping was platonic, so she shouldn't feel embarrassed. And yet, considering how uncomfortable this Richard guy looked, she'd made a faux pas before she'd even introduced herself. "Okay, Tara, that's enough."

Tara tsked. "No, this is fun!"

"Stop, or the cheese is mine."

"Fine." Tara protectively snatched the cheese and crackers from the coffee table.

Lee handed Sunny a glass of champagne with her name engraved on it. "Here. A little social lubricant. Please be nice!"

Sunny ignored the implication that she wasn't always nice. "Personalized glasses?"

"I know!" Lee gave a bashful shrug. "It's extra, but Tonio likes extra."

"Why be normal when you can be extraordinary?" Antonio joined them with a bottle of champagne, popping a cork that made everyone flinch.

"Cheers to that!" Sunny raised the glass as she took a seat next to Tara. "So, Richard. How do you know Tonio?"

"We met through Gabe. Our other friend. Who will be coming. Later." Richard's blush deepened. He met her eyes briefly, leaving her with a flash of robin's-egg blue that made her stomach swoop.

"Richard and I are both Gabe's leftovers," Antonio joked as he refilled Richard's glass. "We're all still friends. Ain't that the gayest shit you ever heard?"

Richard's nostrils flared. "Antonio, what are you doing?"

Antonio shrugged, angling the glass so the champagne wouldn't bubble over. "Sharing fun facts about us. That's how conversations work."

"No, dipshit. *That*." Richard nodded to the champagne in his hand.

"Oh. That." Antonio made a face as he set Richard's glass down and picked up Tara's empty one. "This is me being a good host."

"Tonio." Richard's voice was cold. "Put the bottle down."

Antonio avoided looking at him. "Dicky—"

"Put it down."

Sunny and Tara exchanged a look at the sharp edge in Richard's voice. Lee's smile looked more like a wince.

"Lee is supervising," Antonio explained. "We have an inventory and check-ins—"

"Lee's not responsible for you." Lee tried to interrupt, but Richard silenced him with a glare. "You asked us to be a dick if we ever saw you with a drink in your hand, even if it's not *your* drink. This is me being a dick. Do I need to remind you what happened last time?"

With a sardonic snort, Antonio set the bottle down and slowly backed away with his hands out. "You didn't bring ropes with you, did you? This isn't that kind of party, you know."

Richard smirked. "Pick it up again, and find out."

Sunny was half-tempted to pick up the bottle.

Antonio's sour grimace turned into a wry smile. "I love you, too, Dicky."

"Don't read into it." Richard scowled. "And don't call me Dicky."

"I'll help with refills," Tara offered, cutting the tension and reminding Sunny that she was not watching the opening of a kinky porno. "Leave the bottle. I'll get another one when it's empty."

"Thank you, Tara-Bear." Antonio crossed his arms, still examining Richard. "I can't decide if I'm offended you don't trust me, or relieved I can go back to ignoring the champagne."

"Babe, I told you you didn't have to," Lee said gently. "You don't have to push yourself."

"Yeah, maybe I should prove I won't be tempted another time, when everyone else won't be wasted soon." Antonio kissed Lee's cheek on their way back to the kitchen.

"So." Sunny sipped her champagne to calm her racing heart after watching this unexpectedly bossy man bully Antonio into submission. "You dated Antonio's other friend we're meeting tonight?"

Richard's face immediately pinkened again, a drastic contrast to the glint in his eye from scolding Antonio. "Gabe and I dated briefly in college, but we were meant to be friends. We work together at an investment firm."

"An investment firm?" Sunny grinned, thrilled to find a topic that was a turnoff after confirming the bossy blond who was into rope play was probably queer. Birdie would murder her if she got involved with a white boy, but Richard was checking a lot of Sunny's boxes. "So you get rich with other people's money?"

Tara sighed heavily. "No arguing, Sunny."

"I manage our retirement accounts division, so yes, my team maximizes gains to protect our clients' futures." A corner of Richard's mouth twitched into a smirk as his blue eyes met hers again. "And what do *you* do, Sunny?"

Unsure if his dry tone was sarcastic, Sunny crossed her arms. "I'm a software engineer, but as a hobby, I've started developing apps that could do some good in the world and selling them to organizations who could use them."

Since she couldn't—or no longer wanted to, rather—go to Blanche's every time she and her mother argued, Sunny had found a new escape in creating apps. Even if Blanche wouldn't say anything, Sunny shouldn't take advantage of their poor boundaries when things were already tense between them. Birdie didn't complain about the apps as much as she did her gaming, and Sunny had managed to squirrel away a couple grand in her Vagina Fund.

"So you create supply and hope there's a demand?" Richard's smirk deepened, looking almost charming against his square jaw. "That's a very idealistic approach."

Sunny perked up. Annoying Tara and teasing Antonio had lost their sparkle after a while. This Richard seemed clever enough to be a challenge. "And yet I've sold every app I've made. If I can see an issue in the world, there's probably someone cooler than me who could use my tech to help solve it."

"Really telling on yourself there." Richard sipped his champagne.

Sunny shrugged. "I know my strengths. Convincing people to do something they don't want to do is not one of them. But I can create things for people with social skills to use."

"And you trust them with your creation. Again, very idealistic."

"I'd rather be an idealist than a cynical capitalist." Sunny huffed. "Let me guess—you grew up in some bougie place like Driftwood, and you've got a trust fund that you resent because it makes you feel like you're not a self-made man, but you still use it."

"I miss when we weren't talking," Tara muttered.

Richard was practically smiling. "I don't think taking advantage of my trust fund makes me any less of a self-made man."

Sunny scowled. "It literally does."

"That was a trans joke. I'm literally a self-made man."

Sunny's cheeks burned. *I did not clock him as trans.* "I think for it to count as a joke, someone has to laugh."

"Strange, I haven't laughed once, but you've been full of jokes."

Blood boiling, Sunny's jaw clenched, and her fingernails bit into her palm. This was the most fun she'd had in months. With a scoff and a toss of her hair, she said, "Big words from a rich boy who circle jerks over the stock market for a living. Must be nice to have the luxury of play money to lose for funsies. Meanwhile, the other ninety-nine percent are struggling."

"So a rise in stock returns due to increased cash flow *doesn't* suggest an improving economy? Strange, most economists would think so."

Sunny's retort—a thoroughly researched lecture about how the stock market was bullshit—was interrupted by a singsong of "Happy New Year!" as Blanche strolled in, champagne glass in hand. They were stunning as always, wearing a low-cut black jumpsuit that hugged all their curves and their blonde hair up in a high ponytail, emphasizing their graceful neck. Sunny made herself look away, glaring at Richard again instead.

Antonio followed, setting another plate of cheese in front of Tara. "Blanche, this is Richard. Call him Dicky."

"Pleasure to meet you." Richard rose to shake Blanche's hand. "Do *not* call me Dicky."

You didn't get up to shake my *hand, Dicky.* "Blanche, perfect timing! You can help us win a debate we're having," Sunny exclaimed, drawing

Richard's attention away from Blanche. "He seriously works as, like, an investment banker!"

A slow grin spread across Blanche's face. "Do you, now?" They scanned him up and down, practically purring, "Hey there, handsome."

"Seriously?" Sunny should have known better than to expect Blanche to put her before a potential client.

"Down, Blanche." Antonio flicked water at them from his glass. "My friends are off-limits."

Blanche wiped the water off their cheek with a wink to Richard. "Oh, fine. I'll behave."

"I said help with a debate, not jump his bones!" Sunny protested, glaring at Blanche and crossing her arms.

Blanche's green eyes flicked between her and Richard, whose face flushed bright red. Their half smile edged closer to a smirk. "You'll catch more flies with honey than vinegar, Babygirl."

"I don't want to catch flies." Sunny narrowed her eyes at Richard.

"Nor do I want your honey," he shot back, looking at Sunny up and down with a sneer as he sat back down. Sunny was strangely relieved his attention was back on her instead of Blanche.

Blanche eyed them both with that cool smirk, unreadable as ever. "What's the debate?"

"If stock market performance is a valid measure of economic out-look." Tara supplied around the cheese and crackers in her mouth, her expression as deadpan as her tone. "Thrilling party conversation."

Blanche raised an eyebrow at Sunny. "I'm going to need more cham-pagne for this." They downed their glass and held it out to Tara for a refill, before they perched sideways in an armchair near Richard.

Sunny turned to Tara to keep from looking at Richard's smug face. "Okay, Tara-Bear—"

"Don't call me Tara-Bear."

"What would you like to talk about? Since our conversation isn't up to par."

Tara shrugged. "Don't worry about me. Keep flirting if you want."

"I am *not* flirting!" Sunny scoffed.

Richard coughed, his cheeks as pink as ever. "So, um, Blanche, what do you do for a living?"

Blanche grinned, crossing their legs over the arm of the chair. "People pay me to dominate them, and more people pay me to watch it on the Internet."

His blush somehow deepened. "Th—that's nice. Have you been doing that long?"

"In various forms for longer than I care to admit. I supply a product with a niche market demand, you might say."

Richard ran a hand through his hair, raising an eyebrow at Sunny. "At least someone understands basic economic concepts. Maybe Lee's friends aren't totally hopeless."

His dig didn't bother Tara, who nibbled on her cheese, ignoring everyone.

Sunny scowled, chewing her lip before retorting, "Supply and demand. So advanced. You must have taken Econ in high school."

A smile played at the corners of Richard's lips; they were fuller than she'd expected for a white boy. "Something like that. Why, where'd you learn it? A TED Talk?"

A knock at the door interrupted the comeback she hadn't thought of yet. A moment later, Lee was dragging his sister in by the hand. "It's a New Year's Eve miracle—Jazz made it!"

Tara leapt up with a squeal to give her a hug. "Jazz! It's been forever! You look amazing!"

Jazz did look good, wearing a body-hugging cream sweaterdress. A far cry from the shy first-grader Sunny had met when she'd made friends with Lee in middle school. She was undoubtedly Lee's sister—with the same deep brown skin and handsome features that suited both of them. Jazz even sported close-shaved hair, similar to how Lee used to wear his (which had barely grown in the few months he'd been growing it out, yet he acted like a different person). Jazz's new, grown look suited her. No wonder Luna thought Jazz was too cool for her now.

Jazz greeted Sunny with a hug. "Damn! Okay, titties! Are they bigger than the last time I saw you, or is that dress just that flattering?"

"Aw, thanks! The dress is helping, but estrogen is the gift that keeps on giving." Sunny patted her bust fondly.

Richard stood up, hand outstretched. "Richard Carter. Nice to meet you."

Again, where was my *handshake, Dicky?* Sunny chewed her lip, glaring at him.

"Jasmine Jones, but call me Jazz." She shook his hand politely. "Are you here with Sunny?"

Sunny and Richard both devolved into offended sputters. Finally, Richard muttered, "I'm a friend of Antonio's."

"Oh, sorry. My bad." Jazz winced, covering her mouth with her hand.

Richard waved it off, while Sunny managed to gain some control over her mouth. "As if!"

Jazz turned to where Blanche sat waiting on the armchair, arms outspread for her. "Blanche. You look more beautiful every time I see you."

"Jazzy, you look amazing as always. Love the hair." Blanche leaned into her hug as Sunny sat back down on the couch. Jazz had always been affectionate, particularly with Blanche, who welcomed affection *far* more than Jazz's parents. Mr. and Mrs. Jones were *not* the hugging type. "And the nose ring!"

"I swear you see everything, Blanche." Jazz fiddled with her nose and flipped down a septum piercing. Blanche adjusted in the chair so Jazz could sit on their lap.

Sunny's brief flare of jealousy was surprisingly easy to swallow. Maybe she was over Blanche, after all. "I bet your dad loved that," Sunny teased. Mr. Jones had always been a hard-ass, even before he'd disowned Lee and told a nine-year-old Jazz her older brother didn't exist anymore.

Jazz shot her a knowing look. "You know he don't know about it! He won't even look at me now that I'm bald-headed." She laughed. "But that was the whole point in shaving my hair off. I think I might start letting it grow out again."

Another knock sounded at the door. Antonio rushed to answer it. "Happy New— Are those cheesecake tarts?!"

A deep voice responded. "Yes, and this tray has a dairy-free version just for you."

"Oh, thank god," Richard muttered. "Gabe's here."

Antonio led a tall, handsome, muscular man into the living room, both of them carrying a tray of desserts. "Everyone, this is Gabe. And he brought my favorite dessert! Tara-Bear, you're going to love these!"

Instead of diving for the desserts—or the thirst trap carrying them—Tara excused herself to the kitchen, muttering something about champagne as she ducked around him. The tall man's gaze followed her out, but he quickly turned back to the room with a forced smile.

Sunny was surprised Tara had left. This Gabe wasn't really Sunny's type—thanks to years of crushing on Blanche, she preferred blond, androgynous-looking people more than handsome bodybuilders—but he was undeniably hot. And he could bake? Tara should be drooling over him. But she'd left, and Sunny did need to practice flirting with someone less antagonizing than this Dicky guy.

"Hi! I'm Sunny! Come sit by me!" Sunny patted the seat next to her on the couch that Tara had just left vacant. Gabe's smile brightened, Richard's scowl deepening along with it. Sunny shot him a smug grin.

"Jesus Christ, Babygirl." Blanche rubbed their forehead, then whispered something in Jazz's ear, who snorted and whispered back.

Sunny ignored their matching Cheshire cat grins as she accepted the mini-cheesecake that Gabe offered. "So Gabe, I hear you're an investment banker, too?"

Gabe shrugged, the couch dipping as he sat next to her. "For now. I don't really like it, but it's a job."

Sunny smiled as she bit into the cheesecake. "What would you be doing instead?"

He shrugged again. "Not sure. If I could get paid for playing League or something, I'd do that. But then it'd probably take the fun out of it."

"You play League? Who do you main?" Sunny beamed as Lee, Blanche, and Antonio groaned. Now this was someone she could talk to.

Jazz sidled up as Sunny assembled a plate of snacks at the dining table. "Hey Sunny? Can I ask a favor?"

"Of course, what do you need?" Sunny popped a cheddar cube into her mouth, a little gratified that Jazz was asking *her* for help. Normally everyone went to Blanche or Lee.

"This is embarrassing." Jazz fiddled with a loose thread in her dress. "I was kind of hoping for a midnight kiss tonight."

Sunny laughed. "That's flattering, but your brother would murder me."

"No!" Jazz winced. "Not you, with...Blanche."

"Oh." Sunny froze, unsure how to respond. Jazz must not have been told about Sunny and Blanche's fling. As if being Blanche's secret hadn't been painful enough; the tiny humiliating reminders still sliced her heart like paper cuts all these months later.

"But I don't want Lee to get mad at them, either! So I was hoping that if everyone else was kissing at midnight too, it wouldn't be as awkward or obvious what's happening."

"And what does Blanche feel about it?" Sunny asked carefully.

Jazz's smile, so reminiscent of Lee's, was bashful. "They're fine with it. They suggested it, actually. Something about how it's a thing on TV, but we—or you all, rather—have never done it before, and there are finally enough people who might want to kiss each other here tonight."

Sunny fought the surge of bitter insecurity that Blanche saw Jazz as someone they wanted to kiss, when they had never looked at Sunny that way until she'd forced them to. The damn Jealousy tab that kept popping up was so annoying; she didn't want to kiss Blanche either, not anymore, not truly. Her gut reactions, however, were slow to get with the program.

Because logically, she shouldn't be upset. Even if Blanche *had* seen her that way before, it's not like they could have a midnight kiss while Lee (who only wanted to kiss men) and Tara (who didn't want to kiss anyone at all) watched. She exhaled slowly, closing the Jealousy tab. These were the irrational reactions she needed to work on. She couldn't delude herself again. All the more reason to find a new distraction.

"I just volunteered to help them start the tradition. Platonically," Jazz continued, wincing. "I know Blanche will never see me that way, so this is my one chance to see what it's like."

Sunny's heart went out to her. Her own crush on Blanche had caused her to do plenty of dumb shit before it'd run its course. She huffed. "Who do I gotta kiss?"

Jazz beamed, so reminiscent of Lee that Sunny would risk kissing Tara to keep that joy on her face. "Thank you! Blanche thinks Gabe is totally into Tara, so...Richard?"

Sunny was too unsurprised to care that she was stuck with Blondie. *I don't know what else I expected.* "Tara doesn't kiss people. How do you plan to convince her?"

Jazz's smile was apologetic.

Sunny waited, trying not to fidget under Jazz's expectant look.

Finally, Jazz sighed. "Well... I was hoping *you* would ask her?"

A laugh tore from her before Sunny could stop it. "Are you trying to get me killed?"

"Please?" Jazz clasped her hands together. "You're the only one who has a chance."

Sunny sighed. Her persuasion skills were severely lacking, but Tara's patience was no match for how annoying Sunny could be. "She probably won't do it, but I'll see what I can do."

Jazz threw her arms around her. "Thanks, Sunny! You're the best!"

"Yeah, yeah. I'll take one for the team. Enjoy your kiss with Blanche," Sunny said, patting her back, surprised that the Jealousy tab stayed closed, even more so because she'd meant it. *Just don't do what I did and read too much into it.*

BLANCHE

SUNNY WAS HORRIBLE AT flirting. Watching her laugh at everything Gabe said, and then continue on as if he hadn't said anything, was painful. Sunny could be utterly charming when she wasn't trying to be. But she tried way too hard.

Blanche sighed, swirling their champagne glass, wishing it were a double malt scotch as they finished it.

"You okay?" Lee appeared out of nowhere, hovering over them to refill their glass before they could set it down. "Need to step out for something stronger?"

Blanche snorted, shaking their head as they thanked him. When they'd arrived, Blanche had been on the verge of a drop. Their patron had requested an impromptu session before ringing in the New Year with his fiancée. Blanche had not only been late to the party, they'd walked in with their skin crawling in shame. Thankfully, the joint on the walk over, their friends' company, and Jazz's entertaining commentary had kept them from the worst of it. "No need to worry about me. The host of a party can unwind too, you know."

Lee snorted. "If I relax too much, a fight will break out. I figured you three and Tonio's friends would be like oil and water, but this is more like cats and dogs."

"Oh, it's not that bad. Jazz and I are having a great time. Tara is behaving. Sunny is being..." They paused, unsure of what exactly Sunny was trying to accomplish with her heavy-handed flirting with someone who straightened up like an eager puppy every time Tara entered the room, "...nice."

Lee laughed at that. "To Gabe anyway. I think she'd be at Richard's throat if Gabe wasn't here."

"I rather thought Richard enjoyed having Sunny at his throat," Blanche smirked.

Richard huffed, tapping the arm of his chair next to them. "I may be pretending not to overhear, but I do have ears, you know."

"Have more champagne, Richard." Lee snorted and emptied the bottle into Richard's glass, before disappearing into the kitchen.

Blanche's phone buzzed with a text from an unknown number.

> I thought I told you to end things.

Blanche rolled their eyes, wondering when their patron's fiancée had gotten their number. She'd been a thorn in their side for months; Blanche had already blocked her on their social media and email. Or rather, Tara had, because Blanche couldn't figure out how. Seeing the messages threatening to evict them had stressed Tara out so much that Blanche had regretted not asking Lee instead.

> Tell him to end it.

> You left marks. What will people think?

> Considering the welts are on his ass, I'd be more concerned with why anyone else would see them if I were you.

> We are getting married soon! There will be no room for you or anyone else in our marriage.

> Again, tell him that.

> When my lawyer finds out how to end your lease, it's over. You'll be out of that dump of an apartment, and we're getting a restraining order against you.

> Looking forward to it, sweetheart. Happy New Year!

With a screenshot of their exchange sent to their patron, ordering him to handle his fiancée, Blanche turned their phone off and threw it on the table. The last thing they needed was a threat to take away their shitty apartment—notably, Tara's home—on New Year's Eve. They were making decent money from their SubParty channel, but was that enough to rent an apartment without stressing Tara out?

Blanche frowned as they swirled their champagne flute. Tara would want to contribute, and she already did far too much work supporting the channel and paying the utilities as it was. But Tara was stubborn, refusing to let Blanche pay her. As always, Lee was following her lead, so Blanche had been saving their paychecks in a separate account, waiting for an excuse to give it to them that wouldn't hurt their pride.

"Are you all right?" Richard asked quietly.

"Never better." Blanche leaned over the arm of their chair, smiling as they played with a long strand of their blond hair. They could worry about their patron's fiancée tomorrow. Tonight was for having fun, and the game they had cooked up with Jazz was a great distraction from their problems. "So, Richy Rich, what New Year's Eve traditions does your family have?"

Richard eyed Blanche warily. "Just Richard, please."

"Sorry, I love a nickname, but Richard it is." Blanche sipped their champagne. "So, any family traditions? You act like you come from money. Tell me, what do the elite do to ring in the New Year? Black tie affair? Quiet dinner?"

"On New Years? My parents would invite all the people whose asses they wanted to kiss over, and we would all get drunk and pretend we don't hate each other in front of company."

Blanche raised an eyebrow at his honesty. "So, nothing out of the ordinary."

That got a cackle out of Richard. Blanche had been beginning to wonder if he had a sense of humor.

Sunny broke off mid-sentence from her conversation with Gabe to glare at them.

Pretending not to notice, Blanche murmured, "Well, one tradition I've always wanted to introduce is a midnight kiss to start the year off right. This is the first time there's been more than the four of us, so I'm hoping this is my year." Blanche laid their hand on his forearm.

Richard leaned forward to set his drink on the table to brush off their touch, tugging his sleeve.

If they had been flirting in earnest, Blanche might have taken his blatant rejection personally. But Richard wasn't client material, and poor Sunny would probably implode if Blanche actually had designs on him. "So, what do you think? Anyone here you'd like to kiss?"

His eyes narrowed, searching Blanche's face. "I have a feeling you're going to tell me."

Blanche laughed. "You're a clever one, Richard. You're kissing Sunny."

Richard had a strong poker face. And yet, his lips twitched ever so slightly, his eyes flicking to where Gabe was politely listening to Sunny ramble on about another video game she liked. "And how exactly are you convincing *her* to kiss *me*?"

Blanche caught Jazz's eye, raising an eyebrow in a silent question. Jazz gave a subtle thumbs-up and a sly grin as she chatted with Antonio. "She didn't take much convincing."

"I highly doubt that. We seem to have got off on the wrong foot."

"Rest assured, she barely put up a fight." Blanche fought to keep from grinning. Just like how Tara probably thought avoiding Mr. Tall, Dark, and Handsome was convincing anyone, Sunny was putting on quite a show to prove she wasn't interested in Richard.

Things had been so awkward with Sunny since last summer. But so far this evening, all of her jealous glares had been directed *at* Blanche, not *over* them. Maybe encouraging her to consider someone new was what Sunny needed for their friendship to resume in truth, not just intention. And to think, this had all started as mere musing with Jazz to keep each other entertained, until the threat of Blanche's drop passed and Jazz had gotten her bearings.

"What's the best way to get Gabe on board?" Blanche asked quietly.

Still politely listening to Sunny for far longer than anyone else could without their eyes glazing over, Gabe sat quietly on the couch. Knee bouncing, he stole yet another glance toward the kitchen where Tara had been hiding for hours.

"Don't play games. If he says no, he means no." Richard's voice was sharp, jaw tightening. As Blanche nodded, his face softened and the barest hint of a smile teased the corner of Richard's mouth. "Though, if you ask him to kiss Tara, he'll say yes."

Blanche smirked. "I wish Tara were that easy." There was no chance Tara would kiss anyone at midnight, but damned if Blanche wouldn't have fun trying.

Giggling quietly to themself—their fingers were tingling from so much champagne—Blanche dried their hands with a soft towel before admiring themself in the mirror and making sure their bodysuit was still flattering after they'd had to strip half-out of it just to use the bathroom.

When they finally opened the en suite door, Lee blocked the way, his arms crossed over his chest. "What's this I hear about you kissing my sister?"

Blanche tittered, leaning against the doorframe. Standing was hard; both Tara and Lee poured a generous glass. "I was wondering when you'd come after me."

Lee pushed his glasses up his nose, waiting expectantly.

"You know I'm not trying anything with your sister, Lee." Blanche rubbed his bicep. "We're just having a little New Year's Eve fun." At Lee's raised eyebrows, they hurried to explain, "The kiss isn't the fun bit. Jazz was feeling anxious around so many people, so she wanted an excuse to break the ice. And I need...a distraction from my bullshit."

She hid her social anxiety well, but the way Jazz velcroed herself to whoever happened to be making conversation with her, Blanche especially, always went straight to Blanche's heart. They always made room for Jazz at their side when she needed it.

"I'm not following. How does this require you to kiss my sister, who is nineteen, a whole fifteen years younger than you?"

"Fourteen," Blanche corrected, regretting it immediately when Lee's eye bulged behind his glasses. "Look, it's just a platonic smooch. As a prank!"

"A prank," Lee said flatly.

"Yes!" Blanche rubbed his arm harder, hoping it would soothe Lee's overprotective streak the way it did his anxiety. "You seriously haven't noticed the sexual tension between Sunny and Richard? Jazz clocked it the second she walked in and asked if they were together. It was hilarious!" They giggled with a snort.

Lee screwed up his face. "They've done nothing but argue."

Blanche huffed. "*You* would never argue with someone you liked, but Sunny?"

Sunny had never argued with *Blanche*, but she had always hero-worshiped them, so that made sense. She enjoyed arguing with Tara and Antonio enough that Blanche's speculation didn't feel as wildly off base as Lee seemed to think. They sighed, hoping they weren't deluding themself by seeing an opportunity that wasn't there. "You must have picked up on the mutual lust between Tara and Gabe."

"Oh, I've *definitely* caught Gabe staring at Tara's ass," Lee grumbled. "But Tara hasn't been staring back."

"Yeah, she's pretending Gabe doesn't exist. Same thing." Blanche waved him off. "Anyway, Jazz and I are trying to get everyone else to kiss each other, so I've been pretending I've always wanted to do this New Year's Eve kiss tradition, but we've never had enough people before. Meanwhile, Jazz is pretending to have a secret crush to call dibs on kissing me, to give everyone else the excuse to give in to their desires."

Jazz's "secret crush" might not be entirely pretend, but she had a sensible head on her shoulders. Blanche trusted she could tell a teenage fascination and genuine feelings apart. Unlike Sunny. And if not, Blanche had learned their lesson and would shut it down promptly this time.

"You really think you're gonna convince anyone to do this?" Lee asked skeptically.

Blanche grinned, the sour twist of their stomach easier to ignore with how tipsy they were, though their high from earlier had long since worn off. "We already have. Richard and Sunny were delightfully easy to convince, and Gabe has agreed on the condition that Tara is up for it, too."

Gabe had seemed genuinely concerned about Tara's consent, to Blanche's delight. Now *he* was an opportunity that wasn't wishful thinking. Blanche and Jazz hadn't been able to resist teasing him a little, bantering about how much passion New Year's Eve kisses should have, how long it should last, or how much tongue to use. Gabe had been bright red by the end of the conversation.

Blanche's smile fell when Lee's grumpy face returned, the vein in his forehead twitching as his brows furrowed. "You're not actually going to make Tara kiss him, are you? You know kissing's a hard boundary for her."

"Lee, darling," Blanche kissed his cheek. "You really think anyone can make Tara do anything she doesn't want to do?"

Lee still glowered, but he put an arm around their waist to rejoin the party. "No, just... Don't push this boundary, okay? She'll do anything for you. Or Jazz for that matter."

"That's exactly why Sunny's asking her." Blanche shot him a smug smile, as bubbly as the champagne after hours of conspiring with Jazz. Even Lee's protective grouchiness couldn't dull their mood. They pushed his glasses up for him. "And before you come at me for asking Sunny to do anything, just know that *Jazz* asked Sunny, not me."

Lee snorted.

"This is harmless fun, Lee. I'm honestly surprised this is going as well as it is." Blanche rested their head on his shoulder. Even though he'd moved out, their duckling hadn't gone far, to the relief of Tara and Lee as much as Blanche. "Your party is the most fun I've had in months."

Lee fought a grin. "Yeah, yeah. Flattery will get you nowhere."

Blanche grinned. They knew him better than that.

CHAPTER THREE

TARA

As MUCH AS SHE hated to admit it, the cheesecake thingies were bomb. Tara moaned as she took another bite, inhaling the raspberry compote and mascarpone cheese. It had an interesting grounding note she couldn't identify.

Tara had been hiding—no, *helping*—in the kitchen since Mr. Brown Eyes had arrived, refilling the champagne. All in all, not a bad place to be. She'd had worse New Year's Eves in her life. There was food, champagne, and a conspicuous absence of Mr. Dimples. Whiskey would be more efficient than champagne, but she didn't want to discover how she'd act around *him* while wasted. A decent buzz was dangerous enough.

Of all the people she'd hooked up with over the years, Tara had never expected to see Mr. Redwood Tree again. She'd tried to forget him, but forgetting a mind-blowing hookup had been harder than expected. Even when she was fucking other people, he always lurked in her mind as the bar she tried to reach. And now he was way more real than she ever imagined he'd be.

Finding out he and Antonio were childhood best friends had been a shock. Tara couldn't pretend she didn't remember him; when he'd dropped back into existence two months ago, the recognition had been glaringly mutual. Luckily, *Mr. Best Head I Ever Got In My Damn Life* had played along with her assertion that they'd never met before, and she'd successfully avoided him since. But Lee wanted them to be friends with Antonio's, so that plan was out the window.

Tara downed the rest of her champagne to quell the hot flush of shame from how she'd ended their…interaction last year. He'd been sweet, and she'd been a "fucking bitch!" as he'd called her, deservedly so. In hindsight, he had been perfectly within the boundaries of normal socially acceptable behavior. Just not Tara's boundaries, and how could he know that?

She fidgeted with the knot on her wrap pants. She'd have to be polite, but pointless conversations were so painful, even after she'd practiced with the small talk bullshit a lot since their hookup on her birthday last year. Not that she'd tried to date or even hook up with anyone since Lee had moved out; Tara felt no happiness in her vice anymore, just attention. And she wanted happiness now, like Lee had. But Mr. Dimples dropping back into existence in the worst possible way had shaken—

A polite cough made her jump.

Tara whirled around, another cheesecake thingy halfway to her mouth. Mr. Brown Eyes was standing alone with her in the small kitchen.

His long hair hung loose, soft brown-black curls cascading down his chest. Her fingers twitched, recalling how that soft hair had twisted around her fingers. His striking features—Roman nose, heavy brow, and deep-set eyes—were even more stunning than in her fantasies.

"It's hard to get you alone, Kitten." His deep voice made her knees weak. "I was—"

"It's Tara," she bit out. "I've been avoiding you."

He shook his head with a mirthless smile. "Finally got your name at least. Can—"

"Here for more champagne?" she offered coldly, setting down the cheesecake thingy.

Mr. Redwood Tree frowned, but he held out his empty flute with a shrug. She steadied his glass as she refilled it, their fingers grazing.

"Look, it's obvious you don't want to talk to me—you run away anytime I'm in the same room," he muttered, thighs stretching his chinos as he shifted his weight. "Honestly, I'm not sure I should talk to you, either. It's a me problem, as usual."

A pang hit Tara's chest as she poured, drawing a sharp breath, reminded of how heartless her parting words had been the first time they'd met.

Tugging a hand through his hair, his brow creased as those brown eyes met hers, sending her heart fluttering. "But, I felt compelled to tell you there's a game afoot. The—"

"Okay, Sherlock, who talks like that in real life?" She couldn't stop the sarcasm from leaving her mouth.

Frustration flashed across his face. "I'm trying to be nice. Can you let me talk?"

"What's stopping you?" Tara crossed her arms stubbornly, even as she scolded herself for being petty.

"You are!" he hissed as he stepped closer. She didn't step back. "Can you shut your fucking mouth for a goddamn second and let me talk?"

Motioning for him to continue, Tara picked up her cheesecake thingy to quiet the anxiety woken by his frustration. At least he hadn't yelled.

His thick brows furrowed. "Sorry. That was uncalled for."

Leaning back against the counter, she took a bite. The flavor over-whelmed her again. She closed her eyes as a moan escaped her. *Dammit. These are good. Is it nutmeg? Not cinnamon.*

Embarrassed, Tara forced herself to look into his eyes with whatever dignity she still had. "Sorry. I wasn't trying to interrupt that time."

His eyes trained hard on her mouth as he edged closer. "I wanted to tell you," he murmured, "that there's a plan for everyone to kiss at midnight."

Tara blinked, uncomprehending. "And?"

With the slightest shake of his head, Mr. Brown eyes muttered, "That entails you and I kissing."

Tara froze, her jaw clenching. This had Blanche written all over it. Lee wouldn't do this; Blanche knew her "no kissing" rule, but only Lee had been there, helped her fight off the creep forcing himself on her. Neither of them had ever talked about that night again, aside from the occasional vague reference. Some things were better left unexamined, for both their sakes.

She shoved down the memories with a deep breath, reminding herself that Blanche probably had good intentions. They always pushed her to expand her comfort zone, which was admittedly tiny. From their perspective, Tara's resistance to kissing was just another boundary like her other million boundaries.

Mr. Brown Eyes leaned close, murmuring. "I'll make myself scarce at midnight. I don't want to spoil the fun, but I didn't want to blindside you."

She looked up at the intoxicating coffee-brown eyes searching her face. "Did... Did you remember?"

"That you don't kiss? Yeah. Blanche and Jazz seemed pretty adamant that we couldn't get away with a peck on the cheek, so I figured I'd warn you," Gabe said, like it was nothing. As if he hadn't just shown her more consideration than Tara had experienced in months of dating.

It might ruin Blanche's fun, but Tara could show him some consideration in return. "Look, I know you don't know us, but you don't have to do shit if you don't want to. Blanche was just giving you a hard time. Tell them to fuck off if you want."

Gabe leaned in closer. Her heart pounded, defenses rising, but his mouth moved to her ear instead of her lips. Strangely, disappointment swirled with her relief. "All the same," he hesitated as if debating whether to finish his thought, "I'll uh...make myself scarce in the en suite bathroom five minutes before midnight. You're welcome to join me."

Tara's eyebrows rose as her body flushed hot. "Huh?"

Gabe huffed out a sardonic laugh, tugging his curls again. "I really thought I could keep myself from doing this. But you just had to fucking moan, Kitten, and I've wanted to hear that sound again a thousand times." Those coffee-brown eyes she'd dreamed about for months were staring into her soul. "Look, if getting eaten out sounds better than watching everyone else kiss at midnight, you know where to find me."

Tara swallowed hard, her gaze darting to Gabe's lips. "We shouldn't." Her thighs clenched as heat pooled between them anyway.

"You're right. This is a terrible idea." His thick fingers twisted the ends of his loose ringlets. God, the things those lips, those fingers had done to her last time. "But I... I didn't think I'd— I *accepted* that I'd never see you again, and if I did, I'd probably be a raging asshole. That's not really an option if our best friends are together."

Tara shot him a skeptical look. "And hooking up *is*?"

Gabe shrugged. "Not at all. But, the offer stands. If you want."

She did want. Very much. She didn't *want* to want, but her desire was screaming louder than her brain was scolding her for being stupid. Tara was breaking so many of her rules, but with Gabe's pretty eyes looking at her like she was a four-course meal, she couldn't remember why her rules were there in the first place. "As a rule, I don't get involved with people I know."

Gabe raised an eyebrow. "You don't do repeats either if I remember right. You ever break your rules, Kitten?"

"Only when I want to." At his pained wince, she added, "Which I do! It just has to be a onetime thing." *Fuck. What am I doing?* "They can't find out about it. Or the first time. Especially now that we know what we are to Lee and Tonio."

With a forced half smile, Gabe nodded, his stunning eyes cloudy with resignation. Slightly better than the wince, but not enough. Those eyes didn't plead with her, didn't beg like they had the first time they'd met. "I figured. Tonio would give me so much shit if he found out I missed his first performance because I was on my knees with my face in your cunt."

Tara's thighs clenched at the memory. "Can we do ten minutes?"

His dimples appeared as an earnest smile erupted across his face. *There.* "I won't need ten minutes to make you come, Kitten, but I'd go down on you for hours if you let me. I'll be in the en suite ten minutes before midnight. I hope to see you there." Gabe stepped back, eyes dark with want as he raised his glass. "Thanks for the champagne, Tara."

The sound of his honey-deep voice saying her name had her biting back another moan.

"Hey, Tara-Bear?" Sunny asked sweetly, poking her head into the kitchen.

"No."

"Bitch, you don't even know what I'm going to say yet!" Sunny scowled and held up her glass. "I just want a refill."

Tara looked at her skeptically as she handed the bottle to her. "What else? You don't use your nice voice unless you're up to something."

Sunny emptied the bottle into her glass. "Well, now that you mention it, Jazz wants to know—"

"No."

"You don't even know what it is!"

"Fine. What?" Tara already knew what Sunny was about to ask.

"I think Jazz—who is basically our sister, remember—has a crush on Blanche and wants to kiss them at midnight. But if only Jazz and Blanche kiss, Lee would flip out. You know how overprotective he is. So she asked that we kiss—"

"I'm not kissing you."

Sunny scoffed. "You *wish* I'd kiss you! No, Jazz was hoping we'd kiss Tonio's friends. I figured you'd pick the tall one. But Gabe said he'd only do it if you wanted to."

"And you drew the short straw to ask me?" Tara's heart softened in a surge of gratitude. If Gabe was anyone else, he wouldn't have warned her. For most people, a New Year's Eve kiss was just a meaningless kiss. It was, as far as anyone but Lee knew.

"I'm the only one who could take you if it turned violent," Sunny teased.

"How do you feel about it?"

Sunny shrugged. "Wal-Mart Draco Malfoy has nice lips."

"I thought we were boycott—"

"Do *not* cisplain my own ethics to me." Sunny huffed. "Fine, Nordstrom Rack Justin Bieber Circa 2015 has nice lips. Not that I've been looking."

Tara snorted, sipping her champagne. Sunny hadn't been *looking*; she'd been drooling. "I was more asking about Blanche kissing someone else. You guys were together not that long ago, and you have a jealous streak. Are you sure you're ready for that? I'm sure Jazz would understand if you explained it."

Sunny scowled again. "I'm over any romantic feelings for Blanche."

"If you're sure." Tara shrugged.

"So does that mean you'll kiss Gabe?"

"Not a chance in hell." Tara paused. "But for the sake of getting you to shut up, sure."

RICHARD

WHERE THE FUCK IS Gabe? Did he seriously bail? And Sunny? And Tara? Richard was standing awkwardly by himself as midnight neared. Well, with Antonio, Lee, Blanche, and Jazz, who had paired off to watch the television as some drunk D-list celebrities counted down the last few minutes.

"There better not be any tongue," Lee warned.

Blanche held up their hands. "I would never."

"I trust *you*. That was directed at Jazz."

Jazz shrugged. "Worry about your own damn mouth. Don't stress about what I'm doing with mine."

"Jazz..."

"Lee..." she mimicked as Antonio and Blanche snickered.

Richard shifted uncomfortably, unsure how to engage in this conversation. He and his brother weren't close; he didn't know how to insert himself into another sibling relationship, especially when he barely knew Lee and had just met Jazz.

"Lee, you are going all big brother on her again," Antonio sighed, as the clock counted down from sixty seconds. "Jazz, I promise to kiss him long and hard enough to make him forget he has a little sister, so you and Blanche can swap spit all you want."

Jazz and Lee both cringed.

"Again, this is just a peck for the sake of a New Year's tradition. And a little fun manipulation among friends," Blanche added, glancing at Richard standing off by himself. "But I'm not sure how effective it was. We seem to be missing some mouths."

Richard stuffed his hands in his pockets, unsure how to respond.

To his relief, Sunny appeared with thirty seconds to spare, standing uncomfortably far away, yet still somehow too close to him. She glanced over, her eyes flicking down to his mouth. "So apparently, we're kissing."

Richard couldn't read her expression. Someone looking at his lips was a sign they were interested, or so Gabe had told him once. But she was about to kiss him, so maybe that rule didn't apply? His stomach twisted. "So I've been told. Have you seen Gabe?"

"No, and Tara's pretending to be sick in the bathroom." Sunny rolled her eyes. "If Gabe asks, it's nothing personal. Tara doesn't kiss, but she's too proud to back down from a challenge."

"Probably for the best then. He seems to be hiding, too. If Tara asks, also nothing personal. He's a hopeless romantic. Kissing actually means something to him." Richard remembered to smile at the end to show he was teasing.

Sunny's lips twisted as if she were faking her own smile. "Weird. For the record, this doesn't mean anything."

"Agreed." Richard was still shocked that Sunny had agreed to this. He'd had worse New Year's Eves than kissing a beautiful, witty woman at midnight, though. A meaningless kiss was more than acceptable.

The others loudly counted down from ten, while Sunny and Richard stood in silence. As everyone screamed "Happy New Year!" Sunny turned to him, a scowl on her face. "Let's get this over with."

Richard barely processed the plush warmth of her lips against his and a brief aroma of citrus before Sunny stepped back quickly. Fingers pressed to her lips, a rosy blush blossomed on her cheeks.

He resisted the urge to pull her back and kiss her properly as Sunny bolted to the kitchen.

LEE SWAYED WITH ANTONIO, holding him tight against his chest. His eyes closed as his cheek rested on Antonio's brown curls. "I love you, babe."

Antonio wore the same lovesick smile that had been plastered on his face since the day he'd met Lee. "You've told me that eight times since midnight. I love you too."

Richard swallowed, chalking the sour twinge in his chest up to the champagne. *Never pegged Lee for the sentimental type. Glad Antonio's obsession isn't as one-sided as I first thought.* Antonio was impossible not to love, even for Richard, who'd begrudgingly come to see the frustrating, annoying, and bubbly man as a younger brother.

And Lee was significantly nicer than Richard, so of course Lee would fall head over heels. Everyone did when it came to Antonio. He was like a weed: hard to get rid of, but once he was gone, the colorful flowers were painfully absent. The three years Richard had lost contact with him after his blowup with Gabe had been indescribably bleak.

"You're such a sappy drunk, Angel." Antonio grinned and pulled Lee to the couch, depositing him between Gabe and Tara. The two of them had sat on opposite ends, both pressing into the couch arms as if they wanted to be anywhere but near each other.

Richard had expected Gabe to throw himself at the modelesque redhead with the green eyes and freckles now that she was in the same room as him. He'd been only mildly surprised when they'd reappeared after midnight, a conspicuous number of minutes apart, with Gabe's hair messily braided over one shoulder, and Tara's wrap pants tied completely differently. But no one else had commented on it, so Richard hadn't either.

It was best not to, for Gabe's sake. Richard, along with Antonio, Phineas, Gabe's parents, and Gabe's therapist, had been after him for the better part of a year to start living again. Now that he'd finished his most recent outpatient therapy, Gabe finally seemed to agree with them. Richard wouldn't want to discourage him by calling attention to it; Gabe was understandably cautious about new people. Especially attractive, strong-willed people, and Tara definitely gave an "I don't give a fuck what you think" impression—Gabe's kryptonite.

Lee grabbed Antonio's waist, pulling him onto his lap. Antonio nestled against him, smiling at his boyfriend like he'd hung the moon. Richard's chest twinged again, a fit consequence for drinking so much champagne.

"Makes you want to throw up, doesn't it?" Sunny murmured near his elbow.

Richard glanced down at her. He'd perched on the arm of Sunny's chair so Gabe could steal glances at Tara easier. That was less effective now with Lee and Antonio sitting between them, but Richard stayed put. "I assumed I was nauseous from the champagne, but you could be right. They are disgustingly cute together."

She smirked. "You must be drunk if you're agreeing with me."

Richard bit back his smile, carefully keeping his eyes on her face to avoid staring at her cleavage. "I'm not so proud as to refute hard evidence, no matter how much alcohol is involved."

"Hey, Buttercup?" Lee asked from behind Antonio's back.

"Yeah, Lee?" Tara replied.

"What time is it?"

Tara laughed softly. "Time for you to go to bed. It's almost three."

Richard should feel bad that their company was keeping Lee awake. But then again, Lee had single-handedly gotten him too drunk to drive anytime soon. Muttering about "social lubricant," he'd poured more champagne every time Richard started a new conversation with Sunny. *He did this to himself. I was planning on leaving right after midnight.*

Admittedly, his plans would have changed after that kiss with Sunny. Now Richard found himself wishing he'd brought his glasses and contact solution, so he could stay the night like she would be. Sunny didn't seem to like him much, but based on her reaction, she liked their too-brief kiss as much as he had. *Should I ask for her number?* He couldn't exactly flirt—well, *try* to flirt—with her while their friends were in the room. He'd never hear the end of it; he wasn't exactly suave. There was a reason he was chronically single, despite following all of the advice his friends gave.

"Hey, Tonio?"

"Yeah, babe?" Antonio rubbed Lee's arms.

"What was the last thing we needed to do before the party ended? I can't read it in my brain. You're sober. Can you check it for me?"

"You want me to read your mind, Angel?" Antonio teased. "God, you're perfect."

Richard gagged just loud enough for Sunny to hear. She snickered.

Lee stared up at Antonio adoringly. "Oh! I remembered. You wanted everyone to share their New Year's resolutions before they left!"

"I totally forgot! Who wants to go first?"

Best to get it out of the way. He detested the group activities Antonio thrived on. Richard raised his glass, rising from the arm of Sunny's chair and swaying slightly. "Mine is the same as every year: acquire a pair of genuine Freddie Krueger Dunks."

Sunny scoffed. "Your goal for the year is to spend an obscene amount on *shoes*? Should have guessed a snob like you would be a sneakerhead."

Richard sneered to hide his smile, delighted to find another topic that got a rise out of her. She'd started so many arguments with him that he suspected she enjoyed them, too. He didn't care about the shoes; the rare Dunks were merely an expensive and unrealistic goal so no one would bother him about actually completing it. "*You* wouldn't understand. I will spend as much money as it takes. I've been looking for those shoes for years."

Sunny glared at him. "Hyperinflation in the fashion—"

"Oh god, we'll be here all night if we wait for this to wrap up," Tara interrupted. "I want to scale up my graphic design business. Not sure how yet."

"Cheers to that!" Blanche leaned over to clink their glasses. They were stretched across a chair in Jazz's lap. "I want to grow my subscriber count this year, too. Big Pharma won't pay our rent forever. Jazzy, what about you?"

"I want freedom. Or at least not hide *everything* about my life from Mom and Dad."

"I know we just met, but if you feel you need to hide from your parents, they need to do a lot of the work, not just you," Gabe chimed in. They all turned to look at him. Gabe's red blush deepened against his olive complexion. "Sorry, you probably already know that. Sorry. Resolution. Uh... Maybe leave the house more," he muttered.

Leave the house more, Cooper? Antonio had practically bribed Richard to convince Gabe to come tonight. *Whatever could have changed your mind?* Richard caught Antonio's eye and tilted his head slightly to Tara.

Antonio smirked with a nod. "You should start with coming to Sunny's birthday party next month! Sunny, you don't mind if Gabe and Richard come, right?"

"Why rope *me* into this?" The betrayal stung, but this was exactly what Richard had missed when Antonio wasn't around.

Sunny sputtered. "Uh, yeah, whatever. That's fine."

"Great!" Antonio grinned and changed the subject before Richard could protest. "For my resolution, I want to release my, or rather Carlita's, first album. It'll be a deep house meets Carlita Asada experience!"

Lee tapped Antonio's thigh in excitement. "Can I help? That can be my resolution!"

Antonio kissed his cheek. "Angel, you're producing it. I don't know shit about making an album."

Lee pulled him close, a love-drunk smile on his face again, as Antonio looked around the room. "Who hasn't gone...Sunny! What is your New Year's resolution?"

Sunny smiled broadly. "Meet the love of my life who sees and respects me, wants everything I want, and meets my mother's standards. Easy peasy!"

Tara, Lee, and Blanche burst into laughter.

"Good luck, Babygirl. You had us until the end."

Sunny grinned, dampened by a slight twist as she chewed the corner of her lip. "I know, right? That'll be the day. In the meantime, I'll settle for someone to blow my back out."

Everyone laughed. Richard couldn't help but glance at Sunny, her soft lips and graceful neck, with one loose strand of her inky waves falling gently between—

He turned away, an annoying telltale heat rising in his cheeks.

Blanche and Jazz wore twin smiles that promised more mischief than the thinly veiled kissing scheme they'd come up with earlier. Richard scowled at them, but their smiles only grew wider.

SATURDAY, FEBRUARY EIGHTH

Chapter Four

Lee

Maybe their friends weren't meant to be friends.

Lee sipped his stout, watching Richard sanitize his hands again as he perched awkwardly on the wooden bench in their bowling lane. Was he gonna bust out the sanitizer after every turn? Even for Lee, that was a bit much. And why wasn't he even attempting to engage with anyone?

Not that he could blame Richard for not talking with Gabe or Tara, who were currently arguing about Gabe using her ball on his turn. Again. Still? Had they ever stopped arguing?

Why did everyone have to argue?

He just wanted everyone to have a good time and give Sunny a birthday party on par with a core childhood memory. He'd planned a whole evening for her, full of the things they'd never gotten to do when they were young. Pizza and a couple rounds of bowling, followed by a goth rave at a gay nightclub downtown, which was really more Sunny's scene than his.

Gabe had recommended the bowling alley, but Lee was still on the fence about the place. Not only were they over South (already too bougie), the bowling alley looked like it hadn't been updated since the 1920s. Instead of tacky, colorful carpet and cosmic wallpaper, like most bowling alleys he'd been to, this one had dark wood trim and flooring, whitewashed plaster walls, and leaded glass windows. The whole place was too classy for creating the childhood experience that Sunny never had.

She seemed to be enjoying herself though, chattering on to whoever would listen (Lee), and the other lanes were all adults instead of a bunch of kids running around. He wasn't about to make a fuss.

"Because you keep taking mine!" Tara snapped. "Use someone else's. Or better yet, get your own!"

Gabe hugged the green ball, which Tara had designated as hers, protectively against his chest. "It's just a ball! What's the big deal?"

Who needed kids when emotionally stunted friends were just as annoying? Lee sighed quietly. They were only on the third frame of the first game. He took a swig of his stout.

"...so I'm stuck on what to name this app, you know?" Sunny's question clued him in that it was time to respond. He'd barely been listening as she rambled, but it was Sunny's birthday party, so Lee couldn't let her feel like she was talking to herself. No one else was engaging with her; she'd been especially talkative tonight, even for her.

Lee nodded politely, hoping it looked like he'd been paying attention. "What are you gonna do?"

"What *can* I do?" Sunny shrugged. "There's nothing sexy and snappy about a Kanban board. And every good name I've come up with is already trademarked tech."

Lee caught himself before he could ask what a Kanban board was. He'd asked four times and still didn't quite grasp it.

"Have you looked up synonyms of Agile?" Richard asked, finally breaking his silence. "Since that methodology is what you modeled for the self-help app. It might be a little on the nose, but inspiration might strike."

Sunny shot him a look. "What would *you* know, Dicky?"

Lee tensed, hoping Richard and Sunny wouldn't get into it. So far, they'd behaved, mostly because Richard hadn't taken the bait. To Lee's relief and guilt, Richard shrugged, returning to staring at his feet. Why were his friends like this? Why were Antonio's friends like this?

Luckily Antonio called Sunny to bowl, so she simply tossed her hair in Richard's direction instead of egging him on.

"Doing okay, Angel?" Antonio leaned against his shoulder. "You're up next, by the way."

Lee sighed. "I'd be better if our friends were more...friendly."

Antonio laughed. "They'll get there. Don't worry, what's the worst that can happen?"

"Famous last words," Lee teased, getting up to bowl as Sunny pranced back, excited that she'd hit a few pins this time. He gave her the corniest of double high fives, because that was what people did when they went bowling, even when they were bad at it.

That was the main thing he wanted from tonight: Sunny, smiling and having fun at her birthday party. Not arguing with Richard, or gnawing on her lip because Blanche couldn't be bothered to show up—though their calming presence was deeply missed.

Lee sighed as his ball went to the gutter. Sunny had looked crestfallen when Tara had walked out of their apartment building solo to hop in Lee's car. Not that it was Blanche's fault that their patron had terrible timing, but things had still been a bit tense between Sunny and Blanche; he'd hoped tonight would smooth things over.

His second ball knocked half the pins down. Sunny and Antonio cheered for him, giving him cheesy high fives as he reclaimed his spot between them.

Lee grinned despite himself. Maybe this wouldn't be a disaster after all.

"Don't use my ball! I don't want to wait for it to come back!"

Lee groaned into his stout. Antonio patted his thigh.

"Oh no, your life is so hard. You have to wait thirty whole seconds for the machine to bring it to you." Gabe was cool most of the time, but damn, his sarcasm could be cutting.

Tara snatched her ball up before Gabe could take his turn.

"Seriously?" Gabe scoffed. "Real mature."

"Says the man throwing a fit because he can't use the pretty ball."

Gabe tugged the end of his braid. "C'mon, that's my good luck charm! I've gotten two strikes in a row with that one!"

"Find your own!" Tara moved out of the way as Gabe reached for the ball.

"See? They're having fun!" Antonio murmured, kissing his cheek as he stood to referee. "In their own way. They're just a little short-tempered. We can't all have the patience of an angel."

Fighting a grin, Lee rolled his eyes, turning back to Sunny, who hadn't even noticed he'd been talking to Antonio. She was still talking about...cats? Yeah, she'd moved on to cats.

"Stop—oh shit!"

"Look out!"

Antonio's cry of pain made Lee whirl around. Antonio fell backward, tripping over the bench. His arm hit Lee's shoulder as Antonio tried to right himself. Lee lurched to catch him, losing his grip on his glass as he kept them both from eating shit on the floor.

"What the fuck is wrong with you?" Tara demanded.

Gabe's face turned ashen as he stared at Antonio, who whimpered helplessly in Lee's arms.

"What happened?" Lee asked, his voice catching in his throat. "Tonio?"

"Ball landed on his foot." Richard picked the beer glass off the floor, which thankfully hadn't shattered. He set it on the table before he retrieved the green ball from under the bench and dropped it back on the conveyor. "Antonio, shoe off."

Antonio only sniffled, burying his face into Lee's bicep. His nails were biting into Lee's forearm. Pressing a kiss into his hair, Lee rubbed his shoulder, at a loss for what to do beyond empty comfort.

"Gabe, find an ice pack." Richard turned him toward the main desk, guiding him a few feet until Gabe started moving on his own. "Tara, go find a mop—" he paused, glancing behind Lee. "Or better yet, a bar towel. Paper towels if you can't find one."

Tara nodded and bolted toward the bar.

Lee sat helplessly, overwhelmed and out of his depth. Again, this was why Blanche needed to be here. They were the cool head in a crisis. They'd tell him what to do.

Richard knelt down in front of Antonio. "Tonio, I'm going to see what the damage is. Lee, hold him steady. He's a drama queen about pain."

"Fuck you, I'm not a drama queen." Antonio's scoff sounded more like a whine.

"Prove it." Richard smirked as he unlaced Antonio's rented bowling shoe.

Antonio leaned into him. "You're such an ass, Dicky." Lee wrapped his arms around Antonio, kissing his neck and murmuring something that was hopefully soothing.

With a shrug, Richard gripped Antonio's ankle and slowly worked the shoe off. A bead of sweat dripped down Antonio's temple as he gritted his teeth and dug his nails deeper into Lee's arm. Breath tight in his chest,

Lee did his best to keep calm, feeling spectacularly useless. The other lanes staring at them made his skin prickle.

With a manager in tow, Gabe returned with an ice pack as soon as Richard pulled Antonio's sock off. Antonio winced; his toes were already reddening. "Good timing," Richard rose. "Gabe, you're better at this than me. Figure out if he broke anything."

Gabe knelt as Richard spoke with the manager. He held up Antonio's foot, prodding gently around the inflamed skin. "Can you wiggle your toes?"

Antonio laughed. "Is this my Uma Thurman moment?"

Gabe grinned as he rotated Antonio's foot, checking for his reaction. "Can't be that bad if you're making jokes."

"You broke my foot, asshole!"

"Wiggle your goddamn toes so we know for sure if I broke your foot."

Antonio huffed, but curled and wiggled his toes. "Fine, you probably didn't break my foot. But you're still an asshole!"

"You should still get this checked out." Gabe worked the sock onto his foot.

Antonio shook his head. "No, they're just gonna give me pain meds."

"Look at you," Gabe chided, carefully pressing the ice pack against Antonio's foot. "Last time you sent me to the ER, you were arguing with the doctor that I needed 'the good stuff,' and then you stole it all."

Antonio groaned. "Not my finest moment, but exactly why I'm *not* going to the ER."

"Urgent care, then," Gabe said sternly, glancing up at Lee in a silent question. "Until then, rest, ice, compression, and elevation."

Lee nodded, relieved to have a role to play. "We'll go tomorrow morning. You won't end up with any prescriptions you don't want."

Antonio huffed. "Fine. Thank you."

Tara finally returned, holding the bar towel out to Richard. "Sorry, the bartender couldn't take a hint."

Richard gestured toward Lee. "That goes to Sunny."

Shit, he'd forgotten about Sunny. Lee stiffened, craning his neck around. In silence, Sunny sat behind him, tears streaming down her cheeks as she stared at her lap. Dark brown beer had soaked into her new dress, the stain spreading from neckline to hem. Long strands of hair clung in strings against the wet skin of her neck and chest.

"Sun, I'm so sorry," Lee whispered, his chest aching. "It slipped out of my hand. I didn't mean to—"

Sunny silenced him with a shake of her head.

Tara approached her hesitantly, holding out the towel as if Sunny might bite her if she got too close. Sunny didn't take it. After some hesitation, Tara mopped up as much of the beer from Sunny's skirt as she could.

"Sunny? You okay?" Tara murmured. "I'm sorry, this is all my fault."

"Just go." Sunny's voice cracked. "Please. Just go. All of you."

Lee said, "I should drive you—"

"No. Please. Just..." Sunny sniffled, wiping her cheeks with her fist. "Bring Antonio home."

Wishing more than ever that Blanche was here, Lee looked helplessly at Tara. She stared back like she might burst into tears herself.

Richard coughed politely. "I'll take care of things here. And make sure she gets home."

Lee wanted to stay and comfort Sunny. He wanted to carry Antonio home and magically heal him. He wanted to go back in time and erase the past few minutes before everything had gone left. This was supposed to be a fun night with friends, a celebration for Sunny. And instead, everything was ruined, and there was nothing he could do to fix any of it.

Torn, Lee helped Antonio sit up and got both of their shoes changed.

"I can drive you home," Gabe offered to Tara as he and Lee helped Antonio up. "It's the least I can do. That way Lee can get Antonio home right away."

Before Lee could insist she ride with them, Tara shrugged. "Whatever. Sure."

With one last desperate and hopeless look at Sunny—who still stared into nothing, refusing to look at anyone—Lee helped Antonio hobble to the door, ignoring the stares from everyone else as they passed. His heart split more with every step.

TARA

THE TENSION IN THE car was stifling. Tara tried to find something, *anything*, to break the silence, but words failed her. She couldn't even look at Gabe, instead watching the city pass through the window of his Outback. If the mood were lighter and they were friends, she'd crack a joke about him being a stereotype. But they weren't friends, and Tara's hands were shaking. She had to clench her jaw to keep it from quivering; there was no way she could muster lighthearted anything. She'd probably burst into tears.

The GPS shouted to turn left onto the bridge to cross the river. The click of the turn signal echoed in the quiet.

She'd been planning to ignore Gabe, to pretend he didn't exist. That was the smartest course after they'd agreed not to hook up again. Willpower was not her strong suit, and Gabe was... Well, she was tempt-ed.

The ten minutes they'd stolen at New Year's Eve (closer to eight because he'd stopped to bring her another cheesecake thingy) had been so stupid. Glorious, but stupid. She'd hoped that a quickie would be enough to get him out of her system, that the reality of Gabe wasn't as good as she'd remembered. That he'd fuck her and come, and she wouldn't, and she could tell herself that he was just a normal human, instead of the attentive, talented sex god she remembered.

But Gabe had spent all eight glorious minutes going down on her, making her come so hard she'd cried. Facing him again after that was a new level of humiliation she never wanted to experience again, even though he'd been very sweet about it. Their one-time thing had been an appetizer, not the harsh dose of reality she'd wanted.

To make matters worse, he'd done everything in his power to annoy her tonight. He'd not only stolen the last slice of supreme pizza, but Gabe kept stealing the ball she'd picked, forcing her to watch his thick fingers disappear into the holes and heft it in his giant ass hands. It was a new low, to be jealous of a damn ball. And he'd met her annoyance with teasing, turning the bickering into banter when Tara was trying so hard to *not* flirt with him.

And look where it'd got them. The image of Antonio, sweating and twitching from the pain they'd caused, had imprinted itself on the back of her eyelids. And Sunny... Tara wrung her hands in her lap, picking at a hangnail. She should have been focused on her friend, instead of giving Gabe the attention he didn't deserve. Sunny had been so angry, shutting down rather than spend another minute with Tara.

And Tara had just left her. On her birthday. She shivered as a chill curled in her chest. That wasn't how they worked. They argued and fought, but Tara had never made Sunny so coldly furious before. She should have stayed.

The GPS sent them down her street, past all the fancy new condos to their much smaller, run-down building. For a moment, she felt embarrassed, remembering Lee's comments about how loaded Gabe must be and how nice his house was. But if he looked down on the place she was grateful to call home, then that spoke volumes about his character. She had enough shit to worry about between the angry Sunny she'd abandoned, and the guilt-ridden Blanche awaiting her upstairs.

Tara finally looked at him as she unbuckled her seat belt. His jaw was clenched, fingers tight around the steering wheel as Gabe looked ahead.

She opened her mouth, half-tempted to invite him upstairs so they could get this out of their systems properly. Lee's old bedroom had been fully converted to a playroom for Blanche's clients; she wouldn't have any of his intoxicating woodsy vanilla scent lingering in her sheets. No memories of Gabe would haunt her bed afterward.

Instead, she sighed and said nothing. They'd agreed no more.

Besides, Tara was angry. Fucking him while she was feeling *anything* this strongly would be dangerous. They were stuck with each other for as long as Lee and Antonio were together, and that wasn't changing anytime soon. Probably not ever. "We have to figure this out."

Gabe raised his eyebrows, still not looking at her. "*We* do, huh?"

Her jaw clenched harder. Was he blaming her for this? He'd been the one to—

"I can't hurt Antonio." Gabe's deep voice was raspy. "I mean, we already did. *I* already did. I've already put him through so much bullshit, and tonight I let my shit come before him. I have to put him first. Everything else is irrelevant. This is...whatever. I can't hurt him again."

Her breath caught as that chill curled in her chest again. He looked over at her then, his deep-set eyes shiny in the dim flicker of the streetlights.

"Are you—" Tara caught herself. They weren't friends; asking if he was okay wasn't her place. And she understood. She'd hurt her friends tonight just as much as he had. So instead of arguing, or making sure he was okay, or inviting him up to finish what they'd started on New Year's, Tara simply nodded. She didn't want to be relevant to him anyway. "We'll just...focus on them, then. Pretend nothing else ever happened."

Gabe shrugged, his working jaw not hiding the tremble of his lip.

"Thanks for the ride." Tara slammed the door behind her.

Chapter Five

Sunny

Sunny gnawed on her cheek, willing the burning behind her eyes to keep from becoming tears. Her makeup was probably ruined already. If one more person asked if she was okay, she might cuss them out. All she wanted was to go home and sob in bed. In private, without everyone staring at her like she was an alien.

This was officially the worst birthday party she'd ever had.

Everything had gone wrong. Everything that could have *possibly* gone wrong did. And here she was, wearing ugly bowling shoes and a dark beer stain on her new lilac dress. She wrinkled her nose at the bitter smell, cold seeping against her stomach and into her bra. The empty chairs of their lane stood out like a sore thumb against the rest of the alley, full of families and friends laughing and playing together, having fun without a care.

Sunny was an outsider at her own birthday party.

"You look like you could use a drink."

Sunny glared at Richard, the sole survivor of the disaster. Out of everyone, he was the last person she'd expected to stick around.

Rented bowling shoes in hand, Richard stood a few feet away, his crisp white sneakers back on his feet. Her stomach twisted; he was ready to bail on her too. Her resentment was unfair; she'd told everyone to go. She just...couldn't take the staring. Telling them to go had been the only way to get everyone to stop looking at her.

Luckily, Richard's gaze was directed at the table, where her stuff was strewn everywhere. His usual bored expression was modified only by his slightly raised eyebrows. Compared to his blond hair brushed back too neatly and his spotless navy chinos, Sunny felt even more disheveled.

"Don't tell me I fucking look like I need a drink, Dicky!" she spat, trying to hide her hurt behind the banter expected of her. Her eyes burned again, and she screwed them shut.

Sunny jumped when he touched her arm. His brow was creased in concern when he glanced at her. This tender expression was unusual; he'd previously been all sneers around her. "I didn't mean it like that. I meant to say, let me buy you a drink before we go. You deserve it after that shitshow."

Sunny choked on her laugh, losing the fight against her tears. Luckily, they merely welled up instead of streaming down her face. "That was a shitshow, wasn't it?"

From the start, her birthday had been doomed. Blanche hadn't bothered to show up, sending Tara with a present and an excuse. As if a gift would make up for their absence. Even *if* the leather choker with a cat charm was cute, Blanche's presence would have meant more than any gift. That was their post-breakup agreement: to keep showing up for each other. But Sunny came second to work. Just like she always had, even when they were dating.

Then everyone had ignored her completely, other than Lee, who had only half-listened. She'd kept trying to find different topics so he wouldn't be completely bored, but she should have known better. They'd never had anything in common; their friendship was rooted in history, not shared interests. She should have let him get drawn into the bickering between Tara and Gabe, like everyone else. Sitting quietly on the sidelines would have been fine with her, but he'd been so determined to make her feel special that Sunny thought she should try for his sake.

The final straw had been the beer. The bowling alley was overwhelming—with the loud crashes and the cheering and the music. Antonio's pained yelp, followed by the cold sticky splash down her neck and chest, oozing into her lap, had broken her. No one had even noticed her freeze, unable to cope with how overwhelmed she was, until Tara had pushed the sticky dampness into her skin. And then they were all staring like she was an animal in the zoo, instead of their friend fighting to keep her composure.

So she'd told them to go. And they had, and it hurt. Lee, she understood; Antonio's skin had turned a ghastly shade of gray. He was lucky his foot wasn't broken.

But Tara hadn't even argued back, just took Sunny's anger with resigned acceptance. Somehow her silence hurt worse than everything else. Tara always argued with her, always bluntly shared her honest thoughts. That was how their friendship worked.

"Lift up your foot."

Sunny blinked. Richard knelt before her, hand cradling her ankle as he unlaced the rented shoes on her feet.

Too stunned to do anything but comply, she lifted her foot, staring in confusion as he took her shoe off and slid her boot over her foot. "Dicky, watch your sneakers."

Richard looked down at the creased toes with a shrug. "They're just shoes."

"Spoken like a rich man," Sunny teased, but she was touched. For someone who, by all observations, was a snob and a sneakerhead, he was ruining his otherwise mint-condition shoes to do something nice. For *her*.

Richard looked up at her with what almost passed for a smile. "If I were Gabe, I'd say 'if the shoe fits,' but that's low-hanging fruit, and I'm above awful puns."

"Of course you are." Sunny rolled her eyes, shifting her weight as his fingers closed around her other ankle. She firmly ignored the swoop in her stomach while his robin's-egg blue eyes lingered on hers as he knelt before her.

Richard finally looked away to lace up her boots. She should have felt embarrassed or angry that he was tying her shoes for her, but Sunny couldn't find it in herself to protest.

"Why are you doing this?" she asked quietly when he rose. Strange that where her friends should be laughing and celebrating her stood someone that she was surprised had shown up in the first place. Richard had been strangely polite compared to New Year's, refraining from making any classist comments under his breath as he'd traded his Jordans for rented bowling shoes. The bare minimum of politeness, but half of her wished he'd taken any of the openings she'd given him to have another argument.

"Consider it a birthday present. I wasn't sure what to get you." Richard wrapped a hand around her elbow. "Shall we?"

She ignored how warm his hand felt through the sleeve of her dress as he led her away from the crashing of the bowling lanes, past the billiards clacking and the murmur of conversation, to a quieter room. The mostly empty dining room was drenched in the aroma of fried appetizers that all bars seemed to serve, with an undercurrent of stale cigarettes lingering from when it was still legal to smoke inside. The blue glare of a sports broadcast on mute and neon beer signs lit the room. It was a quiet relief compared to the overwhelming excess of the lanes.

Richard sat her down at the bar and passed her a few napkins.

Sunny dabbed helplessly at the beer stain on what had been a cute dress, cringing as the cold damp pressed into her skin. She pulled the tight fabric away from her body as she crumpled the napkins around it.

The bartender came over, long hair pulled into a high pony and her smile wide. "What can I get for you—oh, your dress!" Her grin fell. "Let me help with that, sweetie!" She quickly wet a bar towel and reached over the bar to dab at the stain on Sunny's stomach. "That's so stunning on you, too! Such a shame!"

"That's okay." Sunny leaned away to dodge the towel. Her dress was already clinging to her enough—she'd rather have the stain dry and set than have a stranger with a wet rag get the already-gross cashmere even grosser.

Richard cleared his throat, pushing the bartender's hand down against the bar. "I'll take a ginger ale." In a softer tone, he added, "Order whatever you want, Birthday Girl."

The bartender perked up again. "Oh, happy birthday! You can have a free shot on the house. Our specials are up there." She pointed to the sign above her with a wink. "Though I'd probably give someone like you a free shot anyway."

A free drink should have brought a smile to her face, but tonight it was just enough to keep her from crying. Sunny quickly scanned the menu. "Can I get a Blow Job for the shot and a vodka cran with Grey Goose?" If Richard was paying, she'd make him splurge a little. "You don't mind, right Dicky?"

"My treat." His cold expression returned as he turned to the bartender. "Leave the towel."

The waitress raised her eyebrows, tossing the towel on the counter as she left to make their drinks.

"Dicky is a great nickname for you." Sunny picked up the damp towel. She probably *should* try to blot the stain. It might not be as bad if it was of her own volition. Sunny huffed. She really *would* need a drink after this. "You're kind of a dick."

"You're welcome for stopping her." Richard scoffed.

Sunny snorted. "And here I thought you were just being rude."

"She was being rude first."

"What? How?" The waitress had been perfectly friendly.

Richard shook his head. "You shouldn't let tannin stains dry in cashmere."

"Such a snob..." She cringed as she pressed the damp towel to her sternum, hating the fresh layer of cold and wet over the sticky, chilled damp.

Strange that her new frenemy—who irritated her more often than not—was being almost considerate today. Not that she didn't enjoy their lively debates on New Year's, but she'd never admit that. She liked the crooked smile he tried to hide when she made a good point, and the smirk when he got the best of her. He didn't need to know that her stomach swooped whenever he turned to her out of the blue, saying something incredibly classist, as if he was *trying* to get a rise out of her.

But this was Richard, no point in overthinking his attention, nice as he was being at the moment. She wouldn't do another one-sided relationship like the one she'd had with Blanche. Instead of another distant, emotionally unavailable partner, Sunny wanted euphoria. Someone to yearn after her. A simp who would embrace all of the family expectations and responsibilities that came with loving her. *That'll never be Dicky.*

"I'm sorry your party turned into a mess." He patted her arm awkwardly.

"Lee must be so pissed." Sunny snorted. "They ruined his whole itinerary. He loves planning shit like this."

"Bowling is a choice." Richard added hurriedly, "Not judging, just a far cry from the barhopping most twenty-somethings did when I was younger."

"How old are you?" Sunny asked.

"I turned thirty-one in January."

"Oh, yeah, you're way too ancient to remember your twenty-somethings." Sunny teased as she moved the towel to the stain on her lap. "Lee and I never got to have a Standard American Birthday Party when we were kids. My mae said it was a waste of money, and Lee's parents were too strict to let him enjoy anything."

Sunny loved and appreciated her mom, despite how stifling she could be. Birdie had been through more than anyone should've had to experience, but she still made sure Sunny and Luna felt loved, if not always seen. According to Sunny's grandparents, her mother had been a free spirit until the accident that took Sunny's father and brother. She'd since embraced the traditions she'd previously fought against.

There were pictures of her and her brother in party hats when they were young, eating cupcakes at an amusement park, a smile on everyone's face—even her mother's. But every birthday Sunny remembered was spent at temple, followed by a quiet family dinner that Birdie had decided was their birthday tradition. Sunny went with it out of love for her mother, but that didn't stop Sunny from longing for that normal kid experience everyone else had.

"Mae means mother, right?"

Surprised, Sunny shot Richard a smile. "Don't tell me you speak Thai, Dicky."

Richard shook his head. "No, just super basic greetings from when I've been with my family. I butcher the tones."

"Of course, you've been to Thailand. I haven't even been." Her dress was still smelly, but the worst of the stain had lifted. She set the towel on the bar. "You're right. Mae means mom. Her name is Birdie. Well, Taksa-orn, but she goes by Birdie."

"Do you have another name, too?" Richard paused. "If that's rude to ask, ignore me."

"Good thing I already think you're rude," Sunny teased to hide her wince. "Sunny is the nickname my phaw gave me when I was little. Mae says my legal name can be a girl's name too, but I don't really use it, and I dunno if I want to change it. Mae's the only one who calls me that, and that's only when she's mad at me."

Before Richard could respond, the waitress brought over their drinks, including a second shot for Richard. "Here, I messed up the first one. Your boyfriend can have it on the house."

Sunny stiffened and opened her mouth to correct her, but Richard simply thanked her dismissively and raised the shot to Sunny as the waitress walked away. Instead of arguing, she picked up her shot and clinked it against his. When Richard raised the glass to his lips, Sunny burst into laughter.

"That is *not* how you do it, Dicky. *This* is how you drink a Blow Job." She set the shot glass on the bar, wrapped her lips around the rim, and tilted her head back with practiced ease. Sunny swallowed it smoothly; she and Tara had drunk a lot of these when they were younger. The novelty of the shot was made sweeter with the nostalgia.

With a wary look, Richard tried to imitate her. He sputtered out a cough as he swallowed it down. "Jesus Christ! What is that?" He gagged, a hint of whipped cream escaping the corner of his mouth.

"What, too big for you to take?" Sunny teased.

"It wasn't the size, it was the content!" he retorted snobbishly, wiping his full bottom lip with his thumb. Sunny couldn't tear her eyes away as his thumb disappeared into his mouth to lick it clean. "Is that cream? That's awful!"

"It's a blow job!" Sunny couldn't keep the smile off her face. "If you're good at it, something creamy usually goes down your throat. Weren't you and Gabe a thing? Don't tell me you never sucked him off."

Richard scowled at her, but his eyes had a hint of laughter. "Trust me, he never had any complaints. Although, Gabe was the one and only cis guy I've dated, so it's been a while since I gave anyone a blow job."

"Oh, so Gabe turned you straight?" Sunny teased, hoping he wouldn't think she was flirting. *Am I flirting?* She shoved the thought away. Rich assholes were not a viable port in the perfect storm of her love life. Even ones with square jawlines and pretty blue eyes, who bought her a drink on her birthday.

Richard huffed and shook his head. "Gabe opened my eyes to many things, but straight? No, I am not *opposed* to being with men, but women and non-binary people are generally less annoying. As attractive as they can be, cis men and I typically don't interest each other."

"I wish I had that problem."

"Oh, so *you're* straight? You were projecting, I see."

If she wasn't misreading his tone, Richard was teasing her. Sunny scoffed, pretending to be offended. "No! You obviously don't have to weed through the chasers to find a decent lay. I have low standards, but being fetishized is beneath me. It's easier if I avoid cishet people."

Silence fell over them. Sunny sat awkwardly, sipping her vodka cran, searching for something to say that wouldn't bore him like everyone else, for anything they might have in common. But Richard spoke first.

"I always wanted a regular birthday party too," he said softly. "When I was a kid, I mean. Not now. I wanted a party at a skating rink or a zoo. Hell, even a sleepover like they had in the movies. But my birthday always ended up being about my dad somehow."

"What, did you have a gala instead?" Sunny teased. "That's the richest-sounding thing I can think of."

"The dress code was usually black-tie, so basically." Richard's blue eyes met hers. "I don't want to sound ungrateful, but I wanted my birthday to be about me. I don't know if any of the kids there wanted to be my friend, or if they were forced to be there like I was. And those fucking dresses my mom made me wear." He scoffed at the memory.

Sunny would never fully understand, but she resonated with the resentment in his voice. "Sounds like we both had to put our parents first," she said softly. "Not that I mind. I love my mae. But that didn't make it any easier when kids stopped inviting me to their birthday parties because I didn't have one to invite them to. Mae never understood why I wanted one." Sunny sipped her drink to clear the lump in her throat. "That's why Lee planned this. We were both outcasts in school, mostly because of our parents. Neither of us had many friends. I *still* don't, even if he grew up to be Mr. Sociable. He gets it."

Richard was less awkward when trying to comfort her this time. He touched her hand on the bar, squeezing her fingers in sympathy.

Sunny left her hand where it was, confusion whirling with a profound sense of being seen. She never expected to find *Dicky* commiserating with her and holding her hand.

Socioeconomically, they stood in opposite corners of an economist's scatterplot. Their stereotypes were a Cinderella story waiting to happen, except Dicky was no prince charming, and as the proud breadwinner of her family, Sunny was in no need of rescue. Sure, she wanted a partner, but she wanted someone who would join her family, not take her away from it.

Even if she was a romantic at heart, a relationship wasn't just about the feelings. Love wasn't enough. One person wasn't just connected to one person. They were connected to their families and friends, to their ancestors and descendants, to society as a whole. Relationships created a shared responsibility to everyone in their lives, not just a single link to one person.

That was what had been so uncomfortable about dating Blanche; they'd needed to keep Sunny secret, away from every other aspect of their life. Sunny couldn't have that again, not if she was committed to someone. If it was just fun or casual, sure, that could be a secret. It was better that way; her mother didn't need to know about casual flings. But commitment? A partner? They needed to fit into Sunny's life. They'd need to earn her mother's approval.

So Richard wasn't an option, even if he was acting nice. *Although if he ever wanted to fool around, I might consider it.* Sunny scolded herself. *He isn't an asshole for one hour, and I'm ready to let him hit? He's just being polite.*

Although, he wasn't always an asshole. While not her usual type, besides being blond and relatively androgynous, Richard could be funny. The muttered sarcastic comments about their friends, just loud enough for Sunny to hear, had been a highlight of New Year's. And he wasn't bad looking. He kept his straight hair styled neatly, and his obnoxiously blue eyes were... interesting. He was well-built, with straight shoulders and a trim figure. And he always dressed annoyingly well, usually in some designer label or other.

Above all, Sunny had tried especially hard not to notice his lips. They were full and ridiculously soft—a fact confirmed during their kiss, which had been strangely gentle. Sweet even. Completely opposite from their arguments and bickering.

Richard cleared his throat, raising an eyebrow. He'd caught her staring directly at his lips as she'd zoned out. Heat flooded Sunny's cheeks. She was probably bright red, and it wasn't entirely the alcohol's fault.

His hand was warm, still resting on hers. Maybe the shot had given her liquid courage or a wave of vulnerability had hit her, but she turned her hand over and intertwined their fingers together.

A blush erupted on Richard's face, leaving two rosy patches on his fair cheeks. It was adorable, reminding her of New Year's again. He'd been pink before they'd kissed at midnight, and downright scarlet afterward. Like then, the flush crept down toward his neck. Like then, she was so close to his full pink lips and blue eyes and neat blond hair that she wanted to—

Sunny tore her eyes away and pulled out her phone. "I should go home."

"I can drive you."

She shook her head. "I can Uber. You've already been way too nice. It's getting weird."

"Then text me when you get home. I promised Lee."

Her heart beat a little faster. "I'd need your number to text you."

Richard held out his hand for her phone. She passed it over to him, imagining how hard he'd blush if she sent him pictures of her tits. *He is flirting with me, isn't he? Am I reading this wrong? I probably am. I don't even know if I'm flirting.*

He handed it back. "I'll walk you out at least. To make sure you get in the car and the driver doesn't look like a serial killer."

"Predicting that based on appearance sounds like profiling." Sunny grinned as she hopped off the barstool. "But...thanks, Dicky. For saving my birthday. Never thought I'd say those words to *you* of all people."

He snorted as he threw a fifty-dollar bill on the bar—way too much, but if he wanted to overtip that was his business. And he had been rude to the bartender when she'd only been trying to help. Richard picked up her winter coat and the gift bags with the presents she'd completely forgotten about; she hadn't even noticed that he'd gathered her belongings for her.

Sunny smiled at his blush when Richard's guiding hand slid from her elbow down her forearm, pausing at her wrist. She laced her fingers through his as they left. After all, no one they knew was there to notice.

Sunday, February Ninth

CHAPTER SIX

ANTONIO

"I CAN NEVER WEAR heels again." Antonio winced, adding another pillow under his foot. Pain radiated up his leg. For the first time since he'd left rehab a year ago, Antonio wished he hadn't sworn off pain relievers. No muscle he'd pulled onstage, back pain he'd woken up with, or headache after a long night of bad dreams had made him regret that decision as much as the dull ache throbbing from his toes. "How am I supposed to go on stage like this? Or worse, get around during passing time?"

While nothing was broken, his nail beds had turned black overnight. His normally brown toes looked deep purple, clearly swollen in the afternoon light. But he could wiggle all of his toes and rotate his ankle normally. The urgent care doctor had reaffirmed Gabe's assessment that he'd be fine with rest and to come back if it wasn't getting better within two weeks.

"Maybe take it easy on the choreo for a while. And wear steel-toed boots to school." Lee kissed his forehead, an ice pack in hand. "Here, time for cold treatment."

Antonio squeezed his eyes shut in anticipation. Fighting a moan, he flinched from the sharp chill as Lee carefully wrapped the ice pack around his toes.

"Are you sure you don't want Aleve or anything? CBD ointment?" Lee pleaded, seeing through his mask of attempted bravery.

Antonio shook his head. The jump from Advil and Benzos was gaping, but he didn't want to take the first step unless it was an absolute emergency. "Not today, not tomorrow. That's the promise I made to myself. No pills. No nothing." He forced a grin. "Straight edge, baby! Punk as fuck!"

Lee snorted, his mouth twisting as he rubbed Antonio's leg. "I hate seeing you like this."

A tentative knock sounded on the door. Lee left to answer it, returning moments later followed by Tara. Head hanging low, her short mop of red curls covered her eyes.

Pushing himself up higher on the couch, Antonio waited, giving her space. For as much as Tara complained about Lee's tendency to apologize for things that weren't his fault, she was just as bad. Tara hadn't caused his injury; she'd been hanging onto the bowling ball for dear life. And yet here she was, looking guilty as sin.

"How's it going?" she muttered after a few seconds.

"It's been better." Antonio's chest buzzed with affection as he waited for her to work up the humility to apologize for something she didn't need to. As Antonio's oldest friend, most of his annoyance was saved for Gabe. Tara might have stubbornly hogged the ball, but Gabe had kept using it when she'd told him not to. Most people would have just found a different ball. But Gabe was a poorly socialized dumbass.

Their bickering might have been lighthearted flirting if they were anyone else, but neither Tara nor Gabe did anything lightheartedly. In the rare moments Gabe wasn't staring at Tara while she pretended he didn't exist, they antagonized each other. Antonio could taste the sexual tension, and it was painfully overripe.

Collapsing in the chair, Tara sighed after an awkwardly long silence. "I'm so sorry. I feel awful. I should have just let him use the damn ball. Seriously, is your foot okay?"

"They might have to amputate," Antonio said seriously, laughing a little at Tara's shocked face. "I'm kidding, Tara-Bear. I might lose some toenails, but nothing's broken."

"Anything I can do to make it up to you?"

Another knock sounded at the door. Lee gave Tara a warning look as he went to get it. "You might have to start with being nice, Buttercup."

She scowled as Gabe walked in, a serving dish in hand. A mouth-watering aroma of apple and cinnamon filled the room. *Oh, he's forgiven.*

Glancing at Tara, who looked everywhere but at him, Gabe set the platter down on the coffee table. "Your foot okay, Tonio?"

"Yeah, no thanks to you, asshat."

"I'm sorry. It got out of hand." Gabe raked a hand through his long hair, nervously playing with the brown ringlets that hung down to his waist.

Antonio shrugged. "I've done worse to you, I suppose."

Gabe's dimples framed his charming smile. "I still have a BB pellet somewhere in my left ass cheek."

Antonio laughed. Gabe had gotten stitches more than once due to Antonio's dumb ideas when they were kids. "Good! You need to be reminded what a pain in the ass you are sometimes. So what is this peace offering, Master Baker?"

Gabe tried to hide his laugh. "Tonio, that joke stopped being funny when we were fifteen. But it's tarte Tatin. Mom's recipe." He nudged it closer to Antonio.

Antonio wiped the corner of his mouth before he started drooling. "Lee, Angel? Love of my life?"

Lee was already headed to the kitchen. "I'll get the dishes and coffee for everyone. You want tea?"

"Yes please!" Anything that might keep him awake at night alone with his thoughts, or make him jittery and anxious, was not part of his sobriety plan; herbal tea was as crazy as he got these days. Even with Lee there to help him, Antonio didn't want to give his dark thoughts a chance to intrude. Or his digestive system room to act up.

An awkward quiet fell over the living room in Lee's absence, while Gabe and Tara took turns glancing at each other. Antonio hoped their silence would win out today; he didn't have the patience to referee the two most stubborn people in his life. They'd ignored each other at New Year's, but Sunny's birthday had brought out their annoying sides. Antonio had spent most of last night trying to keep them from causing a scene, and the moment he'd looked away, he'd ended up limping home.

His hopes for peace were dashed when Gabe opened his mouth. "So where's *your* peace offering?"

"Wasn't aware I needed a bribe," Tara snapped, "An apple pie can't buy forgiveness when you don't deserve it."

"This is not apple pie. It's a tarte Tatin," Gabe snipped back.

Tara flushed, red spreading down her neck. Whether it was embarrassment or anger, Antonio would rather not find out.

"Can you two just stop?" he interrupted, tossing his hands up. "You came to apologize for taking your petty bitching too far, and here you are, bitching over who had the better apology! Look, *I* am not the one you should be apologizing to! *Sunny* is the one whose birthday was ruined! That had to hurt worse than some squished toes."

The two of them at least had the humility to look chagrined. Sunny had texted Lee that she'd made it home safely the night before, and Richard had done the same in the group chat Antonio had with him and Gabe. But even though they both knew Sunny was fine *now*, they'd all still left her there in tears. Antonio's chest twinged.

Gabe and Tara stared at the floor.

Tara broke the silence first. "I need to apologize to her too. I will."

"Thank you, Tara." The strain in her voice was mollifying. "And you, Gabey? You'll apologize to Sunny next time you see her?"

Gabe nodded. "I feel bad that we ruined her birthday."

"We?" Tara muttered under her breath.

"Yes. *We.*" Gabe's voice was sharp.

His glare went unmet as Tara looked at the coffee table, her hands pressed between her knees. "If *you* had just gone to find another one instead of constantly stealing mine—"

"Staaaahhhppp!" Antonio sighed heavily. He hated being the peacemaker. "You're worse than my seventh graders! Maybe you should apologize to each other!"

They exchanged glares. Neither seemed ready to give in, both refusing to be the first.

Lee returned with a tray full of steaming mugs and dessert plates. He set it down gently, the clatter of cutlery on the ceramic echoing in the lingering silence. "We all good?"

"We're good," Tara replied, finally looking directly at Gabe. "I'm sorry. I let my stubbornness get the better of me. It didn't matter if you used the ball or not."

Gabe swallowed heavily, staring her down. "I'm sorry I kept using it after I knew it bothered you. I should have used a different one. Tara." He said her name like a dare.

Tara's swallow was audible in the quiet of the room.

Ugh, they need to fucking bone already! Why they hadn't yet was beyond him. They weren't prudes. Gabe had always been a horny ass motherfucker, and Tara's body count may have rivaled Antonio's if he'd ever bothered to keep track. Why keep dancing around their obvious mutual thirst?

"Good, we're all mature adults!" With a clap of his hands, Antonio redirected the attention to himself. "Can we eat, please?"

"I've lost my appetite." Tara stormed from the room. The front door slammed shut a second later.

Lee chased after her. "Buttercup, wait up!"

Antonio glared at Gabe, crossing his arms. "Why are you such a dick?"

"Me? I was just giving as good as I got." Gabe wouldn't meet his eyes.

"No, you were a complete and utter ass yesterday. Worse today! You're better than this, Gabe," Antonio scolded. For all Lee's anxiety that his friends would be rude to Antonio's friends, it was *Gabe* who was acting uncharacteristically dickish. "Seriously, what is with you? This is worse than high school, and you were a raging twat back then! This is worse than *Richard*."

Gabe sighed, his fingers tangling in the ends of his hair again. "I'm not trying to start anything. Maybe *she* should—"

"Will you stop blaming her? Tara is a person with feelings, not a punching bag for whatever the fuck is going on with your moody ass." He jabbed an accusing finger in Gabe's direction. His sternum burned as embarrassment turned to anger, flames spreading the more Antonio spoke; Gabe had upset Tara and, by extension, his future husband. "You're supposed to be the sweet, easygoing friend, but your pissy attitude just caused Tara to walk away from apple pie or *tarte Tatin* or whatever the fuck it is! I've never seen her turn down any food ever, let alone fucking *dessert*. Don't be a dick just because you're in denial that you're into her!"

"I'm not!" Gabe retorted, running his hand through his hair.

"I don't know what you think is happening, but Tara isn't the problem. Tara's a good person, Gabe. She's not hurting you. She's not bullying you. Until you open your damn mouth to start shit, she pretty much ignores you completely!" Heat creeping up his neck, Antonio took a deep breath to calm himself, humming his Intentions Song to mellow his anger back to a manageable flame. "Just give her a fucking break, Gabe. You do with literally everyone else in your life. She's got her own issues. She doesn't need to deal with yours, too."

Gabe's brown eyes blinked wildly. His shoulders heaved, jaw working back and forth.

"Are you okay?" A flash of worry doused Antonio's anger. He couldn't tell if Gabe was about to explode or burst into tears. *You pushed him too far. You did it again.*

He didn't have many memories of New York. But the memory of the cold text message he'd gotten from Gabe after a fight much like this one, telling him they could no longer be friends because of how Antonio had treated Gabe's then-girlfriend, still haunted him. "Sorry. I took it too far. Talk to me?"

Gabe stood up. "Sorry. We're okay. I— I just need a moment. Sorry again." He strode quickly to the door to leave just as Lee returned, sans Tara.

Lee pushed his glasses up. "What's with Gabe?"

"Angel, I appreciate you. So. Much." Antonio sighed, throwing his arms across his face. Frustration itched at his brain, making him wish he could chase after Gabe like Lee had with Tara. *Maybe it's good that I can't walk.* Gabe had seemed pretty wretched; he probably did need space.

Lee pulled Antonio's arms away from his face to kiss him soundly. Antonio softened as he let Lee ease his frustration, anger, and worry. Kneeling on the floor next to Antonio, Lee took Antonio's hand in his.

Antonio smirked. "You're not proposing when I'm injured, are you?" Lee had said he'd propose after six months of living together; it'd only been four. It'd be very unlike Lee to rush into a big decision. Any decision really.

Lee shook his head with a laugh. "No, just less awkward to sit here because you're hogging the couch. We haven't even been dating for a year. I could still change my mind."

"Lee!" Antonio whined, disappointment flickering in his chest. He'd been ready to elope for months, but he was being patient. There was no point in rushing; they had their whole lives ahead of them. "You better ask soon so I can do the big public grand gesture proposal. I just need to decide if I should choreograph a flash mob or hire a plane to write our names in the sky."

"Oh, no. No. Both of those sound hella corny," Lee teased. "I would definitely say no."

Antonio tsked. "Whatever I come up with, it'll be the best fucking proposal of your life, Angel. You'll be so touched that you won't even consider turning me down."

"Hopefully it's the *only* proposal of my life." Lee kissed his hand before settling to the floor, leaning against the couch. "Gabe okay?"

Antonio let out another deep sigh. "I hope so. I was a little harsh with him, and he's sensitive." Sensitive was an understatement some days, albeit he'd been better the past couple months as Gabe had wrapped up his DBT program. But Gabe wouldn't want his business shared, so Antonio left it at "sensitive." What Antonio knew and remembered about Gabe's mental health only scratched the surface, anyway. "Is Tara okay?"

Lee shrugged, pushing up his glasses. "She said she needed some space before she lost control of her emotions. Which I suppose is good, because the Tara I used to know would have just punched him."

Antonio smiled affectionately. "You did tell her to be nice. Honestly, they got along better today than I expected after how they acted yesterday. Maybe forcing our friends to hang out and be nice to each other is actually helping them."

Lee opened his mouth, pausing. "I have what might be a bad idea."

"Is your idea to knock some sense into Gabe so he's not so much of an ass to Tara?"

Lee shook his head. "No, it's not to constantly supply Tara with snacks either, because Richard and Sunny's arguing is annoying, too. They're less intense because they argue about really boring shit, but it'd be nice to hang out all together without any arguments or ethical debates. New Year's was *so* much." He pushed his glasses up. "Tara and Sunny used to fight a lot. They only learned to get along because Sunny was constantly around. So, maybe, we keep creating opportunities for them to hang out? Like, finding excuses to force them to get used to each other. Who knows? They might just become friends."

"*Or* more than friends." Antonio nodded, imagining how hard Tara would blush if Gabe let her see his sweet, affectionate, dependable side, instead of the resentful asshole. Maybe with enough time, Gabe would get his shit together and stop embarrassing himself. If dragged to these get-togethers, Gabe might finally see that he was ready to live a little.

And Richard could... *Well. Dicky's gonna Dicky.* Blanche had insisted he and Sunny were flirting when they'd filled Antonio in on their New Year's kiss plan, but Richard wasn't suave enough to flirt. *Unless being a snobby douche is his way of flirting.* Antonio paused. *You know, it probably is. No wonder he's always single.* Regardless, Richard would see through this plan in a heartbeat and mess with it. Probably double down and argue with Sunny even harder.

"Uh, if that's what they want," Lee said. "I just want less conflict. And they'd be happier with more good people in their lives. Like we are!" He kissed Antonio's hand. "All of them limit themselves so much. It'd be nice to show them that they don't have to push everyone away."

Antonio's heart melted. If their friends becoming friends (or more) was what Lee wanted, then damned if he wouldn't be the most support-ive future-husband and help him achieve it. "We should get Blanche in on this."

Their New Year's Eve/Housewarming party had been a little awk-ward, but it would have been significantly worse without Blanche and Jazz's scheming. Throwing their friends all together at once had led to several arguments, and Tara drinking champagne by herself in the kitchen. The fun parts—including the strangely tender and completely unexpected midnight kiss between Richard and Sunny—were almost entirely courtesy of Blanche and Jazz.

Richard wasn't affectionate, especially around other people. Antonio had never seen him kiss anyone other than Gabe, and that was *always* initiated by Gabe. *Hell, I had sex with Richard, and he never kissed me! He just bit me.* "How do we keep them from just ignoring each other the whole time?"

"What if we're late to shit?" Lee suggested. "Like we tell them to meet at six somewhere, then say we're 'five minutes away' for half an hour, so they have time alone to talk."

"That could work. Though I doubt they'd believe you could ever be late to anything." Antonio tapped his chin. "What will our excuse be? Like, if it was just me? Sure. But no one will believe the guy who was fifteen minutes early to our first date is suddenly late to everything."

"Hey, I was not the only one fifteen minutes early to our first date," Lee teased. "You wanted to record an album. We could strategically let time get away from us when we're working on it, so that way it's not a lie. Then text that we're running behind so they feel obligated to stick around and make small talk." He snorted. "Or at least run out of things to argue about."

Antonio squealed with delight, no longer caring about the friendship plan because he'd totally forgotten about his album. "Yes! I have the tracklist planned out, but that's as far as I got. You're the best." He cupped Lee's face to pull him in for a tender kiss.

Lee pulled away too soon. "This isn't going to backfire on us, is it? Is this manipulative?"

Antonio shook his head. "Of course not! We're just creating an op-portunity. They're making their choices. Whether they choose to get along—or get together—is up to them."

Tuesday, February Eleventh

CHAPTER SEVEN

SUNNY

"What do you wish for Sunny, Luna?" Birdie lit the candle stuck into Luna's cupcake, holding back the billowing sleeve of her blue silk top she'd worn to temple, so it wouldn't fall in the marinara sauce left on her empty dinner plate.

Every birthday, the Boonmees made the hour-and-a-half bus ride to the suburbs to make merit. There were closer Buddhist temples in Bellamy, but "their" temple was one of the few that practiced Theravada traditions, with resident monks from Thailand. Birdie insisted they make the journey, as if bringing alms to these monks specifically somehow earned them bonus merit. Sunny wasn't sure it worked that way, but it made her mother happy. Besides, this temple had given her father and brother a proper funeral after their untimely death, so they could leave offerings where their ashes were interred, too.

"Mae, you know this isn't how you do birthday candles, right?" Luna asked, already changed out of her dress clothes and back in her uniform of a pastel hoodie and leggings. "Sunny is supposed to make a wish and blow out the candles herself."

Her little sister was fighting a losing battle. Birdie knew the "right way;" she just liked her way better. Luna was young though, just a freshman in college, and she still wanted to fit in. Sunny had given up on correcting her mae's interpretations of American traditions when she was still in elementary school.

"I don't want Sunny breathing all over my cupcake."

"Mae!" Sunny protested, fiddling with the too-tight collar of her blouse. She didn't care about the candles, but it was the principle that her own mother wouldn't eat a cupcake she'd breathed on. "I *made* the cupcakes. What's the difference if I blow out the candles?"

Birdie shot her a look. "Exactly. You're not the best cook. I'm already putting my life at risk."

Sunny huffed in mock-offense; she hated cooking enough that she was bad on purpose. Everyone knew it, and Luna liked cooking, so Sunny only cooked on her birthday.

Luna snickered. "At least she didn't try to make seafood again this year."

"Hey, I do the cleaning for a reason!" Sunny kicked her sister under the table. "If you don't like it, *you* cook my birthday dinner instead."

Birdie tutted, "Sunny, calm down. We're teasing. The pasta you made was edible." She raised her eyebrows to point at Luna's candle. "Luna, make your wish for Sunny before the wax drips."

"I wish you...have fun this year." Luna blew out the candle as the first drop of wax rolled down the side. "But for the record, we're not supposed to say the wishes out loud either."

"How else will Sunny know what we wish for?" Birdie shook her head and lit her own candle. "I wish that you get a promotion at work, and that you meet a nice woman, preferably Thai but at least Buddhist, who aspires to motherhood." She blew out the candle before either Luna or Sunny could protest.

"Mae, that sounds more like a wish for you than Sunny." Luna met Sunny's gaze with a sympathetic eye roll. Sunny gave her a half smile back.

Birdie shrugged. "I want the best for our family. Don't you?"

"Yes, Mae," Sunny and Luna said in unison.

Yet another opinion of Birdie's that Sunny had given up trying to change: her plans for Sunny. Not so much about marrying a woman and having kids. Sunny was attracted to people of all genders; marrying a woman wasn't the issue. But being with someone who saw her as a wife, a partner, an equal—not a husband—was her priority. That is, *if* she somehow managed to find a cis woman in Bellamy who was willing to be Birdie's traditional daughter-in-law *and* love Sunny as herself. Sunny's vision for her life was diametrically opposed to her mother's out-of-touch vision of her future.

"Can I make a wish for myself?" Sunny asked, already knowing the answer.

"No, eat your cupcake."

"Yes, Mae." Sunny picked up her cupcake and paused. *I wish to become more myself this year.* She breathed the wish into her cupcake.

That wasn't how wishes worked either, but this was her own unorthodox birthday ritual. Instead of blowing out a candle, Sunny exhaled a wish, the same one she'd been making every year for longer than she could remember, into the funfetti frosting before licking it off. Though everything her family wished for her—and the millions of things she wished for herself—seemed impossible, the positive intentions sent into the universe for her were a comfort.

Her phone buzzed with several incoming texts. Instead of their normal group chat, Lee and Antonio had started a new one. This one included a new unknown number, and one labeled Dicky that she'd been trying not to think about.

Lee: Happy Birthday Sunny!

Antonio: Happy Birthday!!!!

Antonio: Hope everyone is free on Saturday! I snagged y'all a VIP table for Confession's Palentine's Day Drag Show!

Antonio: There's no getting out of this.

Saturday, February Fifteenth

Chapter Eight

FEELING PAINFULLY EARLY AS the only nonemployee in Confession's upstairs venue, Richard waited patiently for the bartenders to finish their conversation to order a ginger ale. He wasn't a big drinker, but he wanted something to hold to occupy his hands. Someone would push a drink or two on him later—probably Gabe, although Lee seemed to have the same "generous" habit—and he didn't want to make a fool of himself tonight.

The neon lights, erotic art, and plants that normally decorated Confession's brick and wood beam interior were joined by red and pink genitalia balloons. A few hearts were thrown in, but even those had nipples or assholes drawn on them in Sharpie.

Arriving promptly at nine as Antonio had instructed, Richard had only felt even more awkward sitting by himself in the VIP section. He'd gotten up to get a drink to stand near other people, instead of alone in a sea of empty chairs.

That only he had been told to come so early was suspicious. Richard grew even more suspicious—but not displeased—when the host showed Sunny to their VIP table across the still-empty room. He turned to the bartender and added a Grey Goose and cranberry to his order.

Of all of Tonio's stupid ideas, I'm not that upset about this one. Normally, Richard would have grumbled and made a fuss about going to Antonio's show. And he *had* grumbled and made a fuss, completely ignoring the new group chat. It would have been suspicious if he hadn't. Antonio had threatened to visit Richard at work for lunch before he'd finally agreed to show up tonight.

He enjoyed giving Antonio a hard time—he was always going to come, especially once Antonio mentioned Gabe would be there. But Antonio didn't need to know that. Secretly, Richard was grateful for the chance to see Sunny again. And she looked just as stunning as she always did. *There is no "always," you've met her twice!* Her maroon sweaterdress flattered her curves. A heart-shaped cutout in the neckline made her generous cleavage impossible to miss.

As he walked over, Richard let his eyes linger on her long wavy black hair, tumbling down over her shoulder, before getting her attention by gently scolding her. "You never texted me that you made it home last weekend." He slid Sunny the vodka cran as he sat next to her.

She blushed. "Oh. I thought you were just trying to be nice. It was very unlike you."

Richard snorted. "I would have texted you to ask, but I don't have *your* number." He'd considered kissing her last week when they had that...moment between them, but he wasn't sure she wanted that. Especially after she'd just been crying. Giving her his number seemed like a safe option to test the waters.

But Sunny had never texted him.

If that was because he hadn't clearly communicated his interest, or if she wasn't interested, was unclear. Richard hoped it was the prior. Flirtation wasn't exactly his strong suit, so it was entirely possible.

"Dicky, are you asking for my number?" Her smile widened, a mischievous glint in her beautiful eyes. Richard hadn't worn makeup in years, but he appreciated the work she must have put into hers. Shades of blush pink and the same maroon as her dress accentuated her dark brown eyes. The wings of her eyeliner were sharp and perfectly matched.

"I thought that was obvious." He sipped his ginger ale. "I needed your number to ask you out for a drink."

She laughed. "Oh? And here I thought I was reading too much into it. I really shouldn't have chickened out on texting you those nudes."

Richard's cheeks burned. "You'd have gotten a lot more than a drink if I'd gotten nudes."

"Oh my, I'd get dinner too?" Sunny teased.

"Dinner would just be the start."

She tilted her head. "I can't tell if you're being sarcastic."

"No sarcasm intended." He stared at his drink to avoid feeling exposed by her thoughtful gaze. Richard normally wasn't this forward, but something about Sunny demanded his attention. Sure, she was attractive, but many people were attractive. Few were anything more than mildly interesting to look at. Admittedly, attraction had deepened into *more* last weekend. His resolve to let things develop organically, if they ever developed at all, had crumbled after Sunny's disaster of a birthday party.

The hurt in her eyes, the tears staining her cheeks, had made him want to fix everything. The anger in her voice, telling everyone to leave her alone, had demanded he comfort her. Then the apprehensive way she'd bitten her lip, when she'd laced her fingers through his, blew past what little reservations he'd had left. He'd needed to make Sunny happy. Happy enough to argue with him again, tease him, challenge him, flirt with him. If she was flirting, anyway. Though Richard was fairly confident she was after the nudes comment.

That bartender rudely hitting on Sunny right in front of him had been the moment Richard had realized he needed to do something, instead of waiting around for someone to notice him. He normally wasn't one for affection, like holding hands at a bar. But if anyone would be comforting Sunny after that disaster, Richard wanted it to be him. Not a pushy bartender.

"I'm confused. We've spent most of our time arguing. Is that what does it for you? Ethical debates? Classist degradation?" Sunny put her chin in her hand, leaning in closer as her eyes, so dark brown they looked black in the dim light of Confession, captured his.

Richard hesitantly put his hand on her thigh under the table, nudging his fingertips against the soft wool hem of her dress. "Whatever it is, it's working."

"Well, doesn't this look cozy?" A cool voice interrupted them.

Richard reluctantly removed his hand from Sunny's thigh as she jumped away.

Blanche draped themself in the chair on Sunny's other side. "What, no debate about inheritance taxes, or how designer labels are secretly funding fast fashion?"

Sunny laughed. "How did you guess what I was just about to say?"

"Oh, so you two *aren't* getting along? Sorry, my mistake." Blanche smirked. "Don't worry, I won't tell a soul that you don't actually hate each other."

Richard was grateful. As much as he wanted to see where this *thing* with Sunny was going, having a natural conversation would be impossible with Gabe and Antonio dissecting his every move and giving advice he didn't ask for. They were too damn supportive. He didn't want prying eyes and intrusive questions.

Speak of the devil. Gabe shuffled through the crowd toward them. The room was filling up; Richard's skin buzzed from the murmur of conversation. To most people, Gabe probably looked ordinary, but the signs of wallowing were obvious, especially after Gabe had been eerily quiet at work all week. His long hair was pulled into a messy bun, so he probably hadn't washed it, and he wasn't paying attention to his surroundings, catching his foot on a chair as he passed. There was a toothpaste stain on his navy blue sweater, and his khakis had obvious wrinkles.

Richard would never have noticed those things on anyone else. On himself, yes, *he'd* never leave the house with a toothpaste stain. But neither would Gabe, who was surprisingly vain when he wasn't in the throes of an existential crisis. *That's uncharitable. Stop thinking like Dick. Depression isn't wallowing or an existential crisis.*

Without a word, Gabe pulled the remaining chair out with a scrape and fell into it.

"Rough day, Gabe?" Richard asked cautiously.

"Shit, sorry. Hi, everyone," Gabe muttered.

Richard exchanged glances with Sunny and Blanche. They also looked concerned. *If people who barely know him can tell something is up, he must be going through it.*

Blanche tentatively touched Gabe's arm. "Gabe, you want a drink or something?"

Their touch pulled Gabe out of his daze. He sat up straight. "Oh, please, allow me." He turned to Sunny, finally meeting someone's eyes. "I'd like to apologize for my behavior last weekend. I let myself get out of hand. Please let me make it up to you."

Mouth parting in surprise, Sunny waved him off. "Oh, apology accepted! But my birthday didn't end up that bad after all. Antonio had the worst of it. The bridge water is already around the bend."

Gabe's return smile didn't reach his eyes, but the tension left his shoulders. "Still, let me buy your next round."

Richard bristled—*he* wanted to buy Sunny's drinks. But Gabe was being nice, and if it would help Gabe get out of his funk, he should be encouraging. So, in a way, it'd be *kind* of him to distract Gabe from his mood. Richard grinned. There were nicer ways, but goading him was the most fun. He waited until Blanche and Sunny had reluctantly told Gabe what they wanted to drink, before adding, "You know what I drink, Gabey."

"Wasn't talking to *you*, Dicky." Gabe flipped him off as he walked away.

"Don't call me Dicky!" he called after Gabe, pleased he'd gotten a retort from Gabe. There'd been a long stretch during Gabe's last relationship where Richard couldn't get any reaction out of him at all. He had been robotic. It'd been terrifying to see someone as sweet and dorky as Gabe barely existing, a ghost of himself.

His empty seat was filled by Tara a moment later. She presented Sunny with a plastic shopping bag. "Happy Galentine's Day."

Sunny squealed. "A present? But I didn't get you anything!"

Tara shook her head. "No, this is to make up for your birthday."

"Tara-Bear! You didn't have to!" Sunny made a heart with her hands before digging into the bag. "Is this Discounted-Day-After-Valentine's chocolate?!"

Richard's mouth twitched at her enthusiasm.

"I know you love chocolate, especially chocolate on sale." Tara grinned.

Sunny's eyes lit up as she inspected the various heart-shaped cardboard containers, reading the flavors inside. *50% Off!* stickers covered each box.

Her perusal of the chocolates was interrupted by Gabe depositing their drinks on the table. Somehow, he had carried five glasses by himself. Moments like this made Richard feel dysphorically small. Not that he was short. Five-eight was a perfectly reasonable height for a man. Gabe was just a giant, hands included.

As the conversation of the crowd—well over capacity with every chair full, and dozens of people standing around the back—dug its nails into Richard's ears, Gabe slid a gin and ginger in front of him despite his earlier protests, like Richard knew he would. Surprisingly, he also slid a drink in front of Tara. Maybe Gabe wasn't completely hopeless.

Gabe stared down at Tara. "You're in my seat."

Richard huffed. *Christ, Gabe.*

She avoided his gaze, unmoving. "It was open when I got here. Find another chair."

Gabe gestured around the now-crowded room. "There are no empty chairs."

Tara took a sip of the drink he'd brought her. "Stand, then."

He scowled. Despite the frown, Gabe looked more energized now than when'd he walked in with a cloud of depression hanging over him. More alive at least. More light in his eyes.

"Tara, be polite. You can share until a chair opens up." Blanche suggested airily as if it were nothing.

Richard bit back a cackle at the indignant expression on their faces, but Sunny didn't bother to hold back her laugh.

Tara sputtered on her drink. "Excuse me? Share? He'll hog the whole thing with those giant ass thighs of his."

"Looking at his thighs, Tara-Bear?" Sunny teased her.

Richard joined in the laughter as Tara's face turned red.

"Sit on his lap then for all I care. Or he can sit in yours." Blanche rolled their eyes. "He's too tall to be standing. He'll block my view."

Somehow Tara blushed harder, her cheeks almost matching her hair. Begrudgingly, she scooted over so Gabe could perch next to her on the chair.

"See? That wasn't so hard," Gabe teased.

"Don't talk to me," Tara snapped.

Richard caught Sunny's eye, exchanging a mischievous smirk. Gabe was, historically, very good with romance. For some reason, Tara brought out all his sharp edges, instead of the doting sweetheart he knew Gabe to be.

In fact, Gabe was acting more like Richard usually did. It was unsettling to see his own behavior mirrored back like this. *We don't need a second asshole in this group, Gabe. Get your shit together.* Richard would have to improve his typical dating behavior with Sunny. If he got a chance with her, anyway. He'd have to be less himself, less like his dad—perhaps more like Gabe *should* be acting or, God forbid, Antonio—if he wanted this to work.

Sunny tore the cellophane off one of the boxes. "Let's start with this one!" She popped a raspberry dark chocolate truffle in her mouth before offering the box to the table.

Richard tried not to stare, unsuccessfully. Hopefully the chocolate was distracting everyone else, because he could not tear his eyes away from her pretty mouth.

"Am I allowed to eat my apology gift?" Tara asked. She waited for Sunny's nod before taking a salted caramel heart and eating it with a moan. "Thank fuck. This is so good."

Sunny passed the box to Gabe, who declined with a polite wave of his hand, before passing it to Blanche. Gabe glared at Tara who was pressed against him, still loudly chewing her candy. "An apology gift, huh? Some might call that a bribe."

Richard lost the fight against an eye roll.

Tara chewed the caramel even louder, their faces inches apart. "So the drink was from the goodness of your own heart?"

Jaw tightening, Gabe's face flashed with emotions, none of them good. Richard's heart went out to him, even if he didn't understand why that had struck a nerve. Knowing Gabe, he needed time to get his thoughts together.

Richard cleared his throat, preparing to say something horribly snobby so Sunny could help him diffuse the situation. Even their most childish debate would be less intense than whatever was about to leave Gabe's mouth. *Maybe I let Gabe isolate himself for too long if he can't remember how to act.*

Channeling the worst parts of his mother, Richard said, "I don't believe it counts if it was on sale. A *real* apology gift should warrant paying full price."

Sunny took the bait, smirking as she licked the chocolate from her fingertips. Her pretty mouth lightly sucked on her thumb. "Chocolates are so marked up for Valentine's Day. The discounts the day after are closer to their true value. I would have been offended if Tara had put her hard-earned money toward overpriced candy."

Fighting a smile, he glanced toward Gabe and Tara. Their tension as they sat pressed together hadn't slackened, but at least their attention was drawn toward Richard and Sunny. *Saving your ass as always, Cooper.*

Richard turned back to Sunny, happy to buy Gabe some time to calm down, especially if it meant more time arguing with Sunny. "Chocolate production is notoriously labor intensive. It's better to pay full price, so the money goes to the farmers and workers who create it." His argument was trash, but Richard didn't argue to win.

"In a utopian society. Unfortunately for us," Sunny leaned forward as she spoke, the heart-shaped cutout in her dress making her cleavage impossible to miss, "we live in a capitalist hellscape where oligarchs hoard profit. The farmers never see gains, just violence and exploitation."

"So by eating this chocolate," Richard took one from the box without looking and almost spit it back out. *Dammit. Coconut.* He forced himself to keep eating the horrifying texture without breaking eye contact. Her smile widened as he gagged on the candy in his mouth.

"I'll give you a minute," she laughed as she ate another piece of chocolate, carefully inspecting the reference guide on the back of the box. The awful taste and texture were worth the delight in her eyes. The grin on Gabe's face didn't hurt either.

Richard continued after washing the hellish flavor down with the last of his ginger ale, "So by eating this chocolate, aren't you contributing to the problem?"

"I'd argue it'd be worse from a moral perspective to pay full price. By buying the leftover discounted chocolate that doesn't bring in as much profit, I use my purchasing power to ensure a greater percentage goes to the cost of production, instead of lining the pockets of billionaires." With a toss of her long hair over her shoulder, Sunny gave him a smug grin as if she knew she'd won. "Besides, the moral responsibility of ending labor exploitation falls on the companies making the decisions of where and how they source their chocolate, not on the individual consumers who have no transparency when deciding what chocolate to buy."

Fighting a smile, Richard shrugged to concede the point. Even he couldn't pull any decent counter-arguments to that, despite his Ivy League business education and wannabe-tycoon father doing their best to brainwash him. Not that he believed most of the bullshit he'd spouted at her; Richard just liked how she responded. Sunny was delightful to argue with.

"Maybe that should be my next app. A barcode scanner that tells people where their products are sourced from." Sunny turned back to the table, her grin smug with victory. "It'd be a fairly simple UI development, but sourcing the data would be difficult."

"You'd also get a lot of cease and desist orders," Richard added. "Large conglomerates don't share supply chain information. You could include whether or not companies provide that information willingly to encourage transparency, while also covering your ass."

With a flirtatious smile, Sunny pressed her hand to her chest. "As I live and breathe, are you helping me eat the rich, Dicky?"

Richard didn't fight his smile this time, hoping it was half as charming as hers. "No, that wouldn't be self-serving. I've obviously got an ulterior motive."

The lights darkened and the music turned up as the crowd cheered.

"Oh, fucking finally," Blanche drawled.

Richard's pocket buzzed a moment later with a text from an unknown number. Phone under the table, he opened an image of the loveliest tits. Dark areolas peeked out over a red lace shelf bra. The dark room thankfully hid the blush burning across his face.

> That's for the Grey Goose in my vodka cran.

> You deserve far more than vodka for that picture.

> Do more to earn it, then.

Sunny stared adamantly at the stage, her small smile barely perceptible in the dark. Richard ensured everyone's attention was on the show before placing his hand on Sunny's thigh. She bit her lip, still refusing to look at him, and traced the back of his hand with her fingers.

Chapter Nine

TARA

THIS IS TORTURE. TARA's heart pounded as Carlita Asada sang, look-ing shorter than usual onstage in combat boots. Antonio still couldn't get his swollen foot into heels. She should feel guilty about hurting him, but no matter how hard she tried, Tara couldn't give a fuck about anything on stage, not even Antonio's injured toes.

Because Mr. Tree Trunk Thighs was next to her. In her chair. Hogging it, really. And every time she turned toward the stage, her body molded closer against his.

For once, Tara wished an impending panic attack would trigger her flight instinct. Instead, she was uncomfortably aroused, her traitorous body desperate for more contact with his thigh and firm chest. She fought the urge to lean into the arm draped over the back of the chair that wasn't technically around her shoulders, but wasn't *not* around her shoulders either.

Gabe overwhelmed her senses. Their bodies were moving together with every breath they took, his exhale tickling her neck. The vanilla and oak scent of him flooded her nose. Afraid of what she'd do if she let herself breathe him in too deep, Tara kept her breath shallow. Every part that was pressed against him burned.

He cleared his throat, so close to her ear. What she wouldn't give to get Gabe to moan. Or speak, or hum. Anything. God, if his deep voice were to say her name...

As if reading her mind, he murmured into her ear, "Can I rearrange us? My ass is so numb I'm about to fall off this fucking chair."

Her heart racing, Tara simply nodded.

His arms slowly encircled her, gently gripping her waist just under her tits. As if she weren't already horny enough without fantasizing about those hands sliding up a couple inches. While he guided her off the chair, Tara briefly considered resisting. But Mr. Boundaries would actually listen if she told him to stop, and that was out of the question. Gabe wedged his muscular thigh underneath her as he slid fully onto the chair, perching her on his leg so she straddled his upper thigh.

Oh, what fresh hell is this? Tara swallowed, forcing her eyes to stay on the stage, unable to process who was up there or what song was playing. Without question, she would be replaying this position with her pillow and vibrator later. She was half tempted to rub one out on his leg right now. But Gabe had accepted her declaration that they wouldn't be hooking up again with more grace than she'd felt, and she'd respect that.

"This okay?" Somehow their new position brought his honey voice even closer. His deep timbre dripped into her ear and down her spine, turning Tara into a puddle. Was this asshole *trying* to turn her on, or just oblivious to the effect he had on her?

"Green," she whispered back, in case he was being annoyingly hot on purpose. Two could play at that game. He wanted her, too. Hopefully—*no, not hopefully. No more!*

His lips curved into a smile against her ear. "Make yourself comfortable. You feel tense."

This motherfucker *was* doing it on purpose. Tara wanted to lean against him, to have his arms wrap around her and pull her tight against him. To have his fingers massage her clit through her leggings. Or better yet, just fuck her like this. Sitting in his lap would be even better with his cock inside her. Even if they were in public, in front of everyone.

She exhaled sharply as Gabe's thigh twitched under her. Tara would not say no right now if he asked; if they were strangers, she might suggest it.

But no, she had to figure out how to be acquaintances with him. That was all they could be, despite Lee's insistence that they would all be best friends before long. Friends were off-limits, and Tara seriously doubted if she could ever platonically appreciate the gorgeous human she'd fantasized about for months. Anything more than reluctant acquaintances would get messy. And as fun as messy sounded, they couldn't cause any more problems for Lee or Antonio. They'd done enough damage already.

Tara tentatively leaned back to settle in and get comfortable, immediately regretting it when a whimper left her throat.

Gabe inhaled sharply. Had he heard her? He must have. Forcing herself to ignore how good his thigh felt under her, Tara settled herself against him. Her back pressed into his chest as embarrassment burned through her; her leggings were soaked.

Jesus, I'm going to ruin his pants. She had been wet for him already before he'd put her on his lap. Maybe this was why people wore underwear. *I need to get myself under control. We talked about this. No more.*

Tara had not expected her attraction for Antonio's best friend to grow exponentially in the few times they had hung out together. She thought she'd had it bad for him, at least physically, when they were strangers. But now that she knew him personally? Now that they had agreed they wouldn't fool around again? It was like having the most delicious cake in front of her and she wasn't allowed to eat it, making it all the more mouthwatering. Cake that somehow always got under her skin, no matter how determined she was to ignore its existence.

Gabe exhaled hard against her neck as Tara's heart hammered in her chest. She wondered if he could feel how her pulse coursed through her body with every heartbeat. Considering how hard his own heart was beating—and how hard his cock was growing against her—he must be able to feel hers too.

It's a little gratifying knowing he's as miserably horny as I am. Maybe I'm not out of his system either. She at least managed to resist the urge to grind against the erection pressing against her ass. His cock felt just as massive as she remembered. Not that she'd ever seen it, but it had split her in half from behind for an impressively long time.

"This brings back memories," Tara teased before she could stop herself.

"Sorry," he whispered. "I didn't expect you to make yourself *that* comfortable. Just, uh, ignore that, please. I'm so sorry."

Tara turned her head, her mouth against his ear as she stubbornly avoided glancing at their friends. It was dark, but she'd lose her nerve if the ever-observant Blanche was watching, and leaving her current seat was out of the question. "Considering your pants are gonna be soaked when I get up, I won't hold it against you."

Gabe exhaled a laugh through his nose as she turned back to the stage. "You already are, Kitten."

"You have the corniest lines, dude." Tara chose to not comment on the nickname. She had strong feelings when Gabe called her that. Mixed feelings, certainly, but all heated. Anger that he dared call her the nickname he'd given her when they first hooked up as strangers, when she had refused to give him anything more, not even her name. Yet there was also something soft and gooey that melted in her chest because he still called her Kitten. She should ask him to stop. Except he always made sure to never say it when others could hear.

"What do you want me to do with my hands?" Gabe asked.

Oh god, what a question. Her mind raced with the possibilities. *Choke me, pull my hair, stick three fingers inside my cunt and your thumb on my clit.* "Uh...huh?" she asked instead.

"I don't want to make you uncomfortable, but it's awkward to just hang them at my side. Can I touch you? Like, platonically I mean," he rushed to explain. "I—I just realized how that sounded. Sorry."

"Sure, I don't care," Tara responded, sounding calmer than she felt. "Just not—"

"Not your wrists. I remember, Kitten."

Any anger from the nickname was overwhelmed by whatever happy gooey shit was happening in her chest. *Of course, he remembers.* Almost no one she'd tried to date in the months following their first hookup had ever remembered her two simple rules: no kissing on the mouth, and no pinning her hands down.

Moments like this made her wish they were strangers again, free to see this attraction through. If sex happened again—*please let it happen*— Tara stiffened. *No, I'd just mess it up. This is Tonio's best friend. Don't fuck this up for Lee.*

Gabe wrapped his arms around her hips and pulled her close, his chin settling on her shoulder. A soft sigh escaped her; that stupid gooey shit was stronger than ever. Relaxing against him, Tara let this soft new feeling linger, enjoying the quiet moment between them without arguing and insults.

Maybe this was what it would be like if she'd gone back to his house that first night, when they were still strangers. If she had somehow managed to not ruin whatever connection they might have had together. If Tara could have let herself experience the intimacy shit Lee and Blanche always wanted her to try, like she longed for whenever other people were happy together.

Even though she and Gabe would never be friends or lovers, if she ever wanted something like Lee and Antonio had, she would want it to be with someone like him. Someone she could share quiet moments with, who made her feel wanted and respected and worshipped.

Tara tentatively rested her hands where his were wrapped around her hips, and laced her fingers between Gabe's.

He drew in a sharp inhale.

"Color?" she asked, wondering if she'd crossed a boundary and hoping she hadn't. The lines were so blurry for them, and he'd been cuddly and shit with her first. Besides, Lee wanted them to be friends, and Tara held hands with her friends. And, even though she wanted him too much to ever be his friend, Gabe had really warm hands. Hers were always cold.

"Green," he breathed out, his thumb gently rubbing against her own.

"You looked cozy during the show," Blanche noted as they walked home arm in arm afterward. The sharp February wind had pushed them together for warmth as they crossed the footbridge over the Mississippi back to Eastside. The ice under their feet crunched in the shadows cast by the streetlights.

Tara wrapped her peacoat tighter around her, reminding herself to look for a parka the next time Sunny dragged her along thrifting. "I don't want to talk about it, Blanche."

"Of course you don't."

As soon as the lights had come back up for intermission, the spell had been broken. The person holding her wasn't the hypothetical Mr. Brown Eyes That Might Have Been, it was Gabe Cooper, Antonio's best friend. The stark reminder that her vice had collided with Lee's growing social life had exploded into a clusterfuck of pesky emotions under the bright house lights.

She had put some distance between them by strategically knocking a glass of ice melt into his lap where she'd left a noticeable wet spot. It had the added benefit of quickly eliminating his lingering semi, though

Gabe hadn't appreciated her quick thinking. Their quiet moment had devolved back to bickering like it had never even happened.

Fortunately or unfortunately, a chair opened up during the second half. They put as much distance between them as they could, while still trapped on the same side of the table.

"He is genuinely nice, you know," Blanche tried again.

"Yeah, to everyone but me," Tara mumbled.

"Isn't he? He bought you a drink earlier, even though you waited until he left the table to join us. I wonder how he knew your favorite?" Blanche trailed off suggestively.

"Lucky guess." Tara's heart fluttered, threatening to break through the Sexual Attraction boundary she had firmly drawn around Gabe. Tara *had* been lurking, waiting for a chair before joining them so she wouldn't have to stand awkwardly like she'd made him do. And he'd still bought her a drink, the same drink Lee had gotten her on her birthday last year: Black Label with a splash of Coke.

"If you say so." Blanche put their arm around her. "You could be nicer to him. He's sweet when he's not flirting with you. Reminds me of another stubborn asshole I know."

"Who, yourself?" Tara grumbled.

They squeezed her close. "All I'm saying is that you use your thorns and prickles to drive people away, but you have the prettiest flowers if you get through the bramble. So ease up on the thorns. Better yet, show him your flower!"

"Blanche!" she protested. "Stop talking about my *flower* or how thorny I am."

"Thorny, huh?" Blanche laughed, squeezing her shoulders. "Just keep an open mind, babes. You wanted practice dating and connecting with people right? Well, Gabe seems open to *connecting* with you."

Tara snorted, but didn't respond. Her chance of "connecting" with Mr. Brown Eyes was over the moment she'd found out he was Antonio's friend.

CHAPTER TEN

RICHARD

RICHARD SPOTTED SUNNY NEAR the entrance of Confession. Thumb hovering over her phone, she scrunched her nose in displeasure.

"You look like you need a ride."

She jumped, but a shy smile bloomed when she saw it was him. "Is that an offer to drive me home, Dicky?" At his nod, her smile turned shy. "Thanks. The surge prices right now are astronomical."

"Luckily, you still have credit from earlier," he teased, zipping up his coat. He held out his hand, strangely craving her touch and nervous that she'd reject it.

But Sunny put her hand in his, allowing Richard to lead her to the parking ramp a block away. The mist of their breath frosted in the February chill.

"Were you serious about taking me to dinner?" she asked tentatively as they walked.

He gripped her hand tighter. "I thought that was obvious. I'd like the chance to get to know you better. Without the chance of being interrupted or...analyzed by everyone. Not that Gabe could have paid any attention to us tonight."

Sunny laughed. "Yeah, I don't know how they did it, but Blanche was slick with that chair thing. Tara looked so cute and horny."

Richard snorted. "Antonio must have had something to do with it. I imagine that's also why we were told to be there half an hour before anyone else." He gestured with their joined hands. "Not that I'm complaining. I enjoy talking to you. Just preferably without the audience."

"Well, there's a diner on the way… Could we grab a bite now?" Sunny suggested. For how smart and confident she was when they were arguing, the shyness in her voice was endearing.

With a nod, Richard unlocked his SUV.

"A Range Rover?" Sunny whistled. "I'm going to have to tuck and roll when we get to my house. This will get stolen in my neighborhood the second you put it in park."

"Why do I get the feeling that you'd be the one stealing it?" Richard asked wryly, opening her door for her. Opening doors seemed like something Gabe would do. If Richard wasn't going to be himself, he should probably try being sweet instead.

"Don't ask questions you don't want the answers to, Dicky," she teased as she climbed into the passenger seat. "And don't open my door for me. That's weird as hell."

"Understood." Richard hurried around the vehicle to turn on the heated leather seats once the engine hummed to life. "So what's the name of this diner?" He fiddled with the console, bringing up the map.

"Uh… Denny's?" Sunny replied as if it should be obvious. "Are there other diners open in Bellamy this late at night?"

Richard shrugged, typing in "Denny's." Six locations came up in the Bellamy metro. He didn't want to assume, but after her comment about his car getting stolen, he guessed the location in Eastside was where she meant to go. But if she *didn't* live in Eastside, that could be a faux pas he would not recover from.

He hovered over the screen, hoping she'd tell him. "Can't say I go to many diners. The last time I went to a Denny's was in college."

"Too good for America's Diner, Dicky?" Sunny touched the correct location on the screen, the Eastside location as he'd guessed, near Antonio and Lee's apartment.

"Too sheltered for America's Diner would be more accurate." He snorted mirthlessly. "If my parents knew Gabe and I had gone to a chain restaurant in Hartford, they would have cut me off. If that wasn't bad enough, we were high out of our minds during finals."

Richard's mom had never allowed him to go to Bellamy without her, let alone set foot into Illinois. He'd grown up with stories of murderous addicts leaving dead bodies in the streets of Eastside, and homeless men who would do unspeakable things to him. He sometimes wondered what his parents' skewed reality was like, where New York was peak civilization, and East Bellamy was a vile cesspool.

It was probably yet another example of his parents' tendency to control his choices. Barbie wanted Richard to marry a rich man with a penthouse on the Upper East Side, like she had. She'd married Dick to finance her socialite lifestyle, and now she was a lonely, bored housewife, safe and isolated in a gated community in Driftwood. Richard couldn't blame her for wanting more for him, but he wished she'd consider a future where he was happy being himself.

The diner wasn't far from Confession, merely a ten-minute drive across the river. He pondered how to stretch their time together in silence as he drove, hoping for inspiration, another meaningful commonality to spark a conversation with her.

Sunny didn't speak either.

It didn't feel appropriate to egg her into a debate when they were on an impromptu date, and he was shit at carrying a normal conversation. Richard had only ever made himself practice professional conversations. Asking Sunny about herself, without sounding like he was interviewing her for a job, was not in his skillset.

It was a common criticism from his exes: he couldn't sweet talk or flirt, treating everything like a transaction. And, with most of his exes, the feedback was valid. Romance wasn't his forte, nor his priority. *It'd be nice, I suppose. Tonio seems happy.*

Before he could come up with a good icebreaker, they were parked at the diner and he was following Sunny inside. *Maybe she'd want to come over sometime? Do I need to talk to her more before that? Or maybe ask her on a proper date first? Would it be rude to say this isn't a proper date?* The host brought them to a booth with their menus and took their coffee order.

"What's good at Denny's?" Relieved he had finally found a "small talk" topic, Richard paged through the menu, peeling apart pages glued with what he hoped was syrup.

"Do you want breakfast food or dinner food?" Sunny asked.

"Breakfast, I suppose." The overly-edited pictures of pancakes looked slightly more appetizing than the burgers loaded with bacon.

"I'll order for us," Sunny told him, matter-of-factly. "I'm torn between the French toast slam and the loaded nacho tots, so we'll share both."

Richard nodded, grateful to put the sticky menu down. Both options sounded like he'd have stomach pain for several days. Normally, he'd insist on something that wasn't deep-fried. But if it made Sunny happy, Richard could deal with the indigestion later.

The server came over with their coffees and took their food order. Sunny dumped several flavored creamers into her mug and grabbed six sugar packets from the dispenser. Richard raised an eyebrow at her as he sipped his decaf with one plain creamer.

"Don't judge me," Sunny said, not looking up as she stirred in the fourth sugar packet.

"I'm not judging. Just observing," he replied, before amending, "Well, no, I *am* judging. Do you want some coffee with your sugar?"

Sunny shot him a look. "I prefer my coffee like my lovers, hot and sweet, not bitter."

"Oh, I guess I'm out of luck then," Richard drawled sarcastically.

"You're so forward," Sunny teased as she tore open two more packets.

"I'm usually not." He usually admired people from afar until some-one—usually a woman who found his argumentative nature funny in-stead of abrasive—pursued him. It worked well enough. At least until they realized he wasn't the mysteriously aloof millionaire they wanted; Richard was an awkward, stubborn homebody.

With Sunny, distant admiration wouldn't work fast enough. But he had no idea how to pursue someone; his attempts to get Gabe to notice him back in the day had been humiliating. Luckily, Gabe had taken pity on him. Everyone else Richard had dated since had led every step of the budding relationship, including its inevitable end shortly after.

Sunny examined him over her coffee cup. "You don't do the normal song and dance, where I need a secret decoder to guess if you're actually interested, or if I'm being delusional. To be honest, I didn't think you liked me until last weekend. And suddenly I'm getting felt up under the table."

"Says the woman who likens affluence to immorality, but still sent me a titty pic because I bought her a drink," he teased.

Sunny blushed as a small smile spread across her face. "I like Grey Goose."

His chest tightened at her endearing expression. Richard wondered how to move the conversation where he wanted, how Antonio or Gabe would make their intentions known. "I want to get to know you better. Not just as a friend, I mean. Unless you'd prefer that. You can tell me if I'm coming on too strong." Another embarrassing burn crept up his cheeks.

She shook her head, that shy smile blooming. "You're not coming on too strong. I just don't do this very often. What do you want to know?"

Richard smiled, doubting that someone as stunningly beautiful as Sunny wasn't hit on every time she left the house. "Careful with giving me a blank slate. This might quickly turn into an interview." *Better to wave my red flags, let her know what she's getting into.* Richard pondered about what to ask. "Tell me what is most important for me to understand about you." *That's a terrible question. Talk about an interview.*

"Deep question right off the bat, Dicky. I appreciate that." Sunny's full lips pursed in thought. "I guess I'm still not very confident in who I am. Like, I'm figuring it out, and I've come a long way, but I doubt I'll get to be fully myself for a long time."

"What's getting in your way?"

With a sigh, Sunny wrinkled her nose. "Lots of things. Not to be that trans girl whose whole personality is being a trans girl—not that there's anything wrong with that. Intersectionality and all. Our gender informs our whole existence, etcetera, and you're trans so I figure you won't judge any TMI—but I want to get my upgrade, you know?" She gestured below the table. "And until that's done, dysphoria is super shitty. Like, it's better than it was when I was younger, but I'm still not wholly me. And my mom is somewhat supportive, but she has such high expectations that I feel like shit for wanting to put myself first. She's totally fine with kathoey people—not that I identify as kathoey personally, but it's easier for her to think that way about me—as long as I fulfill my familial duties, you know?"

Richard shook his head. "To be honest, no. I get the dysphoria part, but tell me more about the second part." He had been to Thailand with his family, but they didn't venture out of luxury resorts. His dad had never allowed him to come along to the business visits that had brought them to Thailand in the first place, even though his younger brother got to. His experience of Thailand was as sanitized as the rest of his childhood had been. He owed Gabe a life debt for breaking him out of Pleasantville.

"Kathoey is like a third gender in Thailand, usually people who'd be considered trans women and femme gay men here. But not all trans women and gay men are kathoey, and some people find the word offensive while others embrace it as their identity." Sunny paused, her eyes focused on her coffee. "That's weeds in the forest, though. Anyway, queer and trans people are generally socially accepted there, so you'd think she'd be fine with me being trans, right?" Sunny looked at him expectantly.

Richard mixed a shrug and a nod to show he was listening.

"And in her defense, she probably would be, except my older brother and father both died when I was little, so I'm the only AMAB person in the family. In the US, at least. So I have to be a dutiful son and continue on the male line, basically." Sunny paused again, brow furrowed as if mentally getting herself back on topic. "I mean, there's more nuance to it, but it's hard to explain without giving you a deep dive into Buddhism, Thai culture, and some serious psychoanalyzing of my mom's trauma. Anyway, I suppose she can't think of me as her daughter because she needs me to be her son.

"It might be different if we had more family here, but it's just my mom, my little sister, and I. And since my dad was an only child, we financially support his parents and my mom's family, who all still live in Thailand and can't work anymore. My mom carries a lot of guilt for leaving her family and asking my dad to move to the US, so supporting the family takes priority over my gender-affirming care." Sunny held out her hand as if to stop an interruption that wasn't coming, at least not from him. "I don't mind, of course! I've never met them in person, but I still love my family, you know? It's just, when do I get to support myself?" She blushed. "Sorry for the monologue, but you asked. It's the honest answer."

"So you've essentially been 'man of the house' since you were a kid. While also figuring out your gender and dysphoria. And balancing your family's needs with your own. That would be challenging to navigate." Richard made sure to obviously air-quote the "man of the house". He didn't want Sunny to think he saw her as anything but a woman. Social dysphoria was its own slow poison. One of his exes had subconsciously treated him like a butch lesbian, then got upset when he'd called her out on it. It'd been one of the few times where he'd ended things. There were only so many times he could take his anatomy being prioritized over his gender identity in a relationship.

"Yeah, since I was six." Sunny stared into her coffee. "It took me so long to figure out why I was uncomfortable being what my mom needed me to be. I felt so guilty because I should want to take care of my family, but internally I was screaming that it was wrong. It still feels wrong. Not that taking care of my family feels wrong, more so the reason *why* I need to, if that makes sense?"

Richard nodded, unsure of what to say. He had his own share of gendered expectations, but no one *relied* on him to fulfill them. His mom could get over him quitting the pageant circuit or not finding a husband in college; Sunny had a very different relationship with her mom, who relied on her more than anyone had ever needed Richard. He couldn't imagine facing that kind of pressure as a child. Sunny seemed so carefree when they'd met; he'd have never guessed she'd been through everything she'd just shared.

Her pretty dark brown eyes suddenly snapped to his. "I'm sorry. Stop me if I start monologuing again. I usually try to keep it all in my head."

Richard shook his head, bringing his coffee to his lips. "No need to apologize. I asked. How did your mom take it when you came out?"

Sunny smirked. "She dragged me to a fertility clinic and had me freeze enough sperm to populate several small countries."

He choked on his coffee. "What?"

She laughed at his reaction. "My mom is...particular about her way of doing things, and she will tell you if you don't meet her expectations." Sunny snorted derisively and leaned in closer. "Picture being eighteen and a freshly cracked egg who barely understands why you hate touching yourself, and your mom asks what kind of porn you like because you didn't produce enough sperm last appointment."

Richard grimaced. "That's disturbing."

Sunny laughed again. "You're not wrong. Funny how there's money in the budget for the fertility clinic, but I'm on my own for any surgeries." She sighed quietly into her coffee, taking a sip before she shrugged. "Anyway, her intentions were good, and she pays for my HRT, so I give her a pass. She just didn't want me to take any 'drastic action'—meaning my vagina upgrade—before making sure I can still reproduce in some way." She winced. "Don't get me wrong, I want kids one day, when I'm ready, but not *that* many."

Richard tucked that revelation away as she continued.

"But other than that, she's fine with me expressing myself how I want, as long as my tits aren't hanging out. The biggest issue is she uses my Thai name when she's upset that I'm not being a good son, and I told you before how it kind of gives me the Ick." Sunny bit her lip, any hint of a smile fading. Richard's chest twinged in sympathy. "I like being

Sunny, you know? It's cute, and feminine, but anytime I'm disobedient, suddenly, I'm...not that anymore."

Richard sipped his coffee for longer than necessary, wondering what the proper response might be. He settled on a compliment, if only to get her smiling again. "Well, even if she doesn't use it enough, Sunny suits you."

Sunny brightened. "Thanks. Dicky suits you too," she teased.

With a sigh of relief that he'd brightened her mood, Richard shook his head as she laughed. He hated the nickname Antonio had given him, but he couldn't bear to tell Sunny to stop using it. It didn't annoy him as much when she said it.

"Well, aren't you two the cutest?" The server brought their food over, apparently overhearing only the teasing compliments, and thankfully none of the deeply personal conversation. The smell of grease hit his nose. His stomach turned at the oily sheen over the platters of food. "Is this your first date?"

"I suppose," Richard replied politely, glancing at Sunny as she put their plates in front of them. *See? We could be a couple. That bartender just wanted to flirt with her.* She gave him a tight smile in return.

"Late-night dates are always the best." The server winked as she walked away. "You kids enjoy."

"So, Dicky." Sunny arranged their plates so they got half of each dish. Richard doubted he could eat that much. Or any of it. *Mom would throw a fit if she saw me now.* "What is important for *me* to know about *you*? I gave you my whole fucking life story. What about you?"

Richard tentatively took a bite of hashbrowns, undercooked and drowning in oil. Chewing, he considered. Her response to his question had been very insightful. Normally, he hated giving anyone potential ammunition against him. But, fair was fair. His exes had all told him he was emotionally unavailable; maybe it was time to start opening up. He cringed internally. He should *try* to be better, be less of an asshole. If *Antonio* could find someone as well-suited for him as Lee, maybe Richard should follow his example.

After swallowing, he replied, "I have achieved everything I need to earn my parents' approval and respect as their son."

"Any luck?" Sunny asked, covering her mouth as she chewed a huge bite of nacho tots.

"Not at all." A sardonic chuckle escaped him. "All I've managed to do is *lose* their approval and respect for me as their daughter. They think

I'm a total failure." He poked the hashbrowns with his fork. "The silver lining is that I finally removed their opinions from my self-assessment of success. I've stopped caring what they *actually* think of me and instead ask myself: If I were cis, would they respect me? Would I have their approval? Would they be proud of me? And I would. I've outshone my younger brother in every performance metric in life, not that they care. To them, Connor can do no wrong. In actuality, he's a complete degenerate."

Richard tried to keep the bitterness from his voice. He'd worked hard on detaching his self-worth from what his family thought of him. *No need to lose that because of fucking Connor.*

He ticked off the achievements that his parents valued as he spoke. "Meanwhile, I was valedictorian and captain of the varsity soccer team in high school, graduated summa cum laude from Yale, and have an MBA and MS in Economics from Columbia. I became the youngest managing director in my firm's history, and I'm on the board of several nonprofits. But do my parents care? Not at all."

"Um...I took a coding boot camp at a community college." Sunny laughed nervously, looking down at her plate and pushing her tater tots around.

Richard blushed, realizing how he must have sounded. "Sorry, I wasn't trying to brag. Those are the things my *parents* care about. How they measure success. Or would, if I were cis. But they want me to be pretty, compliant, and marry into a family with high earning potential, a good reputation, and connections. That was supposed to be Gabe, but everyone knows that's *never* going to happen, other than my dad." Richard rolled his eyes before staring at his plate. As beautiful as they were, Sunny's eyes had flicked back up to him as he spoke. This topic was too close to his underbelly to feel so examined.

"And since I'm not doing that, they neither respect nor approve of me. Meanwhile, Connor is a creep who skates by on Dad's charity, does nothing with his life, and somehow is the favorite." Richard scoffed, gripping his fork tightly. "And yet, after achieving all of that and *still* not earning their approval, I no longer care to have it. I respect my own actions and the path I've chosen, and I am proud of myself. That's what matters most these days." Richard shrugged, playing with the hash-browns. "Still working on getting the 'what would Dad think?' or 'what if Mom hears about this?' out of my head sometimes, but that's what therapy is for."

When he quieted and glanced up, Sunny was still giving him that long, examining look that made Richard wonder if he'd said too much, or perhaps the wrong thing. But Sunny snapped to attention and tore into a piece of French toast. "Do they love you at least?"

He blinked in confusion. Love wasn't for family; love was for his friends, for people he could be himself around. So, Gabe, Antonio, and Phineas. The three people in the world who truly saw him were the complete opposite of him.

Well. Shit. No wonder all of my exes felt like our relationship was transactional, if I was supposed to act like them instead of my parents. Antonio's relationship blueprint, new as it was, sounded exhausting; Lee had the patience of a saint. Phineas was possibly worse at relationships than Richard. And Gabe's style was suffocating. Some people might want utter devotion, but not Richard.

When they were fake-dating in college, Gabe insisted on acting like the perfect boyfriend, buying him gifts, walking him to class, and—to Richard's annoyance—holding his hand. Gabe had played the devoted partner in all ways except sex; they'd stopped sleeping together after Gabe finally got Richard to accept that he was trans. The denial and his parent's influence had been strong, but Gabe's support had been stronger. Even if it meant they were no longer compatible, romantically or sexually. Once Richard had acknowledged the dysphoria that came from bottoming, it was impossible to ignore. And Gabe needed the physical intimacy that made Richard's stomach turn and his skin crawl.

None of that was anything Sunny needed to hear though. That fact that he'd only been truly loved by a total of three people wasn't relevant to the conversation about his parents, nor something he particularly cared to admit.

"I don't honestly know if my parents are capable of love. My father values success, and with success comes approval and respect. My mother values her social status, so she needs me to be her clone so she can pretend she's a perfect mother." It was a terrible explanation; if only it were that clear cut. But that was the closest description of their mentality Richard could provide.

"They sound like shitty parents. No offense," Sunny added, probably realizing how bad that would sound to most people.

Richard appreciated Sunny's bluntness. The delightful slips of her tongue mirrored his own thoughts, ones he kept inside except around his friends. "No offense taken. They are. I admire some of their values, but a normal childhood would have been nice."

"You seem fairly well-adjusted despite everything," Sunny teased.

Richard couldn't hold back the cackle that erupted from him. No one had ever described him as well-adjusted before. *Everett will get a kick out of that.* "Oh, trust me, I've got plenty of issues. Red flags galore. Just a fair warning, I've been told I'm an emotionally unavailable asshole by several ex-girlfriends. And my therapist on occasion."

Granted, Richard had never shared as much with those exes as he just had with Sunny. And his therapist's refreshing honesty was why Richard resonated with Everett so well. Richard realized he was pushing the food around on his plate. Even the last few bites of hashbrowns and overly-buttered French toast would probably be a regret tomorrow. "You should take this home."

"Are you sure? You've barely eaten it. Didn't you like it?" Concern flashed over her face.

Richard didn't like it, but saying that would be rude. "It's just late for me to be eating. As my unofficial personal trainer, Gabe keeps me on a tight food regimen. I know I'll never have a body like his, but his workouts help with the dysphoria. At least until I can start T and start building muscle mass more easily."

Sunny choked on a tot. "Wait, you're *not* on T?"

Richard shook his head. "I know. My doctor has the prescription ready for me whenever I tell him I'm ready for it. I just...can't yet."

He didn't want to freak Sunny out by telling her why he hadn't started T yet. Even he knew better than to bring up kids on the first date.

"No, I meant, you pass really well considering you haven't done any hormone treatment." Sunny blushed. "Not that you *have* to pass unless that's something you want to do. And like, obviously you're a man and masc." She huffed. "I'm just going to stop talking now."

Heat crept into his cheeks again. "Tonio taught me some vocal exercises to speak in a lower register. And Gabe is helping me with targeted weight lifting to build muscle in the right areas. Between that and top surgery, the only thing I can't do without T is grow a beard." He stroked his imaginary whiskers jokingly.

"Oh no, no beard. We can't hide that blush of yours," Sunny laughed.

Being teased by someone other than Antonio was nice. Everyone else took him too seriously. As much as he liked having a serious reputation,

Richard wasn't a complete stick in the mud. Sunny saw through his sarcasm and into his dry humor.

"I should take you home," Richard said, sighing inwardly. It was getting late and he'd already taken up more of her time than he deserved.

"My place or yours?" Sunny winked.

Somehow his cheeks burned hotter. That damn blush was always his downfall. He hadn't dreamed beyond a good night kiss, but if she wanted to...

"I'm teasing, Dicky." With one last smirk, Sunny got up to find a box for the leftovers, while he paid at the register.

They stepped outside to gently falling snow. The fresh flakes coating the frozen pavement squeaked under their shoes.

Richard held his hand out to catch the fluffy snowflakes. It reminded him of the few happy parts of his childhood. Sledding. The rare snow day on his birthday. The nanny making him hot cocoa. His glasses fogging up when he stepped inside after making a snowman.

He turned to Sunny, who had a scowl on her face.

"Uh oh. Don't tell me you hate snow?" Richard teased, spinning around as they walked through the parking lot. Snow always brought out the kid in him. Hopefully Sunny would see that as a green flag and not a red one.

"Don't tell me you *like* snow?!" she retorted, wrapping her arms around herself.

"Winter is my favorite season."

"Spoken like someone with a car." Sunny scoffed. "Snow is cold. And wet. And stressful. Have you ever tried to get on a bus with a three-foot bank of snow in the way?"

"I've never been on a bus." Richard unlocked the car in case she got there before he did. "I'm going to have to convert you. You'll come around."

"And if I don't?" Instead of hurrying to get out of the snow, Sunny kept pace with him, smiling as Richard caught snowflakes on his tongue.

"Hard dealbreaker," he teased, unable to keep the grin from his face. "Sure, it's stressful, but snow is a vital part of the ecosystems in the Driftless Area."

"Okay, nerd."

They climbed in the car, still lightheartedly teasing each other. As they drove the deserted streets to Sunny's neighborhood, he shared the good memories that made him like snow. How as a kid, he would pretend the car was at warp speed like Star Trek when the flakes attacked the windshield. And how he had once found a little kitten in the woods behind his parent's house from a paw print trail in the snow.

Maybe his coffee hadn't been decaf, because Richard was rambling. Luckily, Sunny didn't seem to care. She teased him for being a Trekkie and excitedly asked what happened to the kitten, rambling on in kind about how much she liked cats.

It was nice to talk about nothing important after such a heavy conversation. Not quite small talk, but not quite deep. Merely interesting topics. It was surprising how easy Sunny was to talk to without an audience like Antonio there to tease him. He didn't want the ride to end.

"Okay, I'll consider changing my opinion about snow," Sunny finally agreed without agreeing as he slowed to a stop in front of what he presumed was her apartment. "On the condition that you take the city bus somewhere."

"Oh, tough bargain." His back itched in a telltale sign of impending anxiety sweat, but Richard pushed the question out in a rush before he could overthink it. "Are you busy Friday?"

"I'm free. Why? We gonna ride the bus?" Sunny unbuckled.

Richard snorted. "I was thinking we could watch a movie. Together. At my place?"

Sunny turned to him with a smirk. "Are you asking me to come over to Netflix and chill?"

"Well, I'd buy you dinner, too."

Sunny shot him a confused look. "Oh, I was joking about the Netflix and chill, but you're serious? You want me to come over for a dick appointment?"

"I wouldn't be that presumptuous, but I suppose so." He had never heard the phrase "dick appointment" in his life, but it seemed self-explanatory as slang for a casual date. He wouldn't have asked her to come over if he didn't want her company. Romantically or otherwise, Richard wanted to get to know her.

Sunny studied him carefully, her dark eyes narrowed, bottom lip between her teeth. "Want me to bring anything?" she finally asked.

"Just yourself." Richard considered his next words carefully. "And, if you want, an overnight bag. You're welcome to stay over."

Sunny's lips pursed in thought. "Let me try something." With that, she leaned forward, brushing her lips against his for a fleeting moment.

Richard recovered from his surprise as quickly as he could, chasing her soft lips. He captured her mouth, sucking gently on her bottom lip like he'd been dreaming about since their too-brief kiss at New Year's.

Sunny gasped into his mouth and let out the softest squeak.

He backed away, in case her squeak was a protest. But she grabbed his coat and pulled him back, sliding her tongue between his lips, tasting of rich syrup and saccharine coffee.

Relieved, he caressed her neck as they devoured each other, thumb pressed gently against her fluttering pulse. Her citrus perfume drowned out the smell of the leftovers. Her soft skin and glossy hair were silk between his fingers, and her soft gasp when he bit her lip was angelic.

They paused for air eventually, though how long it'd been, Richard had no idea. He pressed his forehead against hers as they panted. His chest burned as if he'd run a marathon.

"Damn, Dicky, you kiss like you mean it."

"If I kiss you like I want you, then I do mean it."

Sunny leaned in and kissed him again. He took that as a yes, Sunny would be coming over on Friday. He made a note for himself to text her his address when he got home. Richard smiled as he buried his fingers in her silky hair and pulled her closer.

Friday, February Twenty-First

Chapter Eleven

Sunny

As Sunny IMed her least favorite coworker, her phone vibrated between her knees. She ignored it, along with the humming from the fluorescent lights overhead, the smell of popcorn that someone had made in the breakroom earlier, and the chair squeaking from one of the greige cubicles around her, all devoid of decor and personality per company policy. If she let herself pay attention to all of the annoyances around her, she would snap. At Greg, probably.

He deserved it, but he was chummier with their boss than she was, so ignoring everything around her was safer; she was already frazzled. Spinning side to side in her chair with her feet tucked under the wheels, Sunny reread her message before hitting send, hoping she sounded nice enough, but honestly not caring that much if she did.

Greg was the bane of her existence: inept, out of touch, a little transphobic and misogynistic but never blatantly enough to call him out, and overall, useless. He'd sent her an email with some failed test scripts without explanation or question, not even a hello. Or a subject line to figure out what she was looking at. Her knees vibrated again, and again, and again while she stared hard at the screen, waiting for a response.

She didn't need to look at her phone. The deluge of notifications buzzing in her lap was from her gamer friends, starting the usual Friday arguments about who wanted to play what this weekend. They used to have a schedule, back when she first started playing with them years ago. But now there were so many new people and new games that every weekend had become a clusterfuck of arguments and scheduling arrangements.

She huffed as Greg's head bobbed across the sea of cubicles toward the bathroom, instead of responding to her IM. He'd be at least fifteen minutes. Checking her phone while she waited, the chat scrolled by with jokes, arguments, and memes faster than she could read. Ignoring it, Sunny instead sent a DM to Black_Hawk, her online BFF.

Sunnywith0meatballs: How much longer you think they'll take?

Black_Hawk_Up88: Until we inevitably play League again? Three hours at least. I miss when we had WOW Wednesdays and shit. We didn't spend hours debating what to play.

Sunnywith0meatballs: Lmao put it in the chat.

Black_Hawk_Up88: They know I always want to play WOW.

Sunnywith0meatballs: True. You're so predictable

Black_Hawk_Up88: Like you're any better, Minecraft hater.

Sunnywith0meatballs: I need all my avatars to have curves. Lol. Doesn't matter anyway, I'm busy tonight so I don't care what y'all do.

Black_Hawk_Up88: You're flaking on me? We had such a good streak going!

Sunnywith0meatballs: I flaked the past two Saturdays too. Didn't you notice?

Black_Hawk_Up88: No, I also flaked lol. Strangely, socializing instead of my usual excuse of depression.

Sunnywith0meatballs: Ew. How was peopling?

Black_Hawk_Up88: It wasn't awful. I'm trying to be better about going out lately.

Sunnywith0meatballs: I have a TMI question.

Black_Hawk_Up88: Oh no. I hate when you have TMI questions.

Sunnywith0meatballs: Rude. Have you ever had a FWB?

Black_Hawk_Up88: Are you coming on to me again?

Sunnywith0meatballs: You wish! This sort-of friend sort-of propositioned me. And I'm not sure if I should do it, and I can't go to my IRL friends with this one because they are also friends with this person. Like, I'm not interested in them romantically, but they are kind of hot. And they're a great kisser.

Whether or not to go through with this…*thing* with Richard was probably something she should have figured out before Friday. Sunny chewed her lip. She'd been ignoring the Doubt tab in her mind all week, but it kept popping back up every time she thought about what would happen after work today. Would she go to Richards? And if so, what would happen there? Or should she go home as usual? And no matter what she picked, would she regret it?

This was definitely something she shouldn't be unsure of, especially considering her overnight bag was sitting in the back corner of her cubicle. Richard had already texted her his address earlier that week. It was the only text they'd exchanged since Saturday; her risky pic was still visible without scrolling. The sight made her burn from humiliation all over again. She still hadn't responded, unsure if she would even be going. Considering there was only an hour left of work, she should probably decide.

In the car, after their impromptu not-date and after *that* kiss, she had taken him at face value when he'd said to pack an overnight bag. But after a week of debating if she should, or wondering if she'd missed a social cue somewhere, she was increasingly unsure if he'd been serious. His dry sense of humor made it hard to decipher sarcasm from truth. And if there was one thing she'd taken from her fling with Blanche, it was that Sunny read into things too much. She didn't want to do that again.

Black_Hawk_Up88: Sounds like there are already benefits.

Sunnywith0meatballs: Kissing and a dick appointment are two very different things.

Black_Hawk_Up88: True! Kissing is way more intimate than sex lol. Well, my (not) extensive FWB experience isn't great. I had one fuck buddy in college that worked out well, but the rest ended with my heart broken.

Sunnywith0meatballs: Is it worth the risk?

Black_Hawk_Up88: As long as you're on the same page, I'd say go for it. As long as neither of you catches feelings when the other one hasn't. That shit sucks. Especially when you have mutual friends. It gets messy.

Sunny snorted. Wasn't that the truth? "Messy" was an understatement for her "thing" with Blanche when she had caught feelings for them, while they had merely tolerated her attention. She didn't want to do that again. This was supposed to be her year to shine, not waste time with one-sided feelings. But Richard wasn't Blanche—another understatement. Blanche had been sweet and patient with her, listened to her feelings and encouraged her to flourish.

And while she *thought* she and Richard had shared some sweet moments last weekend, he had ended their not-date with an invitation for a meaningless hookup. She winced at the memory. It had hurt in the moment, considering she thought they'd just bared their souls to each other. But in hindsight, he'd done her a kindness. He wasn't going to be the simp she wanted in a relationship, and her mae would never approve of him.

Besides, she'd practically been a nun since Blanche had broken up with her. All of the toys and supplies she'd invested in when she was with Blanche had gone mostly unused, gathering dust in the ugly backpack Sunny kept tucked under her bed, so Luna wouldn't be tempted to borrow the bag. Her one attempt at the dating app game a few months ago had ended with several chasers and literally no one else in her messages. Even if he wasn't relationship material, Richard at least saw her as a person.

Sunny was long overdue for a good time, and the risk of deluding herself into heartbreak again was low with Richard, who, again, hadn't texted all week other than his address. Not even a hello or anything. He was a very good kisser, and he could host. She sighed as the Doubt tab finally closed. *I guess I'm fucking doing this.*

Sunnywith0meatballs: Oh, there is NO chance of catching feelings.
Black_Hawk_Up88: Then why not? Go for it. Get some.
Sunnywith0meatballs: You're a bad influence on me. If I could tell my IRL friends about this, they'd talk me out of it.
Black_Hawk_Up88: Good thing we're not IRL friends, then.

Sunny snorted. *See? This is why I go to Black Hawk for shit like this. Lee would never be this supportive of me. He'd just call me delusional again.*

"Hey, Earth to Sunny." She jumped as Greg waved his hand in front of her face. "You said you have a question?"

She sputtered out an apology, looking up at her monitor and the six replies Greg had sent back in return to her IM. "Sorry, zoned out. What were these test scripts for?"

Muting her phone to silence the still-buzzing notifications rolling in, she tried to listen as Greg rambled, searching between his words for what he expected her to do about it. But a new tab in her mind opened, mapping out the walk to Richard's apartment.

Sunny double-checked the address, craning her neck to look up at Richard's building. The late afternoon sun reflected off the gold accents embedded into the sandstone walls of the old art deco building. *This is it, I guess.* She rucked her backpack higher on her shoulder. As fancy as the building was, with stone carvings flanking the door and a tile sunburst mosaic encasing the entryway, at least it was an older building. She'd pegged Richard for someone who'd live in the ugly "luxury" condos, clad with cheap fiber cement panels.

As she walked in, a receptionist greeted her from the front desk, eyeing Sunny over her glasses. "Can I help you?"

Sunny looked warily at the middle-aged white woman in a dark wool pantsuit. *If she thinks I'm a delivery person, I'm going home.* She was already uncomfortable going to Richard's place, let alone dealing with a receptionist who dressed nicer than she did. "I need to get to apartment 903?"

"Ah, you must be Ms. Boonmee." The receptionist looked at her questioningly.

Sunny nodded, confused at how this woman knew her name.

The receptionist beamed. "Splendid! I was surprised to see a new name on Mr. Carter's guest list. He never has visitors. You'll be on this elevator." She gestured to her left as she rose from behind the desk. "I'll buzz you up, sweetie."

"Uh... Thank you." Unsure what to think of the whole situation, Sunny obligingly followed the woman to the elevator.

The receptionist pressed the button for the ninth floor and swiped her ID badge. "Enjoy your evening!"

"You too!" Sunny hoped her smile covered her dumbstruck expression as the doors closed. *I swear, if this opens up to a fucking penthouse, I'm going home.* She wasn't signing up to be the fuck buddy of some ultra-rich asshole. *Just a regular-rich asshole is bad enough already. What am I doing here? This is going to be so awkward.*

The doors opened to a normal-looking apartment hallway, if significantly less dated than her building's dingy green carpets and peach wallpaper. Instead, the art deco inspiration continued, with geometric ginkgo-patterned carpet and gold accents on the navy walls. She approached 903, took a deep breath, and knocked.

Within seconds, Richard opened the door, annoyingly put together as usual. His button-down was crisp, his blond hair swept neatly over his ear, grazing his square jaw.

"Hi."

"Hey."

They stood there, looking at each other. Shifting under his gaze, Sunny regretted not dressing up. She'd come right from work to save herself a bus ride back to Eastside and a potentially intrusive conversation with her mother. So she stood, in her khakis and plain navy sweatshirt—her work drag, as Antonio called it. She couldn't exactly go to the office wearing the fishnets and low-cut dress she would prefer to wear to a dick appointment.

Still, it would have been a confidence boost to dress a little more femme than this. She hadn't packed a change of clothes either. This morning, she'd convinced herself that Richard had been sarcastic about the overnight bag. So she'd decided against it. Well, she brought makeup remover and a toothbrush—just in case—but not clothes.

"Are you gonna let me in?" Under any other circumstances, Sunny wouldn't mind his blue eyes on her all day, but standing in the hallway in silence was getting awkward.

"Sorry." Richard gestured to invite her in.

Sunny looked around the gray monochrome minimalist aberration as she toed her shoes off. She grinned. *This* was what she'd expected from Richard. But even as she took in his decor, she had to admit it was tasteful. The black leather Chesterfield sofa and armchairs looked comfortable. The warm gray walls highlighted the abstract painting hanging over the walnut console table. But the books on the shelf were stacked too neatly, the row of candles on the coffee table too perfectly aligned.

He held out a pair of slippers for her. "Here. The floor can get cold."

Sunny smirked, ready to tease him for... For what? Being polite? Considerate? No snappy banter came to mind, so she simply thanked him and slid them on. The black and gray sunburst pattern on the floor tile must have inspired the rest of the decor. Sunny was a little disappointed; she couldn't talk shit about Richard gentrifying an old building if his decor was actually nice. "I should have known you'd live in a place with a receptionist, Mr. Carter."

Richard blinked, his lips pressing into a thin line that almost passed for a smile. "You met Briony at the front desk, I assume? Even though this place is mine outright, my father insisted on a secured entrance, so he could pay the property manager for updates on my comings and goings in case I reflect badly on him. I pay the security team to only pass along what I want them to."

"So, not me, you mean?" She set her backpack down on the coffee table, intentionally letting it fall so it nudged the candles out of line.

Richard raised an eyebrow. "To say they wouldn't approve is an understatement."

"Great." *Good thing this is just a hookup then. I don't want to be a secret again.* Sunny had read far too much into every interaction with Blanche, deluding herself they had felt the same. She wouldn't make that mistake twice. Anything Richard said, she had to take at face value. This was just a dick appointment. "What do you do for fun, Dicky?"

Richard blinked.

Sunny gestured to his sparse apartment, looking for something to tease him about. "You have no personality in your decor. Like, it's nice, but it's a showroom. There's no sign of who you are. So, what do you do for fun?"

The corners of Richard's mouth twitched, creating a ghost of a smile on his face. "Aside from work?"

"Work is *not* a hobby, Dicky." Sunny scoffed to hide her laugh.

The ghost of a smile turned corporeal, the smallest crooked grin gracing his face. "I enjoy working. But, I go to the gym with Gabe. I nap. I read."

"Napping is not a hobby." On her way over to the bookshelf, Sunny tugged the neatly folded throw blanket draped over the back of the sofa so it crumpled on the seat. The bookshelf was stuffed full, titles ranging from cookbooks to poetry to fantasy epics to non-fiction. A seahorse sculpture sat on the top shelf. "What do you read? And if you say business cases, I'm leaving."

"I won't say it then."

Sunny glared at him over her shoulder.

"That was a joke," he explained.

"Is it a joke if I don't laugh?"

Richard wore a full smirk now. "I've been into Taoist poetry lately. Yuan Mei, in particular, has a delightfully complex meaning even in the lightest of passages."

"Great bedtime reading." Sunny rolled her eyes when she saw the books were categorized by genre and alphabetically. The spines all looked broken in, even the most boring of the non-fiction books. Either Richard bought his books used, or he'd actually read them.

"It puts me right to sleep." That line between Richard's dry humor and sarcastic truth was so fine, Sunny never knew which side he was on. "Does that pass muster? Or is poetry worse than Harvard Business Review?"

"Well, there's no financial self-help books, so I guess I can stay." Sunny pulled a well-worn copy of bell hooks from the poetry section and pretended to look at it, before putting it with the non-fiction. She managed to switch two more books before Richard's hand around her wrist stopped her from pulling out an unabridged *Les Miserables*.

"What are you doing?"

Sunny put on her best innocent expression. "Seeing what books you have, Dicky. It's a great way to get to know someone."

"And putting them back in the incorrect spot is a key part of the process, I suppose." His hand tightened around her wrist.

Sunny fought her grin, tipping the thick book onto its spine as he pulled her hand away. "I have no idea what you're talking about."

Richard's hand tugged her wrist, pulling her around to face him. He stepped closer, backing her against the bookshelf. Sunny's heart raced as his blue eyes narrowed. "The candles and throw were one thing. The bookshelf is off-limits."

With a heavy swallow, Sunny reached up with her free hand to stroke his cheek. "You can't control everything, Dicky." With a grin, she ruffled his neatly combed hair so it fell over his eyes.

Richard closed his eyes and exhaled slowly, letting out the softest frustrated groan Sunny had ever had the pleasure of hearing. He shook his hair out of his face, his bright blue eyes captivating like a patch of clear skies on cloudy day. Her stomach swooped as he stepped ever closer. She swallowed heavily, breath catching, as his thigh claimed the space between hers. The bookshelf dug sharp lines across her shoulders, her hips, her thighs. "Sunny. The bookshelf is off-limits. Be chaotic anywhere else, but not the books. Or the shoes."

"Fine." Sunny's response came out breathier than she'd intended. Her heart pounded as he pressed against her. "Not the books."

She leaned in to kiss him, but Richard pulled back with an expectant look.

A smile broke across her face. "Or the shoes."

"Good girl."

Shivering, Sunny whimpered against his lips. "Don't call me that."

"But you liked it." Richard finally kissed her back, sucking her lower lip ever so lightly.

She had liked it, but a praise kink would have to be unpacked when Richard wasn't pinning her against the bookshelf and kissing the daylights out of her. His tongue parting her lips drove all thoughts out of Sunny's head. His hand sliding up her wrist to twine his fingers through hers erased her nerves.

It wasn't until her own gasp of pleasure from him sucking her neck reached her ears that she realized they hadn't discussed anything yet. "Dicky. What are we doing here?"

Richard froze. "Oh. We can move to the couch." He guided her toward the sofa.

Sunny snorted, pressing her fingertips against her tingling lips. "No, I mean, what are we doing? Like, boundaries, preferences, limits, what we want out of this, etcetera?"

He smirked. "Besides the books?"

"And the shoes."

Richard pulled her down next to him, kissing her neck again. His exhale tickled her earlobe as he murmured, "I should swear you to secrecy."

"Oh." Sunny stiffened; his bluntness stung. She'd hated being shut out of Blanche's life during their fling, but what she and Richard were doing would never lead to a relationship.

Even if part of her had been a little hopeful after he'd let the waitress think they were on a date, he'd been clear that her coming over tonight was *not* a date. Just a hookup. Which Sunny was fine with—Richard wasn't exactly relationship material as far as she was concerned. But he was a really good kisser and frankly, getting laid was a good way to break the seal now that her heart was relatively whole again.

So it was fine. Keeping this a secret. The two of them hooking up wasn't something their friends needed to know about. And definitely not her mom. Birdie would flip her shit if she found out Sunny was "wasting time" by fooling around with someone she didn't approve of. "All right. This can stay between us."

Richard froze and sat back, brows furrowed in confusion. "I wasn't referencing *this.*" He gestured between them. "But if you want to keep this private, I can respect that. It'd probably make things easier without Antonio sticking his nose where it doesn't belong."

"Exactly." Sunny paused, confused. "Wait, what were *you* talking about?"

His cheeks burned crimson. "Uh, no one except my exes have seen my body since right after I got top surgery. Gabe is probably the last friend to see it, and that's because I wanted a second opinion on how my nipple grafts were healing."

"...okay? And?"

Richard swept a hand through his hair, eyes downcast. "To be honest, they didn't heal well. Gabe sent me the link to a tattoo artist who would fill them in, and I told him I didn't want to do that, but..."

Sunny was still confused. *Get to the point, Dicky.* "So the secret is..."

"You can't tell anyone I have tattoos. Not even your friends."

"Why?" Sunny asked, at a loss for why tattoos had to stay a secret. Not even her mae would care if she came home with one, as long as it wasn't too ridiculous.

Richard's ghost of a smile was back. "I want to see how long it takes before they notice."

Sunny burst into laughter. "Deal. I'm so in! How long has it been?"

"Eight years."

"Eight years?! No one has seen you shirtless in *eight* years?"

"Not *no* one!" Richard retorted defensively. "Only the people I was seeing, and none of them have met my friends or family."

Really? None of them? Sunny wondered if that was another red flag, but that wasn't her problem, as far as a hookup was concerned. "Consider me honored to witness them. Let's see these nips." She gestured to his shirt, still buttoned to his neck.

"It's more than just the nips," he admitted, unbuttoning his shirt quickly. A flash of golden yellow on his bicep peeked out from the sleeve of his white tee as he folded his button-down and set it on the coffee table.

He pulled off his undershirt, revealing a muscular torso covered in ink. On his right bicep, a quarter sleeve of a honeycombed beehive accentuated his wiry muscles. On his left, a black and gray seahorse wrapped down his arm. A deer head marked his taut stomach and rib cage, its antlers spreading along his chest, crowned by flowers. Richard folded the tee and leaned forward to set it on the coffee table, which revealed a dragon tattoo covering his back.

"Damn," Sunny breathed, awed by the artistry, color, and gorgeous body hidden beneath Richard's boring exterior. She'd never expected him to have so much personality under his bougie clothes. "It's *not* just the nips. No one has noticed all of *this*?"

Richard shrugged. "I know, right? I don't make it easy, but it's been close to a decade. I'm starting to feel bad for keeping it from Gabe for so long."

With a delighted gasp, Sunny squinted at his chest to examine the nipple tattoos that had started it all. "Dicky! You have roses for nips!"

Adorably, Richard blushed, matching the dusky pink of his nipples that blended into the petals of the roses that crowned the deer. "Yeah, the artist asked if I wanted 'creative areolas,' and I figured if I'm getting the color filled in, I should get the scars covered up too. He came up with this. Turns out tattoos are addicting."

"I would never have guessed you were hiding all of this under those stuffy shirts. These are all sick as hell." She held out a hand, hovering over his chest, barely catching herself in her eagerness. "Can I touch you?"

Richard nodded. "Yes, just with a finger or two only if you don't mind. I'm not a huge fan of being touched, and I don't have much sensation in the grafts or scars. Which is fine. Nipple play was dysphoric anyway."

With quiet awe, Sunny traced the antler of the deer, feeling the ridge of scar tissue along his ribs and the softness of the inked skin. That she was one of the privileged few who knew this side of him made her heart flutter. She flicked her gaze up and found his blue eyes watching her. The way his plush lips parted when he caught her looking back made her shiver. "Good to know. Anything else I should know? I've only had sex with AMAB people, so I'm a little out of my element. Be bossy with me."

"You might regret telling me to be bossy." That ghost of a smile was back.

Sunny swallowed heavily. Finger trailing along the sea horse's tail, she imagined how the ink would move with his toned shoulders when he pinned her down in his bed. Or flex with his biceps when he wrapped her hair around his fist and smacked her ass. She smirked, hoping "bossy" went as far as she wanted, farther than Blanche ever dared with her. "No, I take direction *very* well."

Richard blushed again. "You might have to direct me too. I'd rather avoid overlapping dysphoria if we can."

"Unless you have a ball fetish, we'll figure something out." Sunny tried to sound more confident than she felt. She hadn't considered the possibility that he might want her to do something that caused her the Ick. What if he wasn't comfortable with anal and wouldn't fuck her? Like sure, a vibe to the muff would do the trick, but she could do that on her own. Or what if he wanted *her* to fuck *him*? "Or if you're a bottom. I can top if I have to, but...not my jam."

"Perfect. I strongly prefer to top." Richard nodded, far too serious for the awkwardness of the conversation. She bit her lip, replaying his voice a few times to make sure she'd heard him correctly. He always sounded sarcastic.

"See? We're figuring this out already," Sunny teased, assuming she'd interpreted his tone right, that she might actually enjoy this hookup. She'd fully expected this to be awkward, until he'd backed her into the bookshelf and kissed her senseless. Her finger trailed back down to the deer tattoo. Following the thorny rose stems that lined his abs, she imagined how they'd flex when he came, moaning her name. "Get naked. Introduce me to your body, and then I'll introduce you to mine."

For a moment, Richard looked like he wanted to argue with her, but he nodded. His blue eyes stayed on her as he unbuckled his belt. "I wasn't expecting us to move this fast, but I suppose it's efficient."

"You're such a fucking nerd, Dicky." Sunny admired the wiry muscles tensing along his body as he lifted his hips to pull his pants off. He folded them neatly along the creases and set them on his other clothes. "Do you have a spiel you give? Or should I ask questions?"

He pulled off his boxers. "I can tell you what I don't like."

"Perfect. Let's hear it."

He pointed to his crotch. "Not vagina or pussy. Just bits, clit, or front hole. A finger or two in either hole is fine, but that's about as much penetration as my dysphoria can handle. Oh, I've been told I get a little rough. Biting, hair pulling, spanking, choking. I can rein it in if that's a problem."

"Sounds hot." Sunny's heart raced at the thought of him biting her neck.

"Was that sarcasm?"

"No." Sunny's laugh was breathy as heat rose in her cheeks. "Bite away, Dicky. Hard as you like. My pain tolerance is very high."

Richard's eyes flicked down to her neck and chest. "Good. If you want to touch anywhere, warn me first so I can mentally prepare. Or at least don't take it personally if I flinch." He winced, checking for her reaction.

She nodded. "That's fine."

His shoulders relaxed as he smirked. "Tell me if I make you uncomfortable in any way. Though I wouldn't expect anything else from you."

"Oh, trust me. I will." Sunny waited for his nod before she slid her hands up his thighs. "Can I blow you? Full disclosure, I have no idea what I'm doing."

Richard's flush spread across his chest, a crooked smile threatening his composed facial expression. "Only if you take your shirt off."

Sunny raised an eyebrow. "You just want to see my tits."

With a shrug, Richard rubbed the back of his neck. "That, and I'm hyperaware that I am bare ass naked, and you're fully clothed. Level the playing field for me, please."

She laughed, tugging her sweater over her head. While she was still shaking her hair out, Richard cupped her tits, thumbs over her nipples. Before she could tease him for his eagerness, his arm slid around her waist and pulled her against him. Sunny groaned, bracing herself with the back of the sofa, as his mouth pressed hot against the lace of her bra.

"These are perfect," Richard breathed as he switched to the other side, fingers digging into her hips. "That damn picture you sent me is burned into my retinas, I've looked at it so many times this week."

Sunny gasped as he bit down, the lace digging into her skin between his teeth. "Dicky, I wanted... I want." She ran a hand through his hair and yanked his head back so she could form words. "I want to get you off!"

The blue of Richard's eyes were thin halos around his dilated pupils. He panted, the faintest of smirks gracing his unfairly pretty lips, "On your knees, then."

"You are bossy, aren't you?" A grin bloomed across her face as she slid onto the floor, sweeping her hair back as she settled between his legs. Despite her bravado, her nerves still worked against her. *I really hope I don't suck at this.*

Richard brushed her hair away from her face, wrapping it around his fist and pulling it tight. A squeak flew from her mouth. She bit her lip to hide her grin, but the arousal thumping through her body was delirium-inducing.

"That's cute." Richard's crooked smile grew. "Get to it."

Sunny wanted to melt into a puddle. This was everything she'd been missing from Blanche—the bossiness, the flirtatiousness, the edge of pain and pleasure, the blatant desire for *her*. She slid her hands up his thighs to explore between the dark blond curls. Glancing up at him to check for an approving nod, she leaned in to taste him. Licking tentatively at first, Sunny grew more enthusiastic as she got used to the texture of his skin and the hardness of his clit. The tangy earthy taste blended with a musky smell she couldn't get enough of. He hissed out instructions to her, telling her where to touch and curl the finger that slipped so easily into him. How to lick just so, when to suck harder, and when to ease off.

While Richard was bossy, certainly, he wasn't giving her any clues if he was actually *liking* it. Sure, he was breathing hard, and his face and chest were flushed bright red. His thighs would tighten around her ears, or he'd thrust against her face. A couple times, he tensed up and let out a sharp exhale that almost sounded like a moan, but Sunny had no idea what was good or bad.

One thing was certain—he really liked pulling her hair. And of course, she let out that stupid squeak every time, because she really liked when he did. Being told what to do, when, and how hard, was a relief. She didn't have to think too much, just listen and learn. It'd be better if she knew he was enjoying it as much as she was, but it was easy to get lost in Richard. To let her mind focus on the task and let the rest of her brain fade into a daze.

After one of those sharp breaths with a hint of a moan underneath, Richard pulled her away. "Okay, I can't take any more."

Sunny frowned, the sting of his words sobering her daze. He was certainly wet enough that she couldn't have been *that* bad. She wiped her chin and lower lip with her thumb, sucking it into her mouth. No wonder Tara liked doing this so much. His arousal was surprisingly sweet. "Well, what should I have done better?"

Leaning forward, Richard buried his face into her neck before he pulled her up, pushing her back into the sofa. He crawled over her with a small smile and a soft daze in his eyes. "Nothing. You are a very quick study."

Richard leaned down to kiss her, but she blocked him. "No, 'I can't take it anymore' warrants some constructive feedback."

"Sunny," Richard shook his head with that confused furrow of his eyebrows. "You were good. Very good. I came twice. I'm just very easily overstimulated."

"How was I supposed to know you came twice?" Sunny shot out even as a smug pride ran through her. "You were giving me no clues. Not even a little moan?"

"I moaned!" Richard protested defensively.

"You exhaled loudly. That's *not* a moan. Let that be *my* feedback for *you*. Let me know that you're enjoying it if I do something right."

Richard's crooked smile returned as he pulled her close, fingers tangling in her hair again. "But you noticed when I exhaled."

"Ugh, you're impossible." She let him kiss her this time. Let herself get lost in his talented lips and tongue as he stole her breath away. When he sucked hard on her pulse point, Sunny moaned so loud it echoed as a demonstration. She didn't bother to try and quiet herself as his hand swept behind her back, unclasping her bra with ease.

"Get naked. Give me your...spiel." He murmured against her neck, lips trailing down her chest.

Sunny blinked, trying to remember where she was and what Richard was asking. *Oh yeah. Shit. I need a spiel.* "I can't give you a spiel if you don't let me think."

Richard snorted and sat back, gesturing over her body. "Go on."

Her lessons from Blanche were so long ago; what did she need to say? She bought herself time as she removed her pants, intentionally tossing them a bit farther than necessary to annoy Richard. But he never noticed; his eyes were glued to her body. She hesitated before pulling her panties off. Being all the way naked around new people gave her anxiety, but the only way to get past it was to do it. She flung her panties toward the bookshelf before she could get stuck in her own head about it.

"Don't touch these bits," she gestured to her testicles, "unless you absolutely have to. Clit or girldick are the more comfortable words for this part. And I've been doing HRT for a while, so the skin is kind of sensitive, and frankly, my clit does not work the way you might expect. Direct touch is usually too much."

Sunny paused, wondering how to put what she *did* like into words. "I usually use dental dams or panties to create a barrier, then touch myself or put a vibrator over it. But if I don't get or stay hard, don't take it personally. On the plus side, I can come multiple times with minimal cleanup needed," she explained with a shrug. "I honestly prefer muff or anal play to get off, but even if I'm not hard, the indirect touch is usually nice. I love nipple play, too."

"Sounds hot." Richard had to be teasing her again; his voice had a hint of vocal fry. "Can I go down on you? It's been a decade since I slept with an AMAB person, so I want to get to know your body before we introduce toys. But I can get a strap and lube if you want."

Normally, getting head was a little dysphoric and frankly, not that effective. But that comment about getting to know her body was one of the sweetest things anyone had ever said to her, and it had come from fucking *Richard* of all people. "It's not my favorite, but we can try it. Change my mind, Dicky."

That ghost of a smile graced his face again as Richard leaned her back into the sofa. His hands gripped her ankles, drawing them over his shoulders. His tattoos framed the smooth skin of her calves. Her heart pounded. The awkward, nerdy exterior that had been hiding an edgy, dominant lover left her off-balance. While Sunny was incredibly turned on (the tattoos were doing things for her), she had expected to feel more confident than she did.

As Richard's eyes and fingers traced her body, her old anxiety started to creep up. The familiar indecision of what she should be doing had combined with the pressure to perform. To orgasm to make her partner feel better about themself, and to make this awkward hookup worth leaving the house. Even with Blanche, sex had always been about Sunny's pleasure, never their shared intimacy. And here she was, desperate to be at his mercy, but stuck in her own head, because she was once again the shy, awkward weirdo who didn't know what to do.

The leather creaked as Richard pulled her down the couch by the hips, folding her in half. Sunny closed her eyes, luxuriating in his teeth biting her neck and earlobe, in his nails digging into her hips. The sting grounded her, quieting her insecurities.

Being ravished on Richard's leather couch wasn't as awkward as she'd expected. And if she'd learned anything from her fling with Blanche, it was that she should enjoy the here and now, the pleasure she was receiving. She might not come, she might come multiple times. She wouldn't find out by psyching herself out and worrying about how she was acting, or if she was performing the way he wanted. She should simply enjoy herself, and him.

Her eyes flew open with a gasp as Richard sucked a nipple into his mouth. Sunny whined and arched into him. Pinching the other only briefly, his hand dragged up to her neck, resting around her throat. Sunny's pulse fluttered under the slight pressure. As with his kiss, she lost all sense of herself as Richard mapped her pleasure. His mouth and hands wandered over her body, finding the spots where his teeth made her gasp, and his pinching fingers pulled moans from her.

Under the onslaught of his exploration, Sunny melted, barely processing anything beyond the bliss he brought her and how hyper-attentive he was. Richard's blue eyes were on her constantly, watching her every gasp and moan. If she didn't know any better, she would almost describe him as sweet. The man with his thumb circling her asshole and his teeth around her nipple, so attuned to her and only her, was not the version of Richard she'd built up in her head.

Richard lifted her hips, finally bringing her clit to his mouth. Sunny tensed, waiting for the strange Ick sensation that always came when anything was too tight around her girldick. Instead, the wet heat of his tongue massaged her gently into his mouth and down his throat. She tightened her thighs around his head as pleasure won out over her dysphoria.

At her whimper, the wariness in his blue eyes turned into a smirk, his nose buried in her neatly trimmed pubic hair. Wrapping an arm around her hips, his other hand snaked between them, pressing against her muff.

She moaned loudly before coaching him. "Spread your fingers just a little further apart."

Richard adjusted his fingers to mimic hers.

"Little to the left? Oh, fuck, that's perfect. Dicky, I'm not going to last long."

He pushed his fingers harder against her in time to his tongue massaging her, lifting her hips higher as Richard rose to his knees to get a better angle. Gripping the couch as all of her blood rushed to her head, Sunny moaned as her orgasm built, electric tension pulsing through her muscles. She cried out as pleasure tore through her body until she was left a twitching mess.

"What is wrong with you, Dicky?" She panted, wiggling out of his grasp as he let her go, a worried expression on his face. Sunny nearly fell to the floor in her desperation to get away from his relentless mouth. "You said you were out of practice but then you do *that*? I was hanging upside down! God, that was amazing..."

With a quiet laugh, Richard shrugged, hands running along her thighs. "Any feedback for me?"

Sunny shook her head. "No notes. You changed my mind."

His ghost of a grin was undeniably smug. "Good. Next time I'll have dental dams, and we can try other things."

She sat up on her elbows. "Next time? So is this going to be a regular thing?"

Richard looked at her carefully, a mask settling over his features. "I'd like it to be."

"Oh." Sitting all the way up, Sunny chewed her lip. That was a pleasant surprise, but he'd said it so stoically that she wasn't sure how to take it. She hadn't expected anything more than perhaps another round tonight, certainly not a "next time." But after the care and passion he'd just shown her, she wasn't going to pass up the chance. With Blanche, she'd practically had to beg to see them. But then again, Richard wasn't Blanche. "Cool, but if this is going to be a regular thing, can we, like, have a schedule? That was my biggest pet peeve with Blanche, I never knew when I'd see them next."

"I wasn't aware that you and Blanche had a history." Richard still wore that cautious expression, his eyes searching her face.

"Well, it's not common knowledge. I wasn't allowed to tell any-one. I figure since we're keeping this a secret already, you can be in the know." Sunny shrugged. "We tried a relationship for like a month last year, but we didn't last long because they always had to put work first. We're still cool, though. Friendship survived the fling and all."

"I see," Richard said carefully. "To be frank, I am somewhat of a workaholic myself. I don't have much free time on the weekdays. However, considering my only hobbies are working and reading, my weekends are consistently available."

"Don't forget napping," Sunny teased. "So, I'll come over next Friday then?"

"Good." That crooked smile was back. "And I'll have dental dams, lube, and whatever toys you want waiting for you."

Sunny climbed into his lap, keeping her hands on the couch in-stead of his shoulders. "Oh, Dicky, now you're speaking my lan-guage. Do you have any straps that vibrate?" If her new fuck buddy was offering her a dicking down on the regular, at least she could take the chance to experiment on his dime.

"I can order one." His mouth found her neck again, sucking hard. Richard's hands slid up her thighs as she straddled him. *My neck is probably one big hickey but now, but honestly, that's what foundation is for. Luna won't snitch if she—*

Sunny gasped when he smacked her ass, all thoughts of hiding Richard's marks vanishing. "Good. I want one with a vibe right on your clit. You're going to moan for me if it kills you."

Friday, February Twenty-Eighth

Chapter Twelve

Richard

RICHARD TOOK ONE LAST frantic look around his apartment, making sure everything was tidy before opening the door. The books were in order, and the candles were aligned and centered again. He'd even spent a few minutes tidying things that weren't normally tidy—the shoes in the entryway were evenly spaced, the throw pillows were symmetrical, and the coffee mugs by the espresso machine were in a neat row. Sunny would enjoy messing those up. Hopefully, that would keep her away from the bookshelf this time.

"Hi." Sunny blushed, just as she had the previous weekend. She was dressed much the same, in a baggy sweatshirt and khaki pants. A far cry from the thrifted scene look she wore around their friends, but seeing her shy smile still made his breath catch. Her makeup was flawless, even after a full day of work, and her inky hair fell in soft waves around her face.

"Come in." Already an improvement from last week; he'd remembered to invite her in. "Are you hungry?"

Richard's plans for last weekend were to buy her dinner and make her feel comfortable, before maybe kissing her if she wanted. That had been quickly forgotten. They'd eaten eventually, but both of them were ravenous by the time their takeout had showed up at ten. This weekend would be different. He couldn't let her think he was just using her for sex.

Even though that particular activity had occupied most of their evening on Friday. And Saturday morning. And once more on Saturday afternoon. They'd had conversations between rounds (and sometimes during), mostly Richard listening to Sunny talk about work, funny stories about Lee, Tara, and Blanche, or a rant about the state of the world. All of which reminded Richard how isolated and uneventful his life was. The best he had were a few dating horror stories, and the rare funny story about Gabe and Antonio that didn't veer into depressing. But thankfully, Sunny didn't seem to mind how quiet he was.

Even their texts over the past week were mostly dominated by her, to his relief. Richard had never been good at texting. Sunny's stream of consciousness, frequently interrupted by links to toys she wanted and memes he didn't understand, gave him plenty to respond to. Thankfully, she didn't seem to take it personally when he took a while to come up with a reply.

"Yes, but I don't want to eat yet." Sunny greeted him with a kiss, ruffling his hair. That should have annoyed him, but Richard was left salivating from the barest hint of vanilla lip gloss and citrus perfume. She stepped around him before he could formulate a response. "I've been craving sushi if you're buying, though."

"I'm surprised you have no ethical qualms about importing saltwater fish to the Midwest," Richard teased, smoothing his hair back. "Or overfishing. Or commercial fish farming practices."

"Oh, we're doing this again?" Sunny laughed. "I'm supporting a local business, and my carbon footprint is negligible as an individual consumer. And frankly, I barely had time for lunch today because of stupid meetings, and I want sushi. So get off your high horse before I eat it."

"So you do want to eat now."

Sunny ruffled his hair again on her way to the sofa. "I was low-key hoping you'd jump me as soon as I walked in again, so if it's all the same to you, I'd rather have you fuck me first."

Richard blinked, willing his brain to produce anything besides static. Maybe he didn't need to worry about Sunny feeling used. "On that note," he tidied his hair and deposited a box in her lap, "your presents came."

Sunny squealed as she opened it, holding up a double-ended dildo in triumph. "Yes! I've been looking forward to this all week!"

Muscles in his stomach tensing, Richard swallowed. He had not been looking forward to *that* all week. The other toys, sure. Especially the lingerie he'd added to the order after she'd left. But the dread of…what, he wasn't sure. It wasn't necessarily dysphoria from the toy—Sunny had checked that it wouldn't give him "the Ick," as she called it, before adding it to the cart. The lump in his stomach came more from being so exposed to someone. Having Sunny see him vulnerable and out of control. He'd barely kept it quiet last weekend.

No, there are worse problems to have than someone who wants to make me come.

Occasionally, he'd been on the other side, where the women he dated had been unwilling to touch him for various reasons, most of them thinly-veiled transphobia. That Sunny was so determined to learn how to pleasure him was… The word escaped him. Nice? Not complex enough. Refreshing? That wasn't it. Validating? Maybe his therapist could tell Richard what he was feeling.

Sunny held up a pair of black lace underwear. "Is this for me, too?"

Richard nodded, still at a loss for what to say.

Sunny cocked her head as she glanced between him and the panties she held up.

Maybe he had overstepped. Maybe it was too soon to be buying her lingerie? Or maybe she thought it was controlling for him to pick things out without her input? He'd thought that was something men did for their partners as a romantic gesture, but Sunny hadn't liked it when he'd opened the car door for her. He couldn't tell if the lines between her eyebrows and how she was chewing on her lower lip were a sign of concentration or annoyance.

But Sunny eventually gave an approving nod. "So like a femme jockstrap? Sick! I'd ask you to send me the link, but there's like a dozen in here."

Richard straightened his shoulders to hide his relief. "I wasn't sure what color you'd like."

She dug through the box, pulling out a large pump bottle of lube and several matching bras, along with a few other toys he'd added on impulse. "Damn, Dicky. All of this is for me? How did you know my size?"

Richard shifted. "Educated guess."

"You must feel up a lot of titties," Sunny teased. "You got the band size right and everything."

"No, but you… We," He paused to figure out his words. "You're a similar size to what I had…before."

"Oh." Sunny's eyes flicked to his chest and down to hers. "Bro, binding must have sucked."

He rubbed his chest, grateful as always, even after all these years, that his chest looked and felt like it should. "Understatement of the century."

She cocked her head again. "Should I pay you back for this? Or are you like rich, rich?"

Richard huffed. "To be completely honest, I am uh...rich rich. I'm not a billionaire or anything, but I work because I enjoy it, and having my own income has allowed me to get out from under my dad's thumb. Using my trust fund for sex toys is a nice 'fuck you' to my dad. So no, don't pay me back. This is for my enjoyment as much as yours."

"Oh, so this isn't for me. This is for *you*." Sunny laughed, swatting his arm with the red panties in her hand.

"It's for *us*," Richard teased. "It's for you to wear, and I get to look at you wearing that."

Sunny laughed again, and Richard found himself smiling. Her joy was so loud. "I'm gonna try these on. Be right back."

While she was in the bathroom, Richard busied himself by tidying up the packaging she'd thrown around the living room. He'd just deposited the last of it in the recycling when she cleared her throat from behind him.

Sunny was leaning against the doorframe, wearing only the red lingerie set and fishnet thigh highs. Drinking in her curves, he stepped slowly toward her, not attempting to quiet the static in his brain at the sight of her. Her toned stomach bloomed into muscular thighs where the lace circled her slender hips. Her full tits were lifted impossibly high on her chest, brown nipples and golden tan skin visible through the red lace.

"You like it?" Sunny spun around, showing off the lacey straps exposing her peachy ass, a teasing grin over her shoulder.

Richard swallowed, worried he was on the verge of drooling. Figuring out the right words to describe exactly how much he liked it was infinitely harder than showing her.

Her ass bounced as his palm connected with a loud smack.

A surprised yelp came from Sunny. She whirled around with a shocked grin on her face. "Damn, Dicky! Warn a girl before you do that. I almost fell over."

"Then this is your warning that your ass will be as red as those panties by the time I fuck you." The rasp in Richard's voice surprised him. "So you might want to get somewhere you can fall over."

Sunny squealed and ran as he lunged for her ass again.

She let him catch her as she reached the sofa, shrieking as he grabbed her around the hips and bent her over the cushioned arm. He kissed and bit and licked down her spine until she was a puddle of sighs and whines under his mouth.

"Stop teasing, Dicky." She shifted, adjusting her hips against the arm of the sofa so her ass was exposed to him. One cheek was red with his handprint.

With another loud smack, Richard gave her one to match on the other, enthralled by the ripple effect through her beautiful, firm curves. Struggling to control his baser instincts, he reached for his phone, tossing it in front of her. "Here, order your food," he said, rolling his sleeves up to the elbow.

Sunny huffed. "You got me all wound up for one little spank?"

"Order your food while I keep going. Because I could do this for hours, and you're already hungry." He snapped the elastic cupping her ass to emphasize his point, grinning as she yelped.

"Fine." Sunny grabbed the phone. "Where do you want to eat?"

Richard rewarded her with a firm smack. "Whatever you want."

"You expect me to make decisions?" Sunny asked. "My brain shorts out every time you spank me."

"Figure it out, Sunshine," Richard teased. "You stop, I stop."

"I'm never going to eat." But she pulled up the menu of some restaurant and scrolled through it, letting out a new delightful sound with every blow he landed—a whimper, a whine, a few deep moans when he struck her particularly hard. Every sound sent a thrill pounding through his veins that left him feeling almost tipsy. Experimenting to identify what would make her cry out the loudest, Richard was so captivated by the reddening of her skin, the loudness of her pleasure and the wiggle of her hips, that he barely noticed when she looked at him over her shoulder, eyes wide and lips parted.

He paused, hand raised. "Are you finished?"

Sunny shook her head, blushing before she turned back to his phone. "Still figuring out dessert. You're just— It's really... Your sleeves rolled up like that is hot." She laughed. "Why am I getting turned on at the sight of your wrist?"

"Imagine how I feel with you spread out like this in next to nothing." Richard hoped she wouldn't look back again; if the burning in his face was any indication, his cheeks had just turned bright red. He gave one final slap to her ass before pulling a bottle of lube from the box on the table. Sitting on the couch, he beckoned for her.

"Are you done already?" Sunny pouted but crawled forward across the cushions, draping herself over his lap. Her red cheeks wiggled in the air. She hissed as the cold gel squirted down the cleft of her ass.

"No." Richard used two fingers to swirl around her hole before pressing slowly into her, easing in and out of her until he brushed against the spot he'd been aiming for.

Sunny cried out, her hips bucking to take his fingers deeper. The phone fell from her hand.

"Focus," Richard teased. "You stop, I stop."

She groaned in frustration and pleasure, choking on the sound as he pressed against her prostate. Blood thrumming under his skin, Richard fingered her methodically, while she struggled to keep her eyes open and focus on the phone in her hands. Sunny was so responsive, her vocal and physical reactions so rewarding every time he touched her. He wanted to tie her up, have her at his mercy while he toyed with her and learned her body. To find the best ways to make her come undone and what would leave Sunny begging for more. Last weekend had been the crash course; now Richard wanted to analyze her.

"Dicky, I'm so close," Sunny whimpered, looking over her shoulder. Her eyes were glazed with pleasure, her lower lip puffy from biting it. "Please don't stop."

As if he would even consider stopping at this point, when she was so close to falling apart in his lap from just his fingers inside her and her clit against his thigh. "Are you done ordering?"

Sunny nodded, blabbering out her yeses and pleas to let her come.

When she begged like that, Richard would give her anything she wanted. "Then go ahead, Sunshine. Let me hear it." He wound a hand through her hair and tugged as he pressed harder inside her.

Her whimper of relief morphed into a loud cry as her body shook and twisted in his lap. He watched, fascinated at the contortion of her face, the arch of her back, the trembling of her thighs. Richard took the phone from her as Sunny's body sagged, thighs still twitching. "You want me to keep going?" He tentatively flexed his fingers inside her as he asked.

She shook her head with a wince. "Not yet. That was amazing. I need a minute to recover."

Richard removed his hand, wiping the lube from his fingers onto her skin absentmindedly as he added an order of edamame and buckwheat noodles to Sunny's cart.

"So, you gonna let me make you come or what?" Sunny asked sleepily, looking at him over her shoulder as Richard rubbed more lube into her cheeks in an attempt to soothe them. He should stock up on aloe.

"Eventually. I had something I wanted to talk about *before* we began fooling around, but you're very distracting." He gently swatted her ass.

Sunny squeaked in response. "This was much more fun than talking. What about?"

"Oh, I made a list." Richard pulled up a spreadsheet on his phone and handed it to her.

"You made a *list*?"

He nodded. "Of different things we could try. With yes-no-maybe categories. I already moved all of the things that trigger my dysphoria to the no list, but if you want to go through it—"

"Dicky, you're such a fucking dork." Sunny grinned as she read the list. "Damn, you're kind of a freaky ass, though. I assume by fisting, you mean, you'd fist me, right?"

Richard nodded. "Yes. All of these assume I'm topping you. Unless they say reverse."

"That's cute. So the 'reverse missionary' in the 'maybe' column means you want me to fuck you?" Sunny winked at him.

Richard shrugged, his cheeks growing hot. "More 'open to it' than wanting it. I doubt we'll be into it."

"Agreed. But we can try it. Eventually. Not tonight though. I want you to moan as loud as you can when you're fucking me with this." Sunny climbed off his lap to reach into the box, waggling the dildo he'd been dreading.

His stomach clenched, the dread pooling. Sunny seemed determined to pull out all of his embarrassing sounds.

At his tight smile that probably looked more like a wince, Sunny raised an eyebrow as she knelt on the couch next to him. "Is it such a chore to let me know you're enjoying it?"

Richard sighed. "It's not that it's a chore..."

"Then what?" Sunny chewed her lip, deflating as she sat back on her heels. "I just... I'm not good at picking up on stuff. Like, I know this isn't the same thing that I had going on with Blanche, but they were always so hard to read. At the time, I figured that if they didn't want something, they would tell me. But they never did, and honestly, in hindsight, it was so obvious they were faking it for my sake, but I couldn't let myself believe that. It's been hard to reconcile that I basically just used someone I cared about for my own needs." She fiddled with the dildo in her hands. "So I need to know that you want this, that you're *enjoying* this too. And even if it's not moaning or whatever, I need some sign that you're enjoying what I do to you."

"I do want you. I enjoyed everything we did last weekend. All of it. And this." Richard gaped, at a loss for words but determined to reassure her. To bring back the Sunny who teased him, instead of the timid woman curling around herself. "I just...don't like how I sound."

Oh, *that* was the knot in his stomach. His dysphoria usually felt more like shame than dread, but he supposed the anticipation might cause that reaction. He wished it was easier to know what he was feeling without expressing it out loud. Or perhaps have a chance to discuss it with his therapist in private, so he could make sure he explained it right.

"Oh?" Sunny cocked her head, still gnawing her bottom lip between her teeth.

Using his thumb to pull her lip out of danger of being chewed raw, he huffed, hoping he could get the words across comprehensively. "I can control my speaking voice to be deeper than it normally is, but not when it's involuntary. And I sound like a bad porno."

Sunny laughed.

Richard shot her a look, torn between relief that Sunny was no longer sad and irritation that she was laughing at him.

"Sorry! I'm not laughing at your dysphoria." Sunny covered her mouth. "Just the imagery was funny. But I get that. I used to practice so I *would* sound more like a bad porno."

"You practiced your sex noises." Richard bit back a snicker; Sunny sounded so natural, he'd never have guessed she'd rehearsed her moans. But she was right, the idea of her alone practicing those glorious sounds was entertaining. Charming, but funny.

"Of course!" Sunny shrugged unabashedly and tossed the dildo at him. "Come on, Dicky. Practice makes perfect. I want to hear you growl."

"I'm not growling."

"Okay, *moan* then. I don't care what sounds you make, just so long as you make them. We have," She checked the phone still in his hand, "half an hour before our food gets here. So, come on, practice your sex noises while you make me scream."

He allowed himself one small huff of mock annoyance before climbing on top of her, pinning her against the couch. Richard kissed her, tongue soothing the puffiness of her lower lip. Because she was right—of course Sunny was right. Even without making the noises he dreaded, he still felt so exposed by her.

Sunny moaned when he scraped his teeth along her neck. "Dicky, I'll need more foundation if you leave as many hickeys as last time. I swear, I had to put it everywhere from the tits up."

A possessive satisfaction curled in his belly. He wanted to mark her, leave reminders that *he'd* made her come undone days after Sunny went home. Even if that meant *growling* or whatever when he made them. With one hand, Richard unbuckled his belt, yanking it out of his slacks. "Send me a link. I'll buy you a case of it."

Saturday, March Fourteenth

Chapter Thirteen

Blanche

"Where's Sunny been?" Tara asked, breaking the quiet of their apartment. The crisp morning light reflected off the windows of the new condo across the street, the only natural light their collection of plants had since it'd been built. Her brows furrowed as she took a puff from the joint Blanche had rolled for her. "She hasn't been here in weeks. It's been so quiet."

Blanche opened the oven door to check the pie, blinking as a rush of hot air blasted the moisture out of their eyes. The crust was a nice golden brown, and it smelled done, they supposed. Not that they knew how to bake. Chas's mom had made this, finding a recipe based entirely on Blanche's memories and preparing it the night before. Blanche had watched the older kids, while Chas and the newest baby had slept. Freddy was working lights at Confession and keeping an eye on things, while Chas was out on leave.

"It has been a while." Blanche turned the oven off and left the door propped open to keep the pie warm until it was time to leave. "Sometime before her birthday, I think."

"Fuck. She's still mad at me for the bowling shit." Tara groaned, burying herself into the throw blanket wrapped around her. Only her hand stayed visible, the joint held lightly between two fingers. "I'm such an asshole."

Blanche took it from her, taking a deep drag to quell their own nerves. A picnic in March, the event Lee and Antonio had contrived to get their friends to hang out, was bad enough. The location made this the worst plan imaginable. And that was coming from someone who had once steered the getaway car from the backseat, so Chas could return fire from the passenger seat after Freddy had gotten shot while driving away from one of Daisy's ill-fated adventures. Daisy, useless as always when her plans went wrong, had panic-laughed in the backseat.

Blanche shook their head, trying to focus. Antonio wanted a damn picnic, and Lee wanted to support him. Thanks to her chronic martyr complex, Tara would be going to the one place in the city where she was practically guaranteed to have a panic attack. "Babes, it's been a month, and Sunny forgave you. She's not passive-aggressive enough to hold a grudge."

At least I hope so. Sunny could still be upset with Blanche for not coming to her party in the first place. She'd *said* she understood that Blanche had to work—their schedule was even worse now that they had to film scenes and create content, on top of their patron and other clients. But Sunny had been acting oddly a few weeks ago when Blanche last saw her. Granted, they had interrupted her and Richard sitting a little too close at Confession. Maybe they'd just ruined the moment by showing up when they had. Blanche exhaled slowly as they curled up in their armchair. *Maybe that's where she's been? Boning Richard?*

Now that was an interesting possibility. They were obviously attracted to each other, though Blanche hadn't been sure if Sunny had noticed. While her unannounced visits had been less frequent since last summer, they'd dropped to almost nothing over the past month.

As tempting as it was to reassure Tara that Sunny might be distracted by Antonio's friend, it was mere speculation. Nothing solid enough to share. Tara would then tell Lee, and that might mean the end to Lee's Kumbaya scheme. And then Tara might stay unhappy in her emotional bomb shelter forever. She needed a push to accept the new people Lee was determined to include in their lives, especially when it came to Mr. Tall, Dark, and Handsome.

"I hope you're right. That'd be another reason to be pissed off at Gabe." Tara rolled her eyes as she reached for the joint.

Blanche took a hit to hide their own eye roll before passing it back. "Sure." Tara had many strong feelings about Gabe, but anger was not chief among them. Reading Gabe's feelings for Tara was harder; his face was expressive, but Blanche couldn't pin down his moods yet.

"Maybe she's getting along better with her mom," Tara suggested. "Or she's out with one of the straight girls her mom's always trying to set her up with."

Blanche laughed politely, assuming Tara was trying to be funny.

"Are you okay with that?" Tara asked. "Sunny dating again?"

They shot her a look and took the joint back. "Don't make it weird, Tara. Of course, she deserves someone who makes her happy."

"So do you." Tara made a face back.

Blanche's heart twinged. They didn't remember how happiness felt, if they had ever known it in the first place. "And so do *you*."

Tara shook her head resolutely. "Don't go there, Blanche."

Blanche appreciated her more now than ever since Lee had moved out, but Tara was not the sweet, empathetic teddy bear roommate Lee had been. She was more of a porcupine who gave surprisingly good advice, but would bristle when anyone returned the favor. Their heart-to-hearts were circles of encouraging each other to open up, while neither of them actually shared anything meaningful.

"You started it, babes." Blanche sighed as the high buzzed under their skin, just enough to make the tugging in their heart easier to ignore. Not tugging for Sunny. Not even for someone to call their own. Just tugging for...more. For control of their own life. For a home their patron's fiancée couldn't evict them from. For peace. Though they'd gotten a text recently that said simply, "You win," so perhaps they wouldn't have to worry as much about that. Not that life under their patron's thumb was peaceful by any stretch of the imagination.

Blanche swallowed the sourness in their chest.

They just had to keep working on their channel. Throwing themself into work had helped to bury their feelings after Daisy died. It would work again, and Lee's fun little plan to get Sunny and Tara to shack up with Antonio's friends was a nice distraction from the future Mrs. Big Pharma. Who was and always would be the future Mrs. Big Pharma, even if they were officially off at the moment. Mr. Big Pharma would never let anyone go, especially someone who made him look good.

"Are you gonna be okay today?" Blanche asked quietly.

"I better be. After all, having this picnic on the island was my idea. Lee couldn't make up his mind about the location." Tara shrugged. "I want to be okay today, so I'm gonna be okay. The joint will help. You?"

Blanche forced a smile. "Why wouldn't I be?"

Tara's face softened as she held out the smoking stub. "Because I'm not the only one with hard feelings about the island. When this stupid picnic is over, you wanna visit Daisy?"

Squeezing Tara's hand before taking the end of the joint, Blanche said, "Only if you're up for it. There isn't much of Daisy left on the island."

Tara huffed. "There isn't much left of the camp either, but it's still in here." She tapped her temple. "Daisy is too."

"I love when you try to be a therapist," Blanche teased. But Tara was right. Maybe if Tara was up for it, they could spend some time by the sandstone outcropping, where Daisy's ashes had been scattered years ago. "Shall we?"

"Oh shit!" Tara grabbed her phone to check it, overdramatically. "Is it that time already? Oh no, I still have to get a pie. Just go on without me, I'll go buy one and meet you there."

Blanche's eyes ached from rolling them so hard. For all of Tara's big talk about confronting her hard feelings about the island, she was still avoiding Gabe like the plague. They would never understand why Tara, who could so easily pursue short-term pleasure, resisted anything that might make her happier in the long run. "As if you didn't forget a pie on purpose. You can't avoid him forever, you know."

"I don't know what you're talking about." Tara slipped out the front door before Blanche could call her out on her bullshit.

With a sigh, Blanche pulled their coat on, wrapped their pie in a tea towel, and followed her down the stairs. The camp had never been home for them the way it had been for Tara, but it had been a refuge whenever Daisy and Blanche had needed to disappear. Hopefully it would be a refuge again today, providing some reprieve from the stresses of Blanche's life. And if not, well, at least they could go see Daisy.

Chapter Fourteen

Sunny

"Is Lee seriously late to his own stupid thing?" Sunny steamed. "Who has a picnic outdoors in March? It's freezing. And for Pi Day? That is next-level nerdy. And Lee, Mr. 'On Time Is Late,' isn't here yet? Why are we here?"

Richard, who stood silently with a pecan pie in hand, simply shrugged. He looked annoyingly put together in his cream sweater and black leather jacket with a pair of matching Adidas on his feet. "Honestly, this is typical Antonio."

They waited for the others in the "new" riverfront park, at the picnic pavilion where Antonio had told them to meet. The park was a short bus ride from her house and within walking distance of Blanche's, but it still felt wrong to gather here. Did Antonio know their history with the park, or was Lee being inconsiderate of Tara's feelings? Sunny might seriously hurt Gabe if he couldn't keep his mouth shut today. She huffed, cold air turning to mist around her mouth. "Doesn't mean it's not annoying."

Richard gave her that ghost of a crooked smile that sent her heart fluttering. "Tonio's always annoying."

"You're so...reasonable, Dicky." She wanted to be annoyed, and he was ruining her attitude.

"That was sarcasm, I presume."

"Yes, that was sarcasm." Sunny fought a smile. "Just let me be annoyed at Lee, okay? Is that so much to ask?"

Richard's lips twitched, leaning against the end of the picnic table. "I'll give you three minutes to work yourself up about Lee being late."

To her displeasure, Sunny flushed. His bossy flirting got under her skin in the best way, even though she was grumpy. But they were in public and waiting for their friends. Richard couldn't exactly follow through with his hinted consequences like usual. She sat on the picnic table next to him, shooting him an annoyed look. "It's not just because he's late, you know."

Richard mimicked her scowl. "I *don't* know. You told me it was none of my business."

A snort escaped her. "It *is* none of your business." It was Tara's business. And Blanche's. And Lee's, who should know better than to make Tara come here. Normally Lee was the one who protected Tara from those hard feelings, and now he was dragging her into them? And for what? Because his boyfriend wanted to eat pie outside when it was forty degrees? *And* they were late?

"Regardless, you're supposed to hate *me* today, remember." Richard nudged her. "Can't have them thinking we get along."

Sunny tsked, smiling despite herself. "I love when you tell me what I'm supposed to feel."

"Now, *that* was sarcasm."

Sunny rolled her eyes. His detached humor was annoyingly charming, despite how dry and serious he could be. Finding new ways to make Richard lose his composure was fun. She'd stayed at his place every weekend for the past month and always found new ways to unravel him.

Richard's life was too structured. The huffs of annoyance that left him when he found yet another spoon on the counter, or the toilet paper flipped backward, were adorable. Without complaint, he quietly tidied up in her wake and slapped her on the ass. A win-win as far as Sunny was concerned. Her favorite (non-sexual) sound was his quiet groan of frustration when she messed up his hair as she walked in the door. He always looked too nice for their Friday (and lately, Saturday) nights together. He'd learn eventually that she preferred him messy—

"Okay, time's up. Be annoyed at me instead of Lee. We'll need to argue if you want this to stay a secret."

"Fuck you, Dicky," Sunny laughed. *Dammit, I spent none of that time annoyed at Lee.* "Typical man. What are you going to do next, tell me to smile?"

"That's perfect." Richard gave her that ghost of a smile that melted her heart. "But maybe save the good one-liners for whenever Antonio finally graces us with his presence."

"Being this late is very unlike Lee. I'm suspicious." Sunny set the French silk pie she had "made" on a picnic table. She'd picked it up at the Perkins closest to Richard's condo last night, but she wouldn't admit it to anyone. Well, anyone but Richard, who was sworn to secrecy much like everything that transpired between them. That hadn't stopped him from teasing her because Antonio had specifically said, *"Bake your favorite pie for Pi Day"* (even though he'd stolen her idea and paid for both of their pies).

"You have every right to be, Babygirl." Blanche's voice made Sunny jump. They set a steaming pie on the table next to Sunny's. "This is a foolish idea."

"Wow, that looks good. What is it?" Sunny sniffed the steam. "It smells like stew."

"Pasty pie. Grandma Rose's specialty. Pie courtesy of Chas's mom, but I technically put it in the oven." Blanche pulled their parka tighter around themself.

Sunny raised her eyebrows. "And you remember the recipe?" Blanche's grandma had passed when they were thirteen.

"It's just steak, onion, potatoes, carrots, and rutabaga. Lupe found a recipe pretty quick once I remembered what the fuck a rutabaga was." Blanche shrugged, hugging themself as they forced a half smile. "I figured everyone else would bring something sweet."

Richard set his pecan pie down with theirs. "May I ask why we should be suspicious that they're late? And is it something Antonio came up with?"

"Surprisingly, *Lee* is the mastermind here. Antonio just came up with today's bullshit." Blanche paused, green eyes flicking between Sunny and Richard. Their half smile stretched into a grin. "The plan is to organize social events to force the two of you, as well as Tara and Gabe, to spend more time together and get to know each other better. The goal is to get you to stop bickering and, hopefully, bone."

"Please, as if!" Sunny tittered. "That's the dumbest idea I've ever heard! Like I'd ever think of *Dicky* that way!"

"Could have fooled me," Blanche snorted, unzipping Sunny's jacket and pulling her collar to the side. Hidden beneath it were several dark hickeys from last night that Sunny had *thought* would be hidden without makeup. "You two don't exactly need encouragement, do you?"

Sunny huffed, her stomach souring as Richard looked at the ground instead of at her. She hadn't wanted Blanche to find out about her situationship with Richard at all, let alone in front of him. Other people knowing made it...real. After several weekends of being treated like... Well, like a girlfriend (even though that wasn't what she was), Sunny was at serious risk of catching feelings. Other people knowing about that, Blanche especially, would only make it more painful when this situationship eventually fizzled out.

Richard crossed his arms, still looking at his feet. "I take it you're not supposed to tell us about this master plan, seeing as you're their accomplice."

Blanche shrugged, inspecting the teeth marks imprinted on Sunny's collarbone.

"I knew that chair thing was too perfect to be an accident." Sunny wanted to flatter herself by thinking Blanche might be jealous that Richard had marked her as his (even though she wasn't his). But Blanche had never wanted Sunny in the first place, so their involvement in getting Sunny laid by someone else was no real surprise. More surprising—and confusing—was Lee being the brains behind this. He liked to make plans for his friends, but usually aimed for meaningful, not manipulative. "Was the New Year's kissing shit your doing, too?"

Their silence was all the confirmation Sunny needed, making her wonder if Jazz had lied about her crush on Blanche, too. Though, if she was being honest with herself, Sunny didn't really care. She hadn't exactly needed much convincing to kiss Richard that night. Or to send him a picture of her tits after only a few minutes alone together at Confession.

As usual, Blanche's half smile was unreadable as they prodded around the love bites that Sunny had triple-checked wouldn't be visible with her jacket zipped up. She was going through foundation as fast as they went through lube. Richard had offered to leave marks in less visible places, but she liked seeing the evidence of how much he wanted her throughout the week.

"How could you tell?" Sunny gestured to her neck, shivering as the cold March breeze found its way into her jacket.

"Nothing was visible, but I had a hunch. And you have foundation on your scarf." Blanche's half smile turned into a smirk. "Don't worry.

I won't tell anyone anything. I'll just hint to Lee that he doesn't have to try so hard to get you two to stop arguing."

Sunny shook her head. "Don't! Promise, Blanche, you won't say a word. We don't want anyone sticking their nose in our business. Besides..." Sunny scrambled for a reason that would keep Blanche quiet, exchanging a look with Richard. He had finally looked up, his blue eyes alarmed. Blanche knowing was bad enough. If Lee knew, and therefore Antonio knew... "Wouldn't messing up their plan be fun?"

Lee would be full of judgy opinions and well-intentioned advice if he found out. Opinions she could handle, but they'd be scrutinized by all of their friends, and neither she nor Richard wanted that. Privacy was imperative. She and Richard got on better than she'd expected; Richard was surprisingly sweet. But they didn't have a real relationship. There was no point in their friends treating it like one.

Their lives were too disparate to bridge, even if Sunny could begrudgingly admit she might like him. Richard had been upfront that his family would never approve of her, and if Mae found out... Her mother would make Sunny break up with him, and she wasn't done with Richard yet. She wanted the fun to last, before their families came between them.

Richard emphatically nodded his approval. "You could play for both sides. Plot and counterplot."

Blanche eyed Sunny thoughtfully, their all-seeing green eyes digging into her soul the way only Blanche could. "That does sound fun." They paused. "Just a quick word of advice, maybe leave less visible marks? It won't be winter forever." They side-eyed Richard.

He nodded, blushing that adorable deep red. "Tell that to Sunny."

"Blanche, what are you saying to poor Dicky now? I can see that blush from here!" Antonio's voice rang out from the footbridge. He and Lee had arrived at the perfect point in time as far as Sunny was concerned. She stepped away from Blanche, zipping up her coat.

"Oh, nothing that poor little Dicky here doesn't want to hear." Blanche's placid half smile was frustrating more often than not, but Sunny was relieved to hide her own expression and let Blanche do the talking. "Don't worry. I'm not corrupting your friend too badly."

"Could everyone stop calling me Dicky?" Richard protested.

Sunny bit her lip as she pretended to fuss with her pie. She called him Dicky all the time, and he never said a word about it...

The taste of iron flooding her mouth let her know she was stressing over nothing. She enjoyed annoying him; why should she care if he was annoyed by her nickname for him? She closed that tab, trying to regain control of her face.

Lee set down a stack of plates and napkins. "Are you okay there, Sunny?" Gesturing to his lip, he eyed her thoughtfully.

"What pie did you bring?" Sunny couldn't fool him, especially with the forced smile on her face that Lee always saw right through. Hopefully, he wouldn't press the change in subject; Sunny wasn't a very good liar, especially when lying to her oldest friend.

"Sweet potato. Out of season, but nostalgic." He took the lead she'd given him, granting her mercy from his nosiness. "Antonio brought key lime."

"Honestly, this is the weirdest idea for a party you've had, Lee."

"It's a great idea!" Lee checked to make sure Antonio was out of earshot before lowering his voice. "But it *was* Antonio's idea, so I'm mostly saying that to be a good boyfriend."

Sunny covered her laugh.

In his regular volume, Lee said, "A math teacher he works with roped some of the teachers into making their favorite pies for his classes to judge for Pi Day, so Tonio spent the last month making dairy-free key lime pie to practice. He thought we should all be included in the experience, and I'm not going to complain about eating sweet potato pie." Lee lowered his voice again. "Because I'm so damn tired of key lime."

"Okay, shady." Sunny giggled. "Did he win?"

"No!" Antonio interjected. "Apparently middle schoolers aren't refined enough to have taste yet. They all voted for French silk or apple."

"Well, as someone who brought French silk, I'd have to agree with them," Sunny said imperiously, even though lemon meringue was her favorite. Antonio didn't need to know French silk was the only pie left at Perkins last night after Richard had claimed the pecan. Maybe Tara would take the leftovers home.

Richard unobtrusively leaned in once Lee had stepped away, and the conversation was drawn away from her. He crossed his arms and murmured, "A counterplot? Genius."

"Careful, Dicky. They might think you like me if you keep talking like that." Sunny narrowed her eyes and scowled, in case anyone was watching. She bit her lip to keep from smiling at his praise.

"Fake arguing, outstanding." Richard shook his head with a sneer, "I'd kiss you if it wouldn't give us away."

"Don't you dare! Not if you want to pull this off." Sunny rolled her eyes with a huff. "How long can we get away with fake-hating each other?"

"With Antonio? Until we tell him. Gabe will catch on sooner, but I don't want him to know."

There was a twinge in her chest at Richard's words. Her face fell. "Oh?"

His eyes narrowed, but Richard's voice softened. "Their plan has merit where he's concerned. Gabe needs a push to get out of his comfort zone. He's been hiding too long."

Sunny scolded herself for feeling relieved that Richard didn't want to keep her a secret because of her. "Tara's going to murder them when she finds out."

"All the more reason to keep it a secret. This is so fun." Richard gave her one last fake sneer. "Stop biting your lip. You're already bleeding."

Sunny bit her lip again to annoy him. "You can't do anything to stop me, bossy ass."

"I can later." His blue eyes narrowed on her lip.

"Who says I'm going back to your place?" Sunny teased, curious what "later" might entail.

"You will." With a barely-there smile that made her squirm with anticipation, Richard turned to greet Gabe, who deposited a beautiful quiche on the table, greeting everyone politely. Sunny hadn't seen him since the night at Confession a month ago. When she'd sent Richard a pic of her titties, made him buy her Denny's, spilled her life story, and kissed him.

Sure, they'd done a lot more than that in the weeks following. She actually enjoyed hanging out at Richard's apartment. They'd eat takeout, argue, and share stories about their lives. It was almost like they were friends. Except with way more fooling around. Richard was very forward and generous in the best ways. But she was still surprised at her boldness that first night. At long last, Sunny had felt the kind of bravado that Tara usually exhibited with her sex life. It was liberating.

"No Tara today?" Gabe asked.

Speaking of Tara and her potential sex life...

"She's on her way," Blanche said. "Just getting a pie."

As if summoned, Tara half-jogged to meet them, panting out her apologies for being late. She set a Perkins box down on the table to wrap her peacoat tighter around herself, shoving her hands in the pockets. "Sorry, that took longer than I thought."

"Is Perkins your secret family recipe?" Sunny teased, intentionally keeping her tone light so Tara wouldn't feel antagonized. Tara's audacity at not even hiding the fact that hers was store-bought was impressive. The night before, Sunny had taken all the chocolate curls off and smooshed the whipped cream around to make it look homemade.

Tara's smile didn't quite reach her eyes. "Nah, Anne would have used the Sanderson five-finger discount."

Taking a page out of Blanche's book, Sunny forced on her best half smile. *Tara's voluntarily talking about her mom? It's worse than I thought. We need to eat now before Gabe opens his mouth.* Sunny tried not to judge people for their intelligence, but Gabe was *such* a dumbass himbo. While he treated everyone else kindly, he acted like an immature little boy pulling his crush's hair around Tara, who drooled over him when his back was turned. *The himbo charm.* Gabe was certainly nice to look at, and Tara was a hedonist.

But today? Today Gabe trying to flirt would spell disaster.

Before Sunny could suggest they eat, Gabe cut in with a snide tone, looking over Tara's shoulder. "You know, the rest of us actually made ours. You couldn't *try* to make an apple pie? It's an easy recipe."

"It's not a competition, Gabe." Antonio started to interject, but the damage was done.

"Some of us know fuck all about baking, asshole!" Tara managed to mutter before her forced smile fell, replaced with a far-off look in her green eyes that was not good. Turning on her heel, Tara headed to the bridge without another word.

Lee followed after her, calling her name as he shot Gabe a glare over his shoulder.

"What the hell is your problem?" Sunny turned on Gabe, seething. The first thing she'd learned about Tara was don't fuck with her food. Granted, her first interaction with Tara was stealing her cookie, so it was a lesson quickly learned. She still remembered the sting from Tara pulling her hair.

Gabe shrugged. "What? It's just a question!"

Richard sighed, rubbing his forehead. "Jesus Christ."

Antonio had turned on Gabe too, an accusing finger pointed up at his friend. "Seriously? You told me you'd behave today. And you can't say she started that. This was all you!"

"I didn't know she'd take it personally." Gabe fiddled with the end of his braid.

"Cut the shit, Gabe!" Antonio's voice rose. "It's fucking apple pie! Dessert! We talked about this! You're not an asshole—you're the sweetheart!—so what's your fucking problem?"

"We are in public!" Blanche hissed in a singsong voice, a fake smile plastered to their face. They waved politely at two middle-aged white women glaring at them.

Sunny forced her own smile, anxiety souring her anger. The optics of a group of queer people, most of whom were people of color, yelling at each other in the park—*this* park—was not ideal. Hopefully they hadn't seen Lee chasing after Tara, too.

This part of Eastside had never been *that* safe, but now it was unsafe for a different reason. The homeless encampment that had existed on the island for decades had been bulldozed to make a park as part of "city revitalization" efforts, the people displaced by white women with their lattes and poorly-trained dogs. The whole city was still on edge from the riot that had erupted the night of the eviction, even five years and counting later. It wasn't safe to be racialized or queer, a sex worker, homeless, an immigrant, or mentally ill anywhere in Bellamy, but especially not in *this* park.

"Sorry." Antonio forced a laugh, throwing an arm around Gabe until the women turned away. Talking between themselves, the pair continued shooting the occasional glance in their direction.

"Look, Gabe," Blanche murmured in a soothing tone, putting their hand on Gabe's arm. Sunny swallowed—Blanche's calm voice was scary; they only used it when they were on the verge of losing their temper. "You don't know Tara that well yet, but you may have noticed food is very important to her. Sacred even. She didn't have the resources growing up to learn how to cook. Quite frankly, you should be glad she didn't attempt to—that girl manages to burn water in the microwave." They softened. "Just please keep any value judgments about food to yourself. Can you do that?"

Gabe nodded. "Sorry. I didn't know."

"How could you have, darling?" Blanche patted his arm, smiling tightly. "But it was a dickish thing to say, so maybe try not to be a raging asshole. Okay?"

Before long, Lee and Tara headed back their way, hand in hand. Sunny wished she had Lee's touch with Tara; he could calm her down with a hug, while the best Sunny could do was stick food in her mouth and distract her until the threat of a panic attack passed. Affection didn't come naturally to her. She never really understood their clingy, codependent friendship.

"That was quick," she noted to Blanche. She hadn't expected Tara to even come back.

Blanche hummed in agreement. "She's getting a better handle on herself lately," they murmured. "She hasn't had a panic attack yet this year as far as I know. It's a record. Also, we're both a little high."

"Of course." Sunny snorted, then asked quietly, "You okay? I thought Gabe was about to get a taste of Work Blanche."

"Oh, it was close, Babygirl." Blanche shook their head and let out a slow breath. "I'll be fine when we're home. I can't imagine how Tara feels with so many memories here, but coming here was her idea, so I'm staying out of it." Their half smile returned, which was strangely reassuring, even though Sunny still didn't know what feelings hid behind it. At least Lee wasn't being *totally* inconsiderate of Tara's feelings, even though Sunny didn't understand why Tara had suggested they come here at all.

As Lee and Tara walked up, Antonio announced cheerily that everyone would get one slice of each pie to bring home, going on about how he'd wanted them to have a true picnic, but it was fucking freezing. Sunny was impressed that he'd gone from pissed off and yelling at Gabe to happily pretending nothing was amiss. *Teacher skills, I suppose. Or drag queen skills. There's a lot of transferable skills between the two.*

"So, do I want to know why you two were so late?" Sunny asked Lee as he deposited a slice of sweet potato pie onto a pie tin for her.

"We were recording a song for Antonio's album. We got caught up and lost track time," Lee replied smoothly.

Too smoothly. It wasn't a lie, but it certainly was rehearsed. Lee was even worse at lying than she was; they had to have planned this carefully. "You lost track of time from...Antonio singing?"

Lee fought a grin. "I didn't say he was *singing.*"

Sunny laughed. "Oh, you were fooling around."

"Let's just say, I'm really looking forward to listening to the recording later." Lee refused to meet her eye.

"That makes more sense." She still didn't believe him. He may have been telling the truth, but it wasn't the whole truth. Unfortunately for Lee and Antonio, they were so transparent that Sunny would have picked up on their plan all on her own, even if Blanche hadn't told her. Surely someone as suspicious as Tara would have figured it out by now.

Sunny glanced over at Tara, who was talking to Gabe at the other end of the picnic table. An extra slice of quiche had made its way onto Tara's plate. Her cheeks were more rosy than the cold weather accounted for. *Unless she's too distracted.*

Lee

"Okay. So, to recap, today was a disaster." Antonio spun in the chair, rubbing his eyebrows with a makeup remover wipe after the show. Carlita's padding and a red bodycon dress were still on, but the traces of his alter ego were slowly disappearing. He kicked his heels to the floor, muscles tensing in his calves as he stretched his ankles.

Their long cardigan trailed over the cabinets like a waterfall as Blanche reclined on the countertop lining the back of the Control Room at Confession. "Oh, I don't know about a 'disaster.' Sure, it could have gone smoother, but there was a lot of progress. Tara didn't leave. Gabe feels guilty. Richard and Sunny didn't even argue."

"Yeah, but they barely spoke!" Antonio protested. "And when we got there, *you* were having a moment with Sunny! Like, if you have a problem with her getting together with Richard, or you're jealous or something, speak up!"

Lee cringed; Blanche took accusations of being jealous seriously.

Sitting up and wrapping their cardigan around them, Blanche glared. "If I wanted Sunny, I'd have Sunny. That's not going to happen, nor do either of us want it to. Did it occur to you that *I* was trying to make *Richard* jealous?"

Antonio winced sheepishly. "No, Richard never minded sharing Gabe. Although they weren't truly dating. Why? You think he was jealous?"

Blanche smirked, leaning against the wall with their arms still crossed. "You saw how red he got."

"Aren't we just trying to make them get along?" Lee pushed his glasses up. "Like, less fighting? I don't want anyone to get mad at us because the universe is pushing them together, and it turns out to be us the whole time."

Antonio waved his hand. "Sure! I want everyone to get along. But Gabe has it bad for Tara, and she'd be good for him. So I wouldn't be mad about them getting together."

Lee sat silently; he wasn't so sure that *Gabe* would be good for *Tara*. Normally a little moody, he was generally nice. But Gabe had been an outright dick to Tara earlier. Tara would have dished it right back, if they'd been anywhere else but the island.

He still felt weird for making Tara go there, but she had insisted she wanted to. Lee had intended to be a buffer for her, knowing she'd be fighting hard feelings the whole time. But Gabe had opened his mouth before Lee could stop him. They'd warned him to be nice, but it wasn't like Lee could tell him *why* it was so important; Tara would never forgive him for sharing her personal business with someone she didn't trust.

"I want them to bang," Blanche declared. "Tara and Gabe. Richard and Sunny. Hell, vice versa could be fun, too. I'm tired of the residual sexual tension. Let them fuck it out and become friends that way."

Lee still didn't see the sexual tension between Richard and Sunny. Unless Sunny had somehow learned to hide the longing looks she used to give Blanche, she wasn't feeling Richard. She just glared at him.

"How about this?" Blanche suggested, "Next time, instead of a structured event, we bring them somewhere where they can mingle. Get away from inquiring eyes, so to speak?"

"What did you have in mind?" Lee asked.

"Remember Tara's birthday plans from last year?"

Lee nodded. They'd planned to go to an arcade, just the four of them. Except that was the weekend Antonio had started at Confession, so Lee had to move the party to work. Which had worked out just fine as far as he was concerned; he'd kissed Antonio for the first time that night. "You think an arcade is a good place to mingle?"

"How is Gabe at arcade games?" Blanche asked Antonio.

"Obsessively good." Antonio pulled the breast pads out of his bustline and tossed them to Lee, who tucked them carefully into Antonio's drag bag. "He used to hang out at the arcade after school."

"But probably not better than Tara," Lee added, Blanche's plan coming into focus. Tara could never say no to a game. She was a sore loser and winner, but she'd always play. Even with Gabe, who fortunately never minded losing to Lee. "Honestly, Gabe low-key sucks at every game I've played with him. Tara could beat him at shit like Mortal Kombat."

"So maybe we start at the arcade, and then move somewhere where they could disappear for a while?" Antonio suggested. "We could try going to the club we were supposed to bring Sunny to? Stormé's has a sick dance floor, and Gabey loves dancing."

Lee and Blanche burst into laughter. "Tara can't dance to save her life," Lee said. "She will find a spot to sit, someone will eventually hit on her, and she'll disappear for ten to twenty minutes and come back reeking of sex."

"Convenient." Antonio eyed Lee, a smile playing on his lips as he slowly rucked his dress up to pull his stockings off. "Stormé's also has a lot of dark corners to disappear into."

Lee's blood pulsed as Antonio's smile turned suggestive.

"Then that settles it," Blanche said, clearing their throat. "Tara's birthday is our next event. Lee, you just have to convince Tara to invite Richard and Gabe."

"I can probably make that happen, but would they come?" Lee asked, finally pulling away from Antonio's hazel eyes undressing him while he slowly stripped Carlita away and revealed the man he loved underneath. "Especially Richard? He looked so uncomfortable at the bowling alley." *Richard and Tara need to interact more, though. At least Sunny and Gabe talk.*

"Dicky likes to feel useful," Antonio said, back to twirling in his chair. "I could probably rope him and Gabe into giving people rides. Oh, Gabe's mom invited us to that fancy shindig coming up. I can get her to convince them." His face lit up with a grin as he came to a halt. "Babe, we could ride in Dicky's Range Rover! Okay, so, Dicky can chauffeur us and Sunny, and Gabe can pick up Tara and Blanche. He probably feels guilty about today, so he'll bend over backward to make up for it."

"Does Gabe have a nice car? I want to ride in a Range Rover," Blanche asked.

Antonio grinned apologetically. "Sorry, he's got a station wagon."

Friday, April Tenth

Chapter Fifteen

Richard

"Is that Blanche?" Richard asked Antonio quietly, spotting a familiar bleached blond updo at a table across the ballroom. Gabe's mom had roped them into attending a gala fundraiser for an organization helping young adults recover from opiate addictions. Seeing Blanche here, and not sitting at their table, was unexpected.

Leaning on the shoulder of an older man, Blanche wore an ivory evening gown that made their bronze skin gleam as they laughed along with him. They didn't look like themself, but Richard couldn't quite place his finger on what was different.

There was no way Blanche could have heard him, but their attention was drawn his way. With a wink at Richard, they quickly looked away, a fake smile plastered on their face.

"Yes, but pretend you don't know them," Lee replied from Antonio's other side in an equally hushed tone. He fiddled with the cloth napkin in his lap. "They're working. If you happen to be introduced, this client insists on she her pronouns for Blanche, and he pays the rent, so best to go along with it."

Antonio added, "Apparently, he's on the board and needed some eye candy to dangle in front of his ex, who's the chairwoman. She broke off their engagement, so he's trying to make her jealous. She's the one in red sitting across the table." He shook his head. "I love rich people drama, but I would not want to be in Blanche's shoes right now."

Gabe's mother Miriam, ever the philanthropist, had donated enough for a table and invited Richard and Antonio, each with a plus one, as bait to get Gabe to come. In the two years since Richard and Gabe had moved back home, getting him to leave the house had been like pulling teeth. Unless a certain redhead was invited, but Gabe would not appreciate it if Richard let that slip to his mom.

Richard had hoped that Antonio would suggest inviting Tara and Sunny as part of his transparent meddling. Or that Gabe would invite Tara himself; they'd seemed to come to a truce at that stupid picnic. But Gabe had suggested Phineas come along instead, who sat next to Gabe's dad John across the table.

Richard had reluctantly given up his plus one so Phineas could bring a date, as inviting Sunny alone would expose their relationship. Not that Richard cared; he was following Sunny's lead. She wasn't ready, and the chance to mess with Antonio could not be missed. Besides, Sunny would have had a field day picking apart the hypocrisy of the sponsors being mostly pharmaceutical execs, Blanche's client included.

Not to say the organization wasn't a worthy cause; Richard trusted Miriam's judgment regarding philanthropy. If she thought the organization was worth donating to, he would too. Still, Sunny would take one look at the luxury and question if it was necessary to spend this much to raise money.

Tara wouldn't exactly fit in at this dinner, either. Though Richard found Tara delightfully refreshing. An honest, blunt person who did exactly what she wanted and nothing more. Richard envied her in many ways. But here? He could only imagine the snide comments from Gabe and Tara's angry retorts. Most of the time, Gabe acted like he didn't *want* her to like him— Honestly, that sounded exactly like something Gabe would do.

Richard glanced at Gabe, seated between himself and Miriam. His dad, John, was on her other side. Gabe looked better tonight than he had lately: clothes tidy, long hair clean, and the patchy stubble he'd been sporting finally shaved. Hopefully, he hadn't just done it to spare himself a lecture from his mom. Gabe's disheveled appearance at Confession in February, and at work the past few weeks, had him concerned. But he wasn't completely neglecting himself again, so Richard hadn't pushed it.

"If I'd known Blanche was going to be here, I would have made you two invite Sunny and Tara," Antonio said in a louder tone than necessary.

"Who are Sunny and Tara?" Miriam asked, taking a bite of her rice pilaf. Her brown eyes looked between Gabe, Richard, and Antonio expectantly.

Richard kicked Antonio's foot under the table, who immediately kicked him back harder. Putting Miriam on the scent was low; she had a penchant for being too encouraging.

"They're my friends," Lee explained. "We've been trying to get these two to be nice to them, but they mostly just argue."

"There's no need to bring me into this." Richard shot him a look. Lee wasn't wrong, but his fake arguments with Sunny were not something Miriam needed to know about. The arguments were an act, but he couldn't *say* that yet.

"Can I meet them?" Phineas asked, to an immediate chorus of "no", including from his date, a pretty white woman named Signe.

Miriam gently smacked Gabe's shoulder. "Gabey Baby, I didn't raise you to be an asshole. If you don't have anything nice to say, get to know them until you find some common ground!" The hint of a Queens accent tinged her words. It always got stronger the more upset she was. "And you, Richard, I thought you were trying to *not* turn into your father."

Richard bristled, but just replied with a sullen, "Yes, ma'am." He was *nothing* like his father, especially where Sunny was concerned. He was determined to be a better version of himself—better than his parents—so he could be what Sunny needed. Getting a text from her made his day. Friday nights were the highlight of his week. He was reluctant to hope in excess, but their futures were...not unaligned. He wanted more than anything to make this work.

But he couldn't explain all that to Miriam when he hadn't even told Sunny that.

Besides, he wasn't even *that* rude to her. Sunny's strong reactions were just for show. And he was always polite to Tara, although she mostly ignored him.

Richard wondered what he'd have to do to win *her* over. They'd have a difficult enough time with their families whenever Sunny decided to reveal their relationship. She shouldn't have to deal with her friends questioning her choices too. Lee was apparently trying to set them up, so he was presumably supportive, but Tara was hard to read. And Blanche? Richard had no idea where to start *that* conversation. But it'd be best to get it out of the way.

"Sunny and I have had many perfectly nice conversations," Gabe attempted to defend himself against his mother. "She's developing an app. We talk about video games, and uh... Well, other things? Lots of things!"

"Tell your mom about the conversations you've had with Tara," Antonio teased. "Or how you crushed my foot with a bowling ball."

"Gabriel Fucking Cooper!" Miriam scolded him, her voice hushed, but her childhood nanny's accent still leaked into it. "A bowling ball?"

"He was trying to flirt with Tara," Antonio added. "I was the collateral damage."

Gabe glared at him. "Dude, seriously? I was *not* flirting. And that was an accident. I already apologized, and you said we were cool! You've done way worse to me before!"

Richard was glad to have the heat off of himself. Miriam had become his second mother, and honestly, a far better one than Barbie. They were polar opposites, but that was the appeal. Miriam was affectionate, enthusiastic, and generous with everyone, even strangers. Even her brown curly hair, big brown eyes, and short stature were drastically different from Barbie.

More importantly, Miriam held Richard to his own standards, not hers. Barbie and Dick expected him to be what they wanted. Miriam and John listened to him and what he wanted out of life.

"Why didn't you invite her, Gabey? If she puts up with you after *that*, I'd love to meet her!"

"All the more reason for me to not invite her, Ma."

"I'm not complaining," Phineas chimed in, rescuing Gabe from his mother's rant. "If it means we got to tag along. Right, babe?"

Signe smiled from where she sat between Lee and Phineas. "Yes, thank you so much for inviting us! You've been so welcoming." She was a little too polished to be genuine; Richard could spot a fellow pageant girl from a mile away. But she seemed to have a decent head on her shoulders, compared to the poor choices Phineas usually made. *So she'll be gone quicker than normal.* Women looked at Phineas and saw a hot, rich, lawyer, but instead found an insecure workaholic.

Richard and Phineas had bonded during freshman year of college over figuring out who they were, while struggling against their parents' standards. Phineas's dad wanted a son who followed in his footsteps: a lawyer, with a future career in politics. His mom wanted her prince to find his fairy tale princess, meaning no real woman would ever be good enough. Instead of figuring his shit out, Phineas had crafted a fake version of himself who fell in love with women his parents would like. When it inevitably fell apart, he hooked up with strangers his parents would not like. Phineas wanted someone to love him for who he was, and an ambitious trophy wife to satisfy his parents, all in one.

In Richard's experience, those were mutually exclusive. Phineas needed to prioritize his own happiness, not his parents. Barbie and Dick would never approve of Sunny, but Richard had stopped seeking his parents' approval a decade ago. He was happier with her than he'd ever been trying to make his parents proud of him.

"It's been a pleasure to have you along, Signe." Lee smiled widely at Phineas's date.

She beamed back, laying her hand on Lee's arm. "It's not every day a girl gets to sit between two attractive men at a gala."

Lee rested his hand on hers. "I've always been curious about what woman would catch Phin's eye, and I have to say, you are way out of his league."

"Man, don't ruin this for me," Phineas said. "Signe still likes me for some reason."

The three laughed. Antonio didn't join in. He pouted, shooting glares at Signe and Phineas. It was reminiscent of their first, incredibly awkward hangout with Lee, the one that Phineas had unintentionally crashed. When they'd first met Lee, Phineas had been an ass, Lee had been tense, and Antonio had glared at Phineas the whole time, like he was glaring now. Since then, Phineas had always talked like he and Lee were bros, hanging out with mutual friends—sans Antonio—fairly often. Richard had found that hard to believe, until he saw them getting along so well tonight.

"You okay, Tonio?" Richard asked, more curious than caring. But it was probably good to check. He'd sat between Antonio and Gabe on purpose; Antonio might need emotional support at a gala focused on addiction, and Gabe might need it being at such a formal event for the first time since moving home. Not that Richard was any good at providing emotional support, but both Antonio and Gabe would pretend they were fine so that they wouldn't burden each other. With Richard between them, they could focus on themselves.

"Thank you for asking, Dicky." Antonio leaned against him, taking his hand. "I am having a lot of uncomfortable feelings."

"Oh no!" Richard pulled his hand away. Antonio was so damn touchy, almost as bad as Gabe. "Hold hands with your boyfriend, not me."

Antonio sent a pouty look to Lee. "I would, but he's busy. Talking to *Signe*."

"You can't possibly think he's flirting with her." To anyone sensible, Lee was over the moon in love with Antonio and not attracted to women. But Antonio was not often sensible.

"Not seriously, but jealousy is easier to manage than the other shit in my head right now, so I'm focusing on that," Antonio muttered.

"You could have just said no to this, you know," Richard sighed. Antonio challenged himself so hard when he didn't need to, while Gabe had to be dragged along. At this point, Gabe's lack of confidence was the biggest obstacle to letting himself live again. Meanwhile, Antonio's unquestionable determination was usually his undoing.

"Maybe, but I can handle it." Antonio shrugged, shooting Richard a mischievous grin. "And pretending to hate this bitch helps."

Richard snorted. Sunny would also be upset if she were here, and *he* was sitting next to Signe. Just as upset as he would be if Sunny was flirting with anyone else, not that she'd pick up on Phineas's relentless charm. Richard bit back a smile. Sunny never picked up on when anyone flirted with *her*, but the one time someone delivering their food had been a little too friendly with *him*, she'd turned into a complete brat.

It'd been adorable, watching her pout and whine until he'd convinced her that he liked *her*, not the food delivery person. This of course involved fucking her, and saying her name when he came. Richard still felt weird about so much talking, but the "practice" was enjoyable; they'd made a "dirty talk" category on their yes-no-maybe list. Sunny would tell him what she wanted to hear, and she reacted gloriously when he said it.

Antonio took advantage of his lapse in concentration, wiggling under his arm. "You should have invited Sunny to come with you, Dicky. I'd rather sit with her than this fake bitch."

Richard stiffened as Antonio wrapped his arms around his waist. "Lee, get your boyfriend."

A smile erupted on Lee's face at the sight of Antonio, clinging to Richard. "Oh, babe, have I been neglecting you?"

"No, I'm fine. Dicky's taking care of me," Antonio said primly.

Richard pushed Antonio away again as Lee pulled him close. "Don't call me Dicky."

Lee nodded in his direction, asking Antonio, "Did you ask yet?"

Richard narrowed his eyes. "Ask what."

Antonio grinned and lowered his voice. "Well, Tara's birthday is coming up. You and Gabe are cordially invited. We're going to an arcade and then dancing at a club downtown."

That solves that problem. Sunny had been brainstorming how to convince Tara to invite him and Gabe along. Lee and Antonio's meddling had taken care of the conundrum.

"No." Richard had to act the part.

"Gabey, will you come?" Antonio pleaded. "You love arcades! And dancing!"

Gabe shrugged. "Sure. Sounds fun."

"Great! So we can count on you both to help us carpool?" Antonio grinned.

"I presume you're ready to blackmail me," Richard drawled sarcastically.

Antonio tapped his chin, as if pretending to consider it. "Funny, I *do* have a video of a certain someone singing Katy Perry at karaoke. It'd be a shame if that were to circulate on my Instagram. Coincidentally, your mother follows me."

Richard glared. "Fine." He wouldn't normally care what Antonio posted about him, but Sunny also followed Antonio. And his red-faced drunk rendition of "Firework" was not what he wanted her to see.

"I knew you'd see sense, Dicky." Antonio gripped his hand. "You'll pick up Sunny and us, and Gabe can pick up Tara and Blanche."

Richard pulled his hand away. *Convenient. I can pretend I picked Sunny up first.* "Whatever. You owe me."

"Gabey, you should bring a cake too." Miriam chimed in.

"You are a Master Baker, Gabey." Antonio laughed at his own joke.

Richard and Gabe exchanged a look. They hadn't realized Miriam could hear the hushed conversation, but nothing about Antonio was ever truly hushed. A glance at Phineas's tight smile was enough confirmation that the whole table had heard. Richard's gut twisted. But Phineas wasn't ready to give up his indulgences, and Antonio had to choose his sobriety, so Richard could only give a sympathetic wince.

"And I'll bring a cake," Gabe sighed.

Lee grinned. "Tara does love sweets."

"I'm aware."

"Took you long enough to figure it out," Lee muttered into his glass.

An announcement came on that the silent auction would be closing in fifteen minutes.

"Gabey Baby, you should check to see if you're in the lead for that vacation to Hawaii," Miriam suggested brightly. She'd swiped his phone earlier to bid on his behalf, deciding that her son needed a getaway from Bellamy. As with all of her ideas, Miriam steamrolled her way into making her good intentions reality. Poor Gabe usually got squished in the process.

"Ma, for the last time, I'm not going on a vacation," Gabe huffed, playing with the ends of his hair. "I'd need someone to watch Hippo, and I don't want to go alone."

"We can watch Hippo!" Miriam suggested. "And besides, Hawaii is romantic. I'm sure you'll find someone special to go with if you ask!"

"Ma..." Gabe buried his head in his hands. "Don't start."

"Dearest," John, Gabe's dad, finally spoke up, "Gabe doesn't want us involved in his love life, remember? Although, she has a point. A vacation would be good for you, Gabe. You deserve a break."

Richard had almost forgotten John was there. He was impressively quiet, like always. But still, he should be hard to miss. He was as tall and striking as Gabe, but thinner, more wiry than muscular. Miriam wasn't a large woman by any means, about Antonio's height and an average build, but her personality made her larger than life. John tended to happily fade into the background, until he had a reason to emerge from her shadow. A trait Richard had done his best to study, so he could do it too. Though he'd deny it if anyone ever asked, he'd also mirrored John's hairstyle; John's slicked back cut was much more flattering than the high and tight his father and brother wore.

It still surprised Richard that his dad was so determined that he marry Gabe. John was a father figure to him now, but he wasn't exactly what Dick should want in a father-in-law for his "daughter," considering Dick's obsession with good social connections.

As a ward of the state since toddlerhood, decades before the Indian Child Welfare Act was even a bill, John had been placed in a Native boarding school. The few official records he'd found had listed his ethnicity simply as Indian. If he had any family or official tribal connections, John had no way of finding them. Other than Miriam, his AIM buddies, and old friends from school, Gabe's dad had no "good social connection" that Richard's dad could exploit.

And yet, Dick Carter was obsessed with the idea that Richard would marry Gabe.

Miriam was just that much of a force of nature. Or at least, that's what Richard liked to believe, so he didn't have to psychoanalyze his father too deeply. She overcame the scandal from when she'd eloped with John and moved from the Upper East Side to Bellamy in the '80s. Since then, Miriam had built a reputation as a determined and passionate businesswoman. Her investments always paid off. She was a good judge of character, with a quick grasp of potential risks and benefits. Richard understood why Dick wanted *her* to be his mother-in-law.

But Miriam would never do business with Dick, even if Richard had married Gabe; she loathed Dick Carter. Fortunately, Miriam had looked past who his father was and still taken Gabe's socially awkward friend under her wing.

"Ah, see? You're still in the lead, Gabey. It's a sign!"

"Ma, for the last time, I'm not going to Hawaii, even if I win the stupid auction."

Richard caught Phineas's eye, asking him silently. *Can Gabe go to Hawaii?*

Phineas shook his head. *The appeal got postponed,* he mouthed back.

"Gabe, maybe your parents would like a vacation to Hawaii," Richard suggested, downing his wine to soothe his nerves and rescuing Gabe from Miriam's relentless pressure. The courts were too damn slow, and Richard didn't trust Gabe's ex to leave him alone; Phineas had barely managed to keep him safe in Bellamy.

Miriam laughed, her brown eyes crinkling. "Richard, you're so sweet. We couldn't possibly! We have so much work to do."

Gabe gave Richard a thankful look as he refilled Richard's wine glass. "I dunno, Ma, a vacation might be good for you. You deserve a break, too."

John laughed. "He's got you there."

With a sip of his wine, Richard checked his own phone to make sure he was still in the lead for the dinner at a newer Michelin-star restaurant in Chicago. It'd be the perfect weekend getaway for him and Sunny. Maybe when it was warmer, so she could wear something low-cut, and they could be together in public. Walking arm in arm and taking as many cute selfies as Sunny wanted at all the touristy places she'd like to see.

And they wouldn't have to worry about anyone finding out about them.

Richard frowned as the wine rolled over his tongue, dry and bitter from the tannins. Normally, he preferred that, but at the moment he had a taste for something sweeter.

Chapter Sixteen

Sunny

"Why am I here?" Tara grumbled from across the clothing rack. "I should be working."

Sunny's fingers flew over the hangers, sliding them down the metal rack to inspect and touch each garment. Shopping so late on a Friday felt odd, but Sunny didn't particularly want to go home. Friday nights were Richard's now, but he was "busy" or whatever.

"You work too much." She forced a smile at Tara, instead of nursing her jealousy that Richard was out with their friends without her. "Besides, I need your objective opinion about how hot I am when I try shit on."

Sunny was surprised Tara had lasted this long without complaint. Normally she grumbled the whole time, and they were at their third thrift store of the evening, having taken the bus to Driftwood after the selection at her usual stops had been underwhelming. For Tara especially, this was a lot of time in public. She hadn't even bought anything but still dutifully carried Sunny's tote bag, stuffed with finds from the first two stores. Then again, they hadn't been thrifting since January because Sunny had been spending every weekend with Richard. Maybe she was being more patient because it'd been a while.

Tara grinned. "I'll just be less mean if it looks good."

"Exactly." Sunny examined a black A-line halter dress that would barely cover her ass, but she didn't plan to wear it in public. Despite her shaky but growing confidence in her sexual prowess (thanks to her arrangement with Richard), her body looked great. And Richard would appreciate the dress.

She added it to her already full cart.

"You're going to buy all of that?" asked Tara. She peered into the cart as Sunny draped a couple items over the edge. "Won't your mom be pissed?"

"She won't know about half of this. My Vagina Fund pays for femme clothes, the money my mae knows about pays for my work clothes." Sunny shrugged.

Tara grimaced. "Can we go try stuff on? We're gonna be here til close if I don't stop you."

With a laugh, Sunny pushed the cart to the fitting rooms, taking stock of Tara's findings—a maroon sweater and a pair of gray shorts. "Is that all you're getting?"

"Yeah, just something for my birthday."

"You go first then. Then you can tell me I'm hot when it's my turn."

Tara rolled her eyes, closing the door to the fitting room behind her. Sunny pulled out her phone, hoping Richard had texted her. He had, just a moment ago. She grinned.

> I'm taking you to Chicago soon. Tell me what weekend you're free.

> That almost sounds like you're asking me on a date.

> I have no idea where you got that idea from.

Her smile fell. As if she needed the reminder that she was already reading too much into their arrangement...

> Would you like to come on a romantic weekend trip to Chicago with me?

Sunny's heart skipped a beat. She bit her lip to hide her grin. "Romantic" was new vocabulary. Maybe he was starting to read too much into this, too? *Confusing, but I'm into it.*

> You're just trying to get more nudes, aren't you?

Always. Every time you text me, I hope it's another picture of your gorgeous tits.

> Are you drunk?

I have had two glasses of wine, so I will concede that I'm slightly tipsy. But I do want to take you out on a real date eventually. Regardless of alcohol consumption.

> What, Denny's doesn't count as a real date?

It definitely counted. Great first date. I have to top it (and you) for our second.

Wait, Denny's was *a date? Is he being sarcastic?* Richard's replies didn't fit the rules they'd established for their FWB situation. *Did I get something wrong, or is he really drunk?* Reconciling the terse, sarcastic Richard with his sweet, flirty texts would only give her a headache. But she was trying to take everything at face value…

Maybe he's better at writing than talking? I'm certainly better at reading than listening. The spark of hope that had died when Richard had wanted her only as a secret booty call reignited. *Well, fuck it, let's see how far I can push this.*

> I usually save romantic weekend trips and fancy restaurants for at least the third date.

Then I'll take you on a second date soon. Let's go out for drinks, and I can cook you dinner after. Wine and dine you.

> And then recline me? ;) I didn't know you cooked, Dicky.

> Keep your expectations low. The only thing I can cook is pasta. But yes, reclining is also on the agenda for the evening.

> You really know how to woo a girl, Dicky. Agendas…so hot.

So are we, like, talking? In a situationship? Not just hooking up? If the smile on her face was any indication of how she was feeling, she wasn't mad about the shift. Just confused.

"Who are you texting?" Tara asked.

Sunny jumped. "No one. I was just looking at memes."

Tara looked skeptically at her from where she leaned on the fitting room doorframe, arms crossed. "I've been standing here for a hot minute while you're cheesing at your phone. Must be a helluva meme."

Sunny ignored her, instead taking in her outfit. Figuring out where she stood with Richard would have to wait.

The clothes Tara had picked flattered her scrawny frame. The maroon sweater was clingy in all the right places, and the deep v showed off her collarbones. The shorts made her hips look wider, giving Tara the illusion of a waist despite her rectangle silhouette.

"Turn around?"

Tara turned slowly.

Sunny whistled. "Your ass looks edible in those shorts. Gabe will lose his fucking mind."

"Sunny!" Tara protested. "I'm not trying to look edible, especially not for *Gabe*. I just want to look hot on my birthday!"

Sunny ignored her again. No point in trying to convince Tara that she did, in fact, want Gabe to eat her. Tara could be frustratingly and willfully ignorant of her feelings when she put her mind to it. But only horny feelings could get Tara to wear anything but athleisure.

She opted to tease her instead. "My only concern is you look like a fucking nerd. Do those elbow patches match the shorts?"

Tara scowled. "I like elbow patches."

Sunny laughed. "I didn't say it looked bad. You just look like a nerd."

"Good thing I'm wearing it to an arcade then, isn't it?" Tara went back into the fitting room to change again. "Speaking of grouchy, what's with you and Richard? I never thought I'd meet someone you argue with more than me. You're usually nice to people. Is that like some weird flirting, or is he actually getting under your skin?"

Sunny was glad Tara couldn't see her blush. "Ugh, flirting? As if! He's so annoying."

Richard *more* than got under her skin. Richard got under her fingernails when she scratched his back. Richard got deep inside of her when he fucked her for what felt like hours. Richard took over her senses when she went down on him. Richard was wriggling his way into her heart with his dorky laugh and sweatpants and glasses that he only wore at home, and those soft snores at night when he held her. Richard was sweeping her off her fucking feet with talk about romantic weekend trips and fancy restaurants.

Sunny groaned. *Oh, fuck. Did I catch feelings? Dammit! Ten minutes ago, we were just fuck buddies! I wasn't supposed to do this to myself again!*

And she couldn't tell anyone about it. No one knew other than Blanche. While they were still friends, Sunny wasn't particularly keen to tell her ex about her growing feelings for her new fuck buddy, who she may or may not be in a situationship with. Even if this fling had already lasted longer than her whole relationship with Blanche. Even if Richard spent more time with her most weekends than Blanche had in the whole month they'd been together. Even if she had more fun when she was with Richard than she could ever remember having in her life.

Dammit, I didn't want to be a secret again, and here I did it to myself. But she didn't want a repeat of Lee's dressing down after her breakup with Blanche. He'd been right. She really should be smarter about catching feelings with people who were doomed to break her heart.

"Earth to Sunny!" Tara was already back in her joggers and hoodie. "Where did you go?"

"I was just thinking about how annoying Richard is." Sunny rolled her eyes.

Tara laughed. "Sure, you looked *real* annoyed there, Sun."

Sunny fought her blush. "What's with you and Gabe anyway? Is that some 'weird flirting' y'all got going on?" Tara would deny it, but Sunny needed to change the subject. Get the focus away from her before she blurted out everything racing through her head.

Tara frowned. "No. He's such an ass."

Sunny shrugged. "He's nice to me." They'd had a great conversation at the picnic about the product supply chain app she'd been working on. Gabe was a great listener, until he started a conversation with Tara.

"Well, good for you." Tara scowled, but there was no heat in it. "It's like everything that works to manage my shit gets thrown out the window as soon as he opens his mouth. He just rubs me the wrong way."

"Maybe tell him how to rub you the right way?" Sunny teased. "Just tell him what he does wrong. If you were fucking him, you'd tell him how to do it better, wouldn't you?"

Tara blushed as red as her hair. "I mean, yeah. But telling him to choke me harder is way funner than telling him off for mocking my lack of basic life skills. What am I supposed to say, the only thing my mom taught me how to cook was heroin?"

Someone from the other fitting room cleared their throat pointedly. Tara and Sunny both rolled their eyes. *I forgot we're in the nice part of town.*

"Did I rub you the wrong way when we first met?" Sunny paused as she picked out dresses to try on. "That's probably a question I should have asked years ago, huh?"

Tara laughed as Sunny went to the dressing room, closing the door behind her. "All the fucking time. It was like you just smashed all of the buttons in the elevator. Poor Lee."

Sunny wiggled out of her clothes and into the black minidress. "Good thing he wasn't brave enough to tell me off, or we'd never be friends. How did you handle me back then?"

"I cussed you out," Tara said. "And Lee gave me snacks."

"So do that with Gabe. Cuss him out. Bring snacks. Or better yet, make *him* bring snacks."

"Ugh, he's *such* a good cook. No joke, I cried when I ate that quiche," Tara laughed.

Sunny admired herself in the mirror of the fitting room. The skirt barely covered her ass. She posed and snapped a pic to send to Richard. She set her phone back down with a smile and stepped out to show Tara. "What do you think?"

Tara's eyes narrowed. "Turn around?"

Sunny turned slowly as Tara had done.

When she looked at Tara again, she was fanning herself. "Damn, your ass looks amazing in that." She paused, her mouth open.

"But?"

"Your tits look flat as fuck." Tara tugged on the halter top. "Maybe if you add a dart here, it'll help? Blanche will know how to fix it. You paid too much money for those big tiddies to let them look sad."

The fitting room next to them coughed even louder.

Sunny ignored them, chewing her lip. Should she ask for Blanche's help? Since their breakup, she'd been reluctant to rely on them as much as she used to. But altering an outfit seemed like a healthy, time-bound way to ask for help, versus using them for escapism. "Yeah, good idea, Tara-Bear!"

Tara shifted as Sunny grabbed another outfit. "So...how are things with you and Blanche? They just keep saying everything's fine."

"Oh, we're good! I think? Way less awkward now than it was at first. It's more comfortable for me anyway." Sunny pulled on a go-go dress she'd found. The wavy mod lines formed an ombre of muted earth tones; not really her color, but Sunny couldn't resist a good vintage dress.

"How'd you get there?" Tara asked, her voice soft. "To where it's more comfortable."

While maybe not the most effective method, Sunny had simply pretended that they'd never had a relationship, and they'd both stopped any flirting. Thankfully Blanche had gone along with it because they wanted to be her friend again, just as much as she wanted to be theirs. "We just kept showing up and getting through it. It was hella awkward. It still is sometimes, but forcing ourselves to be friends worked eventually."

Tara made a noncommittal hum.

"Why do you ask?" Tara didn't have any exes, nor had she slept with any friends. Sunny zipped up the go-go dress and posed as she swung open the stall door to show Tara. "You tryna smash after seeing my ass in that dress? Am I about to go three for three with y'all?"

"Fuck no!" Tara laughed as she took in Sunny's appearance. "That one isn't bad. Makes you kind of shapeless, though."

"Oh, we can't have that," Sunny groaned.

"Exactly! Show off the tiddies!" Tara teased.

The fitting room next door opened and an older white lady stepped out, glaring at them with another "hem-hem."

"Would you like a cough drop?" Sunny offered, letting the sarcasm drip into her obviously fake sweet tone. "It sounds like you have something in your throat. I've got some lozenges that really help clear out the judgment."

The lady just sneered and walked away.

Tara grinned. "You're so much nicer than me. I was just going to flip her off."

"Remember you said that next time you're annoyed with me." Sunny grabbed the next dress and returned to the dressing room, just as her phone buzzed with a Venmo notification: *Richard Carter paid you $100 for Buy that dress. LMK if you need more.*

A laugh burst out of her before she could stop herself.

Thank you, Mr. Carter. The dress is only $6 though. You're so out of touch.

Spend the rest however you want, just wear that dress for me next Friday.

Sunny laughed again.

"You okay in there?" Tara asked.

"Yeah," Sunny said. "Just a meme."

She changed into a red bodycon dress. It fit like a glove, hugging her curves with an off-the-shoulder sweetheart neckline. She took another pic and sent it to Richard. *He might as well see what he's paying for.* She stepped out.

Tara's mouth fell open. "Damn, Sunny, that completely hides your annoying personality."

"Thanks, Tara." Sunny spun around. "Are you sure you don't want more stuff? It's your birthday coming up after all. Let me treat you to a little Goodwill shopping spree."

Eyes narrowing, Tara crossed her arms. "Why? I was shitty as hell to you on your birthday."

Is she still worried about that? So much had changed since her birthday, and she'd moved on from any hurt feelings long ago. Still, Sunny probably shouldn't tell her that she was feeling generous because Richard had sent her $100 for an ass pic. "Water under the duck, bitch! Go find more shit to buy."

To Sunny's complete and utter shock, Tara hugged her. "Thank you."

Sunny froze. Tara never hugged her. She hugged Blanche and Lee all the time, but not Sunny. "What's happening? Are you high? Do you need a snack? I have granola bars."

"Shut up, Sunny. Just take it."

Sunny shut up and hugged her back.

"What kind of granola bars, though?"

BLANCHE

"Don't you clean up nice." Blanche sidled up to a familiar silhouette at the bar, carefully draping the slit of their gown as they perched on a barstool. "Buy a girl a drink? My money is still in my date's bank account."

Gabe was nursing a glass of wine by himself, his slim fit suit highlighting his broad shoulders and triangle frame. Or it had at the beginning of the evening, when they first saw him from across the room. Now he looked tired as Blanche felt, hunched around his glass with his suit rumpled. "Wine okay?"

"That sounds like a smarter choice than scotch."

Gabe flagged down the bartender. "Black Label?"

Blanche laughed with a nod. "Neat, please. How'd you know?"

His smile didn't reach his eyes. "Just a hunch. Rough evening?"

The asshole who paid their rent usually didn't trot Blanche out as arm candy when he and his off-and-on fiancée were fighting. Horrifically, Blanche had to spend all evening pretending to like him. It was exhausting. "I've had worse."

"Where's your date?" Gabe asked. The bartender deposited the glass in front of Blanche.

Blanche took a sip, rolling the smooth burn over their tongue. They exhaled in relief. "Fucking his ex—well, probably his fiancée again by now—in a closet somewhere. He brought me to make her jealous, and let's just say I earned my pay tonight." They wondered if Gabe was a cuddler, because his shoulder looked inviting to lean on. They took another drink instead of asking. "Thank you. I needed this. No date of your own? Didn't you want to invite Tara?"

Gabe shook his head with a scoff. "And I came over here to get away from my mom."

"I'm teasing, Gabe." It was strange, having real people around when they were working. At least Gabe seemed to be on the same wavelength: tired and ready to leave. "I don't really want to talk about Tara. It's weird enough having Lee around when I'm working. I hate to say it, but I'm glad he's pretending not to know me."

Gabe gave them a sympathetic look. "I imagine it's hard to get in the right headspace for this kind of stuff."

Blanche scoffed. "Not to break client confidentiality, but normally I'm not fawning over that piece of shit like a stupid lovesick girl. Quite the opposite."

Normally, the asshole would prostrate himself on the ground and confess his sins, while Blanche punished him with a paddle and hot wax. At least the deaths he'd caused and the lives he'd ruined weighed on his soul, even if he came to Blanche to absolve him of guilt instead of changing. The clients they recorded with were so much more pleasant to be around. If they had a choice, they'd drop all of their shitty clients, their patron especially. But Blanche had backed themself into a corner with him. *Something I can look forward to when I finally save up enough to get out of this mess, dropping the horrible people who use me.*

Gabe nodded. "Hard to do a long scene like this, especially when you prefer to dom."

Blanche quirked an eyebrow, relieved for the distraction from the tense dinner they'd just endured. "Speaking from experience?"

"Unfortunately. I'd rather not talk about it though."

Blanche nodded, burning with curiosity. Like most dominants, Blanche firmly believed that kink should help the participants, or at least do no harm. Not everyone had the same mentality. "I won't ask. Not to plug my own channel, but I have a few videos about handling scenes gone wrong. I can send you a link if you want."

Gabe shook his head. "Thanks, but that's what my therapist is for."

"Let me know if you change your mind." Blanche wondered what exactly he was in therapy for. If Gabe had a mental block or trauma he was working through, that would explain why he was such a dick to Tara, when he obviously didn't want to be. "You know, I was hoping you and Tara might hit it off, but I don't know if you'll be good for her."

Their stomach twisted as their words hung over them like an echo.

Stiffening, Gabe's brows furrowed. "What's that supposed to mean?"

"Tara needs stability." Even that was probably more than Tara would want them to say; Blanche felt guilty enough for meddling already. *But if Tara's progress is at risk...* Blanche put a hand on Gabe's arm. That usually calmed him down. "Don't get me wrong, you have chemistry together. And Tara is overdue for a good time, which I imagine you'd be happy to provide. But Tara needs support. Safety. Dependability."

Gabe's jaw clenched. "I'm fully aware I've been an asshole to her, Blanche, but that doesn't make me a threat. I apologized, and I intend to be better."

Blanche winced. "I didn't mean—"

"No, you did mean. And you're right. Tara and I would not be good for each other, which is why nothing is going on between us, and nothing ever will. I don't know why everyone insists otherwise." He threw back the rest of his wine and set the glass firmly down on the bar.

Blanche grasped his forearm. "Gabe—"

"Excuse me." He shook Blanche's hand off and stalked toward the exit.

As soon as the doors closed behind him, another voice spoke behind them. "You brought up Tara." Richard took Gabe's spot at the bar. Though his appearance was neat as usual, his expression was just as tired as Gabe's, which was odd. He was normally a closed book.

Blanche sighed. "Just tried to have a little heart-to-heart when I'm in a shitty headspace."

He wrinkled his nose.

"I know. Terrible timing, and I should have known better. I tried to warn him that she's emotionally fragile, so he should be careful and patient with her. I just went about it the wrong fucking way and instead, told him that he wouldn't be good for her."

"Ah. Yeah, that probably didn't go over well." Richard snorted. "He'll be fine with some time to process and honestly, that might be what he needs to hear. He won't hold it against you. Probably more pissed at himself that he's doing a shit job at hiding his feelings."

Blanche sipped their scotch, the burn less soothing against the sour churn of their stomach. "I thought the booze would be enough, but tonight's going to be a weed night."

"Gabe's mom always has some in her purse. Want me to ask?"

With a laugh, Blanche shook their head, wanting more than anything to say yes. Sadly, they needed to stay present to get through this evening. "That surprises me. She looks so classy from a distance."

Richard smirked. "She is classy, just wound tight."

"The poison is enough for now, but thanks." Blanche glanced at Richard's watch. Their own phone—currently in their patron's pocket—would be full of new text messages from his fiancée by the time they got home. "I only have a few minutes before my date stages an argument, and I get to storm out of here anyway."

"Ah. Not enough time to warn me off Sunny, then. I'll reschedule."

Blanche leveled a look at him, unsure if he was being sarcastic. "You don't need my blessing, but you have it if that wasn't clear."

Richard shot them a confused look. "I figured you'd tell me to back off."

"Would you?"

"Of course not," Richard huffed. "But she told me you two used to be involved, so if you have something to say, might as well start the conversation."

Blanche scoffed; neither Blanche nor Sunny were acting weird anymore, but everyone else still was. "We weren't suited. I love her as a dear friend, and I want the best for her, but trust me, I lay no claim to her or her choices for herself." They finished off their scotch, sighing through the burn. "And you're a good choice. You challenge her. In a good way. She needed more of that than I could give her."

Richard's thoughtful look was too intense for their current emotional state. Blanche's stomach twisted, made more sour with the scotch. They looked away as their now-disheveled date sidled into the ballroom and beckoned to them. *Like I'm a fucking dog.*

"Ah, showtime." Blanche carefully stepped off the barstool. The seam of the high slit stretched tight around their thighs. "Just be good to her. Because I'm still her friend, and if you hurt her, I will have something to say. Probably along the lines of 'any last words.'"

Richard nodded before Blanche turned away, draping their least favorite headspace over themselves. Acting like a jealous girlfriend was their literal nightmare.

Tuesday, April Fourteenth

Chapter Seventeen

Antonio

Antonio's chest heaved as shame suffocated him. Adrenaline coursed through his body, sending tremors through his muscles. He glared at his phone on the coffee table, where he'd tossed it as if it burned him.

"Babe, you okay?" Hands massaged his shoulders. A kiss landed on his neck.

Antonio stiffened.

"Oh, shit. No, you're not okay." Lee's face swam in his vision, kneeling in front of him and taking his hands. "Antonio? You're safe at home. Are you with me?"

Antonio blinked, trying to focus on Lee, who hummed while pressing a steady rhythm into Antonio's palm. He took deep breaths to steady himself, taking in his surroundings to place himself. He'd felt *Lee's* hands on his shoulders, *Lee's* kiss on his neck. No one else's. "Sorry. Forgot where I was."

"You don't need to apologize. Bad memory?" Lee asked softly.

Antonio nodded, swallowing the nausea. The demons hadn't been this bad since he'd first gotten out of rehab well over a year ago. This used to be his normal? This was awful. No wonder sobriety had been such a struggle. He rubbed his chest with one hand, the other gripping Lee's thumb that still pressed steadily against his palm. "Why do I have Scissor Sisters in my head?"

Lee shrugged with a smile. "You hum to yourself when you're upset, and that's been stuck in my head all day. Want me to hold you?"

Antonio nodded again.

Lee sat on the couch and pulled Antonio close. "Want to talk about it?"

He crawled onto Lee's lap, reassurance washing over him as his boyfriend's strong arms held him tight. "No, but I'm going to."

"You don't have to if—"

"I'm going to," Antonio insisted, dread churning his stomach. If he didn't tell Lee now, the guilt would fester and build until he snapped. He couldn't afford to let himself break. "Because it kind of concerns you, and I don't like how I'm feeling, and you're going to have something reassuring to say to make me feel better."

Lee pressed a kiss into his shoulder, in that spot he always did that reassured Antonio that Lee was there with him, grounding him, supporting him.

Antonio took a breath, trying to decipher what was real and what was his imagination. What memories were true and which were intrusive thoughts, whispered by his demons. Even seventeen months sober, he still couldn't tell the difference sometimes. So he started with the facts he knew for certain. "I got a message from a producer who works at Household. He saw the video of us dancing to 'Trade You.' He wants in."

"Seriously? Household as in Household Records? The production company?" The excitement in Lee's voice was apparent, even under his careful tone.

Antonio huffed. "Yeah, but no. *Household* isn't interested. This guy who happens to be a producer at Household is interested. Independently. And it'd be stupid to say no. This guy's got like eight Grammys, for fucks sake!"

"Okay. That sounds like good news, so far. What's the rest?"

Antonio groaned, rubbing his chest again as shame burned through him. The messages had started off innocently enough: a "hey, long time" from a mutual he had vague memories of meeting when he'd lived in Brooklyn. But shame had quickly crept in, and he couldn't remember why. Then the guy's messages had all but confirmed that Benzos had erased some memories that Antonio preferred to forget. "I'm still figuring that out. Maybe I'm freaking out over nothing. But I think he propositioned me? And if the memories in my head and the subtext in his message are anything to go by, it's not the first time."

Blurry memories of an exciting introduction, a blow job in the back of a car, and Antonio rationalizing that he would have done it anyway, even if the guy hadn't promised him anything, flashed through his head. Worse were the memories of staring helplessly at the texts of "Where are you?" and "I set this meeting up for you. You're making me look bad." All the while, he'd been frozen on the floor of his apartment, numb with anxiety.

Antonio waved his hands, humming to himself to clear his head. He'd wanted to leave Old Antonio's self-sabotaging tendencies behind in New York, but his worst habits were part of him, even now. "And I may have taken him up on it before. And apparently fumbled the opportunity he gave me after. Because of course, I did."

He wasn't sure if the memory of blocking a number after getting a text that read "Look, you gotta get your shit together. You wasted a great opportunity." was real or not. Or if that was from a different moment of self-sabotage. Because Antonio had always been the reason his music career had never taken off.

"Oh."

"Yeah." Antonio exhaled. "Can you...read it? Tell me if I'm reading too much into this? I still don't know if these memories are true or not."

"You sure?"

Antonio nodded, refusing to look at the phone as he unlocked it with his thumb. His own judgment on his past was harsh enough; he couldn't bear the disappointment in Lee's eyes. He buried his face in Lee's neck instead, breathing in the peace and reassurance that Lee's familiar presence always brought him.

"No, yeah, he's definitely asking for head in exchange for a foot in the door." Lee's voice was sharp and clipped. "And I'm guessing that 'don't fumble this like last time' means your memories might be real."

"Fuck," Antonio groaned. "How could I be so stupid?"

"Don't do that," Lee said, quiet and gentle compared to the edge in his voice a mere moment ago. "You're not stupid, Tonio." Lee tossed the phone back on the table and held him tight. "You made the best decisions you could while you were operating in a whole different set of circumstances than you're in now."

"Easy for you to say. How many guys have you sucked off to advance your career?"

Lee let out a sardonic snort. "Well, not to advance my career. But Auntie Alitrice never asked where I always found the money for her meds."

"Oh." Antonio sat back, squeezing Lee's hand.

Lee squeezed back. "Oh. And as Blanche has reminded me many times, I did what I believed I had to do, and you did what you believed you had to do. There's no shame in that. And now you have an opportunity to decide what to do, in a better headspace than you were then."

Antonio jerked around to look at Lee. "You're not suggesting—"

"No! I'm not suggesting you fly out to New York to blow him! The fuck? No! We don't need him." Lee shook his head emphatically, pushing his glasses up. "Let's figure out what our options are. We can block him and forget this ever happened. We could send the screenshot to his boss and try to MeToo the creep."

Antonio scoffed. "Yeah, and get blacklisted before we even finish the album. We're nobody, and I can't be the only one who got acquainted with the backseat of his car. Or any of the dozens of cars belonging to men with a little bit of power and money in the music industry."

Lee rubbed his back. "Right, but it is an option, and if that's what you want to do, I would support you."

But that would mean Lee would never have a break. Half the reason Antonio wanted to do this album in the first place was for him to get this experience. He leaned into Lee's shoulder. "I think this could be a good opportunity for us, if he's serious anyway."

Lee's sigh was heavy. "While I hate the idea of working with this guy, we do need more support. I'm doing what I can, but I don't have the connections or experience he does. So a third option, then: we tell this guy that if he wants in, he's got to be professional. And since interacting with him is obviously not good for you, *I* deal with him. If you're comfortable with that, of course. If that's too much, we can keep thinking. I'm sure he's got competition out there who could use this as leverage, if we wanted to work with someone else instead."

"One of many reasons I love you." Antonio's heart melted. "You always know what to do."

Lee bumped his forehead against Antonio's. "Yeah, no, I never know what to do. But I can overthink enough options for you to decide what to do. What do you think?"

"What do *you* want to do?"

"I want you to be happy, healthy, and all your dreams to come true." Lee pressed a quick kiss to Antonio's cheek.

Antonio laughed. "That's not an answer."

"It's not my call."

Antonio glared at his phone again. Lee might be unwilling to make the decision, but Antonio's choice would impact him too. They needed backing, and Lee needed to build his network. Antonio would be foolish to say no, even as his skin crawled with the idea of saying yes. But the idea of letting Lee down made his heart break, and that was worse. Besides, if his memories were right, it was a miracle this guy would even give him another chance in the first place. New Antonio didn't self-sabotage, and here was a chance to prove it.

"Ugh, I feel like such a sellout! What's a professional way to tell this creep to keep it in his pants if he wants in?"

RICHARD

"ARE YOU DONE YET?" Gabe unceremoniously dumped his messenger bag and blazer into one of the empty leather chairs across from Richard's desk.

"You don't have to wait for me." Richard tore his eyes away from his daily reports to glare at Gabe, who collapsed into the chair across from him. The sun hung low in the sky, casting an orange and peach glow through his office and across the cubicles beyond the glass walls.

Gabe propped his feet up on the oak surface, which had been spotless and bare other than the technology essential to do his job, before Gabe had put his *shoes* on it. "Yes, I do. Otherwise, you'll be here all night."

"Get your shoes off my desk. That's unsanitary."

With a huff, Gabe kicked his shoes off before putting his socked feet back on the desk. Somehow, this was worse than the shoes.

"Seriously." Richard leveled a look at him, shifting in his chair to alleviate the pain in his lower back. "I don't want your nasty feet on my desk."

"My perfectly clean feet will get off your desk when your workaholic ass comes to the gym with me." Gabe's grin was smug.

"You are free to go to the gym without me." Richard turned back to his reports, trying to focus on the meaningless numbers in the dataset, blinking around the irritation from his contact lenses. His concentration had been off all day, an unfortunate side effect of his cycle starting the day before. Most of the time, he was at peace with his choices regarding his transition. But the second day of his cycle always made him want to stab his uterus, preferably with a syringe of testosterone.

Gabe groaned, dramatic and moody as always. "Dicky, we do this every day! I'm not going to the gym without you. Partly because you work too damn much, and your workday ended an hour ago." He pressed his hands together in plea. "But mostly because I get anxious working out by myself when it's busy. Please stop working and come with me!"

His begging was ineffective. If Gabe was actually upset, he would hide it, not ham it up. "You're an extrovert. Make more friends. And don't call me Dicky." Richard pulled a rubber band out of a drawer and fired it at the sole of Gabe's foot.

"Ow! Fucker!" Gabe dove for the rubber band at the same time as Richard. Richard cackled and held fast to his end.

"Everything okay in here?" Richard's boss, Sheila, leaned in the doorframe of his office. A bemused smile on her face, she crossed her arms, the sleeves of her blue pantsuit wrinkling.

"Oh, hey, Sheila," Gabe greeted, because he was on first-name terms with everyone in the office. Even though Gabe worked in a different line of business, several levels below Richard in the company hierarchy.

Sheila smiled affectionately as neither Richard nor Gabe let go of the rubber band. Even if she was too nice to let it impact her opinion of him, this was not the impression Richard wanted to give his boss. But damned if he would let Gabe win. "Gabe, are you distracting Richard again?"

Richard huffed out a "no" at the same time as Gabe proudly nodded. "Yup!"

"Good. As long as it's HR-appropriate, distract away. He works too hard."

"That's what I said!" Gabe beamed, while Richard scowled.

"Richard, do your reports in the morning. You know I won't read them until the afternoon." She held up her hand to stop his protest. "I know you transferred from the New York office, but you've been here long enough to know we don't live at the office in Bellamy. Go home, Richard."

"Yes, ma'am." He waited until Sheila was out of earshot before snapping the rubber band against Gabe's fingers. "Way to go, Cooper. You made it worse. She already thinks we're dating."

"Ow! She does not." Gabe shook his hand.

"She does. A lot of people do, actually." Richard ticked off the evidence on his fingers. "You come to my office anytime you're bored, and we leave together every night. Neither of us talks about dating anyone. You're the 'gay best friend' for half the office, but you keep turning down their invitations to set you up with the other gay men they know. Sheila has asked me several times if I want to update anything in my HR records." With a glare at the unrepentant Gabe, Richard turned back to his reports. He'd email them in the morning, but he'd finish them tonight. He was not a morning person on a good day, let alone during his cycle. "It's getting weird. We're not doing the fake-dating shit again."

Many times when they'd pretended to be together in college, well-meaning young women would quietly approach Richard after parties, saying that Gabe was cheating. Richard played his role well, heavily implying that their relationship was open because he couldn't keep up with Gabe's voracious sex drive. Which was true, kind of. They were not compatible. Not that Gabe was ever aware that he had a wingman. It was Richard's gesture of thanks for being a supportive friend, while he figured his shit out without his parents breathing down his neck.

Richard stared blankly at his spreadsheet. *Maybe I could try something similar with Tara. How would I pull it off now as a friend, instead of a fake partner?*

"You know, maybe you *should* talk about your dating life." Gabe fiddled with the rubber band. "You know, make friendly conversation with the people we see every day? Let your coworkers get to know you? You scare people, dude."

"You make it sound like I have people lining up to date me." *Honestly, it's a miracle Sunny likes me.* "Maybe *you* should start dating again, so you have something to talk about with your flock of straight girls. Perhaps you could ask a certain redhead out."

Richard's phone buzzed in his pocket as Gabe groaned in frustration. "Don't start."

> Can I come over? Sorry. It's not Friday. I just need quiet, and Mae is a lot. Blanche has a client, so I can't go there. Not in the mood for Lee and Tonio.

> Of course. I'm still at work, and I'm about to go to the gym with Gabe, but I'll text you when I'm on the way home.

> Thx.

> Is everything okay?

Sunny didn't respond, which worried him. Richard was a little put out that he was third on her list of places to go when she was upset, but at least he was on the list. He pulled up a food delivery app. Regardless of his twinge of hurt, if Sunny was upset, he should take care of her. And if Sunny was in a bad mood, she would want tacos.

Gabe pulled the rubber band around his fingers. "Even if I *did* date, which I'm not going to, especially not *her*, I wouldn't talk about it at work. Maybe *you* should open up a little. You actually have a love life."

"News to me." Richard added a flan to Sunny's usual order. Sunny always wanted one every time they ordered tacos for dinner and would remove it from the order at the last minute. Richard impulsively added churros with chocolate sauce for himself. They might make him sick, but deep-fried dough with chocolate sounded like heaven. He already felt like shit, so why not?

"Considering whoever it is you're texting managed to distract from your damn reports, it sure *looks* like you have a love life."

Richard glared at Gabe. "That's none of your business."

Gabe grinned triumphantly, his fingers steepled in front of him. The tips were turning purple from the rubber band wound tightly around them. "Just observing."

Richard shut his laptop without saving his reports and stood up. "Let's go."

Gabe stood up and pulled helplessly at his hands. "Wait, Dicky. I'm stuck."

"Hurry up, Cooper. I don't have all day."

"You're such an ass, Dicky! I waited for an hour for you." Gabe let out a frustrated groan. "Hold on! I need to put my shoes on."

"Oh, Mr. Carter! Are you just getting home? I thought you were here already." Briony greeted him as he approached the front desk.

"No, just getting back now. I should have a food delivery."

"Yes, here. Smells delicious." Briony paused and then added quietly, "The thing is, your guest arrived about an hour ago. I assumed you must be home and sent her up."

Richard froze. "An hour ago?" He'd only texted Sunny that he was leaving the gym fifteen minutes ago. When he'd offered to pick her up, she didn't respond. It normally took her half an hour to bus over from her mom's apartment. But if she'd gone upstairs over an hour ago...

Briony nodded, a concerned look on her face. "She didn't seem well."

Fuck. I should have skipped the gym. "Thank you, Briony. As usual, I hope this stays between us."

Briony nodded. "Of course, Mr. Carter. Luckily she arrived after the day shift left."

Richard nodded politely in parting. The plastic bag irritated his skin as he gripped it too tightly. He jammed his finger against the "door close" button in the elevator, willing it to go faster.

After an eternity with his blood rushing in his ears, the doors opened to reveal Sunny sitting on the floor outside his door, hugging her knees. Her eyes were closed, and the cat-ear headphones Lee and Antonio had gotten her for her birthday covered her ears.

Richard cleared his throat loudly.

No response. Her eyes stayed shut.

The elevator doors closed behind him. He probably shouldn't just touch her without warning to get her attention. He pulled out his phone and texted her instead.

Her eyes opened, looking at the phone in her hand before she noticed him standing at the end of the hallway. Sunny scrambled up. "Hi. Sorry."

"I didn't know you were here already." Richard approached cautiously.

"Sorry." She backed up as he neared the door, staying out of arm's reach.

"No, Sunny." He huffed softly as he unlocked it and beckoned her in. "Don't apologize. *I'm* sorry. I would have come sooner if I knew you were waiting already."

"I just didn't want to be a hassle. I'm already here when I'm not supposed to be." Her voice was unusually timid as she took off her shoes.

"You're not a hassle, Sunny. But you sat in the hallway for over an hour when you're obviously upset, and I went to the fucking gym. I should have been here." He set the plastic bag on the coffee table and dropped the rest of his belongings onto the armchair. It wasn't the normal routine, but that was out the window anyway.

Sunny hovered by the doorway. "Sorry."

"Sunny, if you say sorry one more time, I'm going to eat your flan."

She perked up. "You got me flan?"

Richard cackled, relief washing over him that his Sunny was still in the timid, scared woman standing in front of him. "If you're good and tell me what is going on instead of apologizing one more time, I may even let you eat it."

To his relief, Sunny scowled, as if she hadn't been a shadow of herself mere moments ago. "Just an argument with Mae. The same one we've been having for years. I just can't be around her when she gets like that. She doesn't even pretend to listen to what I want. She says she only cares about what's best for me, but it happens to be exactly what she wants from me."

"What do you need?" Richard asked, unsure what Sunny would want when she was so on edge. He didn't have a script for this. Normally when she was grouchy, she wanted some quiet time to stew, followed by a distraction. But Sunny normally wasn't sad like she was now, and she'd had an hour alone in the hallway because he was an asshole who hadn't rushed home.

She rubbed her eyes. "Can we just sit quietly?"

Richard nodded and led her by the elbow to the couch. "Do you want to be held?"

Sunny nodded.

Richard sat and gathered her in his arms as she curled around him. She shook quietly and sniffled, while he ignored the ache in his back and thighs as best he could.

But Sunny noticed him shifting under her. "What's the matter with you?"

He grinned at the annoyance in her voice, where he'd expected timidity. He breathed through a cramp. "I'm fine. Just a combination of leg day with Gabe and cramps."

"You did leg day during that time of the month? That's intense."

"It was. And if you don't mind, it's just my cycle, not 'that time of the month.'" Richard had briefly considered telling Gabe that he was on his cycle after the second set of Romanian Deadlifts. But Gabe had been in such a good mood for a change that Richard hadn't wanted to make him go easier for his sake.

Sunny sat up, her hair hanging over her face, and gestured for him to move back. "Here, I'll be your heating pad."

Richard leaned against the arm of the sofa where she indicated, trying to catch her eye. But her hair hid her face as she nestled against him, resting her shoulders on his abdomen.

"I do this for Luna sometimes because Mae doesn't like when we take medicine unless we absolutely need to. Typical Mae always knows best." Her voice cracked, and she cleared her throat. "Wouldn't T make this go away?"

"Probably, but the biology of it isn't actually that dysphoric for me. More the social aspect." Richard paused, wondering if it was still too soon to admit how much he wanted kids, but it seemed as good a time as any. "I plan to be the birth parent for my future kids, and T might reduce the chances of conceiving. It might not, but I don't want to risk it."

That had been a confounding variable in his journey, part of the reason it had taken him so long to figure out who he was, despite knowing he was a boy for longer than Richard could remember. Boys didn't have babies, so he obviously couldn't be a boy, because he wanted to have them.

Except that was exactly the case. He was a man, and he wanted to have his own goddamn babies. Despite his physical dysphoria about his outside, his reproductive organs were strangely, inexplicably exempt from that feeling of wrongness. His second puberty could start later in life, and he'd deal with the imposter syndrome of never feeling "trans enough" until then.

To Richard's relief, Sunny merely chuckled. "I can totally picture you with a dad bod."

With a smile, Richard gently pulled her hair back from her face and neck. His chest ached at the red rims of her eyes, smudged with mascara. Burying himself in her inky waves to breathe her in, he sank into the soft citrus aroma that always floated around her like a halo. She nestled deeper into him as he tightened his arms around her.

He wished he could bring Sunny peace right now, like she always brought to him. Even as chaotic as she was, putting everything in the wrong place and constantly messing up his hair, her presence made his mind so still. Like being in the eye of a tornado.

"Are you sniffing my hair, you weirdo?"

"You smell nice. Like oranges."

Sunny snickered. "It's this tangerine shampoo that Mae got in bulk because it was Phaw's favorite. We've still got a lifetime's worth." Her voice was still breathy and strained, but she seemed to be back to herself.

"I like it." Richard nuzzled her hair again. "I'm sorry you and your mother argued. I'm here for you in whatever way you need."

Sunny sniffled and reached over for the tacos on the coffee table. "You've already done so much. Why are you so amazing?"

Richard didn't know how to answer that he wasn't. He was merely trying to be someone better than himself, following other people's examples of how to act, instead of hiding in the safety of the bare minimum for once. Sunny made him want to leave the armor of the cold distant asshole he'd let himself be for too long. Instead of answering, he buried his face in her hair and held her close.

"Oh, did you get me churros, too?"

He gripped her wrist before Sunny could bite into one. "Don't you dare. Those are *my* churros."

Relief washed over Richard as Sunny's shaking came from laughter, instead of tears.

SATURDAY, APRIL TWENTY-FIFTH

Chapter Eighteen

Lee

Do all arcades have this many kids in them? As a herd of screaming preteens ran past, Lee shook his head and took a long swig of beer. He tried to catch Tara's eye to exchange a shady look, but she simply ate her pizza. Shoulders dancing as she chewed, Tara remained unfazed by the chaos and the horde stampeding around her. Typical, always happy as long as she was eating.

Though, she'd always had a soft spot for kids. Tara had even babysat Auntie Alitrice's monster neighbors when they were hard up. Lee had done many *many* things his aunt wouldn't be proud of, but he always found better ways to make money than *babysitting*. He'd never come close to *that* point of desperation.

While being around this many kids gave him hives, at least Tara was having fun. Which was a relief, because Lee was determined to make sure the redo of her botched birthday party plans from last year was a success. He'd put himself on referee duty—watchful for signs of an argument about to break out, instead of joining the conversations buzzing around their table.

Hopefully, with their new friends—and Jazz, miraculously—this would be even more fun. Going to an all-ages place meant that Jazz could join them for Phase One: pizza, arcade games, and drinks. Lee had never expected his little sister to actually make it, but he was glad she was here. Jazz needed more time around regular people. And thankfully, she was too young to join them for Phase Two: dancing at a club that wasn't Confession.

As much as Lee loved his job, he didn't want to go to work after he'd asked for the day off. Or worse, embarrass himself in front of his coworkers. And he absolutely planned on embarrassing himself tonight. Stormé's had dungeon nightclub vibes, compared to Confession's neighborhood bar ambiance. He was looking forward to dancing with Antonio, and maybe finding a dark corner somewhere. Feeling each other up around friends was weird enough; if their coworkers were watching? Worse, if his *sister* was there too? No way in hell.

Looking away as Gabe glanced up, Lee pretended to inspect his beer glass, hoping Gabe wouldn't pull him—or rather, Tara next to him—into the conversation.

Gabe just shot them a quick smile and returned to his conversation with Blanche and Jazz.

Lee exhaled, ignoring the guilt mixing with his relief. *Maybe this foolish idea I had is working.* Tara had been suspiciously agreeable when Lee had asked if he could invite Richard and Gabe along, which was a hopeful sign. Unlike Antonio and Blanche, Lee didn't actually expect anyone to get together. They all needed more friends, so he'd consider it a win if everyone stopped arguing.

And so far tonight, there'd been no arguments. Probably thanks to the cheesecake Gabe had brought, drizzled with raspberry sauce and fudge. Though how exactly had Gabe guessed Tara's weakness for cheesecake? Tara had blushed and stammered out a thanks. Lee was so used to watching out for her bad moods, it was hard to figure out her good ones.

"Lee, guess what?" Jazz asked from her seat next to Blanche, a proud grin on her face. The short hair and the septum ring had completely changed her, making Jazz look more her own age (honestly, *too* grown) than the modest tradwife their parents wanted her to be.

"You get something else pierced? A tattoo maybe?" Lee hoped she hadn't gotten a tattoo. His own tattoo from when he was her age was embarrassing. The wolf print on his lower back was supposed to be his way of "reclaiming the narrative of being disowned," like he was some kind of lone wolf. Someone really should have told him it was corny, but it was too late now. At least Antonio had finally stopped howling whenever he saw it.

Jazz laughed. "No, I got a job! I'm working part-time at the Science Center library. Opened my own bank account too!"

"About fucking time!" Lee teased. Baby steps away from their father's domain, but at least she'd have money of her own. Sometimes Jazz's stories helped Lee see the silver lining of being kicked out so young.

"That sounds amazing, Jazzy!" Blanche gave her a half hug. "How is the employed life?"

"Oh my god, it's so nice! I get to talk to real people. I made a friend at work—Mimi, and her roommate Teddy is so cool! They've been inviting me to catch up on the secular music and shows I've missed out on," Jazz gushed. "And the best part is? Dad thinks I'm doing an internship there for class credit, so he doesn't even know I'm getting paid."

"I'm proud of you, Jazz. Even though I can't believe you never listened to secular music before." Lee knew their parents would freak if they found out about any of it. Hopefully, Jazz wasn't putting herself at risk.

"I know! I've been missing out." Jazz's smile fell.

Thankfully Blanche asked her about what music she liked as a distraction, but Lee's heart still went out to her. Their parents had given up on him and instead stifled her. If they hadn't kicked him out, maybe they'd both have a healthier balance of support and independence. Like he had now with Antonio. Sure, they spent all of their free time together, but they *liked* spending time together.

Except now. Damn. Where'd he go? It took him a moment to find his boyfriend among the chaos of the arcade. Antonio had teamed up with Sunny against Richard at the foosball table, his tongue sticking out between his teeth and nose wrinkled in concentration. But based on the sour look on Sunny's face, they were losing to Richard, even two on one.

It was nice to see Sunny brought down a peg. She always won every game. Finally, she'd met her match.

At least in foosball.

Lee still didn't see any chemistry between Sunny and Richard, unlike Blanche. Maybe he just couldn't get a good read on Richard, but he didn't seem to be into Sunny at all. And Sunny wasn't acting like she did when she'd had a crush on Lee or Blanche.

A middle-aged white man dressed in flannel with a baseball hat approached the table nervously. Their group hushed amidst the screams of children around them. Lee's shoulders tensed as the man tapped Blanche on the shoulder. "Sorry to interrupt, but are you Blanche Van Horne?"

Blanche asked cautiously, "Who's asking?"

"Sorry, I just want to tell you what a big fan I am," he stammered out nervously. "I'm one of your subscribers. Would it be too much to ask for a selfie?"

Blanche's guarded look burst into a big smile. "Oh! Aren't you the sweetest? Yes, of course!" They rose, sweeping their bleached blonde hair over their shoulder before putting their arm around him.

The man squealed, a sound Lee had not been expecting from someone who looked like him. "Oh thank you! My wife is in the bathroom, so I won't take up your time, but I had to tell you your channel is amazing. I've found a whole new part of myself that I didn't know I was missing." He brought out his phone and snapped a picture. "Seriously, you've changed my life."

"I'm so glad my content resonates with you," Blanche cooed with a smirk. "Now, be a good boy and run along. We don't want to cause any trouble with your wife, now do we?"

"I'll be good, Your Honor. Thank you again. I'll be sure to leave a big tip." He gave a small wave, scurrying back to his table. A small voice asked, "Who was that, Dad?" from his direction.

"Well!" Blanche sat down with a beam. "Did you hear that? Life-changing. Helped him find himself." They grinned at Lee and Tara fondly. "I'll have to give you two a bonus soon. Without your help with recording and editing, this old theydy would be struggling to make any content, let alone be one of the lucky few who can actually make money."

Jazz nudged them. "It's not luck, Blanchy. You've earned it."

With a reluctant smile, Blanche nudged her back. "And so have Tara and Lee."

A bonus would be nice. He had already bought an engagement ring for Antonio, but it had taken all of his savings (and some of Tara's—he still had to pay her back). The ring was in Lee's pocket now. He'd been carrying it around for a few weeks, waiting for the right moment. Which was getting irritating, because it never came.

Lee had already planned out what he was going to say. He'd had it scripted in his head for months. *"Antonio, you've been my greatest joy since the moment I looked into your eyes. You're the love of my life, and I appreciate you every morning when I wake up beside you and every night when I go to sleep in your arms. I don't have much to give besides my heart, so I'm offering you my hand and asking for yours. Antonio Flores, would you do me the honor of marrying me?"*

Lee was tired of waiting. Maybe he had to create the right moment, instead of waiting around for it. Tomorrow. No, he'd be hung over. Sunday. *I could serve him breakfast in bed?*

Tara laughed, drawing him back to the conversation and away from his proposal plans. "You may be technologically inept, but you're nowhere close to being an old theydy, Blanche. And you don't need to pay me! You've let us stay with you for so long, it's the least I can do. And I get to practice my photography, even if I have to censor part of my portfolio."

"You do photography?" Gabe asked. He'd been thankfully quiet up until now. Hackles rising, Lee shot him a warning look to be nice. But Gabe's attention stayed on Tara.

Tara nodded. "I dabble. So does Lee, but he leans more toward the audio side of Blanche's operation, especially the ASMR videos." She ate another bite of pizza.

"How did you guys get into that?"

Tara chewed slowly, hesitating to answer Gabe's thankfully polite question. Lee took over, answering for them. "We took a class at the art museum when we were teenagers. We learned different mediums each week. Got us both on track to start our own businesses."

Their unconventional education was a sorer subject for Tara than Lee. The asshats at Bellamy Community College had looked down on her for never attending high school. Which was dumb as hell, because his Buttercup was incredibly smart and talented. And it wasn't like community college was worth gatekeeping.

"Was that program through the Modern Art Institute?" Gabe asked.

"You know it?" Lee was surprised. Gabe was a fitness buff, investment banker, Ivy League legacy kid, and rich enough to drop ten bands at charity galas on a vacation he insisted he'd never take. Familiarity with community youth programs at a modern art museum didn't fit the persona Lee had built for him. *I guess he did go to the same private art school as Antonio.*

Gabe nodded. "I volunteer there. I taught a photography class a couple times, and my mom roped me into leading a youth program, too. She's on the board."

"Oh, you do photography, too?" Lee elbowed Tara, who grumbled under her breath. Maybe Gabe and Tara *could* find something civil to talk about. Either that, or they'd have a photography competition. But at least that would be less violent than bowling. Probably.

Gabe shrugged. "I dabble. It's a creative outlet. Isn't that why you got into audio production?"

A "creative outlet" that didn't make money was a luxury Lee'd never had. "Sorta. I'm lucky I found a way to monetize my calling, even if I haven't gotten my break yet."

He'd spent hours as a kid listening to stolen CDs on his Walkman while hiding in his closet from his parents. Even later, living with Aunt Alitrice, he'd put on music and dance around the house with her to help raise her spirits. Music had always helped Lee cope with all of the hard times, and had brought him to better times with Antonio. Making music had never been a question, but selling the house beats he made was not the most lucrative hobby. Yet. Hopefully, this album credit with Antonio would give him some credibility.

Gabe nodded thoughtfully, turning to Tara. "You work in graphic design, right? Did the program have that too?"

Tara nodded, fussing with her cheesecake. "Yeah. The graphic designer who taught the class sold it as a reliable freelancing gig with minimal costs, which was good enough for me."

"So it was all about the money for you?" Gabe kept his tone light, but Lee glared.

Don't poke my Buttercup. Lee was getting a little sick of how Gabe always managed to find Tara's sore spots. He genuinely liked Gabe, who was kind, supportive, insightful—to everyone but Tara. The considerate-but-moody friend that Antonio waxed poetic about was not the same doucheface who goaded Tara and creeped on her ass constantly. Lee sighed, reminding himself that most people would not find his teasing as triggering as she did. Tara was more sensitive than she wanted to admit, and Gabe was still relearning how to function around people.

Luckily, Tara ignored the jibe and took a bite of the cheesecake instead, sighing with pleasure before answering his question. "And? I want job security. Even when the world is starving, there's always some entrepreneur with a loan from Dad looking for a new logo, or an MLM looking to rebrand. The demand is reliable, and I can be my own boss." She raised an eyebrow. "Not that the investment banker who dabbles in photography as a 'creative outlet' is one to talk about being in a job for the money."

Gabe shrugged, but luckily didn't retort.

Lee searched for Tara's usual tells of dissociation, checking her hands for tension and her green eyes to see if she was still present. She still seemed to be enjoying herself. Lee hoped it would last until the party was over; Gabe was supposed to drive Tara and Blanche home. If it came to it, they could switch cars. But feeling up Antonio in Gabe's Outback didn't have the same "Partition" energy as the third row of Richard's Range Rover.

He once again found himself grateful that Jazz would not be coming with them to Stormé's after this. And that Sunny would presumably be distracted by arguing with Richard in the front seat. *Oh, I should have him drop us off first, so they're forced to spend more time together.*

Lee sipped his beer. This plan had to work eventually. He needed to fit into Antonio's life, and his friends were all he had. This was supposed to be the perfect way to start blending their lives into one, with a seamless group of shut-in friends who he *knew* would get along *so* well, if they could just keep an open mind.

But at this rate, Lee and Antonio would still be playing referee at their wedding.

TARA

"WANT TO RAISE THE stakes?" Gabe's deep voice unexpectedly poured into Tara's ear when she was off by herself playing Donkey Kong. Sunny had finally taken pity on Tara's losing streak and moved on to make Richard her newest victim in air hockey.

Tara stiffened, allowing herself a quick glance over her shoulder. God, his damn sweaters were so... Tara turned back to the game just in time to dodge a barrel. The things she would do to those pecs if that navy merino, stretched impossibly tight, wasn't there. How soft it'd be under her fingers as she pulled it off those broad shoulders— She cleared her throat. "I'm listening."

Gabe's voice was amused. "You pick the game. Loser buys a round."

A drink? She'd been hoping for sex. Tara hit the buttons harder than necessary as she considered the offer. She had no money with her. Just her ID and phone tucked into the useless pockets of her shorts, and confidence that her friends wouldn't let her pay on her birthday. She couldn't afford drinks these days anyway, not with paying all the utilities and bills since Lee had moved out—Tara hadn't realized how draining bills were, until Lee had transferred them all to her name. And then Lee had borrowed the last of her savings for Antonio's engagement ring (not that she'd tell him that).

As "Game Over" flashed on the Donkey Kong screen, she turned to Gabe, her elbow brushing his torso. "It's my birthday. I'm not supposed to buy drinks."

His pretty eyes flicked to her chest as her revealing sweater worked as intended. Gabe's mouth twitched into a smirk. "Better not lose then, Kitten."

A flare of unidentified emotions burned through her. That nickname he called her only when others couldn't hear, the challenge and dare in that addictive timbre of his... Tara couldn't say no even if she wanted to.

Glancing around the arcade, Tara hunted for a game that she might win. After Sunny had kicked her ass so many times already, Tara wasn't confident she'd win anything. Whatever she picked would have to be something cheap. She only had a few tokens left after losing most of hers to Sunny.

"Pinball. High score out of three wins." She held out her hand.

"Deal." Gabe shook it, warm fingers lingering gently over hers.

Tara quickly discovered she was out of her league. "I might have picked the wrong game," she said, wincing as her third "Game Over" flashed across the screen.

"Tough break, Kitten." Gabe teased, still racking up points for his first round. He looked so relaxed as he shot her a smug grin, casual in a way she wasn't sure she'd ever seen. Maybe it was the jeans that clung to his thighs even more than his usual chinos. "Whatever you're having is fine."

With a frustrated groan, Tara turned on her heel, stomping toward the bar as her skin burned in embarrassment. *Fuck, I hope Lee has a tab open.* She ordered two whiskey cokes from the bartender, checking that Gabe was still out of earshot, only to find him right behind her.

He placed a warm hand on her lower back. "It's your birthday. I can't let you pay." Gabe passed the bartender his card.

"Then why make a drink the prize?" Resisting the urge to lean into him, Tara wondered what he would order if she wasn't there. "Not that I mind. I was bluffing. I don't have any money with me."

Gabe snorted, dimples flashing. "I wasn't expecting you to pick pinball, first of all. That's my game." He leaned in a little closer as he spoke into her ear, keeping his eyes on her to check her reaction. "And...I didn't know if you'd be open to what I actually wanted to wager. You have your...rules."

That's what I was hoping he'd say. She swallowed heavily as her heart beat faster. "I'm feeling open-minded tonight. What is it that you *actually* wanted to wager?"

He bit his lip, twisting a hand through his curls as he glanced around to make sure they were alone. Gabe leaned in to murmur in her ear. "If you win, we go to my place tonight, and I'll do whatever you want. Just casual fun between friends."

"Whatever *I* want? That seems like a reward for you," Tara teased, even as Gabe's emphasis on "friends" bothered her for reasons she didn't want to unpack.

Gabe's dimples flashed as he grinned. "Trust me, Kitten, you could leave me hanging all night if you want."

Leave him hanging? No, this man would be completely undone by the time she was finished with him. Tara swallowed hard. "And if I lose?"

"I get to kiss you."

Tara froze. A thin whistle of alarm rang in her head, dulled by confusion. *He knows I don't kiss.* If she was being honest, Gabe was probably the only person she might consider kissing, because he'd respect the boundaries she'd set. And his lips were so... She picked a hangnail. *He didn't hold me to that last wager. Would he hold me to this one?*

As his confident grin faded, she made herself ask, "What kind of kiss are you talking about? Like, tongue and shit?"

"Whatever you want. Just one kiss." Gabe's challenging smirk brought the dimple back to his left cheek. "Scared you'll lose, Kitten?"

With a glare, Tara ripped out the hangnail with a sharp, stinging tug. Of course, Gabe would listen if she set boundaries to his wager. He wouldn't just shove his tongue into her mouth like so many others had. "Are you any good at Skee-Ball?" She held out her hand.

Gabe shook it, holding her hand for longer than necessary. "I'm terrible at it."

"Good."

Despite her insistence that New Year's was a "one-time thing," Tara had been hoping for a replay of last year's birthday hookup since Lee had suggested inviting Gabe and Richard. They'd been getting along better. Maybe she could finally get him out of her system, without any hard or complicated feelings getting in the way.

While it'd be...interesting to figure out the fuss with kissing, to discover what Gabe's plush lips might feel like against hers (hopefully without a flashback), Tara was determined to win. She'd fantasized about his mouth, his fingers, his fucking *thigh* every night for months, and damned if she would pass up this opportunity. With Skee-Ball, she could at least try to throw him off his game with shit-talking.

Which, it turned out, wasn't needed. Gabe was blatantly throwing the game, scoring tens and twenties. For someone determined to bring out her competitive side with his wager, Gabe was unbothered by how badly he was losing.

"You really are terrible at this." Tara laughed when she sank a fifty-point ball, leaving herself two hundred points ahead of him. Safe enough to egg him on without losing, in case he decided to start trying.

"I don't suppose you want to do best out of three?"

"Not when I'm winning like this." Tara grinned as he biffed another throw. "And that was my last token."

Gabe's dimples broke through the fake scowl he failed to keep on his face.

Their friends were surprisingly absent, leaving them to their game. Sunny was playing Richard in foosball again. Lee and Antonio were taking pictures in a photo booth, while Blanche and Jazz laughed together at their table, blatantly people-watching. They were all pointedly ignoring her and Gabe.

Which was a relief. Gabe was different when it was just the two of them. Not just because he called her Kitten and flirted better. He was more open when their friends weren't around. Less irritated and less irritating.

"That's game." Tara spun around with glee as she sunk another fifty-point ball, leaving her close to three hundred points ahead. "Guess you're all mine for tonight."

"Oh, darn." Gabe smiled down at her as she stepped closer.

"Although," Forcing her gaze away from his dimples and pretty smile, she shot him a suspicious leer, "I suspect you lost on purpose."

Red tinged his cheeks, darkening his olive skin. Gabe's only answer was a slight twitch of his smile, his silence speaking volumes. The honest, naked hunger in his pretty brown eyes made her breath catch.

"Why? Decided you didn't want to kiss me after all?" Tara asked, surprised at the timidness in her voice. Her fingertips brushed the impossibly soft wool clinging to his waist.

That intoxicating vanilla and oaky scent washing over her, he murmured softly into her ear, "I very much want to kiss you, Kitten, but when you kiss me, it's going to be because you want to. Not because of a fucking bet."

Chapter Nineteen

Richard

Richard did his best to ignore the itch under his skin from the booming music, and the flashing lights of the dance floor making his eyes burn. Sunny had just started another argument; he had to keep up their charade, instead of burying his face in the safety of her neck like he wanted.

The group had claimed some couches around a lounge table at Stormé's. Antonio and Lee had quickly disappeared to the dance floor, leaving the rest of them sitting quietly around the table.

Quietly, that was, until Sunny called him a label whore out of nowhere.

Richard shot her an offended look. "There's nothing inherently immoral with designer. I am fortunate to have the resources for luxury items, but I would *never* wear labels on my clothing."

"And yet everything you wear is couture."

Richard shrugged, shifting his hand into his pocket. "I can't help it if I look good."

Everyone but Sunny snickered. She scoffed, eyeing where his hand had gone. "As if! You dress like you're fifty."

"And you dress like it's the aughts again." Richard pressed the remote hidden in his pocket with a smirk.

"Who calls it the aughts?" Sunny stiffened, biting her lip. "Excuse me for wearing all the things I never got to wear as a teenager. You know, having fun with my wardrobe? Maybe fun is a foreign concept to you."

"Oh, I have plenty of fun." Before it could overwhelm her, Richard turned off the vibrator he'd put inside Sunny earlier. On their list tonight: mild exhibitionism. Sunny wanted to have sex in public ("like Tara does!"), and while Richard doubted he could ever come in a public place, he was eager to make Sunny lose her mind. "And I do it without telling the world what brand I'm wearing."

"If you two are gonna argue again, I'm getting a drink." Blanche rose, heading for the bar.

"Okay, Mr. Pedantic. You're not a label whore, just a label slut." Sunny crossed her arms.

"Better to dress like a label slut than an actual slut." His heart sank, regretting the words as they left his mouth. He hadn't meant that as a personal slight against her, but Sunny's flinch told him that it'd been received as one.

Sunny stood, her expression clouding. "I, uh, have to go to the bathroom." She scurried away, shooting Richard an unreadable look that made his stomach clench in anxiety.

He'd give her a few minutes before following. And create a distraction in the meantime. He turned his sights on Gabe, who was playing with the ends of his hair, staring off into space in Tara's direction. Thankfully, neither had been paying attention to their bickering, or Tara might have punched him. She should have. "Why aren't you dancing, Gabe?"

Gabe jumped. "Huh?"

"You like dancing. There's a dance floor." Perhaps pushing Gabe was too much too soon, but Gabe used to love dancing and parties. Not sitting quietly on the sidelines. "And yet you're sitting here with the introverts."

Gabe shrugged. "I don't want to dance by myself, and Antonio said he would murder me if I joined him and Lee."

"Because it's impossible to ask anyone to dance with you." Richard tilted his head to indicate Tara, ignoring the deer in the headlights look on her face. "I'm going to the bathroom."

Richard stood up and headed to where Sunny had disappeared. Before he made it to the restrooms, Sunny beckoned him from a dark hallway instead.

"You want to do this here?" Assuming she still wanted to after he'd been an ass. His head thumped with the overwhelmingly loud music, but at least the lights were off here.

"The bathrooms are not public hookup friendly. Or trans friendly. There's no stall doors." Sunny made a face as she led him down the hallway. "Maybe we should have tried mild exhibitionism at Confession."

"I took it too far, didn't I?" Richard asked quietly. He'd tried to tell himself that she was pretending, but the hurt that had flashed through her eyes earlier seemed genuine. "Earlier I mean. I'm sorry."

Sunny shook her head. "You were kind of a dick, but I've heard worse. Mae says I dress like a hooker, but I like showing off my body."

The more he heard about Sunny's mom, the less Richard liked her. But then again, he'd just insulted her, too. "You should wear what you makes you happy—"

Sunny cut him off with a snort. "You don't need to mansplain bodily autonomy or sex positivity to me."

"...and I like how you dress," Richard finished lamely.

"I know." Sunny's smile turned challenging. "But show me anyway."

Richard pushed her against the wall as soon as they were far enough into the shadows of the hallway that he was confident anyone walking by wouldn't see them. Here, the sensory overload from the club was a dull irritation. Or perhaps being pressed against Sunny was the escape he needed.

"I wish I could take my clothes off." Sunny panted. "But that'd be too much exposure."

Richard pinched her nipple through her dress. "I thought that was the point of exhibitionism."

"I want them to hear me through a locked stall door, not see me in the middle of a hallway! I don't want to get caught," Sunny retorted. "This feels so rushed."

"Should we table it for another time?" Richard asked, lips brushing hers.

She shook her head. "No, I'm into it, but it's not what I had in mind."

"Then we'll keep it in the maybe column and try again. Any excuse to bring back this plug." He tapped the remote in the pocket to activate the vibrator inside her. "I like this."

Sunny gasped, squirming against him.

His lips found her ear, taking care to avoid her neck; she'd spent a long time covering the marks he'd made. Richard wedged a leg between her thighs, grinding against her.

Sunny arched into him, her hand tangling in his hair. "That was a dirty trick earlier. I almost came in the few seconds you had it on."

"Good." He reached into his pocket and pressed the button again, grinning as Sunny jerked against him when he turned it up to its highest speed. He left it in his pocket to tweak her nipple through her dress.

"You're such an asshole!" she gasped, pretty lips parting as her face contorted in pleasure. She bucked against him.

"You like it." Richard captured her mouth, devouring her moans as she came.

BLANCHE

FROM THEIR PERCH AT the bar, Blanche had a bird's eye view of their ducklings. Or at least, the dark corners where they'd most recently disappeared into. Blanche smiled into their scotch; Antonio's insatiable love had finally dragged Lee firmly out of his comfort zone.

Beads of light from the disco ball reflected off the carrot-red of Tara's hair. She was laughing as Gabe had his mouth to her ear and his hands on her hips, guiding her to the dance floor.

Blanche nearly spat out their drink, coughing as they tried to swallow it.

Tara?

Dancing?

With Gabe? Voluntarily? And *smiling* about it? Blanche wondered what cataclysm had triggered the apocalypse, because Hell must have frozen over.

"Go down the wrong pipe?" a voice asked.

Wiping scotch from their chin, Blanche turned to the stunning woman on the barstool next to them. A tight dress showed off her curves, her lips a bold red smile against her brown skin. Black curls flowed over one shoulder.

Blanche remembered to blink, all thoughts of Tara forgotten as the woman's eyelashes fluttered. "Must have."

"You need some water?" the woman asked, her eyes taking in Blanche's long legs crossed on the barstool.

They shifted, feeling very exposed in the thin kaftan that had felt so comfortable and flowy, until this woman had started undressing them with her eyes. The high slit no longer stopped at their thigh, instead exposing Blanche all the way to their soul under those doe eyes. "Uh...no thank you."

"Oh." The woman looked confused. "Oh, sorry, are you not into women? I shouldn't have assumed, I guess."

"No, I am! It's just... Uh..." Blanche covered their legs, heat flashing through their body. Damn Sunny for reminding them how powerless Real Blanche was against gorgeous women. They'd gone for years without being attracted to anyone, and here they were blushing like they were thirteen again.

The woman raised an eyebrow. "Are you worried I won't be into you? I don't want to presume, but I'm guessing you're trans or enby or something? You'll find I'm pretty open-minded." She winked.

"It's not that..." God, her eyelashes were *so* long. Blanche shrugged; explaining the "or something" to someone who didn't need to know wouldn't be worth it. "I'm keeping an eye out on my friends."

The woman looked around. "They asked you to sit here by yourself while they have fun?"

"Well, no... But they need someone to look out for them." Not for the first time since they'd arrived at Stormé's, Blanche felt Jazz's absence keenly. If she were here, Blanche would have someone to talk to about Tara dancing with Gabe, and how Sunny and Richard had been gone a suspiciously long time. Keeping Lee's sister company would have been a good excuse not to talk to this woman. But Jazz had only turned twenty last month, and her strict parents expected her home before curfew. Blanche had to exit this conversation gracefully, before they could get talked into anything.

"Do they?" the woman challenged. "Why do you have to be here all alone, instead of having fun like they are?"

Wasn't that the million-dollar question? They didn't have an answer.

As stunning as this woman was, Blanche couldn't risk giving in. If their fling with Sunny had taught them anything, they should not have any entanglements that weren't with clients. Even now, Blanche couldn't bring themself to find out what might happen if they said yes. If it'd be one dance, or one kiss, or one night, or... Blanche downed their scotch. Because she was stunning, this woman, but she *pushed*. Like Sunny pushed, like Daisy pushed, like their patron *and* his fiancée pushed. Tomorrow morning, this woman might push again, and again, and again, and Blanche had been pushed their whole life.

Stomach clenching, Blanche forced themself to smile as they slid off the barstool, digging into their purse to find their lighter and a preroll. "Excuse me. Smoke break."

They headed toward the hallway that would hopefully lead to the back-alley smoking area, if Stormé's still had one since the last time they were here over a decade ago. Daisy had insisted they research Chas's "competition and collaboration" before Confession had opened. Blanche, Chas, and Freddy had been dragged to every gay bar and queer-owned business in the Bellamy metro area.

Soft laughter drew their attention down a side hallway on their way out. Pressed close together in the shadows, Richard smoothed his hair back while Sunny wiped her lipstick from his mouth.

A sour pang twisted in Blanche's stomach. They hurried away before they were seen.

Sitting behind Gabe in his Outback, Blanche silently observed as he drove through downtown toward Eastside. Gabe could barely keep his eyes on the road, and Tara made no attempt to keep her eyes off of him. Streetlights lit their faces with every block they passed. They wouldn't put it past Gabe to forget they were here, but Tara was usually much more guarded.

Blanche smirked as Tara looked away too slowly; Gabe noticed her staring. Tara's blush was visible even without the streetlights rolling over her face, and yet she didn't look away.

"It's a good thing you're not driving, Kitten," Gabe teased affectionately.

Blanche's breath caught in their throat as the sour turn of their stomach, dulled by the indica, roared back to life. *Oh, it's like that.* Tara, of course, would never notice. She probably wouldn't believe it even if he told her. But Blanche recognized it—that soft tone in his voice spoke volumes more than the nickname itself. Guilt panged in their chest for coming down so hard on him at the gala.

"Trust me, you don't want *Kitten* to drive you anywhere." Blanche forced a Cheshire cat grin to spread across their face as they reminded Gabe of their presence in the backseat. He probably hadn't meant to let his heart show in front of them.

Gabe's olive skin went red as he looked at them in the rearview mirror. His mouth opened and closed, as if searching for something to say.

Blanche's smile softened in sympathy. "She's a terrible driver. What exactly happened to your car again, Tara?"

"It was a free car, Blanche. Totally beyond my control that the brakes didn't work properly." Tara's dire lack of emotional intelligence came to Gabe's rescue as she took the bait. "I tried to park it on a hill by the mounds. As far as I know, it's still in the river."

Gabe shook his head with a snort. "You are never allowed to drive my car."

"Oh, come on. You don't want to be my driving instructor? I need to practice. I should get a license at some point," Tara teased.

Tara only had her learner's permit, which she'd gotten after moving into Blanche's apartment. Only with a permanent address had she started with the endless requests for documentation to prove she was in fact, Tara Sanderson. All of her documents, like her birth certificate, were with her mom, wherever she was.

Thankfully, Blanche was an expert at establishing an identity with little to go on; Tara's process went much faster than theirs. It had taken Blanche several years to get their ID with no proof of who they were, and no knowledge of their birth name or parents. And that was just to get a state ID. It'd been worse when Daisy and Blanche went to apply for— *Nope. I may be tipsy, but I'm still too sober to think about her tonight.*

"Ask Lee. You know, your bestie?" Gabe patted the dashboard of his Outback fondly. "This is my baby."

Tara smiled at him. "Lee won't let me drive his."

"If *Lee* won't let you drive his car, you think *I'd* let you? Besides, how pissed would you get if I start telling you how to drive?" Gabe asked pointedly.

"True. I'd crash the car to get you to shut the fuck up," Tara joked.

Gabe laughed as he pulled up to Blanche's apartment.

Blanche unbuckled and opened the door, pausing when Tara didn't make any sign of following. They leaned over to catch Tara's eyes, who glanced at Gabe briefly.

"I see." They turned to Gabe, pointing their finger threateningly. "Don't be an asshole."

Gabe scoffed. "No promises."

"At least bring *Kitten* home safe and sound." *And remember what I said. Please don't hurt her.* Blanche turned back to Tara. "Call me if you need anything." They kissed her cheek.

With that, they stepped out of the car and sauntered up the steps, trying to ease the sour taste in their throat that they couldn't afford to unpack. They would wait up for her. Even when Tara had forced herself to date last year, she never stayed overnight. Her emotions would be everywhere when she came home. Blanche would roll a joint to help Tara process. *Maybe another for me, too.*

CHAPTER TWENTY

TARA

"Do they see everything?" Gabe pulled away from the apartment once Blanche was safely inside. "I feel like I'm being psychoanalyzed constantly."

"Sunny thinks they can read minds, but they're just intuitive. Good at assessing people." Tara shrugged, tugging at another hangnail. "So, yeah, you are being psychoanalyzed."

"Great. I hate it."

"Me too, sometimes," Tara laughed. "Don't worry, they're very discreet. Any secrets they see are safe."

"Is that something you do, too? Assess people?" Gabe craned his neck to check his blind spot as he merged onto the freeway, giving Tara plenty of opportunity to admire his broad shoulders and chest, the luscious mane of brown-black curly hair. His pretty lips and strong nose were made to be ridden.

Tara swallowed. *Saving that idea for later.* "I'm not as good at Blanche, but I scan people enough to stay safe."

"Did you scan me when we first met?"

Tara smiled. "You came across as upper middle class. Queer. Probably single, unmarried at least. Eager to please. Attracted to me." While nothing she had read was wrong per se, Gabe had proven himself to be much more than her first impression. Her scan had not shown her the snide teasing, the cheesecake he'd made for her, the immature ways he tried to get her attention when she tried her hardest to ignore him, or that deep voice calling her Kitten that sent shivers down her spine. She tugged harder at the hangnail, distracting herself with the stinging pain. "How'd I do?"

"You missed the giant red flag that says insecure asshole." His dimples made an appearance as Gabe shot her a wry smile. "But yeah, I suppose that's all true."

Tara waited for him to elaborate, questions burning. But asking would cross a boundary, open a door she wasn't sure either of them wanted open. *Enjoy this. Don't overthink it.*

Easier said than done. She overthought everything when it came to him. Gabe could piss her off until Tara lost her temper. But then he'd look at her like he wanted to eat her alive and she'd squirm with need. Until he'd open his fucking mouth, goading her to prove she was better than him. Even though that same voice, when he got close and murmured in her ear, had his words pouring over her brain and down her body, leaking out of her cunt. And the way he'd held her close against him with his hands roaming over her ass, hard cock against her stomach as they'd danced tonight...

"What was your impression of me when we met?" Tara surprised herself with the question, ripping the hangnail out completely. The happy gooey feeling she got around him made her rules pointless; normally she never have would asked, but she was curious.

Gabe's smile turned wistful. "I just wanted you to notice me."

"Notice you, huh? Is that a euphemism?" Tara teased.

He chuckled. "No, but yeah, of course I wanted that, too. You were interesting, and I wanted you to think I was interesting, too."

"How so?"

"Fishing for compliments, Kitten?" Gabe teased, pulling off the freeway to head back over South.

"No, just curious."

"Well, you hip-checked me so hard that I almost fell off my barstool." Gabe turned off the main road onto a quiet residential street. The streetlights were barely visible through the tree canopy. "And instead of apologizing like a normal person, you said, 'Oh shit, whoops!' in the most frat bro voice I've ever heard, and proceeded to pick a wedgie out of your ass."

Tara laughed. "And you *wanted* my attention?"

"You have a very nice ass, Kitten. Who would blame me?" Gabe's dimples faded. "Honestly, my first impression was that you didn't give a shit about what anyone thought, and I wanted to know your secret." Clearing his throat, Gabe hit a garage door opener clipped to the sun visor as he pulled into the driveway of an older brick house. "Hope you're cool with dogs. Hippo is chill once he's comfortable with you, but he can be scary at first. Just ask Lee."

"You have a dog?" Tara practically jumped out of the car the second it stopped. "Lee never said! Where is the baby? I need to meet him."

Gabe grinned, dimples on display. "Come on then."

Tara followed him into the large kitchen, squealing with joy as a giant gray dog waddled into the room. She let him sniff her thoroughly before sitting on the floor, letting him crawl into her lap while she covered him with pets and kisses. Tara loved dogs. They were safe. They were easy to read and usually listened to the word no.

"Why am I jealous of my own dog?" Gabe muttered as Hippo rolled on his back in her lap, tail whacking the floor.

"Don't worry. You'll get your turn soon." Tara smiled up at him.

He reddened. "Can I get you anything? Water? Wine?"

"Whatever you are having is fine," she said, rubbing Hippo's belly with vigor.

"Hippo, let's go outside." Gabe opened the patio door, and Hippo reluctantly rose from her lap to go out in the backyard. Tara washed the dog hair off her hands, while Gabe uncorked a bottle of red from a wine fridge tucked under the kitchen island. He poured them both a glass.

She took a sip, appreciating the comfortable silence that only existed when they were alone together. Normally Tara wasn't a wine drinker, but warmth spread through her as she swallowed the tannin-rich, yet slightly sweet red. "This is good. What kind is it?" Based on Gabe's snobby streak and the fancy kitchen, it was probably out of her budget.

Gabe blushed again and handed her the bottle.

"Cooper Winery, huh? Did you buy it because it has your name on it?" she teased.

Somehow his blush deepened. "It's my parent's company. They have a vineyard just past Driftwood."

"Oh, damn, your family's got *vineyard* money?" That was so much worse than just snobby wine tastes. She'd just been considering which liquor store would be the easiest to lift a bottle from; Tara couldn't even afford the cheap shit after the recent hike in her student loan payments.

Gabe shrugged and set the bottle on the counter. "They struggled to get it off the ground for most of my life, so it's not as impressive as you're thinking. I went to business school to learn how to help them run it. But they got their legs under them right before I graduated, so I stayed in New York to work with Richard instead."

Tara sensed she was touching that edge of the Too Close boundary again. She gave him space to continue if he wanted, surprised that she actually wanted to hear about his family and shit. Normally, she didn't care to learn about the people she hooked up with.

Instead of saying anything more, Gabe quietly swirled his glass, leaning on the kitchen counter. His warm brown eyes stared into nowhere as he fiddled with his hair.

Tara forced herself to tear her eyes away from him. Looking at him now was causing soft feelings beyond her normal longing; this new happy gooey feeling was annoying. There was no room for soft feelings here. Even if it was their third "one-time thing," this was still casual.

"So, did you do upgrades and shit to this place when you moved in?" Tara didn't know much about houses, but that was something people asked when they went to someone's house. His house looked older, the color palette warm despite the blues and greens that accented the granite countertop and white tiles on the walls.

Gabe nodded, sipping his wine before answering. "Yeah, but you didn't come here to talk about my kitchen." Hippo scratched at the door. "Or meet my dog."

Tara laughed, grateful to fall back into silence. "Sorry, I'm shit at small talk."

"I'm happy to talk about whatever you want, but don't feel like you have to fill the silence for my sake." Gabe opened the patio door, and Hippo quickly found his way back to Tara, flopping down at her feet. "It literally took him weeks before he got that comfortable with me. What's your secret?"

"No idea. I must smell good." She smiled at him over her wine.

Gabe gave her another heated stare. "What do you want to happen tonight? I was going to suggest a repeat of your birthday from last year, but the club didn't even have stall doors."

"This is a better idea." Tara laughed. A year ago, she would never have considered going to someone's house. So much had changed for her since then. *Tara* had changed. She felt lonelier these days, or perhaps she was merely acknowledging it now. She met his stare, remembering one of her many regrets from her birthday last year. "I still haven't seen you. Like naked. I really want to see you naked."

Gabe blushed. "Don't get your hopes up, but whatever you want."

"And I want to suck you off."

He tugged the thick braid hanging over his shoulder. "Kitten, I'm pretty sure *you* won this bet, not me. You don't have to."

Tara stared back into those brown eyes, stepping into his personal space. "I want to. I wanted to suck you off at New Year's, but *someone* was selfless," she teased, pouting a little.

"Sorry that I ate you out instead of whipping out my dick." His smile was confused.

"You should be. Asshole." She ran her hand up the chest she always wanted to touch, tired of keeping her distance.

Gabe apparently felt the same. He gripped her hips and pulled her close, slipping a thigh between her legs. "What else do you want? Besides seeing me naked and sucking my dick?"

Tara pulled the hair tie out of his braid as she pressed against him. His muscular torso was firm against her, the hair in her fingers soft as she unwound it. The vanilla and oak aroma of Gabe that was so familiar in her memories filled her nose. "I want to get off on your thigh." She squeezed his thigh between hers. "You have no idea how hard I came after sitting in your lap that night. How often I've thought about it since."

Gabe whined quietly as he exhaled sharply.

Tara smiled. "I want to touch you all over. I want to sit on your face. I want to ride you. And I want you to lay there and take it all."

His pulse fluttered under the thin skin of his throat. His growing erection stirred against Tara's stomach. "Can I touch you? When I'm laying there and taking it?" Gabe breathed into her ear as she ran her fingers through his hair. "Please let me touch you, Kitten."

"You better fucking touch me." She stood on her tiptoes to gently bite his earlobe, making him exhale a delightful, soft moan into her ear.

"Same stoplight system as last time, Kitten?" Breathing heavily, Gabe slipped a hand under her sweater, dragging hot along her skin to pull her closer. *Fuck, his hands...* "And I got tested a few months ago. No partners since then."

Her inner id cheered at that. *No partners? In months?* A wave of possession crashed over her. *He's mine.* The urge to strip in his kitchen and spread herself across the counter was hard to resist. *But just for tonight,* Tara reminded herself, allowing a compromise with her greedy id. "I got tested a few weeks ago—no issues. And since I'll be occupying your mouth this time, tap once for green, twice for yellow, three times for red."

His Adam's apple bobbed in his throat as Gabe nodded. "Bedroom?" He offered, running his hand through her hair, tugging gently on the crown of her scalp. "I'm this close to tearing your clothes off, but it's weird with my dog literally laying at our feet."

Tara laughed. "Lead the way."

He picked her up instead, easily hoisting her over his shoulder. Her surprised yelp quickly turned into a laugh. He grabbed their empty wine glasses and the open bottle in his other hand that wasn't supporting her hips.

The happy gooey feeling spread through her, even as Tara hung over his broad shoulders while Gabe carried her through his house. *It's amazing what a little respect for boundaries does to my comfort zone.* He would put her down if she wanted. He would listen if she said no. *This fucker really ruined casual sex for me.*

Setting the wine down, Gabe tossed her gently on the bed. Tara giggled, trying to catch her breath. His whole room smelled like vanilla. Like *him*. It was overwhelming. It was her favorite scent.

He turned on the lamp, illuminating the soft green of the walls and the bright white of the duvet underneath her. But she couldn't tear away from those brown eyes, staring down at her like he was deciding whether to eat her or worship her. A hot, desperate anticipation soaked her already-damp shorts when Gabe leaned over her.

"Undress and come lie on the bed." She slipped out from under him before he could cage her between his arms. He'd taken charge the other times they'd hooked up. It was Tara's turn to make him come undone. "Do you have condoms?"

"Yeah, in there." Gabe nodded to the nightstand, folding his sweater neatly on the chair as he undressed. Her eyes traced the muscles rippling across his back, the biceps straining the sleeves of his undershirt. He froze as he noticed her watching him. "Sorry. I'm not the most confident in my body. Would you mind turning around while I did this?"

"Oh, sure." Tara whirled around to stare hard at the white duvet. "Sorry."

"No, don't apologize. It's a me problem."

Tara flushed at the reminder of how their first hookup had ended. "Sorry for that, too."

"Fuck. I wasn't—" Gabe sighed from behind her. The nightstand drawer scraped open, and a condom crinkled as he set it down. "Just... Thank you."

"Not ogling you while you undress is the bare minimum. You don't need to thank me."

"Kitten, you are more wonderful than you realize." His hands brushed her shoulders gently, before running down her back to encircle her waist. She shivered. "Can I undress you?"

Inhaling deeply and desperately to catch that intoxicating scent, stronger with him naked behind her, Tara nodded, leaning against his chest. His skin burned hot, even through her sweater.

Gabe's hands gripped her hips, pressing his erection against her ass as his voice poured into her ear. "These fucking shorts, Kitten. Do you have any idea how much I wanted to tear these off of you?"

"I have some idea." Tara rolled her hips against him, an imitation of how they'd danced earlier. She couldn't dance to save her life. But with Gabe? He'd moved her along with him, and she'd felt free and sexy. All of the things that she'd never understood about dancing before. "But Sunny just bought them for me."

Gabe huffed a laugh against her neck. "They'll stay in one piece." His fingers deftly unbuttoned them and slid down to tease her already-soaked slit. His other hand pushed them down around her hips.

Tara stepped out of them as they hit the floor, groaning as two big fingers sank into her. The heel of his hand pressed against her clit. "Fuck."

"That's the plan, Kitten." His other hand slid up her stomach, cupping her tit, thumb sweeping across a nipple.

Tara's snort turned into a moan as he sucked gently behind her ear. She rolled her hips back against him again, his erection pressing against her bare ass. Gabe wasted no time with teasing; being held by him like this—mouth and hands caressing her, his desire feeding hers—was heavenly.

"Oh, fuck. I gotta get you naked. This is too tempting to just fuck you like this."

Tara would happily throw all of her plans for him out the window, but instead he pulled away, tugging her sweater over her head and dropping it to the floor. He climbed into the center of the bed, beckoning her to follow.

Her mouth dropped open as she climbed over him. She couldn't begin to fathom what he was self-conscious about. Hard muscle built up his chest and shoulders, stretch marks accentuating the muscular mass of his torso and soft curves of his belly. His legs were long and delightfully thick. Dark hair coated his chest and legs and forearms. A delightful trail led from his navel to a tidy thatch of black curls. And his cock...

Her mouth watered. His cock was beautiful. It was bigger than she'd expected, with a lovely brown color that faded into a soft dusky blush at the head. She wondered if he'd let her take a picture, or if that would be too much to ask from a casual hookup.

Tara straddled one of his massive thighs. She touched him softly, taking his cock in her hands. "Has anyone ever told you you have the most beautiful dick?"

With a hiss and a confused smile, Gabe shook his head. "No? It's a decent size, but that's all anyone's ever cared about."

"They're blind and stupid. You're gorgeous. Not just this work of art, but all of you."

Gabe blushed, his smile turning bashful. *Adorable. Those dimples.*

Tara continued her exploration up his body, grinding her cunt slowly against that thigh as she touched him, and he explored her in return. She moaned at the friction between her legs. His mouth sucked her tits as her fingertip traced the shell of his ear. Having him under her was delicious.

"I've thought about this so fucking much, Kitten. Ever since that night you sat in my lap. Can you come like this?"

Tara nodded with a moan, rocking her hips against him. "I've imagined riding your damn thigh so many times when I touch myself. This is way better than my pillow."

Gabe whimpered into her neck as she ground against his thigh, chasing an orgasm that wouldn't take long. Reality surpassed any fantasy. Pleasure rose with every stroke of his fingertips against her nipples, his mouth sucking a mark into her neck. His thigh was soaked with her, their skin sticky and slick under her rolling hips. His moans grew louder as she slowly stroked his cock with one hand and pulled his hair with the other.

Back arching, Tara shuddered as a wave of pleasure hit her, her peak rising with each tilt of her hips against him. She exhaled his name into his ear as she came, thighs twitching around his and her toes curling.

"Fuck, Kitten." Gabe's voice was raspy. "I can't believe you're not a dream."

Tara caught her breath and collapsed into him. She traced his neck with her tongue, his ears with her teeth. Pinched his nipples and massaged the muscles in his chest. Every mole, every muscle, every mark on his body was committed to memory, just in case this was their final one-time-thing.

Working her way down to his hips, Tara noticed silvery scars. Faded and old, they puckered his skin under the damp hair coating his thigh. She had been so taken by his cock that she hadn't noticed them before.

"Oh." Tara traced them gently with her finger. Gabe probably felt the same empty, numb sensation of scar tissue that she did.

"Sorry. Leftover from my emo phase decades ago." He wouldn't meet her eyes.

"You don't need to apologize. I'm just surprised. We match." Tara pulled his hand to her hip, where tattoos covered scars of her own. "Um, checking in. I just got off on your self-harm scars. Unintentionally, of course. I would've asked if I'd known. Um… How are you feeling about all that?"

Gabe's mouth twitched into half a smile. "I would have said something if it was an issue. Most people get grossed out. Or want to talk about my feelings because they think I must be suicidal. You getting off on them was way more validating."

Tara snorted. "I get it. Got mine tattooed for that same reason. I had a lot of feelings that I couldn't handle when I was younger, but that doesn't mean I want pity now."

She'd made hers when she'd lived with Auntie Alitrice, unable to escape her feelings when she was alone in the bathroom. Angry at her mom for choosing heroin over her, at the dad Tara couldn't remember for not sticking around. Frustrated and helpless that she couldn't do anything to cure Auntie Alitrice's cancer, or make Lee's parents love him. Resentful of her lack of place in the world. So desperately alone, other than Lee and his aunt. All of her hard feelings were incongruous with feeling safe and loved for the first time in her life.

After Auntie Alitrice died, she didn't have confusing feelings to run from as survival once again became her priority, and clean bathrooms became rarer. After Tara and Lee had moved in with Blanche, casual sex had replaced self-harm as her vice, her escape, her way to feel in control. Eventually, she'd gotten the scars tattooed over, so people would stop giving her those pitying looks when they ate her out. They always fucking asked if she was okay, like it was any of their business.

"I remember yours from before, but I didn't think," Gabe murmured quietly, his fingers tracing her tattooed scars. "Should I have stopped you?"

Tara shook her head, grateful that he hadn't said anything, then or now. The intimacy of the moment, touching each other's past like this, tore open her carefully packaged feelings. For once, Tara found she didn't care. She let the hurt, the longing, and loneliness swirl through her mind without shoving them away. Here was someone who had carved their own emotions into their skin like she had. Who wouldn't look at her with pity, but with understanding. The new soft happy gooey feeling somehow made all her other emotions manageable, even the fragile ones.

A whirlwind of emotions flew across Gabe's face. Her own vulnerability was looking back at her from his coffee brown eyes as she pressed her lips to the scars on his legs. His beautiful eyes grew watery as she kissed his past hurt.

She had to look away. There was too much of herself in him.

Tara shivered as his fingers massaged her hips and thighs, shifting down the bed before she could get caught up in the pleasure those roaming fingers promised. She already had way too many soft feelings; she needed to take back control. She needed to focus. This was her prize.

Tara nudged his wonderfully thick thighs further apart and settled herself in between them. She tentatively licked the dark blush head of his cock, his wonderful musky scent filling her nose. Desire flared through her as Gabe gripped the sheets under him, her name falling from his lips. She needed to make him come apart, make his whole body feel her, to soak into his soul, not only his skin.

With one hand, Tara gripped the base of his cock as she swirled her tongue around the head, committing to memory his salty taste. How impossibly hard he was in her grip. Sucking dick wasn't her strong suit—she was much more confident in eating pussy—but she needed to make him see stars like he had for her.

Gabe thrust up against her mouth when she sucked hard, moans and breathy "oh fucks" in his deep voice filling the room. She wished she could capture how he looked—biting his lip, his eyes wrenched shut in pleasure.

"Look at me," she said around him.

When his brown eyes met hers—wide and wet with pleasure—she rewarded him by taking him deeper, pumping the base of his cock in time with the bobbing of her head. Tara gripped her thumb tightly in the palm of her free hand, fighting against her gag reflex. His size made it hard to properly deepthroat him, but she needed to take as much as she could. Tara's lips eventually reached to where her fingers were wrapped around him. Her eyes were watering from the effort, throat burning, but she kept her eyes on him. Spit drooled over her fingers.

"Kitt—fuck— Kitten, you have to stop."

With the hand around his dick, Tara stuck her middle finger up. She did her best to glare at him through the tears in her eyes. No way in hell was she stopping.

Gabe's laugh was breathy. "Seriously, I'm so close. I need to last for you. I can't come this soon."

Tara refused to stop his pleasure, no matter how prettily he begged. She tapped his thigh, asking him for his color. She backed off slightly, giving him a moment to call yellow or red. Instead, he tapped his thigh once. *Green.*

Determined, Tara hollowed her cheeks around the head as she massaged his balls and perineum. He came with a shout, filling her mouth. She resisted the urge to spit or gag, or to even swallow; his salty flavor was delicious. Mouth closed and full of his cum, a long line of spit trailed from her lips as she pulled away.

"Shit! I'm sorry! I'm sorry." Gabe was in a frenzy, eyes wild and breath shallow, even though he'd tapped green. "I tried to warn you."

Tara ignored his panic and crawled up his body, straddling his wide chest. Pinning his arms with her knees, she yanked his head back with her fist in his hair.

He went silent, brown eyes wide as he gasped. Her chest twinged with that gooey soft feeling when Gabe swallowed hard, his throat bared to her and spotted with marks she'd made.

She tapped her thigh once. *Color?*

He replied with a single, sharp slap to her ass. Her cunt clenched at the sensation. *Green.*

Still kneeling above him, Tara worked two fingers into his mouth and forced his jaw open. Slowly, she let the mixture of spit and cum drip down from her mouth and into his. Cum drizzled into his waiting lips, across his cheeks and jaw, as she painted him with himself.

"Fuck, Kitten," Gabe groaned out. He chased the trail that clung from her lips and tongue with his mouth, trying to capture it all.

With a proud smile, Tara stroked his cheek, smearing cum further across his jaw. Gabe sucked her thumb into his mouth, staring up at her. His pupils were blown wide in a daze as he licked her hand clean. Bending down, Tara licked the rest of the cum from his face and nibbled along his jawline, sucking on his earlobe where some had dripped off his cheek.

This would be the only time she would have Gabe wrung out beneath her; she needed to remember this, to commit that addictive, salty musky flavor to memory. Last time, he'd just gave and gave and gave. She needed to make his world explode and mind melt, the way Gabe had done to her. To remember every second for later, when she was alone, dreaming of him.

"I'm sorry," he tried again, a little less panicked now.

"Don't you dare apologize." She gripped his jaw in her hand, turning his gaze to her. "I wanted you to come. Besides, I'm about to ride your face until you're ready for me again."

Gabe nodded, breathless as he rearranged the pillows to lay back.

Tara reached over to the nightstand to pour herself a glass of wine before settling in, straddling his face. Gripping the headboard, she rolled the wine over her tongue, swallowing slowly. His tongue worked a long, hot stripe along her cunt, his hands gripping her ass firmly as she ground against his face. Gabe's tongue was everywhere she needed, his nose teasing her clit. Two thick fingers circled her opening before they filled her roughly.

While nowhere close to drunk, a hazy buzzy warmth spread through Tara's body. She closed her eyes with a groan, letting her head fall back when Gabe sucked her clit hard. Pleasure shot through her.

"Fuck, you're amazing at this," she hissed, clenching as Gabe added a third finger. Maybe it was the wine. Maybe it was that she'd been wet and fantasizing about this for hours. Maybe she was still high from her first orgasm and their vulnerable moment. Maybe it was pent-up arousal from sucking his dick, but Tara was already close to another orgasm.

She ground against his tongue and fingers. Pants and moans flew from her mouth as she pushed and pulled against the headboard. Rutting against his beautiful face, she chased her orgasm, her toes curling and core tightening painfully. The deep-set brown eyes between her thighs never left her. Gabe curled his fingers inside her, pushing her over the edge.

Tara came with a cry, tightening her thighs around his head as she convulsed over him. "Holy shit. Oh, that was good. No one can eat me out like you can. You're so good at this."

With a pleased hum, Gabe slowed his licks, replacing his tongue with open-mouth kisses against her clit that sent tremors through her as Tara came down from her high.

"How are you doing? I hope I didn't get too rough."

"You can be rougher with me." He smiled against her as his voice rumbled directly against her clit.

Tara gasped from pleasure. "I'll try not to break your nose," she teased.

"Break it. I don't care," Gabe said in between kisses to her cunt.

"No, I like your nose," Tara said into her glass of wine before she emptied it. She didn't usually try to carry a conversation ever, let alone during sex. But Gabe's deep voice was practically a vibrator. She set the wine glass back down on the nightstand.

"Be as rough as you want, Kitten. I'm just happy to be here."

Her laughter turned into a loud groan as he licked her more firmly now, picking up the pace. His arm wound around her hips, tilting her forward so he could fuck her harder with his fingers.

"Fuck. Gabe. Don't stop." She was starting to talk nonsense again, curses mingled with his name as another orgasm crept up her spine. His fingers filled her completely, pressing everywhere inside her. She gripped one hand into his thick hair and pulled tightly.

Gabe moaned into her, sending shockwaves through her as her back tightened and her belly coiled. Her vision blurred behind her eyes.

"Gabe, holy fuck. I'm so close. Please, Gabe." She clung to the headboard in desperation, nails digging into the grain. Her face pressed against the cool wood as she shamelessly fucked his mouth.

He groaned loudly when she wound her fingers through his hair again, sending more vibrations directly against her clit. Tara cried out his name as she collapsed over him, barely supporting herself against the headboard to keep from falling. Her mind went blank, exploding into nothingness in the way that only Gabe had ever managed to do to her.

Before she could even begin to come down, his fingers wrung another, stronger orgasm out of her. Tara yelped with surprise as her whole body seized. She heard herself laughing and crying and screaming, unable to control herself as white-hot pleasure tore through her body.

Muscles melting into magma, Tara erupted. A geyser gushed between her legs. Her skin burned deliciously, every nerve on fire as she sagged against the cool headboard.

Gabe coughed underneath her, choking.

Tara scrambled off of him, falling on the bed. "Oh my god! Are you okay?"

He was laughing, still sputtering as he wiped his face. "That was the hottest shit I've ever fucking experienced. I just got waterboarded by your pussy, and I'm in fucking heaven."

"What are you talking about?" Tara noticed now that the pillows, his hair, his face, and chest hair were damp. "Did I...?" She trailed off, gesturing to the puddle around his head.

He nodded, a proud grin on his face, those rare dimples on full display. "Squirt directly into my mouth? Fuck yes. Wish I'd been ready for it. Would have fucking drank it all instead of inhaling it." A heavy sigh escaped him. "You're fucking amazing, Kitten."

Tara smiled as she stretched out on the bed, her legs still liquid. "Sorry for almost drowning you. And for ruining your pillows."

"Don't you dare apologize. I'm never washing these again. I'm going to fucking inhale you every night when I go to sleep." Gabe wrapped his arms around the pillows protectively.

"Okay, that's unsanitary," Tara laughed.

"Like you're one to talk! You just spat my own cum back into my mouth." Gabe laughed with her, leaning up on his elbow. "You're literally a walking wet dream. All my filthiest fantasies rolled into one intelligent," he bit her shoulder. "Argumentative," he kissed her collarbone. "Beautiful fucking person." He licked her neck up to her ear. "Who drinks wine while she rides my face."

Grabbing her around the waist, Gabe rolled them over so Tara lay on top of him. She let herself be held. Let him compliment her. Let him pepper her with kisses down her neck and bites on her collarbones and shoulders. She wasn't ready to move quite yet. Instead of talking, Tara pressed lazy kisses to his chest.

"Did I break you Kitten?"

She nodded. "I may never walk again."

"You don't need to walk, Kitten. I'll carry you everywhere."

Tara smiled up at him. "You won't even let me drive your car, and I'm supposed to believe you that you'll carry me for the rest of my life?"

"My car is a lot more valuable than I am," Gabe joked. Tara frowned. "Kitten, I know you wanted to ride me, but are you up for a change in plans? Position-wise I mean. I want to be inside you, but you seem spent after all that." He thrust against her, erection pressing against her hip.

Her legs might be jelly, but her cunt still clenched as she imagined him splitting her in half. "Green. Told you you'd be ready for me."

"You were right, Kitten." He rolled her on her side before reaching for the condom. "SSRIs got nothing on that fucking pussy of yours."

"You have the weirdest lines, dude," she teased, watching over her shoulder as he rolled the condom down that gorgeous cock, shivering with anticipation.

"And yet they always seem to work on you." Gabe kissed her shoulder and gently lifted her leg, giving himself room to push into her from behind.

Tara moaned as he slowly filled her, a delicious burn stretching her open. A hiss of pleasure sounded in her ear as he fucked her slowly. Gabe wrapped his arm around her, rolling her nipple with his thumb as his cock dragged slowly in and out of her.

This position was intoxicating but too soft, too sweet. She needed him deeper, faster. He needed to fuck the soft feelings out of her. She bucked against him, moaning as he gently bit and kissed her neck.

"Gabe, please. I need more of you."

His deep voice, viscous as honey, poured into her ear. "I hear you, Kitten. Facedown okay?"

"However you want. Just fuck me hard."

Gabe rolled her on her stomach, thrusting into her without missing a beat. She moaned loudly as he drove into her, hitting the spots deep inside where she needed him most.

Arm tightening around her hips, Gabe curled around her as he fucked her hard, but still oh so perfectly slow. Curly brown-black hair spilled into her vision, his head pressed into the pillow next to her. That honey voice hissed in her ear, grunting with each thrust, "I was going to be gentle. I was going to play with those cute tits while I fucked you slow. But you're so fucking needy, Kitten."

"Oh fuck, Gabe! You feel so fucking good like this," she choked out, face buried into the pillow so close to him that the corner of his lips brushed against hers.

Tara half turned out of instinct, but Gabe pulled away and sucked her earlobe between his teeth. A frustrated growl directly into her ear made her cunt clench around him.

His body pressed down against her, pinning her to the mattress as he pounded into her faster. His hips were slapping loudly against her ass. Pleasure fluttered every time his cock dragged against her, but it wasn't enough to pull her over the edge.

His deep timbre rumbled directly in her ear as Gabe murmured, "Touch yourself, Kitten. I need you to come again for me."

Wiggling a hand under her, she tried, but the angle was wrong; her fingers on her clit weren't enough. "I can't. I can't get it right like this."

"Tara, you are going to come before I do," Gabe commanded, the hint of desperation back as he reached into his nightstand. Buzzing filled the room. The cool silicone of a bullet vibe slid against her clit.

She let out a sob of pleasure. The buzzing against her clit combined with his relentless rhythm was too much. She wasn't sure how much she could take, but Tara needed it to go on forever.

"You have another one in you, I know you do. Please, I need to feel you come," Gabe panted into her ear, taking it between his teeth. "You feel so fucking good Kitten. Oh fuck. Please, Tara, come for me. I'm so close. You need to come so I can."

His deep voice saying her name in her ear like a prayer, so desperate and needy, was what broke her. She clamped down around him as another powerful orgasm tore through her. His name tore from her lips in an invocation of her own as she writhed under him. Gabe's hips stuttered against her and he groaned loudly, his cock tensing inside her as he came.

Gabe pulled the vibrator away, turning it off and tossing it aside as their shuddering slowed. His weight was still pressing her into the bed, that beautiful cock buried in her cunt like it belonged there. They panted together as he pinned her into the duvet.

Signing contentedly under him, Tara let herself enjoy being surrounded by him. She so rarely had been held like this in her life. She should have felt panicked, but with Gabe, she was safe.

"Sorry, I must be crushing you."

Tara shook her head into the pillow. "I like it."

A ghost of a kiss grazed her jaw as he lifted off of her. "I don't want to smother you."

Tara twitched when he slipped out of her gently and his comforting weight left the bed. The sound of running water splashed in the sink from the bathroom.

She stayed where he left her, the mattress dipping as he returned. Her alarm bells started to chime softly as his arms folded around her middle to pull her close. Tara let him hold her for only a moment before excusing herself to the bathroom, not meeting those brown eyes and the soft smile that followed her as she padded across the rug.

In the cold safety of his en suite, she put her head in her hands as she peed. This rush of fear wasn't her warning of a panic attack. Tara's chest ached, cold and sharp and cramping like a blast of winter air that stole her breath. The happy gooey feeling grew less comfortable now, growing tacky to trap her as the tile underfoot chilled her. Goosebumps prickled her bare skin.

Splashing her face with cold water, Tara gave herself another minute in the bathroom to figure out how to extract herself from the sweet generous man in the warm bed. From the cute house, with the cute dog. All of the things she'd never allowed herself to want, and now found herself undeniably longing for. She breathed, centering herself as she sat naked on the cold floor.

Inhale, 2, 3, 4, 5. She picked up the scattered feelings around her psyche, gathering them around her to be put away.

Exhale, 4, 3, 2, 1. She handled the easy ones first. Pain, hurt, fear, loneliness. The jealous, needy, hard emotions—her id companions who would corrupt any new soft feelings she didn't protect.

Inhale, 2, 3, 4, 5. She put away the longing, growing better acquainted with it, more fond of it, every time Gabe was sweet to her.

Exhale, 4, 3, 2, 1. Tara scooped up all of the soft feelings at once, the happy gooey feeling with them. These didn't need to be identified. Fear wouldn't allow her to do more than put them away anyway. Packing those away as neatly as she could, Tara buried her soft feelings down deep, protecting her fragile side from reality.

Satisfied, centered, and firmly over her moment of vulnerability, she stepped out of the bathroom. Tara steeled herself against the hurt that she'd find in Gabe's eyes when she told him she had to go.

But Gabe made everything easier by falling asleep while she was in the bathroom. She smiled at the breathy snores that interrupted the quiet of the room. Brushing a stray curl out of his face, she gazed at his lips. Parted softly as he breathed deep and steady, Gabe was more peaceful than she'd ever seen.

Tara had considered throwing their game too, half-tempted to let him win, just to see what it was like. Just to see if this lovely, confusing soul, who honored her boundaries more than anyone else, would be the one to show her how wonderful a kiss could be.

But fear had won out, because what if even Gabe, sweet and considerate and oh, so tempting, triggered a flashback? What hope would she have then?

Before she lost her nerve, before she ran, Tara allowed herself a moment of weakness. After all, he'd told her it was okay, hadn't he? That he wanted to kiss her? When she was ready to kiss him?

She pressed a gentle kiss to his lips, surprised at how right the soft skin felt against her own. His faint exhale, scented with her and him and the wine all mingled together, made Tara wish she was brave enough to do this when Gabe was awake. But no amount of longing, or any gooey soft feeling, would prevent a flashback if he kissed her back. When he'd use tongue, and she'd taste the blood and terror—

Tara sighed as she stepped away, pulling on her clothes in the silent room. She quietly closed the door, resisting the urge to get back into Gabe's soft bed. But staying now would make it that much harder to leave before sleep took her. Or worse, she'd scare him with the panic attack when she woke up in an unfamiliar place, with her duffel bag missing.

Besides, staying the night was shit that lovers did. That wasn't what they were.

Sunday, April Twenty-Sixth

Chapter Twenty-One

ANTONIO

Drying his hands on the towel, Antonio admired the now-sparkling kitchen with a happy sigh. The counter and stove were wiped down. The forgotten French toast was ready to be reheated for Lee's breakfast tomorrow, and the leftovers from the takeout they'd ordered for dinner were portioned out for Antonio to bring to work. All of the dishes were washed, dried, and put away, possibly even in the correct places in the cabinets.

Even his *fiancée* couldn't have done a better job. Elation erupted in his chest as Antonio touched the ring that hung on his neck. Lee had picked out a lovely ring—rose gold with a line of small diamonds in a channel setting. A perfect balance of masculine and feminine. He couldn't wait to show it off to everyone.

His grin fell.

Because he couldn't show it off to anyone, not yet. He had to plan and execute Lee's public grand gesture proposal before that ring could move from the chain around his neck to his finger.

Excitement battled with nerves as he brainstormed idea after idea. Lee didn't like corny. But all public proposals were corny. That was the point. Antonio had to find some way to show his love for Lee that was meaningful and sweet, but also authentic and cool enough that Lee wouldn't get any secondhand embarrassment from his grand gesture.

Not that he could outdo Lee's proposal, anyway. Lee had made him breakfast in bed, with the sparkling ring tucked into the strawberry garnish on the French toast. Lee had gotten down on one knee next to the bed and said…something incredibly sweet and meaningful.

Antonio had internally screamed so loudly the whole time that he couldn't remember a single word Lee had said. But he had cried, so it must have been beautiful. Whatever it was. And Lee'd been so cute and nervous, too, choking up when Antonio accepted with a sob. Tears had gathered in the corners of his lovely brown eyes as they'd kissed.

And then they'd forgotten about breakfast and lunch, instead devouring each other. Antonio barely remembered they had to go to work when he realized the brunch show had already started, but Lee had taken the day off for both of them. They'd languished in bed until their stomachs rumbled loudly in the afternoon, when they'd ordered enough Indian food to feed an army. Even now, Antonio wore only the ring around his neck, his drawers, and his house shoes. Lee was in a similar state of undress in the office. Minus a ring, of course, which Antonio now had to buy.

Antonio tucked the damp towel into the oven handle to dry. After their meal, Lee had remembered he needed to finish an update to a track the skeezy producer had asked for. He'd disappeared into the office to make the edits after Antonio had offered to clean up.

Adding "clean the kitchen" and "do dishes" to his side of the whiteboard on the fridge, Antonio checked them both off. Then wrote "Edit music" and "Tonio" to Lee's to-do list, adding four checkmarks next to his name with a grin. How had he ever done anything before Lee had helped him create a system? He certainly wouldn't have remembered to do the edits that their willing-to-be-professional business partner had asked for.

Lee sat hunched over the computer, headphones on and head bobbing. Antonio planted a kiss on Lee's temple as he rubbed his fiancée's shoulders and neck, smiling at the loud groan Lee let out when he dug a thumb into a knot. Lee was always so tense; Antonio loved making him relax. "I don't know how you're not tired of hearing our music yet."

Lee smiled up at him. "I could never get tired of your voice."

"Sweet talker." Antonio kissed his forehead. "Even *I'm* tired of my voice."

"You wanna hear the changes I made?" Lee asked. "Sleazebag wanted a key change in the breakdown and hi-hat on the offbeat."

Antonio nodded, grinning at Lee's nickname for their investor. He was so grateful for Lee's help in making his dreams come true, not only as the producer for their operation, but the buffer between him and his memories. He would never have gotten to this point, probably would never have even recorded the vocals, before giving up. Yet here they were, finalizing the last few tracks. Thanks to his type A work ethic, Lee had managed to not only get the vocal tracks to sound amazing, but he'd finished the whole damn album within a matter of months.

Sitting in Lee's lap, Antonio settled the headphones over his ears. Hearing his own singing voice for the thousandth time this week sounded nauseating, but Lee had worked so hard on it. To his relief, Lee started the song from the chorus before the breakdown.

"If I could trade you, make you see the Trade You,
you'd see the work you need to do to work!"

The chorus wasn't his favorite part of the song, but it was clever enough. Antonio preferred the raunchy couplets in the verses. That was the fun of house. It didn't need to rhyme perfectly, it didn't need a firm structure. And he could sing about sex and dick and all sorts of fun things.

Antonio had written "Trade You" while living in New York, when yet another uptight "straight" man had refused to reciprocate *after* Antonio had gotten him off. It had also morphed into a shady ode to Phineas, even though he wasn't truly trade. He just pretended that everything would be fine, if he could only find a magical trophy wife who met all of his needs and somehow garnered his parent's approval. But Antonio would never admit to Phineas that he'd inspired the song; he was sensitive. And reviewing their contracts pro bono.

While Lee worked his magic, Antonio had been networking with investors and promoters to get support with funding and marketing. The ones he liked were then connected with Phineas (for the contract negotiations) and Lee (for handling the specifics like content schedules and key changes). Antonio had the fun stuff; details and legalese were the worst.

Lee was somehow keeping time by tapping his thighs, even though he couldn't hear the music, knowing the song so intimately he could follow along from the screen. Antonio smiled, leaning into him. He'd never imagined finding someone who could actually turn the music in his head into something with real potential, let alone fall head over heels in love together. Who would put this much energy into a house album in this day and age, let alone one by a has-been drag queen? His fiancée took his music seriously in a way that Antonio hadn't even taken himself.

Antonio nodded along to the music as it hit the breakdown. This was his favorite part of the song. He dropped singing completely here and went into a spoken word rant about how trade guys couldn't even do the bare minimum.

"I don't want your love. I don't want your time. I just want your mouth, you can't even give me that. You want me to blow your mind, but your trade ass is too scared to even suck my dick? Don't come back without written permission from your therapist and your girlfriend!"

The key on the synth was just a half step higher than it had been, but it made a huge difference to the flavor. It tasted more like tamarind, more sour than bitter, exactly the mood he'd been going for. Antonio was annoyed that the creep had suggested it instead of Lee, but the song was better for it. The faint *tsst tsst* of the new hi-hat layer on the offbeat added a sparkle of citrus, bringing a bright, bubbly, grapefruit taste to the song.

Antonio took the headphones off. "In my professional opinion, that shit slaps."

Lee laughed. "Hopefully that asshole agrees. It's our third time changing this song for him. I hope it pays off."

"It will, Angel." Antonio rested his head against Lee's, staying put in his fiancée's lap. "We've put so much work into this, it has to pay off. Who knows, maybe next year, we'll be rich and famous."

"Do you *want* to be rich and famous?" Lee asked, skeptically.

Antonio shook his head. "Not anymore. I'm not cut out for that. I just want to be the best at everything I do."

Lee laughed. "Then I'll do everything I can to support you. Because you are the best, and the world needs to know it, too."

Antonio grinned, sighing with pleasure as Lee's hands slid around his waist to pull him back against the erection growing against his thigh. "Go on."

Lee nodded, kissing down his neck. "The best singer. The best drag queen. The best teacher. The best lover and the best fiancée."

"You and that sweet mouth, Angel." Antonio took Lee's glasses off, setting them on the desk as he turned to straddle his fiancée's lap. Lee kissed him, hand sliding up his thighs to tug the elastic of his drawers. Antonio stopped him, breaking the kiss. "I love you, but I do not have another round in me. Let me take care of you."

Lee pouted, but his hands swept across the skin of Antonio's back instead.

"Close your eyes." Once Lee's eyes were squeezed shut, Antonio settled the headphones over Lee's ears and found the audio track he wanted on Lee's computer: the "accidental" ASMR recording of them fucking in the closet when Lee had joined him to record ad libs. They'd listened to it frequently, recording a couple more risqué tracks before dismantling the equipment.

"Really?" Lee laughed, keeping his eyes closed. "I dunno what else I expected."

Antonio simply slid off his thighs. Tapping Lee's hips to lift up so he could pull off his shorts, he wrapped his fist around Lee's already half-hard dick. Lee's hand gently cupped his cheek. A soft, sweet groan escaped him as Antonio took him slowly into his mouth. Joy fluttered in his chest at Lee's brown eyes smiling down at him, kneeling between his fiancée's legs. His hand trailed down to trace the chain around Antonio's neck.

Antonio's hand found his, tangling their fingers together. He'd never imagined he could be so happy.

RICHARD

"HERE, THIS IS FOR you." Richard held out a small gift bag as Sunny packed up her belongings, scattered around his living room.

"What's this?" She narrowed her eyes, her gaze darting between him and the gift.

"A present." He proffered the bag to her again.

Sunny didn't take it. "Obviously. But what kind of present?"

"You have to open it, Sunny. That's what you do with presents." Richard grabbed her hand and hung the bag on her fingers, steering her to the couch to sit down. He was already overthinking this in the first place; having to explain it would only make it worse.

Sunny huffed as she curled into the black leather sofa. "I just want to know what I'm getting into. It's obviously not a sex toy, because I'm about to go home."

Richard held back a smile as he sat next to her. "Right, those presents are gifts for *us*."

She laughed. "Oh, so this is just for me?"

At Richard's nod, Sunny slowly pulled out the white tissue paper until she found a jewelry box. Her eyebrows raised into her hairline. She yanked the top of the box off and threw it over her shoulder. "Did you buy me a bracelet?"

Richard nodded again as she pulled the delicate gold tennis bracelet from the box. Diamonds twinkled from her fingers.

"I can't take this." Sunny stood up and circled the coffee table, looking at the bracelet clenched in her fingers.

"You can't take this," Richard repeated carefully, skin burning as he tried to wrap his head around her response.

"Are we doing, like, jewelry, now?" Sunny huffed as she paced circles around the couch. "Is that what this is?"

Why was it so hot in here? Richard couldn't decipher Sunny's expression, or her question. But their unlabeled "this" of a relationship could feasibly include jewelry. The bracelet wasn't even the part he was worried about. Maybe the itch under his skin was all in his head. He tried to sound more confident than he felt when he said, "I thought that was obvious," but it still came out a sullen mutter.

"Oh." Red flooded Sunny's cheeks as she finally stopped pacing and stared at him, chewing her lip. "So, this isn't just sex?"

Sweat prickled Richard's back. He choked as he tried to scoff, but it only came out as a squawk, adding humiliation to his overwhelming confusion. "No, of course not!"

"Oh." Sunny froze, halting her pacing. Lips pursed, her head tilted further and further the longer she stared at him.

Richard glanced down at his feet, feeling so exposed in only sweatpants and slippers. "Is that what this is for *you*?" He hated to ask, but he had to know. He couldn't imagine how or when he'd given the impression that they weren't together.

Sunny huffed as she took up pacing again. "Well, maybe at first."

"At first?" Richard's hands trembled. He sat on them, gripping his hamstrings.

"Well, not anymore!" Sunny huffed, stomping around the living room. "No wonder you've been so damn sweet! I thought I was being delusional when I let myself catch feelings. I had no idea you actually liked me!"

"I wouldn't spend every weekend with someone I didn't like." Richard's neck ached from turning to watch her circle the couch.

"Yeah, I get that *now!*" Sunny gesticulated. "But that doesn't mean you can just give me shit like this! This is something the Mafia Boss Billionaire gives Working Class Barbie in a dumb rom-com before he pulls a Sir Save-a-Ho. I like you, but I don't need a white savior."

"I have no idea what that means." Richard let out a huff of his own, trying to quell his nerves and confusion. Jewelry was supposed to be a default gift, but apparently not when he was using her for sex. "So, you don't like the bracelet."

Sunny shook her head. "No! I mean, yes? I do. Kind of. It's a lot, I guess? I don't know."

"I can take that part of it back if it makes you more comfortable," Richard offered carefully. No one else he'd ever bought a trinket for had ever reacted like this. But then again, no one else he'd dated had thought they weren't dating. Richard gripped the fabric of his sweatpants. He would be analyzing every second of every interaction they'd ever had every night for the rest of his life, until he figured out where he'd gone wrong.

Sunny huffed again, her eyebrows raising. "'That part of it?' What else is there?"

Richard gestured to the bag, swallowing hard to steady his voice. "You have to keep looking."

Sunny picked up the bag she'd abandoned on the coffee table. Pulling out more tissue paper, she unwrapped a cat-shaped keychain. A key and an elevator fob dangled from it. "A key?"

Richard squirmed; a key should be self-explanatory. "So you don't have to wait for me when I'm running late from work."

"That was one time!" Sunny protested, hand covering her mouth.

"Shouldn't have happened at all." Richard ran a hand through his hair to cool his scalp. "I was going to give you the key regardless, but then I bought Tara a candle for her birthday, and it felt weird to buy her something but not you."

Sunny looked at him like he had two heads. "So you bought me a diamond bracelet because you didn't want me to feel left out?"

Richard shrugged, still trying unsuccessfully to decipher what was going through Sunny's mind. And his own. When she put it that way, it didn't sound right, but he couldn't quite figure out how to verbalize the distinction. He'd been shopping for Tara, but kept finding gifts he wanted to buy Sunny. And since he wasn't sure what she'd want, he'd settled on the bracelet. His mom always said that jewelry was the best "just because" gift.

"And the key because you don't want me to have to wait in the hallway if I get here before you again?"

Richard nodded. Again, there was nuance missing, but it might take him years to discover the words for it.

"Okay. Sorry. Okay. Okay." Sunny resumed pacing. "Sorry. This has been a very confusing conversation. I'm going from pining after my fuck buddy to getting a key to your place in the span of five minutes, and my brain is not processing this well."

Richard held out his hands. "Sit down, Sunny. You're making me dizzy."

"Sorry." She huffed, her palms slapping against his as she finally stopped pacing to take his hands.

He wasn't sure if her hands were clammy too, or if his anxiety sweat alone made their fingers slip as he pulled her toward him. "Stop apologizing."

"Asshole." She sat in his lap.

Richard snorted as he wrapped his arms around her, pressing a kiss into the bare skin along the strap of her dress. Sunny in his arms always settled him.

"I just..." That timidity that made him want to protect her from everything bad in the world was back in her voice, and Richard hated himself for causing it. "I can't do this, if that's what this is."

Breathing hurt, each pull forced sharp into his lungs. He should have never gotten her a key. What had he been thinking, buying her a bracelet? He'd ruined everything. "You can't do this."

"I *want* to. I do. I just... My mae wouldn't approve. Your family wouldn't approve."

Richard scoffed. "My family doesn't matter."

"But mine does." Sunny fiddled with the key in her hand, her thumb tracing the outlines of the cats. "My whole life, I've known that one day I'm going to have to be the person my mae and my grandparents need me to be. I'm going to have to get married to a nice girl they approve of and have kids. My life isn't just mine like it is yours."

"Is that what you want?"

Sunny's shrug was halfhearted. "Yeah, kinda. I wanna do it my way, in my own time. That's why this wasn't supposed to be serious." She looked up at him, her dark eyes watering. "I thought you just wanted casual, so this could be safe and fun. So when it ended, shit would be awkward, but I would get over it. But I like you, and you make me happy, and I don't want to give this up." Sunny looked at her lap, biting her lower lip.

"Then don't." His thumb was there, pulling it from between her teeth, before Richard could consider if he should.

"Richard..." Sunny sighed.

Richard's heart clenched. She only called him Richard when she was serious. "Give me a chance, Sunny. I know I'm not..." He paused, searching for the words. "I may not be who your mom expects, but I want to get married and have kids one day, too, and parents usually like me."

Granted, not his own, and the only parents he'd ever met were Gabe's and Antonio's. But both the Coopers and the Floreses had taken him in like another son. And well, he had to try, because he wanted her and she wanted him, and that should be enough. It *was* enough, for him.

Cupping her chin to draw her gaze to him, Richard pulled her lip from between her teeth with his thumb yet again. "I'm not saying you need to introduce me to your family right now or commit to a future together, but let me prove that I am serious about you. Let me take you on that date we always talk about, and then never go on because we'd rather stay in than go out in public."

Sunny laughed quietly.

"Next Friday, we'll do a real date. Get drinks at some fancy place after work, and I'll make dinner afterward."

"I still don't believe you can cook," Sunny teased, a smile playing on her lips.

"As long as you only want pasta, I can cook whatever you want." Richard pressed a kiss to her wrist. The key in her hand flashed in the sunlight. "But if you've been under the impression that this was casual, I need to do better. So let me be better."

After giving him a long, contemplative look, Sunny held up the bracelet again. "Are these real diamonds?"

"As if I'd buy anything else."

"You're such a snob," Sunny chuckled and rolled her eyes. "Then that settles it. I can't take this. It's too much. You have to return it." Sunny looked at the keychain in her other hand, two cats forming a yin-yang in her palm. "I'll keep this though. I like the keychain."

"So the gift was *too* nice. Diamonds were the problem." Richard was relieved she was keeping the key. Their undefined "this" wasn't over yet, even if she needed time to think about what she wanted. He should have known Sunny would need something more meaningful than a bracelet. He'd have to find the perfect gift to tell her how he felt. *Since I somehow gave the impression this was just sex.*

Sunny laughed. "Exactly. How dare you spend so much money on an ethically-bankrupt oligopoly like the diamond industry?"

"I should have gotten you a gag instead."

Sunny turned to him with a grin. "Oh, there's an idea for something you can add to the list. A diamond-encrusted gag. Ooh! Or butt plug."

Richard laughed, relieved Sunny was coming back to herself, back to him. "Lab-created, I presume."

"Of course. I don't want blood diamonds in my ass."

Friday, May First

CHAPTER TWENTY-TWO

SUNNY

IS THIS DAY EVER going to end? Sunny pulled back the sticky note covering the clock on her computer. Another two hours and twelve minutes before she could leave the greige hellscape of her cubicle for her date. Brushing her thumb against her smile, Sunny spun in her chair, unable to concentrate on her work.

Why was she nervous? She and Richard had been regularly hanging out at his condo for months. He was buying her diamond bracelets for no reason, and he'd given her the key to his apartment. Meeting for drinks after work shouldn't feel like a big deal.

But it was. It was a *date*. Because they were...together? In a relationship?

Sunny stood up, the chair banging on the cabinet behind her, closing the Richard tab in her head. She needed to move. Thinking herself into circles would do her no good.

"You're looking cute today, Sunny!" Asha, the only person at work Sunny somewhat considered a friend, complimented her as she strolled into the break area for a cup of tea. "Love the jacket!"

"Thanks, Asha!" Sunny spun around to show off her outfit. She hadn't intended to wear anything extra special; she still had to work and therefore had planned to wear the usual boring sweatshirt and khakis. Even Asha never wore anything flashier than a patterned headscarf. Outside of work, Asha was glamorously feminine; both of them dressed down to fit in.

This morning, though, Sunny couldn't help herself. She'd traded a bland sweatshirt for her prized Mugler denim jacket she had scored at the thrift store, and tight black pants that highlighted the curve of her hips.

"Got a date or something?" Asha teased.

Sunny couldn't hide her smile at the question. "No, not really," she lied. "Just getting drinks after work."

"Oh, sounds fun." Asha looked like she didn't believe her. Probably because Sunny was grinning like an idiot. Like she always did when she thought about Richard. Thankfully, Asha changed the subject, telling her about the client from hell she had.

As much as Sunny burned to tell Asha (well, tell everyone in her life) about Richard, she had to keep it to herself. Sunny was in over her head when it came to him, but Richard was still her secret. Telling anyone would make it real, and Sunny couldn't imagine that they'd survive being real. Even if she was absolutely burning to tell everyone she knew, so someone would tell her what to do.

Mae would flip out. Lee would tell her she was delusional and reading too much into it. Tara would say she should just enjoy the sex and not overthink it. And Blanche? Well, who knew what Blanche thought? That would require confiding in them, and Sunny didn't need her ex's approval. She wanted to know what *Richard* thought.

Historically, picking up on emotional cues was not Sunny's strong suit. *I can barely tell what I'm feeling half the time.* She tried to read the smile in his eyes when Richard refused to put it on his lips. To hear the laughter in his voice because his genuine cackle was so rare. He played everything so close to the chest; until last weekend, she'd been under the impression their situationship was casual. On Sunday, his face had been even more robotic than usual, other than the flush of his skin and the tension in his eyes. Even now, they hadn't exactly said what they were. If she took his words at face value, he seemed serious about her. Sunny just wasn't sure she could afford to be serious about him.

If her mae found out, they'd have to break up. If his parents caught wind, he'd have to risk getting disowned from the sound of it. And in the likely event they broke up, Sunny would be left heartbroken. She'd be heartbroken regardless, but a heartbreak now, when they weren't committed, might hurt less than a heartbreak after she'd decided to keep Richard in her life.

Maybe Mae would come around eventually; she needed Sunny, though a lifetime of guilt trips didn't exactly sound fun. And would Richard stick around through that? When he had his own family to deal with? He said he didn't care what they thought, but... She would want to be a part of his life, too. If they did...whatever it was they might do. A future, or whatever. Marriage and kids and all that meant being a part of his family.

Sunny stirred honey into her tea as Asha ranted on. "And he keeps asking for my cell number so he can text me for updates instead of emailing. Like, he already harasses me enough on my desk phone!"

"What a dick!" Sunny sympathized, though she hadn't been listening at all. Luckily, this client was a recurring topic for Asha. "I wish you could end client contracts for being tools."

Asha laughed. "Same. Thank you for listening, Sunny. The guys on my team don't think he's doing anything inappropriate. They just keep telling me it's normal guy behavior, so I'm just crazy, you know?"

Fuck yeah, nailed that. She totally thinks I was listening. "You're not crazy at all." Sunny sipped her tea. "Have you told your manager?"

"Of course! But he told me it's part of working in tech." With a shake of her head, Asha checked her phone. "Time to dash. Got a call with the devil himself."

"Good luck! Maybe record the calls—make him behave."

"Thanks Sunny! You should tell me the next time you dress up. I'll do it with you. Feminine solidarity in this old boys' club, you know?"

"Yes! We totally should!" Sunny grinned. "Want to do it next Friday?"

Asha grinned as she left. "Yes! Femme Friday, I love it. Have a fun date!"

Sunny didn't correct her. *It is a date, after all.* She checked her phone with a sigh. Two more hours. But, she also had a Discord message from Black_Hawk. A chat with him would make the day go faster, and maybe she could ask him about Richard. He knew about her situationship and would give good advice...probably. She opened the message as she walked back to her cubicle with her tea.

Black_Hawk_Up88: Hey Sunny. Can I vent to you about something? I don't have anyone IRL to complain to about this other

> than my therapist, who makes me self-reflect, and I just want
> someone to be blunt with me.
> **Sunnywith0meatballs**: Omg yes please!!! Entertain me with your
> problems!

Typing furiously, Sunny shot off the message before logging back into her computer. She opened her cursor jiggler script, just in case he replied quickly. She knew herself; she'd get distracted. Especially if Black_Hawk let her vent about her problems in return. Considering she was in the midst of her own existential relationship crisis, Sunny doubted she was qualified to give Black_Hawk advice. But he'd asked, and she wouldn't pass up the chance.

His "typing..." status appeared instantly. Sunny settled back in her chair, keeping her phone in her lap where her coworkers couldn't see it. She put on her best "I'm thinking really hard face" paired with "don't bother me" posture, pulling on her headphones for good measure.

> **Black_Hawk_Up88**: Tell me if I'm being a whiny asshole.
> **Sunnywith0meatballs**: You're being a whiny asshole.
> **Black_Hawk_Up88**: Ha ha ha. Thanks. /s
> **Sunnywith0meatballs**: JK! What's up?
> **Black_Hawk_Up88**: Remember the mind-blowing life-changing
> sex conversation last year?
> **Sunnywith0meatballs**: The time you caught feelings for mid-nut?
> **Black_Hawk_Up88**: ...yes. Well, lucky me—it happened again
> recently. Same person and everything. Only now we're like sorta
> friends and shit? And I'm struggling to keep my feelings from
> getting in my way. They don't want a relationship, and I know
> I'd fuck it up even if they did. But they're fucking amazing. And
> I'm trying not to take the emotional gap personally. Like I know
> we need to keep it casual, but my stupid fucking sensitive feelings
> are upset about it.
> **Sunnywith0meatballs**: So how are you an asshole?
> **Black_Hawk_Up88**: I haven't been in the best headspace around
> them and kinda take it out on them.
> **Sunnywith0meatballs**: It can't be that bad. They still slept with
> you.
> **Black_Hawk_Up88**: Well, I've been trying to be better lately
> about not being an ass, and we were getting to a better place, but

then I let my dick think for me. And now I'm hurt and angry (at myself) and that usually turns into asshole behavior.
Sunnywith0meatballs: With that attitude, yeah you probably will turn into an asshole, but so far you're just whiny. :)
Black_Hawk_Up88: Thanks.... T.T
Sunnywith0meatballs: Honestly, if you need to step back from them to protect yourself, do it. You have to prioritize yourself. Mind-blowing sex isn't worth ruining a friendship over. Or your mental health.
Black_Hawk_Up88: Speaking from experience on that with your own FWB situation?
Sunnywith0meatballs: We might be dating now. IDRK. I'm very confused.
Black_Hawk_Up88: ...again?

Sunny choked on her offended laugh. A few heads turned in her direction over the cubicles, but she ignored them.

Sunnywith0meatballs: iorhjtgoirjogs shut up this is different from last time!!!! At least I think so???jiojg oirjgoiejtoifdrjsfjg how dare you
Black_Hawk_Up88: Are you sure it's different?
Sunnywith0meatballs: Yes? I think? I just... I like them a lot. And they like me. But right now it's fun and easy and even though I def caught feelings, idk if it's worth the future angst to let it become serious.
Black_Hawk_Up88: So how do you know when to give up on it or when to enjoy it for what it is? Like, what's different about this one that's making it work when the other one didn't? Asking for myself. This conversation is still about me, remember.
Sunnywith0meatballs: Fuck if I know. My current SO and I will have some angst in the future, but right now it's just fun and easy. So...I guess I'll cross that bridge when we burn it?
Sunnywith0meatballs: I made mistakes with my ex, but it was a good learning experience so I'm not regretful about how it went down. And we're still close friends, so it worked out, but we chose to make it work out that way. It was intentional.
Sunnywith0meatballs: So be intentional? And evaluate if the friendship would outlast the angst of breaking things off. Or if

endless pining would be worth the friendship. Protect yourself with space if you need, but don't shut out room for joy if that's an option.

Black_Hawk_Up88: Sounds like what my therapist said. I'm not ready for joy lmao. Last weekend was an emotional roller coaster. I was vulnerable with them. They were vulnerable with me. And then they just left right after, like it meant nothing.

Black_Hawk_Up88: I keep telling myself they didn't leave me, and it's not something I did, but that's how it feels, and I can't get out of the funk, even though it was my fault because I knew I can't do casual. Sorry, I'm being whiny. Limerence sucks.

Sunnywith0meatballs: It's okay to be whiny and in your feelings. Just don't be an asshole.

Black_Hawk_Up88: lol No promises. So what's your future angst with your SO? If you don't mind me asking. Distract me from myself.

Oh boy, where to start? Sunny wondered how to explain her and Richard's family situations. She didn't fully understand it herself; she'd been trying not to think about it.

Sunnywith0meatballs: Let's just say neither of our families will approve. You know how my mom is. They meet none of her requirements for a future in-law. And their family seems really um... 1% level rich. Elitist. White. And I can't do that world. No offense if you're white. lol

Black_Hawk_Up88: Ha, I can pass. I don't want to, but people see what they want to see when they look at me. So no offense taken. I know what you mean. My mom's family was elitist like that. And my dad was not son-in-law material. But they made it work, even after my mom's family disowned her for marrying someone they didn't approve of.

Sunnywith0meatballs: See, that is exactly what I don't want to happen. I don't want to be responsible for that shit.

Black_Hawk_Up88: It wouldn't be your fault. It's their choice if they want to be shitty parents and disown their child. Your SO and their parents make their choices. You only can choose how to be there for them if their parents do suck ass.

Sunnywith0meatballs: I hadn't thought of it that way. Thank you.
Black_Hawk_Up88: Likewise! Thanks friend. Anyway gotta go, my boss is calling me. Gotta get some after-market trades in before she tears me a new one.
Sunnywith0meatballs: Sounds like some stock market shit. I'll retreat to my coding where we speak English lol

Sunny set her phone down after checking the time. Fifty minutes left. A new email was in her inbox too. Her boss was asking for an update on a script she'd forgotten to work on that she had to finish before she left. *Whoops.*

So Black_Hawk wasn't the white incel neckbeard she used to imagine he was. He had a grown-up job, a presumably active sex life, and went to therapy. And he could relate to her situation, strangely enough, through his parents. None of it was what she'd expected.

They didn't often share personal details with each other—just the stuff that actually mattered. But she was curious to learn more about him, especially with the "passing" comment he made. Sunny "passed" as a cis woman well enough when she had to; sometimes it was safer to pass, especially being a Thai woman. She was subjected to enough sexual harassment for that without the ladyboy comments.

Sunny just wanted to be authentically herself, as a proud trans woman who didn't have to pass. Like she did today. Dressed femme and glamorous and still kicking ass at her job. It was a nice change from her usual work uniform. Maybe she—

Her computer lit up with an incoming IM, asking for an update.
Oh fuck! The script! Focus!

Sunny practically skipped to the new cocktail bar that had recently opened a few blocks from her office. *Bubbles and Fizz. That's some gentrification shit.* Richard sat at a table on the sidewalk patio, the bougiest-looking vodka cran already waiting for her. It was warm for early May; his navy suit jacket was draped across the back of his chair, the sleeves of his white shirt rolled up neatly to his elbow. *Those forearms should be considered public indecency.*

"Sorry, I'm a little late. Had to finish up some bullshit at work." She bent down so he could kiss her cheek. "Thanks for the drink!"

"Busy day at work?" he asked, leaning back in his hair. Tension left his shoulders as Sunny sat across from him.

She shook her head. "No, I wish. It was so slow. I just forgot about it. You know when you're so bored at work that you forget to do the work you have? I shouldn't complain about not being busy, but the day was dragging."

"I can't say I've ever experienced a slow day," Richard said, taking in her outfit. "How unusual. You look...nice. Not emo today?"

Sunny snorted. All of her non-work outfits were admittedly a little scene. But it's not like she'd been able to wear them when she was younger. "You're so charming, asshole. I can't exactly go to work looking like I live at Hot Topic."

"So you wore the Mugler jacket for me, then?" Richard smiled wider. "And here I thought you frowned upon designer clothes."

Sunny rolled her eyes. Of course, he could tell it was Mugler. "Don't flatter yourself, Dicky. I didn't dress up for you." *Liar.* "And it's from a thrift store. I only frown upon paying full price for designer clothes."

Richard made a face. "Someone donated that to a thrift store? That's disrespectful. Good thing you rescued it."

With a laugh, Sunny's manic anxiety from earlier slowly unwound, letting her relax for the first time since Sunday. Richard always kept her on her toes, getting a rise out of her without actually pissing her off. Being with him felt...right. How could she give that up? "So how was your day? Make millions of dollars for a billionaire? Steal from the poor? Send some small mom-and-pop store out of business?"

Richard's blue eyes twinkled in a hidden smile. "No, mostly just meetings that could have been emails. Listened to people complain about regulations that we can't change. Interviewed some candidates for a job they'll hate, that sort of thing. Very middle management day."

"Corporate hell is universal." Sunny nodded. "Did you have lunch with Gabe?"

Richard nodded. "He's been in one of his moods this week, so it was quiet. His flock of straight girls must think we're having relationship troubles, because they've been giving me dirty looks all week."

Sunny laughed. If his coworkers had thought he was dating anyone but Gabe, she might have been jealous. But Gabe, despite his history with Richard, didn't make her feel the least insecure. "Is he okay?"

Richard shrugged. "He'll bounce back. I wish his manager was more understanding. She acts like the people under her should be robots. But there's nothing I can do about it, aside from document everything she says. Gabe won't because he doesn't want to be 'too much.'"

"Has he always been so sensitive?" She didn't know Gabe very well yet. He was nice to Sunny, always asking her questions about her interests and hobbies. But it was always one-sided; Gabe didn't give up any personal details. She needed to get to know him better, especially since he was Richard's best friend.

And to make sure he was good enough for Tara. Gabe may be an attractive himbo, but he could be moody. Tara and emotions were oil and water.

Richard nodded. "He used to be more resilient when we were younger. Staying single for once in his damn life, instead of jumping feetfirst into a relationship, has been good for him."

"That's impressive. Maybe Tara should take a page out of his book," Sunny quipped.

"Oh, is she seeing someone? I didn't know." Richard frowned.

Sunny shook her head. "Oh, no! She only does casual short-term flings. Very short-term. Like an hour, max."

Richard sat back in his chair, scratching his chin. "Hm, that surprises me. She seems like such a homebody, like talking to strangers is painful."

"She doesn't historically do much talking, if you know what I mean. Although, I haven't seen her flirt with strangers in a—" Sunny paused. *That's odd.* Tara had never been subtle about her encounters. When was the last time Tara had hooked up with anyone? Last year? Sunny had thought the slowdown stemmed from her attempts to "date," which really just meant having a conversation before fucking someone. Tara usually told Sunny about her encounters, so she hadn't banged anyone at all as far Sunny knew since...September? Granted, Sunny hadn't hung out with Tara since they'd went thrifting last month. Maybe she was just out of the loop. "Wow, I'm just realizing I have no idea what's going on with her."

Richard's lips twitched. "Have I been monopolizing your time? Want me to bring you to her place, instead of coming back to mine?"

Sunny made a face. "Don't you dare. You promised me you'd cook. You can't back out now." She'd been looking forward to this all week, even if she was unsure where they stood. She fully planned on teasing him for how bad it was, even if it was good.

"Please don't expect anything fancy." Richard picked up her hand and kissed her wrist. "At least not compared to that trip to Chicago I promised you."

Her heart fluttered. *Emotionally unavailable, my ass. Is this what dating Richard is like? He's a fucking simp when he puts his mind to it.* "Can I touch your face?" At his nod, she cupped his jaw and drew his face close to kiss him.

Just as her lips brushed against Richard's, a voice interrupted them. "Sunny?"

Her mother and Luna were gawking at the two of them from the other side of the fenced-off patio. The blood drained from Sunny's face. "Mae! Luna! What are you doing there?" Her chair scraped the concrete as Sunny stood up.

Mae was supposed to be at work; she was even wearing scrubs under her coat. And Luna was supposed to be studying for finals. But no, they stood, still as statues, on the sidewalk amidst the bustle of rush hour foot traffic snaking around them. Birdie stared silently at Richard. Luna's eyes flicked back and forth, widening with realization.

"We're on our way home from the chiropractor. Mae has been having some back pain," Luna explained, stuffing her hands into her hoodie pocket. "So...we should get you home, so you can lay down, Mae! Let's go!"

"Mae, you didn't tell me that! Are you okay?" Worry crept into the maelstrom of panic; her mother usually told her all of her complaints. Repeatedly. *Granted, she hasn't really been talking to me lately.*

Birdie's sharp eyes snapped to her. "You're never home anymore, Sunny. How am I supposed to tell you when I never see you?"

Sunny bit her lip as Richard rose slowly to stand beside her. The guilt trip was already grating, and it had barely begun. "I would've gone with you if you told me. You shouldn't pull Luna out of class because you want someone with you. She has finals soon!"

"It's fine, Sunny. I studied in the waiting room." Luna was always the peacemaker.

Guilt ate at her that she hadn't been there for her mom, hadn't even known she was in pain. *I should be the one to take care of Mae. It's my responsibility. Luna shouldn't have to parent her, too. She's just a kid.*

"Who's this?" Her mom asked in Thai, pointing to Richard with her chin.

Fuck, I didn't think about how I'd introduce them! Sunny gripped the cuffs of her jacket. "Mae, this is Richard Carter. Richard, this is my mother Birdie and my sister Luna."

"Pleasure to meet you, ma'am." Richard stood up, hand outstretched.

Mae didn't take it, staring coldly at his hand. "Is he someone from work?" She spoke English this time, so they could all hear the hint that Richard better not be anyone important.

Sunny sighed, hating that she was being forced to make this choice so soon. She hadn't even had a chance to let herself be with Richard in every sense. He was supposed to cook her dinner, and take her on a romantic getaway. Maybe they'd tell their friends. If they lasted through everything, lasted long enough, maybe eventually she'd work up the courage to let Mae into this part of her life.

But no. Sunny swallowed thickly. Like everything, their relationship was out of sequence. They'd either figure it out, or they wouldn't. It was do it all backward, or not do it at all, and Sunny... Well, Sunny wanted it all. "Richard is my boyfriend."

Richard glanced at her, his face unreadable, hand still outstretched in greeting to her mother. She hoped that hadn't been a misstep. But she wasn't going to lie to her mother and pretend Richard was no one to her. If this was what he wanted, he could witness her humiliation and heartbreak firsthand and decide if it was worth it.

"Boyfriend!" Her mother turned on her, scolding her in mostly Thai with a few English words sprinkled in. "I do so much for you and here you are—directly disobeying me. Disrespecting your phaw's memory! Your grandparents!" Sunny looked at her feet, iron flooding her mouth as she bit her lip. "You're supposed to find a nice girl and here you are kissing this white boy? And calling him your boyfriend? Oh, what will your yâa say? She already thinks I've given you too much freedom! This isn't how I raised you, Arthit!"

Her birth name punched Sunny in the heart. Shame tightened her throat as she struggled to breathe. "Mae, please. Can this wait until we're home?" she muttered shakily in Thai, hoping no one around spoke it. Sunny didn't want to make more of a scene. If she didn't stop her, she'd get yelled at for allowing Mae to lose face in public too. Tears burned her eyes.

Luna came to her rescue and shook Richard's still outstretched hand. "Richard, lovely to meet you," she said in English, a bit too loudly and too cheerily. "We'll have to have you over for dinner sometime. Come on, Mae, let's leave Sunny to her date!" She wound her arm around Birdie's waist and dragged her halfway down the block, before Sunny or her mother could register what was happening.

"You owe me!" Luna mouthed over her shoulder.

"Thank you!" Sunny mouthed back, pressing her hands together in thanks. She did owe Luna. Big time. She'd spared Sunny the humiliation of being flayed alive in front of Richard. Her baby sister wasn't supposed to bear that responsibility, or *any* responsibility. Sunny was supposed to take care of her, not the other way around.

Sunny took a deep breath and stared into her lap. Richard's hand on her back guided her down into her chair. Her emotions were everywhere, pinging around her heart from guilt to shame to fear. "I'm so sorry." A teardrop darkened the fabric of her jeans.

"Honestly, she's nicer than my dad. I couldn't follow what she said, but she wasn't ready to chuck anything like he would have." With a gentle hand on her chin, Richard drew her gaze up. Concern swam in his face. "Are you okay?" He dabbed at her eyes with a cocktail napkin.

Fuck. Her mascara must be ruined, too. "I'm so embarrassed. That's not exactly how I wanted to introduce you to my mother."

Richard gave her a gentle smile. "Not exactly how I wanted to introduce myself either."

Sunny laughed a little. He was being nicer than he should be, given the situation. She shook her head and took a breath to steel her heart. "I was hoping to ease you into meeting them if we ever got there, you know? She's just a lot. *I'm* a lot. I get it if this was too much... If you don't want *this* with me. If you just want to be friends or whatever."

"I don't." Richard frowned. Her heart sank. It must have shown on her face, because he quickly clarified, "I mean, I'm not following your logic. Sunny, I enjoy being with you. I wanted to meet your mom and your sister. I meant what I said last weekend, and maybe these weren't the ideal circumstances, but you warned me that your mom wouldn't approve. That doesn't change how I feel about you." Richard stroked his thumb over her fingers. "And besides, you're my *girlfriend,* not my friend."

"Sorry. We hadn't talked about that yet either." Sunny blushed.

"We should have talked about it sooner, but I wasn't sure if I should press it. Obviously, communication is not a strength of ours. I thought it was obvious we've been together for months now, so call me whatever label you want." His blue eyes looked thoughtfully at her, hand still covering hers.

Sunny's heart thumped in her chest as his calm confidence washed over her. Maybe she'd been underestimating his feelings. Her hope had felt delusional, and she wasn't sure she could trust it. But here, with Richard looking at her like that, being so open with her, she felt foolish that she'd ever questioned this. Even if Mae didn't approve, and may never approve, Richard was here and still caring about her. She could at least pretend everything would be fine, even if it might not turn out to be. With a small smile, she asked, "So, does that mean I can meet your parents?"

"Hell no."

"Oh." Sunny's heart dropped.

Richard huffed. "Sorry. I didn't mean it that way! I meant, no way in hell would I ever subject you to my family. I don't even subject *myself* to them unless I absolutely have to. I haven't spoken with my brother in years, I only talk to my dad when I need something, and my mother and I get together once a year because she insists on a 'girls brunch' for my birthday, and if I don't go, she shows up to my work."

"Oh." Sunny hadn't realized how little contact he had with them.

Richard rubbed the back of his neck. "But, Gabe's parents invited me to a fundraiser for the Modern Art Institute next month."

Sunny's stomach was still in knots, unsure why he wanted her to meet *Gabe's* parents. "Won't Gabe be there?"

Richard nodded. "Probably, but if you're okay with him finding out, I want him to know, too. The Coopers are more family to me than anyone I'm biologically related to."

Sunny's grin widened. "I'd love to, in that case! But I have no idea how to act rich. What do you do at fundraisers?"

"Have dinner. Drink wine. Donate money for a tax break." That ghost of a smile appeared. "You don't need to act rich. Just be yourself."

"That's so cheesy," Sunny teased. "You should still tell me if I do something that makes me stick out, though. I can be myself and pretend I fit in."

"Trust me, Miriam will like you." Richard shrugged. "And eventually your mom might like me. Like I said, she wasn't as bad as my dad would have been."

"Please, that was Mae with an audience." Sunny scoffed and put on a small smile. She couldn't believe he still wanted to be with her after Mae's scene. She owed Luna big. But with a resigned sigh, reality crept back in. "I'm sorry to ruin our date, but I should go home. Might as well get the yelling and guilt trips started."

Richard nodded. "I could come with you."

Sunny smiled. Mae would eat him alive. "No, I'm good at zoning out once she gets going. I'll survive." She swept a stray lock of blond hair out of his eyes. "And if my talk with her tonight goes better than I expect, maybe we can properly introduce you soon? I think she actually might like you, given the chance."

Sunny smiled as Richard kissed her wrist before she could draw away. "I'd like that."

Historically, Sunny kept her friends away from her mom's judgmental attitude. Birdie insisted she needed better friends, ones who would help her grow her career, which pissed Sunny off. All Sunny needed from her friends was emotional support and their company, not a professional network. Out of anyone, Richard had the best chance for her approval. If Mae could look past her expectations, anyway.

CHAPTER TWENTY-THREE

SUNNY

SUNNY GOT HOME JUST as the sun was setting behind the Bellamy skyline. The front door closed heavily behind her, echoing the dread in her heart. She had no idea how this conversation would go. She knew what Birdie would say, but Sunny had no idea what would come out of her own mouth. Birdie would tell her to break up with Richard, citing a million reasons why that seemed perfectly logical to her.

But Sunny didn't want to, so her usual ways of placating Mae—agreeing with her, ignoring her, and avoiding her—were useless. The resentment was simmering already.

Was it foolish to fight for Richard? Would he do the same with his family eventually? Or was Sunny only prolonging the inevitable? Putting her heart on the line now, only for it to break worse later? Even if he wanted a relationship with her, their real lives were still so disparate. If it weren't for Lee and Antonio bringing them together, they would have never met.

How could they create a life together from a single point of connection?

Sunny slipped her shoes off in the entryway, the carpet rough under her toes. So different from the cold tile mosaic of Richard's condo. The slippers he'd bought for her should be on her feet right now. She should be kissing him and messing up his hair. Tossing a spoon in the sink after stealing a single bite of ice cream directly from the container, because it bugged him in a way that he didn't entirely hate.

Beyond their friends, she and Richard had built so many more connections between them. Their debates and stories and lists and their futures. Richard was part of her life now. *Fuck. This better be worth it.* As long as he didn't give up on her when she fucked up, as long as he stayed a part of her life when Mae inevitably gave them a hard time, he would be.

Luna poked her head around the corner. "Oh, you're home."

Sunny shrugged. "Might as well get this over with."

To her surprise, Luna hugged her. "I did what I could. She's watching some hospital show in her bedroom. As if she doesn't spend enough time at work as it is."

Sunny hugged her sister back fiercely. Somehow Luna had turned out so well-adjusted and caring, despite being born into a family reeling from loss, a world of grief and pain and confusion. Mae had been a shell for the first few years after her father and brother died. She'd gone to work, paid the bills, changed Luna, and brought Sunny to school every day, but mentally, Mae was gone. She never smiled, never laughed.

Sunny had done her best to raise Luna, making bottles and teaching her how to talk and use the potty, but it was a lot to ask of a child so young. She'd stopped being a kid to help raise her sister. And now Luna was the one taking care of both of them, practically still a kid herself. *She shouldn't have to do this shit for us.*

"If it gets quiet, come make sure I'm still alive," Sunny said sarcastically.

Luna frowned.

"That was a joke, Luna. Lighten up."

Birdie ignored her when Sunny knocked on the open door of her mom's bedroom.

"Hi, Mae."

Birdie didn't respond, staring at the tiny TV on the dresser with tinfoil wrapped around the antennae, her attention focused on an erectile dysfunction pill commercial. Sunny's irritation spiked at the passive-aggressive treatment. *No wonder Luna is the well-adjusted one. She just has to watch Mae and me to know how not to act.*

"I'm not going to break up with him." Sunny had not expected those would be the first words out of her mouth. She'd been half-expecting to apologize.

Birdie looked at her, face unreadable. "Who said anything about that?"

Sunny's fingernails bit into the skin of her palm. "You didn't have to. I know what you're going to say."

"Oh? And what's that?"

Sunny wasn't sure if it was good or bad that Mae was speaking English. She usually fell into Thai when she was upset. "Because you always tell me I need to put our family first. I have to honor Phaw's memory, and Sky's. To make merit for our ancestors, and support my grandparents in their old age. Find a nice woman, preferably Thai or at least Buddhist, to settle down with and have kids. I have duties to the family that come before my own wants."

She sounded like a resentful teenager, parroting the many lessons Mae—and her father's parents over video chats and long-distance calls—had drilled into her head over the course of her life. "But I like Richard. So much! We have fun together. He makes me happy, and why can't I be happy and still do those things?"

Birdie sighed, rubbing her eyebrows. "I want you to be happy, Sunny. I do. Yes, those were all of the things I would say because I worry for you. There's more to life than fun. Putting family first doesn't mean you can't be *happy*. You have responsibilities that most people here don't. Why waste time when you should try to find happiness *and* father children—"

Sunny snapped, "Can you please stop talking about me having kids for once, Mae!"

Birdie's eyes narrowed.

Sunny buried her face in her hands to escape her look. "I'm sorry. I didn't mean to yell."

"Then what are you trying to say?" Birdie's tone was dangerously cold.

Sunny chewed on her lip. What *was* she trying to say? "I want you to care about me. All of me—the person I am, not just who you need me to be." Her voice cracked. "I'm more than the parts of my body I hate the most." She looked at her mother through the tears welling up in her eyes. "I love our family, and I'm always going to put you first, but I want to love myself too. I want to enjoy my life! The life you want for me will make me so miserable, Mae! I'm never going to be the good son or husband or father like you want me to be. That's not me."

Birdie looked at her for a long moment before she patted the bed next to her. "Come here." After a moment of hesitation, Sunny climbed into bed next to her mother. Birdie pulled her into a hug. "I know I've been hard on you, Sunny."

Sunny huffed a laugh. That was as much of an apology as she would get. It was more than she usually got from her mom.

Birdie sighed. "When I was your age, I was so optimistic. I graduated from university and found the man I wanted to marry. He was smart, handsome, and most importantly, he wanted to move to California, like I did. He was my ticket to freedom, to independence. And we loved each other madly." Birdie's swallow was audible. "Our parents were so upset with us for putting happiness before the family's well-being. But we went anyway. I want to spare you from my regrets. I forgot what was important, and I learned that lesson too late."

"Do you regret coming here?" Sunny asked, unsure if she was allowed to ask questions. Her mother had never told her any of this before.

Birdie nodded. "Yes, in hindsight. But I would have regretted staying, too. I just couldn't have known, even imagined, what coming here would cost us. But being here brought us you and Luna." She squeezed Sunny tighter. "I just wish we could all be together again."

"Me too, Mae." Sunny rested her head on Birdie's shoulder. "I know you miss them."

Sunny missed them too. What little she remembered anyway. It was strange to think about those years of her life. None of it felt real, like her childhood memories were a movie she'd seen long ago. Life before the accident was too easy to be true. Too happy. She vaguely remembered playing Uno with her brother, Sky. Riding on her dad's shoulders. Her mother's laughter. None of those memories would ever happen again.

Birdie sighed. "I suppose you're allowed to enjoy your life. Just so long as you don't neglect your family. You know better than to act like a selfish brat." Birdie teasing her was a good sign. "I don't like you keeping secrets from me. And you know I don't like surprises. Like a white boy kissing you in public."

"I know. He and I just hadn't quite figured out what we were yet, so I didn't know what to tell you. And if it helps, Richard does want kids one day." At Birdie's surprised exclamation, Sunny covered her tracks. "Not that we've talked about having kids together yet! We've only been seeing each other for a few months. Who knows if we'll last that long?"

Based on her mother's smirk, Birdie was backing off. It was more than Sunny could have hoped for. At least she could give Birdie some reassurance that she was still on the same track, even if it'd still be years before Sunny considered having kids.

"We'll have to start saving for a surrogate. Just in case you last that long." Birdie nodded, eyes looking into the middle distance. Probably already doing calculations for the budget she kept in her head.

She hoped they would; Richard would make a good dad. Sunny grinned. "Oh, no need. Richard's got money. And a uterus."

"Eh? Sunny, why didn't you start with that?" Birdie elbowed her.

With a huff, Sunny said, "Because that wasn't the *point*, Mae. It doesn't matter if he's broke and cis, or rich and trans. The point is that I want to be with him."

Birdie sighed. "I don't suppose he's Buddhist, is he?"

"No, he's not religious. But he's been to Thailand a few times."

"That's not the same thing at all, Sunny." Birdie's face scrunched up in confusion.

Sunny shrugged. "It was worth a shot."

Luna popped her head around the doorframe. "Are you both still alive?"

Sunny grinned as Birdie patted the bed on her other side. "Come here."

Luna joined them in their hug on the bed. It'd been a long time since they'd all sat together like this. Sunny couldn't be sure if the three of them ever had.

"Does this Richard want to come to dinner?" Birdie asked.

Sunny grinned, hope welling in her heart. "He does."

"I suppose you could invite him over soon."

Giddiness burst through her chest as Sunny squeezed her mom. "Thank you, Mae."

"Is this a good time to tell you I have a boyfriend?" Luna piped up.

"Ah!" Birdie cried. "Not you, too! Is this one a white boy, too?"

"No, he's Filipino. And *Catholic*." Luna said the word like a dare, a big grin on her face.

"I'm about to ship you both back to live with your grandparents," Birdie teased. "You have it so easy with me."

Luna rolled her eyes. "Mae, that threat stopped working years ago."

Sunny grinned, amazed by her sister's audacity and for growing up so levelheaded and bold. Relieved that her mother was more understanding than Sunny dreamed she'd be capable of. Proud of herself for finally standing up for what she wanted. Family would always come first, but that didn't mean Sunny had to come last.

RICHARD

FLINCHING AS THE PORCH light of Gabe's house blinded him, Richard unlocked the door and let himself in without knocking. Frank Ocean was playing throughout the house; Gabe was indeed in one of his moods. Richard tucked his sneakers in the hall closet so Hippo wouldn't drool on them.

He should have expected Gabe would be wallowing. *Isn't that why I'm here?* Gabe had been a sad sack all week at work, and misery loved company, even if Gabe didn't. Not that Richard was miserable, at least not on the level of Gabe's depression. He just didn't know what to do with himself on a Friday night without Sunny.

"You look like shit," Richard said, walking into the living room.

Hippo wagged his tail, wiggling in Gabe's lap.

Gabe raised his wine glass in greeting from where he was stretched out on the chaise. "Hello to you too, asshole." His wrinkled hoodie was spotted with stains, his joggers covered in dog hair. His hair was in a messy bun, probably hiding the grease from the past week. The patchy stubble was more pronounced in the dim light of the living room than it had been in the office earlier.

"Did you bother to shower after the gym today, or are you only neglecting your hair?" Richard grabbed a wine glass from the liquor cabinet and poured himself a glass from the half-empty bottle of the Cooper house red on the coffee table.

"Can't I just wallow in peace without your judgy-ass comments?" Gabe downed his wine and held the glass out to Richard.

"Wallow away. I'm here to wallow with you." He emptied the bottle into Gabe's glass. "Your show is about to start."

"What show?" Gabe asked defensively. "I don't have a show."

"I won't tell Antonio." Richard rolled his eyes.

"I don't know what you're talking about." Gabe turned off the music as he picked up the remote, turning on the TV just as the opening credits for a drag reality show played. Antonio had ranted many times about how problematic the show was. However, it was no secret that he'd auditioned several times and was never cast.

Richard wasn't a fan, but he knew Gabe's comfort routines by heart. And he'd overheard several conversations about the show (which Antonio had made them swear to never watch), between Gabe and his squad of self-proclaimed "allies" in the office.

Gabe's work friends were mostly straight women who said "Slay, hunty!" and "Yasss queen!", watched *Queer Eye* when their homophobic boyfriends weren't around, and gave Richard a suspicious side-eye when he exited the single-stall restroom. Their "allyship" was undermined by their inability to consider the possibility that Gabe could be bisexual.

Still, they were nice to him, always trying to set him up with their one other gay friend. Gabe always turned them down, using nonexistent plans with Richard as an excuse. This didn't help the rumors that they were secretly together.

Watching reality TV with a sad Gabe was still better than sitting at home by himself, wondering what Sunny was up to, or how her conversation with her mom was going. Richard couldn't remember what he used to do before she came over on Fridays. He'd tried to read, but he couldn't concentrate on anything. He couldn't even nap.

He'd tried to have a conversation in his head with Everett, his therapist. Normally when he didn't know what he was thinking, mentally imagining what Everett would ask helped him focus his thoughts. Except Richard hadn't told Everett about Sunny yet, so it was a little hard to imagine. *I should tell him. He's going to give me so much shit.* Everett had made him promise after his last breakup to tell him about his relationships before they ended.

And while his relationship with Sunny hopefully wasn't over, Richard worried about what it would mean now that her mom knew. Especially so soon after Sunny had been apparently blindsided by the existence of their relationship to begin with. She'd been so shaken after her mom had left earlier; he hated seeing that side of her. His concern had tempered the unexpected glee when she'd introduced him as her boyfriend. But the timid, subdued Sunny, who wouldn't meet his eyes as she tried to give him an out, wasn't the Sunny he knew.

"Since you're here and shit, can we cuddle?" Gabe asked.

"No."

"Worth a shot." Gabe turned back to the TV with a pout.

Richard shot a look at his friend. He did look pitifully miserable. With a huff, Richard stood up. "Lay down. I'll sit on you, but that's all you get."

"I'll take it." Gabe set his wine glass down eagerly and lay face down on the couch, Hippo grumbling in protest. Richard settled cross-legged on his broad back to spread the weight out. Hippo wiggled, readjusting to sprawl across Gabe's legs so that his giant head snuggled against Richard, breathing his gross, hot breath on his leg.

Richard wrinkled his nose. Hippo was good for Gabe, but cats were infinitely superior. And not just because Sunny liked them. Cats were cleaner. More aloof. At least, he imagined they were. He had never had a pet before. Maybe he should get one. Sunny would like that.

Gabe let out a heavy sigh. "Thanks, Dicky. This is nice."

"You want to talk about it?"

"No. I already talked to Joy about it. Did the interventions I'm supposed to do when I'm a mess." Gabe snorted into his arm. "I'm radically accepting my sadness and showing myself compassion by giving myself an evening of self-pity." He craned his neck to look at Richard. "Do you wanna talk about whatever's got you here?"

"No. I have a session with Everett next week. He'll tell me what I'm feeling." Richard sipped his wine and stared blankly at the screen, wondering who anyone was on the show.

"We should learn to talk about shit together so we're not reliant on our therapists forever."

"Probably." Richard was surprised at how much he wanted to tell Gabe about what had happened with Sunny. He might have, if he and Sunny had talked about how they would finally tell their friends, if they never figured out the two of them were together. If he felt more confident that they would *stay* together after what happened earlier.

After all, Antonio's stupid plan had worked, somewhat. Gabe hadn't exactly hidden the hickeys that had appeared last weekend; Tara was obviously the root of Gabe's moodiness. He sighed, eyeing the faded bruise barely visible under Gabe's jaw. That decided it for Richard. Opening up about Sunny might unintentionally pressure Gabe to open up about Tara, and Gabe didn't seem ready for that. And besides, it would be fun to surprise him at the MAI fundraiser.

At least Gabe and Tara had finally made a move, even if it was just sex for now (not that anything was "just sex" for Gabe these days). He was relieved he didn't have to reprise his "Gabe is a sex god" scheme; getting that message to Tara, without making Sunny jealous, would have been impossible.

If Tara had presumably already experienced how good Gabe was in bed and still needed more convincing, perhaps Richard could show her how caring and doting Gabe could be, since he was doing a shit job of it. The trick was not to make Sunny jealous by hyping up his friend's sweetheart side.

Richard's phone buzzed in his pocket.

You are cordially invited over to my mom's house for dinner on May 15th.

I'm assuming since you didn't text the safeword that you don't need a rescue mission.

Lmao yah. You might make it out of Eastside alive.

That's good. I'd hate to think how you'd occupy your Friday evenings without me.

Bold of you to assume I'd miss you, Dicky.

I'd miss you. I miss you tonight.

Books can't compare to these titties?

Nothing compares to those titties. I had to resort to watching reality TV with Gabe. I'd much rather be with you.

Forget me, are you okay? You're being sappy as hell and watching reality shows? <.< Who are you and what have you done with my boyfriend?

A snort escaped him. *How do I respond to that?* The "boyfriend" hit him in the heart just as hard in a text as when she'd said it out loud to her mother.

"Who are you texting?" Gabe asked, a smug grin on his face.

Richard raised an eyebrow at him. "I'll tell you if you tell me who gave you those hickeys."

Gabe quickly turned back to the television. "So who do you think is gonna win this season? My money is on Bootyful, but Beth thinks it'll be Miss Muffet."

"I have zero idea who any of these people are, Gabe." Richard turned back to his phone, trying to come up with a good response for Sunny. "I don't even know who Beth is."

"Beth in Client Relations? Wait, if you don't watch it, then why the fuck did you tell me to turn it on?"

Richard sighed and shook his head. Gabe could be so thick sometimes. "Because *you* like watching it, dipshit."

"Aww...love you too, Dicky."

"Don't call me Dicky."

Friday, May Fifteenth

CHAPTER TWENTY-FOUR

RICHARD

"Mae! Are you serious?" Sunny's younger sister, Luna, coughed as tears streamed down her face. She gulped her water. "Why is this so hot?"

Richard sympathized, struggling to keep his own composure. But he recognized a test when he saw one. Or ate one, rather. He liked papaya salad, but the bite he'd just taken stung his lips and destroyed his taste buds even before he'd put it in his mouth. His nasal passages burned as he swallowed. "Delicious."

Across the table, Birdie's face was stern, but her eyes twinkled. "Thank you. My mother's recipe. Luna's been spoiled by American food."

Luna wiped her nose with her napkin. "It's *never* been this spicy before!"

Sunny laughed, smacking on her food happily. "Get it together, crybaby. Even Richard's handling it better than you."

"I had to go to three different stores before I found the right chilis. You should be grateful I put in so much effort," Birdie said archly, a teasing grin playing at the corners of her mouth. Both Sunny and Luna took after her, with the same high cheekbones and dark brown eyes. Only Birdie's nose was a bit shorter, and her hair had more curl than Sunny's.

Richard forced himself to eat another bite. It was quite good once he got past the spice level, but he would regret this later. Birdie met his eyes and gave a slight nod. So far, she'd been nothing but polite, but he expected an interrogation soon. He'd do the same in her shoes—catch him off guard with the spice, then ask the harder questions when his composure was weakest. His mom had gotten Gabe drunk on wine before interrogating him when Richard had brought him home for the first time in college. Not that Gabe had needed to earn anyone's approval; "bagging the Cooper boy" had been the sole accomplishment his dad had ever been proud of.

"So, Richard." Birdie turned to him, right on cue. "What do you do for work?"

"Mae, I already told you—"

Birdie stopped Sunny with a look. "I am asking *him*."

Richard bit back a laugh at Sunny's disgruntled huff. He liked Sunny's mom more than he'd expected. "I'm a managing director at an investment firm based in New York. I lead the retirement account division here in Bellamy."

"What kind of music do you like?" Luna piped up, scooping curry over her bowl of rice, her papaya salad uneaten.

Richard blinked. He hadn't been expecting Luna to ask questions, let alone softball questions about music. But he could pivot to being relatable. He'd need Luna's approval, too. "Mostly EDM, but I listen to classical when I need to concentrate." He gave a small smile. "I also had a brief obsession with Katy Perry."

Sunny snorted. "I did not know that. That might be a dealbreaker."

"What about religion? Are you Christian?" Birdie asked.

"I was raised Presbyterian, but my family was never very religious. I don't consider myself any particular religion these days, but I enjoy learning about different religions."

Richard's family was a Christmas and Easter family, just religious enough to keep up appearances. He didn't see the point in the charade, so he hadn't bothered since he'd stopped celebrating the holidays with his own family. Antonio's mom, stepdad, and several sisters attended Mass on Christmas, but it was optional. He always stayed back with the equally nonreligious Coopers, Antonio (along with Lee, last year), and the rest of the Floreses.

"What do you do for fun?"

Richard suspected that Luna was trying to save him from Birdie's follow-up questions. "I work, read, and spend time with Sunny and our friends."

"And nap." Sunny's foot nudged his under the table. Richard met her smile.

"Work isn't something you do for fun," Luna protested.

"I enjoy working," Birdie corrected her. "But you are friends with Sunny's friends? That Jones boy and the blonde and the redhead?"

Richard nodded. "Yes. Sunny and I met through Lee, and I've spent time with all of them, Tara and Blanche included."

"What is your opinion of them?"

Sunny sighed. "Mae, don't start—"

Birdie silenced her with another look, before turning back to Richard for his answer.

Richard considered his response carefully. "I find all of them admirable. They care deeply about each other, Sunny included. They're very supportive of each other and are all very...industrious in their entrepreneurship."

"Entrepreneurship?" Birdie asked skeptically.

He nodded. "Lee, Tara, and Blanche all run their own businesses. Even in the few months I've known them, they've all made strides in growing their companies. Lee is producing an album that's releasing this summer. Tara's graphic design client base recently expanded internationally. And Blanche's growth rate has been exponential. They got over half a million impressions with their most recent campaign."

That was the vaguest way he could describe Blanche's line of work. Hopefully, Birdie wouldn't ask more about what they did. Or who exactly Lee was producing the album for.

Sunny shot him a confused look. "How do *you* know all of that? *I* didn't even know that."

Birdie turned to Sunny. "Why didn't you tell me they ran their own businesses?"

Sunny spluttered in response. "I did! What else would 'side hustle' mean?"

"Side hustle makes them sound unemployed and lazy." Birdie retorted.

Sunny tsked. "In what world does 'hustle' mean 'lazy'?"

"Your marketing could use some work," Richard teased Sunny. "As well as listening to your friends when they talk."

Sunny made a face as her family laughed. Richard counted making Birdie laugh as a win.

"So, what's your five-year plan?" Luna asked.

He had been expecting that question from Birdie, not Luna. But he had been expecting it. "Professionally, I want to advance in a direction with influence over risk and ethics decisions in financial services. Greed, human error, and lack of oversight are too common in an industry where people trust us with their future." Richard paused, glancing at Birdie's expectant look. She'd want to know his intentions for Sunny. "Personally, ideally married with children or working toward that goal. However, building a healthy partnership with the right person is a necessary prerequisite."

He glanced at Sunny, more concerned about her reaction to his answer than Birdie's. She stared at her curry, blushing. Hopefully, his response wasn't too presumptuous.

They both wanted kids, but a few months into their relationship was too soon to be seriously discussing marriage and children. Richard didn't want to put a timeline on where he hoped they'd end up. She was half a decade younger than him, after all. She had other priorities.

"Sunny, your boyfriend is way out of your league," Luna teased Sunny. "Ow! Why'd you kick me?"

"You're supposed to make me look good!"

Richard couldn't help but smile. "Sunny is much smarter than I am. If either of us punched up, it was me."

Sunny flashed a brilliant smile in his direction and her foot gently nudged his again. "At least someone's on my side."

Monday, May Twenty-Fifth

Chapter Twenty-Five

Blanche

"Can I please tell Lee and Antonio they don't need these damn events anymore?" With a heavy thunk, Blanche set a deli container of pasta salad on the picnic table. Sunny and Richard broke apart from their kiss without the slightest bit of shame. "If you insist on keeping this a secret, maybe don't make out with each other in public."

"Sorry, Blanche, you want in?" Sunny teased from her perch on Richard's lap. "Hey! Dicky, don't pinch me, it was a joke!"

"What I want is to stop keeping secrets for everyone." Blanche popped open their folding chair in the grass near Richard and Sunny. The reclining lounge (a custom-made gift from a subscriber) was from their recording set. But Blanche's back would not appreciate sitting at a picnic table all day. At least they'd remembered to remove the restraints before they'd collapsed it down and lugged it to the park.

They were back on the damn island near the apartment, only this time by the splash pool, where water poured from comically large flowers and mushrooms. Lee's genius idea for May's event to force everyone to get along was a Memorial Day pool party; this happened to be the closest thing to an outdoor pool in Eastside.

If this scheme kept up for much longer, Blanche would have to take over the planning from Lee and Antonio. It wasn't even warm enough to wear a swimsuit, let alone go swimming. The strong breeze was chilly, and large clouds blocked out what little warmth might be coming from the sun. Not even the most intrepid child dared get in; the splash pool was empty, and all the screaming kids were on the playground across the island.

Before the riot, there'd been a shed where the pool was, the designated bathhouse for the camp. The spot Daisy and Blanche had claimed whenever they'd stayed at the camp was now a swing set. Maybe Blanche should've smoked beforehand, or pushed back when Lee suggested coming here again. They'd thought they could tough it out, but now that unfiltered bitterness was twisting like worms.

There was no need to be here; the plan had already worked. Sunny and Richard were sucking face every time they were alone. Gabe was in love with Tara. Tara was, well, confused and scared. But Tara was always confused and scared, and at least she was horny for him. Which frankly was big for Tara, who previously had taken a "never the twain shall meet" attitude between sexual attraction and interpersonal relationships. Despite her declaration last year that she wanted to "see what the dating shit was all about."

"What other secrets are you keeping?" Sunny asked. "Anything about Tara?"

"It wouldn't be a secret if I admitted I had one, now would it, Babygirl?" Blanche draped themself over the lounge chair. "'Keep it a secret,' you said. 'Please, Blanche.' Secret, my ass!"

"Gosh, Blanche. You're grumpy today." Sunny stuck her tongue out, finally climbing off of Richard and onto her own chair. "Besides, Lee and Antonio are having fun with their little plan, so we figure it'll be fun to see how long it takes them to figure out we're together."

"Oh my god, this is never going to end!" Blanche sighed dramatically, scolding themself for letting their irritation show. Their anxiety for Tara—and themself—must be wearing on their patience, even if Tara had insisted she was fine coming here. Irritation was for clients, not friends.

They peered at Richard and Sunny over their sunglasses to distract themself. "I'm supposed to start a game of Truth or Dare today because we're *children* apparently. Tonio plans on daring you two to kiss, so please pick Truth?"

Richard cackled. "With pleasure. Tonio comes up with the worst dares anyway."

For as much as they complained, the schemes Lee and Antonio kept coming up with were entertaining, even more so to foil them. It was a nice distraction from...everything. From the artificial conversations with their subscribers, the one-sided relationships with the clients who treated Blanche like an employee instead of a person, the threatening text messages from their patron's fiancée that grew more desperate as their wedding date approached. But at least they had this, their friends, light-hearted secrets instead of the heavy ones. Blanche couldn't remember the last time they'd just relaxed in the sunshine.

"Tara didn't come with you?" Sunny asked, looking around.

Blanche shook their head, fidgeting to find a comfortable spot on their chair and wrapping their cardigan tight around themself. "She's finishing up a commission. She should be here soon."

At least that was what she'd said. Blanche believed her, unlike last time when she'd been late to avoid Gabe. Tara had been throwing herself into her work and spending a lot of time shut up in her room. Blanche found themself alone in the living room most days. Their SubParty subscribers were nice for the bank account, but Blanche missed Tara, missed Lee, missed Sunny, missed *people*.

As if hearing their thoughts, Sunny said, "We should plan a night in. Like we used to do. Tara, Lee, video games, pizza. It's been a while since we hung out."

The bitter churn in their stomach eased a bit. "I'd like that. I'm sure Tara would too."

"I can plan something for Antonio, so you can have Lee by himself for a while." Richard offered. "He must be ready to strangle Tonio by now."

"Who's strangling me?" Antonio asked, his timing perfect. He lugged a cooler behind him, while Lee carried a box labeled "Picnic Supplies" and a bag of charcoal.

"Lee, if I were him," Richard said. "You need to spend time apart."

"Why do we need time apart?"

"Because," Sunny crossed her arms, "I'm tired of being forced to hang out with *him*."

Blanche snorted as Richard and Sunny's expressions soured comically. "Richard is bringing you to a strip club or on his yacht or golfing or whatever it is you two do for fun. Lee, you're coming over to play the video game."

Lee nodded. "Hell yeah. Mario Kart night! When?"

"Tonight, if you all are free?" Sunny looked around. They all nodded. "Great, none of us have social lives." She threw her hair over her shoulder dramatically.

"Some of us have grown-up jobs to go to in the morning," Richard sneered.

"I *have* a grown-up job, Dicky," Sunny spat out. "Something more worthwhile than exploiting the working class by gambling away their life savings."

Blanche admired their ability to switch on the bickering at the drop of the hat. From Lee and Antonio's perspective, they were constantly fighting. *Do they do this when others aren't around too? Is this fun for them?*

"Hey, sorry I'm late." Tara hurried over, depositing a couple bags of chips on the table. "Had to send a proof to that client in Belgium."

Lee hugged her tight. "Hope you don't have to work later. Sunny and I are coming over to kick your ass in Mario Kart."

Tara beamed. "Really?" She tried and failed to scowl at him. "I mean, you *wish* you could kick my ass!"

They laughed as Lee set up the picnic, and Tara passed around hard seltzers and sparkling waters. Humming along with a radio that had appeared from the box, Antonio tied an apron around his waist before lighting the grill. With a sigh, Blanche leaned back with their eyes closed, enjoying the patchy sunshine and the sounds of their friends around them. The charcoal smoke wafted through the air as they sipped a mango seltzer. They'd prefer scotch, but the fizzy flavor was pleasant enough. The knot in their stomach loosened a little more, and the tension slipped from their shoulders.

A deep bark interrupted their thoughts. Blanche sat up, pushing their sunglasses up as Gabe approached with a massive gray pittie leashed to his waist, pulling him toward them. "Heel!"

The dog had other plans, dragging Gabe behind him, who struggled to stay upright, balancing a cake pan in his hands. Blanche tensed, their chest bursting with excitement. *No one told me Gabe had a dog!*

To their utter disappointment and jealousy, the dog made a beeline for Tara next to the picnic table. He bumped his giant head against her hips, body wiggling with excitement as he begged for attention. Gabe barely managed to keep from knocking into her, dropping the cake pan onto the table as he righted himself.

"I'm so sorry." Gabe tugged a backpack off his shoulders, setting it next to the cake pan. "He usually never pulls like that."

Tara bent down to kiss the dog's head "Hi Hippo!" she cooed, petting him vigorously. The dog's whole body wiggled as his tail wagged.

Blanche was seething. *That bitch never mentioned he had a dog!* Tara must have met him on her birthday.

Antonio eyed Gabe suspiciously. "Hippo's never greeted *me* like that. In fact, it took a lot of cheese before I could pet him."

Lee laughed. "For real. I had to bribe him with bacon before he let me in the house."

Blanche burned. Everyone knew they loved dogs. And not one person had mentioned Hippo's existence to them? They would have become best friends with Gabe months ago if they'd known he had a *dog*.

"I probably just smell good to him." Tara shrugged, not looking up.

Antonio raised a skeptical eyebrow. "I literally have burgers right next to me, and he didn't greet me like that."

Tara blushed bright red. "Antonio, you don't want to know where your train of thought is going."

"Well, now I *have* to know."

"Dogs have a good sense of smell. You and I have different smells. Especially at certain times of the month?" Tara hinted. "Maybe you would have had more luck winning over Hippo here if you had a uterus?"

She's lying. Her period was always inconsistent, but she'd just had it last week. It was a good enough lie, however, that Antonio wouldn't ask questions. Blanche was impressed Tara had pulled that out of nowhere. She'd never been a good bullshitter.

"No wonder dogs don't like me," Sunny quipped, causing a ripple of laughter.

Antonio rolled his eyes. "I have sisters. You can just say you have your period."

"Gabe, darling," Blanche called, their jealousy winning out over their patience. "Bring the dog here."

Tara kissed Hippo's head and looked up at Gabe. "Might as well give them the leash."

Gabe looked confused when Lee patted him on the shoulder. "You'll get him back. Eventually."

"Okay." Gabe sounded unsure but walked Hippo over to Blanche. "Hippo can take a while to warm up to strangers, but yeah, you can pet him if he lets you."

Blanche held out their fingers to Hippo, who snuffled them delightfully, evaluating Blanche with big brown eyes before jumping up onto the lounge chair. He flopped down heavily between Blanche's legs, his head on their stomach like a pillow.

"Hippo. Seriously. Where are your manners today?" Gabe tried to pull him off, but Blanche stopped him with a light touch to his arm.

"Leave the dog. He's exactly where he's supposed to be." With a content sigh, Blanche smiled down at Hippo, lovingly tracing the wrinkles of his forehead and neck. His wrinkly snout snuffled their cardigan, as if he could learn everything about them through scent alone. They liked to believe that he could. That if anyone could make them feel understood, it'd be this loveable beast who couldn't begin to conceive of their problems, but could still sense their emotions.

After a thoughtful look that mirrored Hippo's, if slightly more confused, Gabe nodded, unbuckling the leash from his waist. Blanche slid it over their wrist and settled in under Hippo. Arranging their legs under his body, they cradled his *big giant goofy woofy* head as they pet him. They whispered praises in his ears as he smiled up at them, tail *thump thump thumping* harder on their feet. Blanche couldn't remember the last time they'd felt so at peace.

Most critters loved Blanche as much as Blanche loved them. They had grown up with farm animals—the dogs who slept in a pile around Blanche on cold nights in the hayloft, the barn cats who left them mice as presents, a royal asshole of a goat who only let Blanche milk her. And when they were homeless and new to the city, stray dogs and feral cats became their protection, warmth, and love until Daisy took them under her wing.

This one was a majestic sweetheart. The tension that'd been souring their stomach for months eased with Hippo's brown eyes looking up at them, the *tap tap tap* of his tail against the lounge chair, the stretch of his paws as he snuggled in deeper against them.

"Gabe, what the fuck is this shit?" Tara had opened the cake pan, looking inside it with disdain. She held up a skewer of vegetables.

"It's a veggie kebab." Gabe gestured like it should be obvious. "I don't know if you've heard of vegetables before, but you can grill them."

"This is a cake pan." Tara pointed at the pan. "I don't know if *you* know this, but cake goes in these."

"Veggie kebabs are healthier than cake." Gabe clearly didn't understand the depth of Tara's love for sweets. "But, I also made cookies. You're welcome." He opened his backpack, pulling a camera bag out to unearth a plastic container.

Tara snatched it out of his hands, tearing the lid off and grabbing a double chocolate chip with glee. "Hell yeah."

"Your manners are worse than Hippo's." Gabe shook his head, bringing the kebabs to the grill where Lee and Antonio were cooking the burgers.

Tara glared. "Yeah, I'm not a dog."

"Clearly. A dog would have some impulse control." A smile flickered on Gabe's face.

Tara flicked him off as she shoved the cookie in her mouth.

Lazily stroking Hippo's ears, Blanche watched her carefully, checking for signs that she might be struggling, but Tara seemed...fine. *Those must be some "cookies" Gabe has.* Maybe they didn't have to worry about her today.

Blanche turned their attention to Lee and Antonio, who were dancing to whatever song was on the speaker and making moon eyes at each other, instead of watching the grill. *Boring. Cute, but boring.* They looked instead at Sunny and Richard, who were deep in conversation.

From a distance, it looked like they were arguing again. Sunny was gesturing angrily at her phone and speaking in a hushed tone. Blanche listened closely, overhearing phrases: "So we're just gonna let Gabe find out when you introduce me to his parents?" and "What do I wear to a fundraiser, anyway?"

Now that's interesting. Fake arguing while having a real conversation. They're committed to this bit. Blanche smiled, tracing the dog's snout with a gentle finger. They wished they could have a dog of their own. They wanted a lot of things of their own, but until they found a new place to live and a way out of their contract with their patron, there was no point in wanting. "Gabe, darling? Can Hippo come to our party tonight?"

Gabe's lost look of confusion was back to Blanche's delight. "What party?"

"Oh, yeah," Richard said. "Tonio and I are coming to your house tonight."

"Thanks for asking, Dicky." Gabe huffed in annoyance. "Do I get a choice?"

"Of course you do. But you're going to say yes," Richard answered. "Unless you want me to drag you both out to the yacht club instead. And don't call me Dicky."

"Please don't make us go to the yacht club, Gabey," Antonio begged. "It's so awkward, and the brightest color there is khaki."

"Sure, fine. Whatever. I don't care." Gabe ran his hands through his hair.

"So can Hippo come over for a playdate?" Blanche pleaded.

Tara laughed. "We'll take good care of him."

After another pensive look at Blanche, Gabe sighed. "Fine. I'm picking him up at eight though. So you two have to be gone by then too." He pointed to Richard and Antonio warningly. "I'm not emotionally prepared for company today."

"You hear that, Hippo?" Blanche squished his face up, and Hippo grinned, his tongue lolling out the side. "You have a curfew!"

"Burgers are ready." Lee set a platter down on the picnic table, dutifully making a plate for Blanche, still voluntarily pinned in their happy place under the dog.

"Do you really not like when people call you Dicky?" Sunny asked Richard quietly, out of earshot from everyone but Blanche.

"You can. I don't mind if it's you." Richard's voice was more gentle than Blanche had ever heard. They looked over in time to see him blush. *I'm going to vomit. That's adorable.*

Adding a heaping pile of chips to her plate, Tara tentatively sat on the picnic bench near Gabe, maintaining a careful distance from him. Gabe was cutting his burger patty up to eat with the kebab veggies, a small portion of the pasta salad doled onto the plate.

"You brought your camera?" Tara asked around the chip in her mouth.

Gabe nodded. "I was hoping to get some good shots of Hippo. But it looks like he's busy with his new best friend." Blanche looked away just as Gabe shot them a look.

He'd probably seen them staring, but could Gabe blame them for being curious? He was so much more relaxed than they'd ever seen, other than the moment he'd forgotten they were in the backseat. They'd been itching to analyze how Gabe and Tara interacted, now that they'd finally indulged in their mutual attraction.

"I'll still try to take some though. Maybe some candids, if people are okay with it. I need more practice on people, not just landscapes." Gabe took a bite of bell pepper.

"Mind if I play around with it later?" Tara asked. "You probably have a nicer camera than me."

He nodded, covering his mouth as he spoke. "Knock yourself out. I'm already trusting you with my dog tonight. Why not my camera?"

"So, this is a good time to ask if I can practice driving with your car, is what you're saying." Tara smiled mischievously.

Gabe laughed. "No way in hell."

Tara shook her head, staring at his smile. "I'll find a way."

Antonio coughed, trying to get Blanche's attention, mouthing the word "game" at them.

Really? Now? They're getting along! Blanche rolled their eyes, announcing in monotone, "Let's play Truth or Dare!"

Antonio and Lee gave them twin looks of exasperation. Blanche shrugged. What more did they want? They could get the game started.

"Great idea Blanche!" Lee said, too enthusiastically. "I'll go first. Sunny, Truth or Dare?"

"Truth," Sunny replied confidently.

"Wait, you always pick Dare! Why did you pick Truth today?" Lee asked.

"I feel like talking. What a stupid question to waste a Truth on." Sunny stuck her tongue out at him. "Antonio, Truth or Dare?"

"Dare."

"I dare you to bring me a cookie."

"That's not a dare. That's just a favor." Antonio was delightfully annoyed already. He still brought her the cookie. "Dicky, Truth or Dare?"

"Truth," Richard replied calmly.

"Seriously? What is with the Truths today?" Antonio scratched his head, visibly frustrated.

Never mind, this game was a great idea. Blanche grinned.

"I am eating and don't want to go run around the park, or hug a stranger, or whatever it is you'd make me do. I hate to agree with Sunny, but you need to pick better Truth questions." Richard shrugged. "Tara, how about you? Truth or Dare?"

Tara eyed him suspiciously, mouth full of burger. "Dare."

"Go stand under the fountain for...let's say fifteen seconds." Richard's crooked grin made him look like a movie villain.

Tara groaned. "Seriously? I didn't bring a swimsuit. Or a towel. I'm not even wearing underwear—these are my only clothes!" She picked at her basketball shorts and baggy tank top with dismay.

Richard looked at her expectantly.

"Come on, dude," she pleaded, resignation in her eyes as she stood up. Tara *always* did the dare.

Blanche exchanged a worried look with Sunny, who chewed her lip. They were tempted to say something so Tara wouldn't stress herself out, but she'd probably be more pissed if they intervened because they thought she couldn't handle it.

"Your athleisure will dry," Richard said, a hint of challenge in his voice.

"Ugh, you're heartless." Tara emptied her pockets and stalked the short distance to the splash pool. Kicking her sandals off before walking into the knee-deep water, she cussed and complained the whole way to the fake flower spout. "You asshole, this is freezing." She jumped underneath, spluttering as water doused her. "Holy shit this is cold!"

"I don't hear counting!"

Tara flicked Richard off and counted out loud, rushing through the "Mississippis". At fifteen, she shook her head like a dog, spraying water out of her red curls as she leapt from under the spout. Tara's clothes clung to her thin frame like a second skin, dripping down her shivering body. "I hate you."

Richard shrugged.

Gabe blatantly stared as she approached, but ever the gentleman, he snapped out of his daze, dug into his backpack, and pulled out a beach towel. *He's like Mary Poppins. How much is in that backpack?* Draping the towel over her head, he shot Richard a glare.

Tara took the towel gratefully, drying off her hair and wrapping it around her before pressing up against Gabe, shivering. Gabe stiffened, but put his arm around her.

Blanche glanced at Richard, who met their gaze with a knowing smirk.

"Truth or Dare, Dicky." Tara glared through the damp curls pressed to her forehead.

"Truth."

"Why are you such a dick?"

Richard snorted. "What can I say, I named myself after my father, who is also a Dick in name and personality. Chalk it up to Daddy issues." He turned to Blanche. "Truth or Dare?"

"After that, no way in hell are you daring me to do anything. Truth."

"Why Blanche Van Horne?"

"My name, you mean?" They waited for Richard's nod before continuing. "I watched a lot of Golden Girls with my grandma when I was a kid. Blanche Van Horne seemed appropriate for my line of work."

Truthfully, Daisy had decided their group couldn't have both a Chas and a Chad, and Daisy thought Blanche Van Horne sounded funny. So

Blanche had adopted the moniker full-time, unless the government was involved. Their legal name wasn't necessarily a dead name, but Daisy preferred to call them Blanche, so that's what had stuck.

No one questioned Chad Hermanson on a form like they interrogated Blanche in real life. Chad Hermanson could be a good (white) man from a good family, with a bright future ahead of him. Not a racially ambiguous trans femme sex worker, who had never finished eighth grade. Blanche kept a boxy suit and a short wig around, in case they ever had to testify in court again.

Bitterness crept back up their throat, but Hippo whined, looking up with big brown eyes. Blanche stroked his head with a deep breath. His weight across their lap was perfection. They looked around, remembering it was their turn to play. "Antonio, Truth or Dare."

"Dare," Antonio said. "And don't ask for a favor." He glared at Sunny, who grinned back.

"I dare you to play a song from your album."

Antonio shook his head. "The only things we've been cleared to share are the snippets you've already heard, but that is the perfect segue to invite you all to the album release party next month! We just announced it on social media this morning." He dug into the picnic supplies box and pulled out some fliers, passing them around.

"I'm pretty sure that's cheating," Gabe said. "It's a dare, you have to do it."

Antonio made a face at him. "I'm taking a *rain check* on it until the album release party." He tapped the flier emphatically to prove his point. "Tara, Truth or Dare."

"Truth." Tara ate a chip, still bundled in the towel under Gabe's arm.

Antonio scowled. "We should have played Dare or Dare."

Tara shrugged. "I'm dared out."

"Fine. What's the riskiest place you've had sex?"

Tara thought carefully, ticking her fingers quietly to herself. A small smile crept on her face, a blush appearing on her cheeks. "Your bathroom."

"What?! You had sex in our bathroom? Who did you have sex with?" Antonio cried, as Lee buried his face in his hands with a groan.

Based on the smug grin Gabe was fighting, the answer should be obvious.

"Uh-uh!" Tara waved her finger. "You asked your question and got your answer." She looked up at Gabe. "Gabe, Truth or Dare."

"Dare."

Tara grinned mischievously. "I dare you to let me drive your car. Not right now. Just like a few hours of practice time."

Gabe's face darkened as he pulled away from her. "Seriously? No. I've said no repeatedly. Stop asking."

Antonio interrupted. "First of all, that's a favor again, not a dare. But second, Gabe, you can't turn down a dare. That's the point of the game. You literally just said that."

Gabe took a deep breath, emotions unreadable. He growled out, "I'm fucking tired of people telling me what I have to do today. It's been one thing after another. I said no. That's it. You can't fucking coerce me into agreeing to something." Gabe's voice rose as he spoke, his hand came up to run through his hair in agitation.

Blanche swallowed heavily, exchanging a look with Lee. They'd never seen him like this. Sad or annoyed, maybe, but not angry.

Hippo whined loudly, wiggling down from Blanche's lap. They let go of the leash, trusting Hippo would go to his human instead of running away. He nudged Gabe's arm until Gabe pet him absentmindedly.

"I'm sorry." Tara's voice was soft as she leaned away from Gabe. A far-off look entered her eyes.

Shit. I shouldn't have let my guard down. Blanche sat up, but Lee beat them to it. Taking a seat across from her, Lee handed Tara the cookie container, keeping his hand outstretched.

Gabe put his hand gently on her back. He lowered his voice. "Fuck. Sorry. I didn't mean to yell. I'm not angry at you, I'm just frustrated because I feel like I'm not getting a say in decisions that involve me. Sorry."

With a cookie in one hand, Tara took Lee's with the other, her eyes starting to focus again. The towel fell away from her shoulders. "No, you're right. I shouldn't have pressured you, even as a joke."

Blanche let out a slow exhale. They weren't sure if Gabe had picked up on Tara's dissociation, but with Lee's help, he'd done the right things. He had de-escalated and replaced the negative input (yelling) with a positive one (affection). The cookie would provide a taste and smell, and Lee's hand was something to touch. The sensory inputs would help ground Tara.

Blanche sometimes wished their years of sex work counted as practical experience to become a therapist. Their favorite clients were the ones who just wanted someone to listen and give advice as they spilled their souls for hours, scheduling regular sessions that rarely involved anything sexual. And they weren't just subs or clients. Blanche helped other sex workers, friends, and Tara more than anyone.

Blanche had met her and Lee almost six years ago in an alley the night of the riot at the encampment, drawn to the sound of hyperventilating and sobbing amidst the sirens wailing. They had talked Tara through her panic attack and listened to Lee's story of how they'd laid awake all night, hearing the shouts from activists until the smell of tear gas and smoke had filled the camp. They'd gotten away but had left almost everything behind.

The three of them had returned to the camp in the daylight, only to find everything burnt, bulldozed, and fenced off. Everyone who had stayed had been arrested, including Walter and Wanda. The whole camp, decades of history, was gone, Tara and Lee's belongings along with it. All that remained was what little had been in the duffel bag Tara had grabbed as they'd ran.

And now here they all were, sitting where Walter and Wanda had parked their bus and built a life. Daisy and Blanche had stayed at the camp a few times when they'd needed to hide from her stepdad; Walter's camp had been the safety net in Bellamy. None of the three counties that made up the Bellamy metro had done shit to replace it.

"Gabe, you should write a review for your therapist," Richard drawled, breaking the uneasy silence. "You used 'I statements' and everything. And you said no to someone? Five stars."

"Shut up, Dicky." Gabe glared. "Look, can we end this stupid game now? I want to get some photos of Hippo before Blanche steals him from me."

Eyes wide, Hippo backed away with his head low, returning to Blanche.

"I'm not stealing, just inviting him over for a playdate." Blanche lazily scratched his ears as they picked up the leash. "Your human says you have to go be a model, my love."

Hippo responded by climbing back into Blanche's lap, rolling onto his back with a whine, legs outstretched in the air.

Blanche smiled innocently at Gabe. "You'll just have to take pictures of both of us."

Rubbing Hippo's belly, they watched Gabe and Tara dance around each other. Getting too close as Gabe showed her some feature or other on his camera, then awkwardly far apart as they debated about composition or color.

Tara laughed, wrapping Gabe's towel tighter around her. The sound was a relief, yet another reminder that Tara might be more resilient than Blanche gave her credit for. That maybe she didn't need Blanche to take care of her. That maybe none of their ducklings did.

Rubbing Hippo's ears, Blanche ignored the sour twist in their stomach.

Chapter Twenty-Six

RICHARD

"Was Lee too eager to go to Blanche's without me?" Antonio hung upside down on Gabe's couch between them, feet over the back of the couch and absentmindedly throwing the Switch controller between his hands. He'd called it quits after one game. Richard was jealous; he played purely for Gabe's sake. "You don't think he's getting sick of me, do you?"

"No," Gabe and Richard deadpanned simultaneously. Lee was crazy about Antonio for some reason, even after living together for seven months. Richard admired Lee's patience. He wouldn't have lasted two days living with Antonio. How Gabe had done it for a whole year, when Antonio first moved to New York, was beyond him.

"I hope you're right. I'd hate it if he was that excited to ditch me. Especially since I'm proposing to him at the release party."

Both Gabe and Richard paused the game and stared down at Antonio, laying on the couch between them.

"What?" Antonio looked back and forth.

"Have you discussed this with Lee?" Gabe asked. "Like, specifically a public proposal? Not everyone likes the attention as much as you, Tonio."

"What kind of future husband do you think I am?" Antonio scoffed. "Of course, he knows it's coming! I've been hinting at it for weeks, ever since he proposed to me last month." He giggled. "He's getting so annoyed. He totally thought I was going to ask during Truth or Dare. But, like, there's public and there's *public.* I want to do this where every-one will see it."

Gabe and Richard shot each other a confused look. Richard rubbed his forehead. "So, he proposed a month ago. You said yes. Now, *you* need to propose to *him?* Publicly?"

"Yeah." Antonio nodded, as if all couples had two proposals. "You know, a grand gesture thing. He vetoed a flash mob though, so you two are off the hook." Antonio sighed lovingly, feet kicking in the air between their heads. "He knows me so well."

"You certainly have an interesting relationship." Gabe was always nicer than Richard was. Whatever would fly from Richard's mouth was not nearly as neutral as what Gabe had managed. "Did he give you a ring and everything?"

"Oh, yeah. Here." Antonio pulled a chain from his shirt. On it hung a rose gold band, with a neat row of clear stones encased in a channel setting. Larger than Lee or Antonio could afford, so probably lab-grown. *Not that it matters,* Richard reminded himself. That was something his mom had drilled into him: always get the certificate for "insurance purposes," and to see how much you were worth to them.

"We're keeping it a secret until the public proposal, so you can't tell anyone. Especially not Tara, Sunny, or Blanche. Or my family. Or your parents. Miriam would *totally* tell my mom!"

"Should you be telling us?" Gabe asked.

Antonio shook his head. "No, but I am going fucking crazy wear-ing this thing around my neck. I had to tell someone! You two can keep a secret. It's not like you hang out with those three anyway, unless I force you to."

Richard coughed, fully planning on telling Sunny.

"I actually suggested that we elope back in September, but he made me wait until he proposed first." Antonio played with the ring, smiling. "In hindsight, it's probably for the best. He probably would have divorced me after we moved in together. He has very high living standards and, well, you guys know me! But we got some whiteboards and worked out a cleaning system. I've even stopped locking myself out of the apartment," he added proudly.

Gabe shook his head as he got up to get dinner ready. "I can't believe *you* clean now. Lee has balanced you out."

Antonio grinned. "Isn't he great?"

"Congratulations, Tonio. I'm happy for you. You and Lee are good for each other," Richard said softly as soon as Gabe left the room. His friendship with Antonio had always hinged around Gabe, but Richard was genuinely happy for his annoyingly perky friend. He'd tried to reserve judgment where Lee was concerned, but after Antonio's whole family had been won over by Lee, staying wary had become a lost cause. Antonio was a goner, but at least he'd fallen for someone who supported him in the best ways.

Antonio elbowed his hip, sending a shock up Richard's spine. "He doesn't even need to tie me to the chair when I'm having bad moments."

"That was one time! You told me to stop you from leaving," Richard retorted.

"I didn't expect you to bring out a whole-ass shibari rope!" Antonio laughed. "I thought you'd hold me and help me process my feelings like Gabe does."

"Because *that* sounds like me." Richard snorted. "If you want to be held, I can tie a weighted blanket around you next time."

"There's never going to be a next time." Antonio paused. "Or at least, I hope not. It's gotten easier. The early days were rough but time, therapy, and Lee have helped."

Richard leaned into Antonio's leg. "I'll be there if you need. Just...in my own way."

Antonio smiled up at him with an unfairly charming smile, considering he was hanging upside down off the couch. "Thanks, Dicky."

"So, tell me about your proposal plan," Richard said quickly, before Antonio could get any ideas like trying to hug him.

"Oh!" Antonio swung his legs around to sit back upright. "You know how I make up, like, songs and shit to remember things?"

Richard nodded. Antonio had often hummed under his breath for as long as Richard had known him.

"I'm turning my Lee Song into a real song. Like, the good parts, of course. Don't need to remind Lee of hard times unless they're *our* hard times, you know?"

Richard hummed noncommittally. Lee had never told him directly about how his parents had kicked him out, but Sunny had. He didn't want to blow their cover by revealing he knew anything about Lee's past.

Luckily, Antonio didn't notice his nonresponse, because Gabe returned with his laptop and camera, sitting down without a word. Antonio chattered on about his plans to surprise Lee with the song during the album release party, while Gabe transferred the photos he had taken to his computer.

Gabe scrolled through the previews silently. But soon he stopped on a photo of Tara. A lovely photo, no doubt. Tara was striking. Not as breathtaking as Sunny, but Richard could see what attracted Gabe to her. Hopefully, he hadn't overstepped today during that damn game. Sunny had said that Tara didn't care if people were nice, but he still felt like an ass.

But he'd handed Gabe a golden opportunity to look good, which he'd mostly taken, other than briefly losing his temper. Gabe and Tara had spent the rest of the afternoon bantering about Gabe's camera, instead of whatever the fuck Gabe usually did to get her attention. Richard counted that as a win.

Richard elbowed Antonio and pointed to the laptop with his chin once he realized Gabe was lost in his head, staring at this picture of Tara.

Antonio grinned before leaning over to Gabe, putting an arm around his waist. "Gabey, you're staring." Gabe leaned into the side hug. "Don't get me wrong, great shot, Tara's gorgeous, yada yada. But you've been staring at that one for a while. Get to the pictures of me!"

Taking the laptop, Antonio scrolled through the photos. Gabe stayed pressed against him, as Richard had intended. He needed the affection that Antonio could provide.

"Oh, wow. Gabey, these are great. Did Tara take this one?" Antonio pointed at a photo of Gabe and Hippo. "She really captured you. You look sexy as hell!"

Gabe groaned. It'd be a cold day in Hell before Gabe admitted he was attractive.

"There are a lot of photos of Tara here. Even more than Hippo." Antonio elbowed him with a smirk. "Hey, speaking of Tara—who do you think she had sex with in our bathroom? Did she just rub one out in there, or did she sneak someone in when we weren't home?"

Gabe snatched the laptop back, putting it away just as the oven timer beeped. Richard tried to catch Antonio's eye to exchange a knowing look. Antonio might not remember them disappearing at New Year's, but he had to have seen the hickeys Tara had left on his neck. Or Gabe's hand on her ass when they were leaving Stormé's. But Antonio just smiled down at the engagement ring around his neck. *Maybe I don't have to try so hard to hide the fact that I'm dating Sunny. Antonio wouldn't catch on even if we were fucking in his apartment, apparently.*

Gabe set the table as they moved to the kitchen. Broccoli, chicken, and cavatappi noodles bubbled in a baking dish. "Bon appétit. Courtesy of my mom. Sorry, I didn't realize it had dairy and meat in it, Tonio. Want me to make you something else?" Gabe turned to microwave one of his health-nut stir-fries that he'd prepared for the week. Richard served himself a small portion of Miriam's home cooking onto his plate and passed the ladle to Antonio.

"No, I love your mom's cooking! Apologize to Lee, not me. He's gotta live with my lactose intolerant ass." Antonio grinned as he scooped up the pasta with gusto, licking his finger where cheese sauce had dripped on it. "You should bring the rest to Blanche and Tara when you get Hippo if you're not gonna eat it, though. This is delicious."

While Antonio shared in *precise* detail how Lee proposed to him, Richard ate in silence, strangely wishing he could share his own secrets. How he had finally cooked for Sunny, and the pasta had been horribly overcooked, but she had pretended it was delicious. How he'd met her mom and sister and somehow passed muster. How he was strangely happy. Not that he'd been *unhappy*, but this strange, easy, joie de vivre was new.

He'd never considered introducing his friends to any of his previous significant others, but they already knew Sunny, and hiding his relationship from them... Well, it weighed on him. The game was starting to feel duplicitous. More so than nearly ten years of hiding his tattoos. Sunny mattered to Richard, and he was actively hiding her from the only other people who did, too.

Everett had also torn him a new one for not telling him about Sunny sooner. And then torn into him again for not telling literally anyone else. If his therapist was that frustrated by him, Richard could only imagine how his friends would react.

"That was heaven in my mouth, and it will be hell coming out of my ass." Antonio patted his stomach with a laugh. "I might sleep on the couch tonight. Don't wanna fuck up this marriage before I even propose. Speaking of, I should go pick up my fiancée. Gotta get my beauty sleep before the last week of school!" He stood up, kissing Gabe on the cheek.

Richard tried and failed to dodge his own cheek kiss. "I don't understand how he has that much energy working at a middle school," Richard said, rubbing his cheek.

Gabe chuckled. "I'd probably yell constantly."

Richard didn't believe that for a second. "You don't lose it on your art students."

"True, but they want to be there. And we talk about art and shit, not real conversations. They're nicer than most teenagers."

Richard sighed. "You're a better person than you give yourself credit for. In fact, I daresay you've been almost happy lately. Or at least you've been bouncing back faster."

Gabe shrugged. "I have been going to therapy for a couple years now. I hope it's helping."

"It is." Richard paused, unsure of how to put the glow in his chest into words without sounding awkward. "I'm proud of you." Still incredibly awkward, but he'd meant it.

"Thanks, Richard," Gabe said softly. "What's with you though? You just gave me a compliment. Are you coming down with something?"

Richard shot him a grin. "Oh, no. Just noticed you've been trying very hard to keep yourself together. Especially around a certain someone."

Gabe tried to play it off. "Who, Hippo?"

Richard's grin grew wider. "Speaking of Hippo, he was unusually friendly with Tara today. It's almost like he'd met her before..."

Gabe tugged his hair. "You heard her. It was probably her period or some shit."

Richard raised an eyebrow at him. "Sure. And someone with their period heavy enough for a dog to smell across the park is going commando and jumping into kiddie pools."

Gabe stiffened and shot him an accusing glare. "You were testing her, weren't you? To see if she was lying? You're such a dick!"

Richard shrugged. "It was obvious she was lying. Maybe I'm just a dick."

"You're not usually that much of a dick." Gabe scowled.

For someone so emotionally intelligent, Gabe could be so thick. Richard sighed. "You're welcome for the opportunity to make you look good."

Gabe's face clouded. "Don't do that. I don't... I know you think you're being helpful, but I don't like—"

"I'm sorry," Richard mumbled when Gabe gave up on trying to finish his sentence. If his prank made Gabe feel this manipulated, should he tell Gabe about Antonio's scheme? Sweat prickled his spine. Was it his place to say something, or should he get Antonio to fess up?

When the indecision and guilt became too much to bear, Richard stood up, taking their plates to the kitchen and covering the pasta with tin foil. "Here. Bring this to your girlfriend when you get your dog, since you won't eat it."

"She's not my girlfriend." Gabe clenched his jaw.

To their mutual surprise, Richard hugged him, drawing Gabe's head against his chest. "Maybe not, but if you want her to be, get your shit together."

Gabe wrapped his arms around him and sniffled as he squeezed tight. Richard let him, even as his skin crawled. Gabe needed the hug. Richard could tolerate how wrong it felt for Gabe's sake. He appreciated that Sunny let Richard hold her without touching him back. "If you tell anyone I hugged you, you'll need another protection order."

"No one cares if you hug people, Dicky."

Richard let go, bending down to put his sneakers on. "Can you offer Sunny a ride home? She usually takes the bus home from Blanche's, and it's getting late."

Gabe shot him a confused look. "Yeah sure, I'll ask."

Richard was a little disappointed that Gabe didn't ask how Richard knew that, or why he cared. But maybe it would plant the seed so that he'd be less surprised—feel less lied to—when he eventually found out about Sunny at the MAI fundraiser. Guilt ate at him, but Richard didn't know what to say. So he left, wishing it was the weekend, so Sunny could come over to ease this paralyzing solitude that left him feeling isolated from the people he loved most.

Chapter Twenty-Seven

Sunny

"I hate this game." Tara frowned as Sunny's Peach came in first. Again. Tara's Waluigi zoomed across the finish line just seconds ahead of Lee's Toad.

Sunny gloated. "I love it."

Lee groaned. "We almost had her this time."

"You say that every time," Sunny teased. It had been months since they had hung out like this. While Sunny was unquestionably a cat person, the addition of Hippo—sprawled on the couch behind Tara, who leaned into him, petting his shoulder fondly—lightened the mood even more than usual. Sunny cocked her head, watching them all from across the coffee table. "Blanche, you should get a dog."

Blanche lay with their legs crossed delicately over Hippo's back, a dreamy smile on their face. "I wish I could, but I'd rather not risk eviction, no matter how cute they are!" They squished Hippo's face, kissing him loudly on the head. "My patron's future wife is insisting her name be on everything. He's moving the lease to an LLC or something to be safe."

"Do we have a backup plan?" Tara tried to be nonchalant, but the tremor in her voice hinted at the depths of her anxiety. "I've got my duffel packed, just in case, but will we have any warning if she finds a way to evict us?"

"Buttercup, I'm your backup plan. Me and Tonio." Lee bumped her shoulder.

"And you don't need to live out of your duffel bag, babes." Blanche played with Hippo's ears. "Even if she takes over the lease, I have a contract that grants me housing, so she'd have to file an eviction and somehow break my contract. My patron says he's on top of it, and he's determined to keep me kept."

"This isn't like the camp. Or Auntie Alitrice's," Lee added. "You won't lose everything again."

Tara grumbled. "Still, I don't want to be a burden. Your apartment isn't exactly built for four people. I'll just save up enough for a deposit for us, just in case."

"I think Gabe has like four bedrooms. Maybe he'd—"

"No." Tara cut Lee off sharply. "I'll save up."

Lee huffed. "Well, in that case, I'll pay you back the money I owe—"

"No, dude!" Tara crossed her arms. "I'll just take on more commissions. Don't worry about it."

"Why do you owe her money?" Sunny asked, doubt creeping in. Tara seemed more anxious about their living situation than she'd expected.

"No reason," Tara and Lee said together.

"Neither of you have to worry, you know," Blanche said, their smile still dreamy as they pet Hippo. "With how well my channel has been doing, I've made more money this year than I ever have."

"Do you need a loan or something?" Sunny asked Tara.

"No, you need to save up for your upgrade." Tara glared at her. "Can we stop talking about money? Or getting evicted?"

Lee and Blanche exchanged a look that Sunny couldn't decipher, and both shook their heads at her.

"Fine, Tara-Bear," Sunny said, interpreting that to mean she shouldn't push the subject. She hadn't been offering up *her* money. Maybe Richard could make a contribution from his trust fund to Blanche in secret. They wouldn't refuse it like Tara would. "What have you been up to lately? We barely talk anymore."

"Why did we have to change the subject to *me*?" Tara scowled. "Since when do we talk?"

"Bitch, we talk. We're friends, remember?" Sunny rolled her eyes. Sure, they hadn't talked as much lately. But last summer, she'd camped out here waiting for a scrap of attention from Blanche. Lee had been off getting busy with Antonio, so Sunny and Tara had spent a lot of time together. Tara would tell her about her dates and listen to whatever had popped into Sunny's brain while they played video games. Just like they were doing now.

Tara shifted in her seat. "I dunno. I haven't been up to anything."

"That is a deeply unsatisfying answer, Tara-Bear," Sunny said. "What, you haven't been doing anything? Not seeing anyone new or going on dates?"

Tara shrugged. "No, not for a while. I've been a homebody. Just working. Why, what have you been up to?"

Secret relationship? Lying to all of you? Falling for Richard? Sunny glanced at Lee. "Nothing either, I guess. I have been dressing up more at work. Asha and I started Femme Fridays. So far it's mostly only resulted in us getting talked over more during meetings. But at least we're cute!" Sunny turned to Blanche. "And you, Blanche? Anything new and exciting going on?"

Blanche shook their head. "Just my channel and clients. I don't have the emotional capacity for anything else these days. Who knew subscribers were so needy?"

Sunny pouted. "Lee? What have you been doing? Besides being holed up with your boyfriend and making music? Please tell me you're doing something fun."

Lee smiled. "Just happy with Antonio, occasionally hanging out with my other friends, and going to Antonio's mom's house for dinner. Our album is pretty much done, so I've been busy doing marketing shit."

"Wow, isn't that romantic?" Sunny eyed him carefully. He wasn't lying, but that smile was hiding something. But she wouldn't press it, not when she was hiding her own secrets. "When did we get so boring? Lee's the only one with a social life, and it's his boyfriend."

Lee shrugged. "I know, it's corny, but he makes me happy. I probably should be sick of him after spending all our time together, but I'm not."

A knock sounded on the door. Tara got up to open it and was greeted by Antonio's hug.

"Hi, Tara-Bear! Gabe was showing me those pictures you guys took today. There was one of you that was just absolutely stun. I mean, they were all stunning, and between you and me, there were a *lot* of you, but this one in particular was wow! Gabey couldn't take his eyes off it."

Tara's face turned bright red. Lee and Blanche exchanged a smirk. Sunny pretended not to notice.

"And the pictures you took of him? You captured him beautifully! He never takes good photos of himself. Well, he never takes photos of himself to begin with, but when he does he makes *such* unflattering facial expressions. It was gratifying to finally get him to admit he doesn't look as hideous as he thinks he does."

"Take a breath, Tonio. You're talking so fast." Lee kissed the top of Antonio's head.

"Gabe made us dinner. I missed you though! I couldn't shut up about you." Antonio wrapped his arms around Lee's waist.

Lee smiled. "Nothing bad I hope."

"Of course not! Just, you know, happy stuff." Antonio winked at him. "Full warning, the food Gabe made had a lot of dairy. And before you talk shit, I'll sleep on the couch."

"Remind me to key Gabe's car," Lee laughed. "But *I'll* sleep on the couch. You have to work tomorrow. Just crack a window, please."

Part of Sunny burned with envy for their happiness, the inside jokes, the comfort they shared so openly. Even though she had that, albeit privately. She wanted to let everyone else into their relationship, instead of the mutual antagonism she and Richard performed. She wanted her friends to hear Richard's dorky laugh, and the sarcastic comments he'd sneak in while she was rambling that made her laugh. To witness the affection he doted on her. And even though she and Richard hadn't exactly discussed how to tell their friends, other than surprising Gabe, she was bursting to tell *somebody*.

The second the door closed behind Lee and Antonio, Sunny grabbed Tara by the shoulders and sat her down next to Hippo and Blanche. "I have something to tell you, and I can't keep it a secret anymore. I need to talk to someone about it. Besides Luna, 'cause it's hella weird to talk about with my little sister." Sunny leveled Tara with a serious look as she sat on the coffee table. "But you have to promise not to tell anyone. Well, you and Blanche can talk about it, but that's it. Not Antonio, Lee, or Gabe—at least not yet."

Tara told Lee everything, but Sunny hoped her curiosity was piqued. Too quickly, Tara said, "Okay, I promise. What is it?"

"Do you actually promise, or are you going to tell Lee anyway?"

"Do you want to tell me or not?" Tara shrugged. "If I think he needs to know, I'll tell him. If not, your secret is safe with me."

Sunny wrinkled her nose. "This is why I don't tell you secrets."

"You talk too much to have any secrets," Tara imitated her snotty tone, even wrinkling her nose.

"Oh really?" Sunny flipped her hair over her shoulder, the words spilling out of her like a dam had burst. "Richard and I have been together since my birthday, and my mom found out a few weeks ago, and it was awful but then she invited him over for dinner, and it went way better than I thought it would, and now Mae is fully on Team Richard. She's been telling everyone back in Chiang Mai about him." Sunny held out her arms. "How's that for having secrets? I've had a whole-ass relationship serious enough that he met the family, and you had no idea!"

Tara gaped. "Wait, *Richard*?"

"Yeah. He's the sweetest. He's so perfect." Sunny's cheeks hurt from grinning, but the relief of getting this off her chest was bliss. "Anyway, he's bringing me to some fundraiser to meet Gabe's parents in a couple of weeks because he doesn't talk to his own parents. I'm strangely getting really nervous!"

"Are we talking about the same Richard who tortured me with the stupid fountain earlier? And belongs to a *yacht club*?" Tara scratched her head, expression still stunned to Sunny's delight. "You hate him!"

"The very same. The one I make fun of for being an evil capitalist, and his designer clothes, and for being an asshole? Yes, that Richard. It surprised me too, but he's sweet and generous and gives great head." Sunny sighed happily.

Blanche looked confused. "Since when do *you* like getting head?"

"Let's not go there." Tara shook her head. "Happy that you're getting some, but TMI. Why can't I tell Lee?"

"Oh! Because Lee and Antonio have this secret plan to hook us all up. That's why they're always late and planning awful parties. To force us to hang out in hopes that we smash one day. Little do they know, we were already doing that this whole time." Sunny clapped with glee. "Anyway, what do people wear to fundraisers?"

Tara held up a hand. "Hold on, still processing. When you say 'plan to hook us all up,' does that mean like *all* of us? Or just you and Richard?"

"Well, and you and Gabe, of course," Blanche added from the couch. "I'm their accomplice, but I've been double-crossing them." They grinned, turning to Hippo. "Don't tell your dad we're trying to make Tara your mom, okay, handsome?"

Hippo snorted in response, tail thumping on the couch cushion.

"Why would they try to hook Gabe and me up?" Tara's brow knit tight in confusion.

Sunny and Blanche laughed. Even Hippo grunted, wiggling in Blanche's lap.

"Because you have it bad for each other?" Sunny said, trying not to sound condescending. But seriously, everyone saw it.

Tara coughed. "No, we don't. Sure, he's hot, but why would he want to get with me like that? I'm a mess."

"Babes, he follows you around like a lost puppy." Blanche waved her off. "Besides, he's a mess too. At first, I wasn't sure about him, but he's won me over. Don't rush into anything you're not ready for, but keep an open mind about him." Blanche turned to Sunny, gesturing at her to ignore Tara's existential spiral. "Tell me about when he met your mom. Does he meet Birdie's high expectations?"

"Well, she saw us on a happy hour date having drinks a couple of weeks ago and flipped out. It was awful." Sunny winced as embarrassment burned through her at the memory. "Like, I even cried. But Mae and I talked when I got home, and she was surprisingly supportive. She invited him over for dinner, and Richard did everything right to win her over. Reassured her that he wants to get married and have kids one day and has a good job and stuff like that."

Blanche's half smile curved into a smirk. "You're talking about marriage and kids huh? This is getting serious."

"I mean, we're not there yet, obviously. It's only been four months. But we both want them eventually." Sunny's cheeks burned.

Blanche glanced at Tara; she was staring at her knees, mouth moving in a silent conversation with herself. "Okay, Tara stopped listening. Tell me the TMI stuff while she's overthinking."

Sunny grinned eagerly, excited to talk about this with someone other than Black_Hawk. He'd reacted much the same as Tara, sending her countless gifs of people with their hands pressed over their ears. "So like, Richard made a list for us, so we can keep track of what we like and don't like. And you know I don't typically like head, but I dunno, the way he does it? Like it's a little Ick at first, but like once we're into it, it's amazing. I wish I could tell you what he does exactly, but you know my brain goes offline. I can't pay attention to shit."

"A list, huh?" Blanche snorted. "Well, let me know if you ever want help negotiating an agreement for anything. My offer still stands."

Sunny blushed. She hadn't forgotten per se, just wasn't sure if Richard would want Blanche involved in that. "I'll let you know. We have some things on our list that are a bit advanced, but we haven't gotten to anything that might go beyond a safeword." She chewed her lip, and could practically feel Richard's thumb pulling it away from her teeth. She rubbed her lip with her own thumb instead. "And not that I'm with him for his money, but dating a millionaire has its perks. Like, anything I want to try, I just tell him and suddenly all of the equipment and a gallon of lube show up. I'll have to send you this lingerie brand he found. It's like a tucking panties meets femme jockstrap situation, so my Ick parts are less Icky during sex."

Blanche's smile was soft, and—if Sunny wasn't reading too much into it—a little sad. "You've got it made, Babygirl."

"I know. I'm... I'm glad we can talk about this. It's been weird not having anyone to go to," Sunny admitted.

"Me too. I'm honored you're telling me now."

Another knock at the door broke Tara's attention, pulling her out of her spiral. She got up to let Gabe in, who smiled shyly, tinfoil-covered pan in hand. "I have leftovers. Want them?"

Tara took the pan, sniffing loudly. "I never say no to food. What did you bring us?" She stepped back to let him into the apartment.

"A pasta bake my mom sent home with me a while ago. I made it for dinner tonight, but we had a lot left over, and I won't eat it." Gabe waved at Blanche and Sunny, who waved back.

"Pasta! Hell yeah." Tara grinned. Setting the pan on the kitchen counter, she stole a peek under the tinfoil.

"Not disappointed that it's not cake this time?" Gabe teased.

"I can never be disappointed with pasta." Tara grinned.

Sunny and Blanche exchanged a small smile as Gabe bent over the couch to pet his dog. "Hippo! I missed you!" Hippo climbed up the back of the couch, tail wagging hard as he jumped into Gabe's arms. His dimples highlighted his grin as Hippo wiggled against him. "Ready to go home, buddy? Did you have fun?"

"He had a great time. He got all of the pets and kisses. He was treated like the king he is." Blanche gave Hippo one last loud smooch as Gabe put his leash on.

"Did you get the dog time you needed?" Gabe asked quietly.

"It's never enough." Their smile fading, Blanche wrapped their arms around themself as Hippo wagged his tail.

"Sunny, do you want a ride home?" Gabe offered suddenly.

Sunny nodded in surprise, wondering how Richard had put Gabe up to this without revealing their secret. "I'd love one. Thanks!"

He turned back to Tara. "You haven't been drinking or anything have you?"

Tara's eyes went wide. "No, it's Monday."

"Want to drive?" Gabe offered. "Y'know, for practice."

Tara's excited beam was quickly overcome by panic. "Yes, but maybe I shouldn't start on actual roads right away."

"Yeah, if *Tara's* driving, no way in hell am I getting in that car!" Sunny chimed in. She wanted a ride, but not at the risk of her life.

Gabe touched the ends of his hair, tugging gently on it. Hippo nudged him, asking for pets instead. He turned to Sunny, hand leaving his hair to give Hippo a scratch behind his ears. "Okay, I'll drive *you* home." Turning back to Tara, he added, "And then *we* can find a parking lot or something, where you can practice for a while."

After a pause, Tara smiled up at him with a nod. He smiled back, a hint of those charming dimples that always appeared more around Tara.

Sunny and Blanche exchanged another smirk.

CHAPTER TWENTY-EIGHT

TARA

GABE'S DISTRACTING DIMPLES WERE long gone as Tara slammed too hard on the brakes. Again. "I don't know why I'm so bad at this."

Hippo groaned from his crate in the back at every lurch, jerk, and sudden stop.

"Honestly, I'm surprised too, Kitten." Gabe scratched his head in frustration. "Maybe let's just stick with the brake for now. Don't touch the gas. Just get used to letting off the brake slowly, and pressing it back down. Slowly."

"That sounds boring," Tara teased. She wanted to go faster, but she heeded his advice and scooted slowly up the high school's empty parking lot. "That's not as bad, right?"

"No, that was great. I think you're moving too quickly from a full stop to adding too much gas and vice versa. You know, ease off the thing holding you back *before* you go full throttle on going forward."

"Thanks for the life lesson," Tara said sarcastically.

Gabe snorted. "My therapist will wonder why I don't take it myself."

As embarrassed as she was that she was still just as tragically awful at driving as ever, it was so easy with just the two of them. Even stressed out like she was now, learning a new skill that she was not immediately good at, Tara didn't feel judged or pressured. Just that familiar longing and whatever the happy gooey shit was. It reminded her of...something.

Tara scooted the car around, adding the gas back in as she started to feel how the car behaved. Her palms were slick around the steering wheel, her anxiety stemming from the stress of driving. Or perhaps from being alone with him, after Blanche had casually dropped that he was…interested in her. Not that it mattered. Even if Gabe felt anything beyond sexual attraction, Tara didn't do emotional stuff.

She may have some soft feelings for him, but Tara needed to keep her distance. At least emotionally. Physically? That was another story. She could ignore her soft feelings if she got another mind-blowing orgasm or four. Maybe if they continued like this, they could eventually be friends, and with enough time—

"I have a wager for you." Gabe broke the silence.

"A wager huh? What's the stakes this time? Anal?" Tara joked.

Gabe exhaled with a strangled groan. "I was going to say loser buys a round."

"What, you don't want me to peg you if you lose?" she teased.

"Peg me if I *win*, maybe," Gabe shot back. "But no, we should keep sex out of the stakes."

Tara's heart froze, slamming on the brake. Hippo groaned in protest. She whirled to face him. "Why? Did I do something wrong?"

Gabe's brow furrowed, eyes wide with concern. "What? No! It's not anything you did."

"Then what is it?" Her voice cracked as her heart leapt to her throat. A mere moment ago, Blanche had said he was interested in her, and here he was, leaving her. She wasn't even good enough for sex? Her chest ached with every shallow breath. "Why don't you want me anymore?"

"Whoa." Gabe silenced her by pressing a finger to her nose, jolting her out of her spiraling thoughts. His brown eyes pleaded with her in earnest. "Can I pause you for a second? I need a moment to get my words in the order I want them, so I don't say the wrong thing and make whatever this is," he gestured in her direction, "worse."

Tara nodded. The nose boop was a little weird, but the surprise of it had stopped her growing panic. Eyes burning, she put the car in park and waited as he took a moment, running his hands through his hair. This was a perfect opportunity to collect herself before her feelings spilled over. Fear and hurt and loneliness were threatening her fragile self-control. Her skin boiled with embarrassment. She hadn't realized she cared if he left her or not. *Fuck. I do like him.*

Inhale, 2, 3, 4, 5. I see the sunset. She put the fear away.

Exhale, 4, 3, 2, 1. I hear the radio. He listens to a lot of R&B. She smiled as the hurt was gently tucked away.

Inhale, 2, 3, 4, 5. I smell vanilla and that oaky scent of him. Loneliness was folded up neatly and put with the others.

Exhale, 4, 3, 2, 1. I feel the seat belt around me, the steering wheel in my hands. She left the happy gooey feeling out, but put Longing away. The gooey feeling had been useful before.

As Tara breathed, her panic settled. How could he abandon her, if he wasn't hers? Sure, she apparently *liked* him, but Gabe wasn't her family. The chill from the prospect of being abandoned again was placated with the knowledge that he had an explanation.

Maybe it wasn't even about her this time. *Doubtful.* A memory of her mother yelling at her to get lost flashed in her mind, sending a flash of shame burning through her. Tara still didn't know what she'd done to make her mom angry enough to abandon her.

Gabe eventually spoke, slowly and deliberately, his gaze on his knees. "I've been hurt by past partners, in ways that left me less in control of myself. So to help me set boundaries and build emotional resilience, I'm starting an EMDR treatment soon with my therapist, and I need to protect myself while I'm doing that." He paused, looking at the dash. "The truth is I like you, Kitten. A lot. And the last time we... After your birthday, I lost what little emotional stability I'd built up, and I think it's because of how much I like you. That kiss..." He shook his head with a huff. "I can't compartmentalize my feelings for you when we're together—I can't do casual with you without breaking. I'm barely hanging on to myself."

The ice in her chest melted, her heart breaking for him instead. Tara played with the hangnail, embracing the sharpness against the pad of her thumb. Curiosity burned, anger simmering at these nameless past partners who had hurt someone she...*cared* about, or whatever. The only questions she could think to ask were for their names and addresses, so that she and Blanche could pay them a visit. But Gabe probably wouldn't find that helpful.

Gabe looked at her, his brown eyes watery and desperate enough to wash all fantasies of violence from her head. "All I can give you for now is platonic friendship. I really, *really* want to give you more than that in the future, if you're at all interested when I'm stronger. *If* I'm ever stronger." He dropped his gaze again and ran his hands through his hair with a bitter laugh. "Especially because you just casually suggested pegging me, and now I will not be able to stop thinking about it. You're fucking amazing, Kitten, and I hate that I met you when I'm the worst version of myself. So sex has to be off the table, but it's not because I don't want you. It's because I want you too much. I'm just starting to figure out who I am again, and I'd lose myself in you *so* easily."

Tara stayed silent, still counting her breaths. He wasn't abandoning her, just protecting himself from her. Her jaw clenched. She could understand that; all of her many rules existed to protect herself from the worst parts of her nature.

"Are you going to say anything?" Gabe asked. His coffee brown eyes sought hers as the late sunset turned his olive skin gold.

Tara jumped, realizing she was staring at him silently because she had no idea what to say. She pointed at her nose. "I'm still paused."

Gabe threw back his head with a laugh, those damn dimples deepening. He poked her nose again. "Fine, play."

Tara gaped for a moment. "I'm sorry for kissing you. I thought you were asleep. Which doesn't make it any better—worse, really. I should have asked."

Gabe shook his head. "I told you I wanted to kiss you. I did—*do*—want to kiss you. If you had asked, I would have let you kiss me a thousand times. But the reality of waking up to you kissing me, and not being able to kiss you back, was like having one of those really beautiful dreams where you wake up crying because it's not real. Bittersweet or whatever. It fucked me up, but that's not your fault. Just a sign I need to get stronger."

"If I'm being honest with myself, I need to get stronger too. Consider me inspired to work on myself." She was surprised with how well she was handling this, even as sadness crept in and her longing screamed at her. *Is this how normal people do this? Ignore their longing because it's for the best? This sucks ass.*

Even a year ago, Tara never would have fathomed wanting an emotional connection like Gabe was suggesting. But now? Now she saw how damn happy Lee and Antonio were, and their joy together made her loneliness darker in contrast. Maybe one day, she'd let herself figure out her soft feelings enough to be open to...whatever it was that Gabe felt for her. "And I would be honored to be your friend. Just warning you, I'm worse at that than I am at driving."

Gabe laughed a little at that. "Can I hug you?" His voice was soft.

Tara nodded, allowing herself to be buried in his arms, letting the smell of vanilla and oak and him wash over her. She blinked back tears as she wrapped her arms around his torso, fisting the fabric of his t-shirt.

This felt like an end. Regret filled her at the finality of his touch.

"So what's this wager you were talking about?" Tara asked into his chest, trying to lighten the air that hung thick between them.

He pulled away, wiping his eyes. She wanted to hug him longer, but Tara sat back in the driver's seat. Gabe looked at her carefully before saying, "I bet that Lee and Tonio will get engaged before the year is up."

Tara fought the urge to respond with a "duh." But Lee had sworn her to secrecy; she should cover for them, at least until Antonio proposed. *God, now I wish anal was the prize. I wouldn't care if I win or lose.* "I have one for you too."

"Oh? And what's that?"

Tara had one card up her sleeve that she hoped he didn't. "I bet that Richard and Sunny will get together before the year is up." She still couldn't believe that was an actual thing, but the more she considered it, the more it clicked. Whenever Lee forced them to hang out with Antonio's friends—Tara's gut surged with a lot of emotions at *that* revelation from earlier, one which she refused to unpack until she was home alone and safe in bed—Richard and Sunny did spend a lot of time together, even if it was arguing. Richard talked to Sunny more than anyone. And Sunny hadn't been coming around as often.

"Seriously? With *Sunny*? It's on. You're about to lose twice, Kitten—sorry, Tara." Gabe shook his head with a forced smile. "So, do you want to try driving home, or should we switch back so I can drive?"

Wondering if that was the last time he'd ever call her Kitten, Tara barely remembered to unbuckle before jumping out of the car. "You drive. I'm not ready to drive on an actual road yet."

Wednesday, June Tenth

CHAPTER TWENTY-NINE

LEE

"Buttercup, want some coffee?" Lee poked his head out of the kitchen, half hoping she'd say yes so he could have some too.

Sitting cross-legged on the sofa in Lee and Antonio's apartment, Tara was working on a commission while Blanche recorded a session with a client. As usual, Lee and Tara had gotten everything set up properly—all Blanche had to do was hit "record" and get their client on their marks—and then come home, where Tara would hang out until the client left. He sometimes missed spending hours with Tara at Confession during the week, but this routine was far superior to the chaos before Blanche had started their channel.

Tara looked up from her laptop. "Little late for coffee, isn't it?"

Lee shrugged. Antonio wasn't even home yet; it couldn't be that late. On weeknights, Antonio went to bed by nine, which was way too early, so Lee would stay up working on his music until at least midnight. "Are you getting old? Is it too late for caffeine now?"

Tara scowled. "I'm not getting old. I just have a morning meeting with some MLM girlboss type."

"Another new client?" Lee asked. "You've been busy. You want tea instead, then?"

Tara nodded. "This one is so needy too. She's so demanding for a shit commission and keeps calling me bestie."

Lee walked back to the living room after putting the kettle on. "Why don't you just, I dunno, tell her no? Or fuck off?"

"Rich advice coming from Mr. Conflict Avoidant himself," Tara teased, shaking her head with a tight smile. "I would, but I need to, y'know, build my brand or whatever. I'm not happy about it, but it'll be good for the bank account."

"As long as your brand isn't being a doormat, Buttercup." He sat next to her on the couch, guilt eating at him. She was hiding her money stress from him again. Stress that Lee had caused. Stress he couldn't fix yet, because the wedding deposits were eating up all of his and Antonio's money. He pushed his glasses up. He had to stay confident the album was an investment. He believed in Antonio, and he trusted that he'd be able to pay Tara back soon.

Tara scowled. "I don't think anyone would describe me as a doormat."

Lee leaned into her. "You act tough, Buttercup but I know you. You're a big softie. I barely mentioned I couldn't afford the ring I wanted for Antonio, and you transferred the difference to me before I finished the sentence. Remember when you gave our sleeping mat to Walter? Or all of the times you sat with Aunt Alitrice during her chemo treatments? Or when you took that awful babysitting job just so you could buy me a cake for my birthday? God, those kids were annoying."

Tara's face softened into a smile. "They weren't that bad. It wasn't their fault their parents were dicks."

"They pulled out a chunk of your hair. And screamed the whole time."

"They were sweet, how they looked out for each other." Tara shrugged. "I dunno. I wouldn't wish my childhood on anyone, but it would have been nice to have a sibling to lean on when I was growing up. They were cute."

"You have a sibling. Me." Lee kissed the top of her head. "And it wasn't all bad, was it? You had good memories at the camp, too."

He knew Blanche and Sunny didn't understand why they kept going back there, but that had been Tara's home. When they needed somewhere safe to go as teens, she had brought him to the encampment. She'd avoided it since the riot, but if Tara wanted to reconnect with her good memories there, Lee would do what he could to make that happen. "And you had fun the other week, right?"

Despite Richard's asshole dare and Gabe losing his temper, Tara had laughed and eaten enough cookies to keep herself happy; she'd seemed comfortable there again in a way he hadn't seen in years. Maybe he was pushing her out of her comfort zone, but Tara's comfort zone was a prison. She'd never leave it on her own.

Tara smiled. "It was weird being there without the bus and everyone, but it was fun."

The kettle whistled, and Lee went back to the kitchen, returning with two steaming mugs of tea. He sat back down on the couch, quietly admitting, "I'm going crazy."

Tara looked at him, waiting.

Lee sipped his tea, his chest tightening, but he had to get this out. "I proposed six weeks ago, and Antonio still hasn't done his back. He keeps dropping hints, and then it never happens. I thought for sure it would have happened by now."

"You took seven months. Maybe he's getting payback," Tara smiled.

Lee groaned. "God, I hope not. This is excruciating."

A key entered the lock. Antonio's voice could be heard from the other side.

"Shh," Lee hushed. "We weren't talking about it. You're not supposed to know."

Tara rolled her eyes. "He *has* to know you told me."

Antonio entered the room, wearing his teacher drag—khakis and a forest green button-down shirt. Still attractive, but a different person from the real Antonio he lived with. "Oh, hey Tara-Bear!"

Tara smiled and waved. "Hey, Tonio."

Her smile fell, and she whipped her gaze to her computer as Gabe walked in behind him, carrying several large boxes. After six months of forcing them to hang out together, Lee had hoped that she could at least look Gabe in the eye by now, instead of freezing every time he was around. He sighed into his mug. They'd gotten along so well just two weeks ago. What had gotten into Tara's head this time?

"Hey Lee, Tara." Gabe nodded politely in her direction, his jaw clenching.

Oh, no, Gabe, too? Lee and Antonio exchanged a mildly exasperated look. *So much for getting along better.* After Memorial Day, Antonio had sworn up and down that Gabe would be over his Tara-inspired assholery. That things with their friends were finally on a more peaceful track.

"We picked up the promo stuff for the album release party!" Antonio took one of the boxes from Gabe. "See? Check out the posters Gabe printed at the museum!"

He unrolled a life-size photo of Carlita. Their album cover was wonderfully campy, with Carlita's arms full of various cuts of meat. A sausage poked suggestively out of her mouth. The full-size Carlita next to Antonio in his teacher drag was bizarre.

"Looks great," Tara said with a laugh. "It's giving meat raffle. Very Bellamy."

"Thanks, Tara-Bear! Exactly what I was going for! No wonder the New York crowd never understood me. Not nearly enough meat raffles out East." Antonio laughed as he rolled up the poster, putting it back in the box. "Lee, Angel, babe, love of my life, could you be a dear and help Gabe bring this into the office for storage?"

"I can do it. I'm already holding most of the boxes." Gabe offered.

"Oh sure, but Lee, can you help him?" Antonio insisted.

Lee gave him a pointed look. Antonio gave him a stare in return.

With a sigh, Lee stood up and kissed Antonio's cheek. "How long do you need?" he asked quietly.

"Give me a minute and thirty seconds," Antonio murmured back.

"So, three." Lee brought the one box that Gabe wasn't holding to the spare bedroom, Gabe at his heels.

"What was that about?" Gabe asked as Lee shut the door behind him.

"I'm sure I'll find out. Sooner than later, preferably." Lee checked the time before leaning on the door. "So...how are you?"

Gabe ran a hand through his hair with a heavy sigh.

ANTONIO

ANTONIO DOVE ONTO THE couch next to Tara as soon as Lee and Gabe had left the room. "Tara, thank God you're here," he whispered. "Can you keep a secret from Lee?"

"No." Tara leaned in with a grin. "Unless it's a surprise proposal I'm not supposed to know about. I could maybe keep a secret about that."

"I knew it!" Antonio beamed. "I'm going to do it at the album release party. Can you get it on video?"

Tara nodded. "Is my phone okay, or do you want a camera from Blanche's set?"

"Phone is perfect. Gabe will be taking pictures, so any video would be wonderful. Just start recording when I call Lee onstage?"

"Gabe knows too?" Tara asked, leaning back, her brow furrowing.

"Yeah, but Lee doesn't know I told Gabe, and Gabe doesn't know you know, so that's between you and me for another two weeks, 'kay?" Antonio checked his phone. Not enough time was left for Tara to process whatever she was overthinking. "Could you also take photos for our Save the Dates? And can you do your thing to make it pretty? We can pay you of course. I'd like to have them ready before the album release party."

"Yeah, of course! No charge though—friends and family discount." Tara's smile was more like a wince, but her voice was bright. Maybe it wasn't about the favor he was asking? Lee'd said she'd been stressed about money, so then why was she turning it down? "I can come to Confession before the Saturday show if that works."

Lee and Gabe entered the room. Antonio squeezed her hand and whispered, "That'd be perfect, Tara-Bear. We'll text out the details."

Tara nodded wordlessly, looking away at her computer as soon as Lee and Gabe joined them. Pulling up her calendar, she added the photo shoot to an already-packed schedule. Guilt roiled in his belly; he could have hired someone else if it was a burden. Lee looked between them, anxiety clouding his face.

To break the tension, Antonio pretended they'd been chatting about the plans for the release party. "Richard is going to help with the merch table. Do you think Sunny would mind helping him?"

"Only if you want a debate about ethically sourcing your merch," Gabe muttered.

"Sunny would *love* to," Tara insisted, still staring hard at her computer.

"Of course, you'd think that." Gabe scoffed.

"I should go." She snapped her laptop shut. "Blanche's client is leaving soon. I can finish up work at home."

Antonio and Lee exchanged a skeptical look. On film days, Tara was normally around long past sundown. It wasn't even six yet.

"Would you like a ride?" Gabe asked, "Maybe another driving lesson if you're up for it?"

Antonio and Lee's hands collided midair as they both reached for each other. Driving lesson? Antonio's chest bubbled in excitement. Gabe was letting Tara drive his car? From the sound of it, not for the first time! Lee's hand squeezed his wrist.

Tara shot them a look, but gave Gabe a brief nod. "Okay."

As soon as the door shut behind them, Antonio jumped up and down with a squeal. "Driving lessons?! Angel! Our plan is working!"

Lee smiled tightly.

Antonio froze, the excitement in his chest quelling a bit at Lee's lack of enthusiasm. "What is it? What's wrong? Gabe is obviously finally making a move on Tara! Why aren't you excited?"

Lee shook his head. "I just had to convince him to stick around and be social, because he was convinced that Tara couldn't stand to be in the same room as him."

"Then why did he ask her to spend alone time with him?" Antonio replayed what he could remember of the interaction. That didn't make sense.

Lee sighed. "I dunno. I just wonder...was this the right thing to do? Maybe I should have told Tara about the plan."

"Angel, you want our friends to get along, right?"

Lee nodded.

"And telling Tara and Sunny what to do usually backfires, right?"

"They're so stubborn!" Lee groaned. "But it kind of backfired anyway, because Sunny and Richard argue even more now, and Tara still avoids Gabe and Richard. I mean, Richard and Tara spoke more during Truth or Dare than they ever have."

Antonio took Lee's hands in his. "Which I think means they're on the right track. Maybe our friends won't ever be good friends, and maybe they won't all get married and live happily ever after like I think they should, but they're all more comfortable around each other than they were at New Year's. Do I think they're ready for Phin yet? No, but I'm barely ready for Phin most days. Trust me, this is working out how it needs to work out."

Lee smiled and pulled Antonio into his arms. "I hope you're right."

"I'm always right."

Lee laughed.

"That wasn't a joke," Antonio swatted his ass with a huff.

Chapter Thirty

TARA

TARA FIDGETED AS GABE pulled off the main road. *This is painful.* The silence was so heavy she could taste it. At first, she'd thought it was just her, that she'd been overthinking everything since he'd ended things two weeks ago. But he'd been mostly silent, too. Other than clearing his throat, as if he was about to say something, but then decided against it. Maybe he was just being polite before and didn't actually expect her to take him up on another driving lesson?

When they'd first gotten in the car, Gabe had said he knew a place that was good for practice. They hadn't said another word to each other on the entire drive from Lee and Antonio's apartment. The wooden sign engraved with "Driftwood Cemetery" flanking the side of the road was unexpected enough that Tara let out an involuntary, "Uh..."

"Sorry if this is morbid. My parents taught me to drive here," Gabe blurted out. He stopped the car just inside the fence line. "To get used to driving on actual roads before I took Behind the Wheel at school. There's usually no one here, and there are stop signs and shit." He fisted the end of his braid, tugging on it. "They always said that cemeteries had the lowest chances of me hitting a pedestrian, and if I did, at least it'd be convenient. My parents think they're funny. They're not."

"Oh, no it's fine," Tara said, unperturbed by the gravestones and mausoleums dotting the rolling hills between heavy oak trees. "It's pretty."

Maybe she should be creeped out that he'd brought her to a graveyard, but that damn gooey feeling told her she was safe with—her body flushed with recognition.

Are you kidding me?! No wonder the gooey feeling had felt so familiar. Her trust in Lee, Blanche, and Sunny—even Antonio now—was a soft happy feeling that bonded them to her heart. *I fucking trust him?* Sure, he respected her boundaries and remembered her triggers and... *Fuck. I do trust him. No wonder I panicked when I thought he was abandoning me.*

There were few people Tara truly trusted, so she'd do everything she could for them. Including skipping meals to pay the utilities, traipsing around thrift stores that drained her battery, or giving all her savings and hours of free labor so they could have their happiest life.

Or tracking down their exes to beat the shit out of them, as she still kinda wanted to do for Gabe.

"Are we gonna switch?" Tara made herself ask after a few moments of silence, her hand on the door handle.

Gabe put the car in park and unbuckled. "Sorry, yeah."

They switched sides, awkwardly dancing around each other as they passed by in front of the hood. Gabe buckled into the passenger seat. "So, did you take Behind the Wheel when you were in high school, too?"

Tara stiffened and fussed with moving the seat up, so she wouldn't see the judgment or pity in his eyes. "I didn't go to high school."

"Oh. Shit. Sorry. I didn't know."

"Lee didn't tell you? We got our GEDs together." She risked a glance at him. Gabe was looking at her with an unreadable expression that thankfully wasn't pity, his shoulders tense in his blazer. Ugh, he looked so good in a suit, with those broad shoulders and massive biceps. *He'd look better out of—* Tara shut that thought down. He didn't want that.

Gabe shook his head. "Didn't know that about Lee, either. Sorry. Shouldn't have asked."

She turned away, focusing on adjusting the rearview mirror and her seat belt. "You didn't know. I figured Lee or Tonio would have said something. I took the test for my learner's permit at a community center, but the actual driving classes were too expensive. Still are." She forced a smile. "Anyway, if you spot any gravestones that say Sanderson, holler. Especially if it says Anne or Carl." The intrusive joke flew out of Tara's mouth before she could stop it. She gripped the steering wheel, resisting the urge to bang her head against it. One little revelation that she wanted

Gabe in her life forever, and here Tara was, making jokes about her hardest truths.

"You have relatives buried here?" Gabe asked.

"Not as far as I know," Tara replied honestly. "And I doubt my parents are here. This looks like a bougie cemetery."

He reached out to put his hand on her arm but drew back at the last second. "I'm sorry, I wasn't aware you lost your parents."

"Lost is a good way to put it. I have no idea if they're dead, dude. I make the same bad joke anytime I go to a cemetery. Or walk past the jail." Tara scoffed. "Sorry. I guess I think I'm funny, too."

Gabe's eyes stayed trained on her, his voice soft. "You wanna talk about it?"

"Absolutely not." She shifted into drive before he could reply.

Instead of prying, Gabe merely told her where to turn, so they wouldn't end up in a dead end or stuck behind a mausoleum. Tara tried to focus on driving, but his presence was stifling.

He seemed uncomfortable too, fidgeting and tugging at his collar. Eventually, he shrugged his blazer off, filling the car with vanilla and that oaky musk that went straight to her cunt. Tara forced herself to keep her eyes on the road, cobblestone amongst the field of graves.

But when he turned himself around in his seat to hang the blazer on the back of his headrest, she risked a glance. His torso was stretched out, shirt clinging to his firm chest and abdomen like Tara longed to do. She swallowed hard and turned back to the road, just in time to see a streak of gray run across the road.

Tara slammed on the brakes, her arm catching Gabe around the waist. "Gabe, what the fuck is that?!"

Gabe's torso tensed, then he turned back around to see what had startled her. Her hand didn't leave him, dragging across his sternum as he turned around.

"That is a coyote." They watched as it ran to the tree line and disappeared into the woods along the river.

"Jesus Christ, did you bring me to the boonies?" Tara laughed. "I didn't know coyotes got this close to the city." The smile on her face faded as his jaw tightened, brown eyes staring at where her hand still touching his ribs. Tara snatched her arm back. "Sorry."

"S'ok," Gabe muttered. "To be fair, we buried people where the coyotes live. Cities, and cemeteries apparently, are their own ecosystems now."

Tara wasn't sure how to respond. The painfully awkward silence fell back over them. It was so tempting to just pretend none of it had ever happened, that he didn't exist, and—

No, if she wanted to be in Gabe's life for as long as he'd let her (and she would be, because she rarely trusted people; Tara had to hang on to those she did) then she'd have to find a way to get along with him. To keep having moments like this where things may be awkward, but they were still easy. Even if it was as...friends, whatever that meant.

That was why she was here, driving his car when she'd rather hide from him. That was what Sunny had said to do, right? To become friends with someone who didn't want more than that. Tara had to show up and be awkward, until it eventually became comfortable.

Tara shifted in her seat, gripping the wheel under her fingers. "Can I ask a favor?"

"Of course."

Tara searched for the right words. Maybe she should have thought about this more. "Sometimes you're two different people. When it's just us, you're sweet, and chatty, and confident. But around other people, you're, well, not."

Gabe snorted. "That's one way to call me an asshole."

"You said it, not me." Tara smiled back. "And I know I'm no better to you, but... Look, if we're going to be...friends, we need to get along. And the Gabe when it's just the two of us is easier to be around than the Gabe who points out all of my insecurities in front of our friends. For the record, I think we've been getting along better lately. I just want it to stay that way."

Gabe's sigh was heavy. "I like that version of me better too. When it's just us, I can pretend I'm someone I want to be. But Tonio and Richard know the me I am, and it's hard to reconcile the two," he murmured, burning a hole in the dash with his eyes. "Sorry I've been an asshole. That wasn't my intention, hence why I'm doing this EMDR stuff. It's past time I learn to manage my insecurities." Gabe paused before he looked up at her, his brow still furrowed. "Can you do something for me, too?"

Tara wanted to smooth it out with her thumbs. Instead, she forced her eyes back on the road, gripping the steering wheel to keep her hands at ten and two. Easing onto the gas, she slowly continued on her loop of the cemetery. "What's that?"

"Can you stop pretending I don't exist?" Gabe asked. "When we're around other people, I mean. You're different when it's just us, too.

Could you at least say hi, or ask how I'm doing, when we're around our friends? Acknowledge my existence?"

Tara nodded. "Sorry. I do ignore you, don't I?"

"You do. So hard." Gabe grinned, the crease in his brow easing. "Not that it's an excuse for me being an asshole, but it'll be easier to fake confidence if you don't hate me."

"I don't hate you."

"I know, Kitt—Tara, but it's hard to remember when you refuse to look at me." Gabe turned away.

"I should probably tell you something," Tara said quietly, turning a corner to make a loop around a pond with a fountain in the middle. "Just to return the favor. Let you know there's a game afoot, as you put it."

Gabe snorted. "Okay, Sherlock."

Tara flashed him a small smile. "We're not supposed to know this, but Lee, Antonio, and Blanche are conspiring to get us together. All of the stupid get-togethers, including the chair thing, have been some elaborate forced togetherness scheme."

With a frown, Gabe fell silent.

The whole situation hurt worse, because Lee had decided he knew how she felt about Gabe, without her input. *And yeah, he had apparently guessed right considering I fucking trust Gabe. And had really really hot marathon sex with him.* But still, this scheme of his wasn't something Lee did. That was more Blanche's style, and even this was extreme for them. The kiss bullshit at New Year's and the chair thing at Confession? Sure, she could get past that because Blanche was just having fun, and Tara could always back out. But to find out Blanche, Antonio, and *Lee* had been doing all of these damn social activities to get her and Gabe together? That stung.

At least Blanche had finally told her, but only after months of helping Lee and Antonio manipulate them. Lee still hadn't said a word, even though he'd had plenty of opportunities. Tara trusted Lee with all her heart. And yet he'd kept this from her, probably rationalizing it because he only wanted what was best for her. Same as Blanche had with the stupid kissing thing at New Year's.

Tara swallowed, pushing herself to keep talking as much as she didn't want to. "To be honest, I'm conflicted about it. Lee doesn't keep secrets from me. He doesn't do things like this. Blanche, yeah, but never Lee. I'm sure he thinks he's helping, but he didn't even talk to me about it. He didn't give me a chance to tell him what I want."

"Tonio absolutely would do something like this. Sorry if he's been a bad influence on Lee." Gabe ran his hands through his hair. "Thank you for telling me."

"You gave me an out at New Year's. It's the least I can do. I'm still processing it." Tara stared into the distance, looking at the road as she drove. "Can you keep it to yourself until Lee finally admits it? Or should I warn Tonio you're about to kick his ass?"

Gabe chuckled. "I will keep it between myself and my therapist for now, but Tonio and I promised to talk shit out..." he trailed off. "I need to process it, too. Right now I mostly feel resentful, so I'm not about to go talk to him now. Tonio might have overstepped, but I can't push him away again."

"Maybe we talk to them together when you're ready?" Tara glanced at him. "Present a united front or whatever? I just want them to butt out."

Gabe nodded but quickly turned back to the windshield. "There's something in the road up ahead." He touched her arm to draw her attention to some folding chairs lying on the road, half covered by a black tarp.

"Thanks." Tara slowed down to avoid the barely visible obstruction. Gabe's fingers still scorched her arm, slowly tracing toward her wrist.

"Why are you doing this?" Tara asked, slowing to a stop.

As if she'd burned him, he pulled his hand away. "Sorry."

"No, I mean, why did you offer to drive me home? Or give me a driving lesson?"

He stared at her, confusion swimming in his brown eyes.

"Don't get me wrong, I appreciate it. It's just, why are you bothering? Why are you going through all of this trouble when you don't...you know?"

Gabe took a breath. "It's no trouble. Friends should be supportive of each other."

Tara nodded, turning back to the winding road through the cemetery. That "friends" cut deeper than she'd expected, and not even this damn gooey trust bullshit could soothe it.

Saturday, June Thirteenth

Chapter Thirty-One

ANTONIO

"Uh...I'll give you two a moment." Tara stuffed an SD card into her camera bag, throwing it half-zipped over her shoulder in her scurry to flee. Behind her, the white faux-brick backdrop, normally used for photo shoots of the cast, hung in Confession's storage room.

"Tara-Bear, don't leave me," Antonio pleaded.

Tara backed out the door with her hands up, her green eyes wide and earnest. "This is between you two, Tonio. Clean up your own mess. Just meet me in the control room when you're done breaking Lee's heart."

With a deep sigh, Antonio turned back to Lee, who wore the most excruciating, heart-wrenching pout. He should have known this would backfire. *What was I thinking?* Antonio took a hesitant step toward his fiancée.

Lee took a step back. "No."

"Lee..."

"You're not getting this back. You gave it to me. It's mine now." Lee crossed his arms, pausing to admire the white gold band on his finger, before tucking it under his arm.

Humming his Intentions Song, Antonio scratched his head, trying to ease the frustration and guilt battling for dominance. "Angel, I need it for your real proposal."

Lee gestured to the empty storage room. "We're in public. Propose."

"I will. Soon. Very soon," Antonio pleaded. "I wouldn't have asked Tara to take photos if it wasn't coming soon."

"I'm tired of keeping it a secret. I'm *so* bad at lying, babe! Why are you making me wait so long?" Lee somehow pouted even harder, his brown eyes pleading.

Antonio winced. "Angel, I want to tell people too. Do you know how hard it is to keep a secret like this from my mom?" He already felt guilty that he'd told Gabe and Richard. But then again, Lee had told Tara. "But you would have hated the million corny ways I came up with that could have come sooner. Trust me, you'll love what I have planned, and I promise you'll get your ring back in no time."

Lee let him edge closer without backing away this time. "I *was* very concerned that you were going to dare me to marry you on Memorial Day."

Laughing in relief, Antonio pulled Lee's hands away from his chest, slipping his arms around his waist.

Lee pulled him close. "How soon is 'soon,' exactly?"

Antonio smiled up at Lee, resting his chin on Lee's chest. "Soon as in 'let me surprise you.'"

"I hate you." Lee worked the ring off his finger and pressed it into Antonio's palm.

"No, you don't." Antonio put Lee's ring back onto the chain with his own and slipped it over his neck. It was the safest place to keep them, until their rings could go where they belonged. *Why are we doing this again? Oh yeah, because Lee loves grand gestures even though he pretends not to.* "Here, it'll be right next to mine until it's time. Right next to my heart."

"So corny."

"You love it."

"I love *you.*" Lee kissed him. "Come on, let's see what Tara wants."

Walking hand in hand, Antonio opened the control room door to find the small space more crowded than he'd expected. Freddie, the light designer, sat in his usual chair with a baby on his lap. His spouse and Antonio's boss, Chas, stood next to him with—Antonio assessed Chas's outfit of bootcut jeans and a long-sleeve chambray shirt—*his* hands on his hips.

Tara sat on the back counter next to— "Gabe, what are *you* doing here?"

"Flirtin' with my husband, that's what he's doin'." Chas crossed his arms and glared at Gabe, who sat in Lee's usual chair.

Tara snickered from her perch on the counter.

Gabe's mouth dropped open. "I was *not* flirt—"

The baby in Freddy's lap cut him off with a grunt and frowned at Gabe.

"That's right, mija, you tell him. Daddy's off limits." Chas's glare softened when he looked at their youngest in his husband's arms.

"That's not—"

Tara nudged his shoulder with her knee. "It's not personal, Gabe. Just let it go."

"Okay," Gabe grumbled. "Sorry for introducing myself to the only other person in the room."

Chas opened his mouth, probably to comment on the obvious sarcasm in Gabe's voice.

"Aren't you supposed to be on parental leave?" Antonio asked Chas pointedly before he could speak. Gabe couldn't have predicted the quagmire of Freddy and Chas's strangely wholesome, yet territorial marriage. "You're not supposed to be back until after the Fourth."

"I came in to restock the dispensers in the Confessionals." Chas waved his hand. "Make sure everything is ready for Bellamy Pride next weekend."

"Yeah, because no one else who works here can do *that*," Antonio retorted. "You left Jackie in charge of that. Let her do her job."

"I'm just checking up on things!" Chas protested.

Lee sighed. "We all know why you're really here. Just go and pretend to restock the Confessionals." He held out his hands to take the baby, as Chas and Freddie left without further argument. "I don't know how I always end up with the baby. I don't even like babies."

"Because you take her every time." Antonio took Chas and Freddy's youngest from Lee's awkward hold, settling the infant against his chest so she could look around the room. Antonio rounded on Gabe. "So, why *are* you here?"

"Tara asked to borrow my camera for your couple's photos. Which, at first, I was a little put out that you didn't want *me* to help. But then she said it was a boudoir thing, and I figured I should wait here. There are some things I don't need to be a part of."

"Boudoir?" Lee asked. "It wasn't—"

Tara shot them both an expectant look and nodded. "*Boudoir.*"

"Boudoir!" Antonio exclaimed. He couldn't wait until all this secret-keeping was over; he couldn't keep track of who knew what. "Right. Like she does for Blanche. I figured you wouldn't want to see the jockstrap—"

Gabe covered his ears. "I don't want to *hear* about it either. I have to sanitize my camera."

"And he's also here because we need to talk," Tara added.

"Talk." Dread filled Antonio's chest at her tone.

Tara nodded. "Do either of you have anything you'd like to tell us?"

Antonio and Lee exchanged a quizzical look. A warning buzz sounded in his brain, a demon telling him he'd fucked up. He silenced it by bouncing the baby in his arms.

"Really? Nothing coming to mind?" Gabe crossed his arms. "Nothing involving the two of us, in particular?"

Antonio shook his head, trying to wrack his brain as to why he was suddenly so hot and his heart was pounding. This felt like an intervention, but he couldn't think of what he'd done to warrant one.

Tara arched an eyebrow. "Anything that might explain why I had to find out from Blanche that you two are trying to make me—and I quote—'Hippo's mom?'"

A whirlwind crossed Gabe's face.

"Oh, that!" Antonio laughed as relief washed over him. "I was worried I did something wrong!"

Lee pushed his glasses up his nose. "Buttercup, I'm sorry. We weren't trying to get you together, just get along better! Blanche took the plan in a different direction than I intended, and I should have stopped them. You just both got off on the wrong foot, and I figured if you guys got to know each other better that you could be good friends, and—"

"Lee, take a breath." Tara hopped off the counter, putting her hands on Lee's shoulders. "I figured you meant well. I get that you just wanted less fighting."

Lee's arms encircled her waist. "I'm still sorry."

Tara laughed and wrapped him in a hug. "I know. Just talk to me next time, okay?"

He nodded. "I'm sorry."

"Stop apologizing, Lee," Tara said, her voice muffled by Lee's chest.

Antonio turned to Gabe. "See? No harm done!"

Gabe pouted. "I'm less forgiving, Tonio. We've talked about this. I specifically asked you not to set me up with anyone."

"Gabe, that was over a year ago, while you were," Antonio shrugged, his hands too full of baby to mime his best interpretation of outpatient therapy, "busy."

Gabe nodded to show he understood, but the arms crossed across his chest tightened as he looked away.

Antonio saw right through Gabe's fake hurt. "Your mother is so much better at guilt trips. You know why your little pout's not gonna work? Because I don't feel bad in the slightest! The plan was to create opportunities for you two to get along, not force you to have a relationship. If that's where your mind went, that says a lot about you."

Frustration flickered across Gabe's face. "But we agreed to talk shit out. Remember? Well, this is something that I'm feeling resentful about, and I don't want it to get between us. Don't meddle with my relationships, friendships or otherwise!"

Antonio winced. "Oh, damn. Maybe you are good at guilt trips." His stomach cramped at Gabe's reminder of their pact when they'd reunited. "You're right. I'm sorry. It's just that you don't let new people in, and you need more people in your life! And so does Richard. And Tara, Sunny, and Blanche are good people. They'll be good friends if you let them."

"You could have just said that instead of coming up with this bullshit plan."

Antonio fought to keep from rolling his eyes. "I did say that. Many times. Did you listen when I did?"

"No, s'pose not. Sorry." Gabe's arms, still crossed over his chest, relaxed. He looked as if he were hugging himself instead.

Antonio's heart went out to him at the conflicted emotions in Gabe's expression. "Here." He held out the baby. "You look like you need this."

"I don't know how to hold a baby." Gabe took her anyway, cradling her against his chest with a wince as she pulled Gabe's hair. "Do I need to support her head or whatever?"

Antonio shook his head. "No, she's almost four months old."

"Which means..."

"She can hold her own head up, but keep an eye on her in case she needs help. Just cuddle her and bounce her if she gets fussy. It'll make you feel better." Antonio adjusted Gabe's hold, pulling his hair into a bun for him to get it safely out of grabbing distance.

"Oh, that is really nice. No wonder my mom wants me to have one of these." Gabe rested his cheek on her downy black hair. "Would Chas let me babysit, even if I don't know shit about babies?"

"After you flirted with his husband? Not a chance in hell." Antonio turned to exchange a grin with Lee. But the wounded look in Tara's eyes, staring at Gabe holding the baby, made him freeze.

"So we agree?" Tara blinked, turning to him before he could ask if she was okay. "No more meddling in our lives? No more trying to set us up with anyone or forcing us to get along?"

"Agreed. Anything else?" Antonio asked, wishing he could read Tara better. "This feels like we're getting off easy, considering it warranted an intervention."

Tara and Gabe exchanged a look. Gabe shook his head.

"No, that's enough," Tara said, the shadow behind her eyes returning. "Just trust us to manage our own lives. Or talk to us about shit."

"Of course, Buttercup." Lee kissed her head. "We will need you and Gabe to help with some *upcoming events*, but I want you there to help me make decisions. Not because I'm trying to force you to get along. Okay? Argue with him all you want."

Tara gave him a wistful smile and nodded. "As if you could stop me."

Tara and Gabe's matching sad expressions made Antonio's heart twinge with guilt. For Tara to be upset with Lee, for God knows how long and not confront him about it, was worrying. He had to be better for Lee's friends. *Our friends, now.* For how many months he'd been saying "our friends," it was sinking in how deep that "our" went. He had to be there for Tara just as much as Gabe. And Antonio would. For both of them.

TARA

"Friends." Tara slammed the front door behind her. *"Friends" is fine. "Friends" is safe.*

Except *safe* shouldn't hurt. *Fine* shouldn't send a pang of longing throughout her chest at the sight of Gabe holding a damn baby. As if she wasn't confused enough by all of her conflicting feelings, he had to go talk about having babies, and they wouldn't be *hers*.

Tara grumbled under her breath as she stomped into the apartment. She'd never even considered having kids before! And she wouldn't start now. If he wanted, Gabe should fill all those extra bedrooms in that giant house with someone who knew what family—*oh god, a family*—meant, not her. Tara picked at a hangnail, desperate to distract herself from the longing that should *not* be making it so hard to breathe.

"Babes? You good?" Blanche looked up in concern, draped over their armchair with their laptop perched on their bare knees, clad only in a barely-closed silk bathrobe. Since Lee had moved out, clothes had become optional.

Tara schooled her features. "Yeah, I'm fine. Just had another driving lesson with Gabe."

"Oh? 'Driving lesson?'" Blanche smirked.

Tara shook her head. "Driving lesson. There's only driving at these driving lessons."

"Oh." Blanche shrugged. "Did he behave? You seem on edge."

Tara set her bag down and collapsed on the couch. "Yeah, we're *friends* and shit now. He just made me drive out in the suburbs, and I'm anxious about driving on real roads. Especially when the speed limit suddenly went up to fifty miles per hour."

"Need to unwind?" They gestured to the pipe on the table.

Tara shook her head. Getting high was too tempting. But she needed to figure this shit mood out. Otherwise, she'd be in a shit mood for the rest of her life whenever Gabe did anything remotely endearing. Even with a couple weeks to process, it still hurt that the one person she'd started to open her heart to didn't want it. Or wanted it too much, whatever the fuck that meant. Either way, Gabe wanted to be her friend, and so Tara had to figure out how the fuck to do that. "No, I probably shouldn't rely on Northern Lights to process my emotions."

"It works for me."

Tara hummed skeptically. "Does it?"

"Who asked you?" Blanche huffed a laugh.

Tara sighed. "I'm not you, Blanche. You aren't the child of addicts. I have to be careful about depending on shit."

"I could be. I was the Family's changeling. Who knows who they stole me from?" Blanche turned to smile softly at her. "But I'm glad you set boundaries for yourself, babes. You're stronger than me."

Tara shook her head. "You're the strongest person I know, Blanche. You've earned a vice or two after all the shit you've been through."

"Babes, have I told you how much I love you?" Blanche rose from the chair to join Tara on the couch. "Even when you have no idea what's going on in my head, you always say shit that makes me feel better."

"Want to talk about it?" Tara offered as she and Blanche snuggled together, her heart clenching in appreciation for their affection. She didn't expect anything other than a "do you?" in response. Blanche never wanted to talk about it. Especially sober.

They sighed. "Well, I should. Only because I don't want you to freak out when you look at your bank account. You and Lee got that bonus yesterday. I tried to keep it under the table and just give you cash, but I have a fucking CPA now, and he insisted I make you both contract employees. I'll have to get you a 1099 when tax season rolls around."

Tara tried to keep up with Blanche's unexpected response. "A 1099? Why? How much is this bonus?"

"Twenty grand," came a hesitant reply.

"Twenty grand?!" Tara cried. "I can't take that much! I can't take any of it!"

"That's what I told Alfie! That both you and Lee refused to accept money, but apparently holding your money for you is illegal, so you're getting paid biweekly now. Your back pay is coming next week, which—don't freak out—is also five figures." Blanche shushed her protests. "I know, you didn't want to get paid, but Alfie insists. Honestly, I still don't know if I trust someone named Alfie, but either way, it's yours. You and Lee have earned that and then some."

"I wanted to do this for free," Tara whispered, tears burning down her cheeks. "You've done so much for us! I need to do something for you. You can't pay me. Especially not that much. That's what I usually make in a year!"

"Trust me. Before this year, I would have said the same thing." Blanche brushed the tears from Tara's face with their thumb, a soft smile on their face. "If the rest of this year goes as well as the past six months, there's another bonus check coming your way."

Tara wiped her nose. "Damn, Blanche, where the fuck is all this money coming from? How rich are you?"

"You've seen my subscriber count. I'm basically a D-list porn star thanks to you and Lee." Blanche shrugged. "I can't buy a house, but I've made enough to need a goddamn CPA."

"You wanna buy a house?"

"Do I want a place that's mine where we can't get evicted at the whim of some rich asshole? Abso-fucking-lutely!" Blanche scoffed. "If I had a conventional job, I'd have enough for a down payment, but no lender would give someone like me a mortgage. I'll keep saving until I can afford a house in cash." Their mouth twisted. "Or until Mrs. Big Pharma kicks us out, in which case, I can pay the rent."

"Can I give you the money you're giving me back to put toward a house?" Blanche had let her live with them rent-free for six years. Tara had to pay them back somehow.

"I wish you showed everyone your sweet side." Blanche hugged her. "But I've done a terrible job teaching you to survive in this world if you'd ever consider doing any work for free. If someone wants to pay you for something, take the damn money!"

They laughed together as Tara got her eyes under control. As if she weren't already a mess with everything going on with Lee and Gabe, this felt too good to be true.

She'd taken out predatory private loans after BCC had denied her financial aid because she didn't have her parents' financial information, nor history in a shelter to certify that she really was an "unaccompanied homeless youth." Blanche had offered to forge something, but both of them had barely understood the FAFSA application in the first place, and Tara hadn't wanted to put them at risk. To suddenly have hope that she wouldn't be drowning in debt for the rest of her life, to not worry about how they'd afford rent or imposing on Lee and Antonio... The relief conflicted with the churn of emotions already overwhelming her.

"Thank you, Blanche." Tara groaned and threw her head back in frustration. "Ugh, I can't stay mad at you."

"Mad? At *moi*?"

"For your stupid plan to get Gabe and me together." Tara hugged them tighter, wishing she hadn't declined the weed now. Without the need to distract herself with work, she'd actually have to process the whirlwind of feelings she'd rather leave unexamined. "I'm grateful you told me, but you didn't even ask if it was something I wanted. And Lee or Tonio wouldn't have even told us if Gabe and I didn't call them out on it."

"In Lee's defense, he just wanted the four of you to be friends."

"So you admit *you* were manipulating us into a relationship?"

"Of course!" Blanche tsked. "I still say you should keep an open mind about him."

Exasperated yet wholly unsurprised, Tara laughed. "No more plotting, please. We're friends. Nothing more."

"But the chair thing was so—"

"Just friends." Her heart broke to say it, but it was true. "Friends" was what Gabe wanted. What he needed. He always respected her boundaries, so she'd respect his. She'd tuck away the longing and the want, and instead appreciate the trust and tentative friendship they'd established. And that'd be enough. Even if Gabe never wanted her again, being his friend would be enough. It had to be, because Tara would probably fuck it up anyway. *And I can't do that to him.* "Please."

"Okay, no more schemes that impact you and Gabe unless you're aware—"

"Blanche! Just friends."

"Fine, no more schemes."

CHAPTER THIRTY-TWO

SUNNY

As they approached the Modern Art Institute, a beacon of glass and light reflecting off the Mississippi, Sunny smoothed the green satin skirt of her dress. It had wrinkled from being bunched in her fists. She'd been to the museum dozens of times, but never as Richard's girlfriend. And certainly not when there were valet drivers, red carpets, and searchlights brightening the dusk of the riverwalk. Part of her wished she hadn't insisted they walk. But she was glad that she didn't have to climb out of his bougie-ass truck in full view of so many people who looked like they belonged.

"Stop biting your lip." Richard's hand pressed against her lower back. "You seem nervous."

"I'm fucking peachy." Sunny tried to laugh, but instead let out a shuddering exhale. "Sarcasm, in case it wasn't obvious."

"We don't have to go."

"Nope. We're practically there." Sunny didn't dare to look at him. He would take one glance at her, see her anxiety, and turn around regardless of what she said. And Richard had been so good about meeting her family. She could do this for him.

"Well, if you need it, the safeword is alligator."

Sunny snorted. "We need a safeword? Is it that kinda party?"

Richard hummed in amusement. "It's for when we want to leave. I accepted Miriam's invite mostly for Gabe's sake, and she knows that, so don't feel obligated to stay for my sake."

Sunny wondered how she'd work that into casual conversation. "Do Gabe's parents know I'm trans?"

"No, I didn't think it was any of their business. But they won't care. They've asked Gabe and Antonio several times for updates on their pronouns." Richard's hand found hers.

Sunny wasn't sure which she preferred, but at least she'd thought to ask beforehand. "So, what do they know about me?"

"Honestly, nothing. I thought I'd surprise them."

Sunny laughed. "You're such a dick."

"I expect Gabe will be the most upset. Miriam and John will simply be excited I'm finally introducing them to someone," Richard said wryly, leading her into the atrium. The soaring hall was filled with random harmonies and dissonance as people walked across the musical tiles embedded in the floor. "Which is exactly why you're meeting them and not my actual parents."

Richard checked them in as Sunny tried not to gape at the well-dressed people around them. Most wore cocktail attire like Sunny, but some were decked out in black tie. Richard and Luna had helped pick out the green satin tea dress she wore, but being next to glamorous women in ball gowns, several of whom she recognized as local politicians and news anchors, didn't help Sunny's imposter syndrome. This party was several tax brackets above her.

The champagne Richard handed her helped soothe the tightness of her throat. "So, what does one do at fundraisers?"

Richard shrugged. "There's a silent auction, some information booths and art displays to look at. Dinner starts in a couple of hours, so most people will network until then."

"Network?" Sunny tittered. "You? I can't imagine you enjoy that."

"I don't." Richard gave her a wry smile. "I was hoping Gabe would be here already so he could handle the randos who want to make small talk, but I don't see him yet. Nor have I seen his parents, but they must be around here somewhere."

"Well, let's look at art, then?" Sunny suggested. She led the way to a series of photographs on exhibit in the atrium. Oddly enough, one featured Gabe surrounded by a crowd of teenagers who had taken the photos.

"This must be his volunteer class." Richard squinted, reading the caption. "His mom roped him into this art program last year, but he seems to like it."

Sunny was about to respond, when a tall blonde woman looking at them caught her eye. The woman gestured to two men—a bit taller than Richard, but who otherwise were a mirror image of him—and pointed at them. "Uh... Dicky, there are three people who look just like you coming this way."

"What?" Richard looked over his shoulder. "Oh shit."

"What?"

Gripping her jaw the way he normally only did in the bedroom, Richard turned her face to him, blue eyes earnest. "Okay, crash course. My mom's name is Barbie, not Barbara, not Barb. She's going to call you fat and make several racist comments that are just shy of being aggressively racist. My brother's name is Connor. Do not let him near your drink, and he's going to fetishize you. My dad's name is Dick, and try not to laugh if you say his name. Better hope he doesn't talk, and if he chugs his drink, prepare to duck. Do not call me by my name, and don't argue when they use my deadname. Do not take anything they say to heart. I'll get us away from them as soon as I can, but the safeword is alligator if I'm not quick enough. And most of all, they don't matter."

Sunny blinked. "Wha—?"

"Lizzie!" The tall, thin woman with bright blonde hair greeted Richard with an air kiss. "Oh, Lizzie. I hoped you'd be here! And you must be her...friend!" She turned to Sunny, a big smile flashing on her face that didn't reach her eyes.

Sunny stared, dumbfounded, her heart pounding.

"Sunny, this is my mother, Barbie," Richard politely introduced her. His anxiety during his rushed explanation was smoothly replaced with a polite mask, eerily akin to Blanche's. "This is Sunny Boonmee, my girlfriend."

Sunny held out her hand politely with a smile. "It's so nice to meet you, Mrs. Carter."

Barbie pulled her into a stiff hug. "None of that Mrs. Carter nonsense. I'm not old enough for that! Call me Barbie, please." Sunny's nose was filled with rose perfume and a strong undertone of wine as she was pressed into Barbie's chest. "I love meeting Lizzie's little friends!"

Sunny shot Richard a look, who gave her a tight wince before introducing his brother and father. Up close, they were practically clones of

Richard, but taller and heavier. His father, wearing a sharply tailored suit and a red tie, barely nodded at them, not looking up from his phone. His younger brother, Connor, wore an oversized suit with a suspicious stain on the pants. He looked at her up and down appraisingly, eyes lingering on her chest.

Sunny smiled tightly, fighting the instinct to cover her drink.

Barbie snagged a glass of wine from a passing server. "So, tell us about yourself. Where are you from?"

Irritation straightened her spine. "Oh, I grew up here, but LA originally. We moved to Bellamy when I was little for my dad's work."

"And where is *he* from?" Barbie looked at her expectantly, almost like she should be raising her eyebrows. But Richard's mother didn't seem capable of microexpressions.

Should I tell her he's dead? Sunny let out a silent sigh. Richard had said they didn't matter, but she could make an effort for his sake. "My parents are from Chiang Mai, in northern Thailand. How about you? Where are *you* from?"

Barbie smiled widely, ignoring her. "Oh, so you're from Thailand! I love Phuket. Connor spent every spring break in Bangkok with his fraternity, didn't you, sweetie?"

Somehow, Connor leered even more at her. "Thailand is great. Everyone is so accommodating. Especially the females. Had a great time on Khao San Road." He winked.

Her stomach turned. Farang boys' experience of Thailand was usually limited to drugs, "massages" and ping pong shows. Sunny just smiled politely and didn't reply.

"Do you go back often? Where's your favorite place to visit?" Barbie asked.

Sunny shook her head. "Oh, I've never had the chance to go myself."

"I'll take you someday," Richard took her hand, squeezing harder than she'd expected.

Barbie laughed. "Oh, Lizzie. You never liked Phuket. You were so self-conscious in your swimsuit with all those skinny Asian women around, and from the looks of it, you haven't slimmed down yet." Her eyes roved over Sunny's body, settling on the champagne glass at risk of being crushed in Sunny's grip. Barbie sipped her wine. "Both of you might need to cut down on the empty carbs before you go anywhere with a beach."

Sunny's heartbeat echoed through her skull. Sure, she was curvy, but those curves were hard-won. She'd fought for them. Put her blood, sweat, tears, and daily hormone pills into them. Paid for some of them. *This bitch thinks my Dicky needs to lose weight? As fit as he is?*

Before she could cuss his mom out, Richard put a hand on the small of her back. "Mom, let's not talk about anyone's weight for once." Richard's voice was impressively calm.

Sunny steadied her face, even as she steamed internally.

"You're always so sensitive!" Barbie laughed a little too loudly, downing her wine glass. "So, where did you do your undergrad, Sammy?"

"Her name is Sunny!"

Barbie waved the hand holding the wine glass with a fake smile. "Oh, right."

Sunny plastered a smile on, ready to fight her. "I have a certificate in Software Engineering from BCC."

"So you never went to college?" Barbie asked. Lips pursed, she flagged down a server for another glass of wine. Connor took two from the tray. "Such a shame. Best years of my life. Dick and I met in college, right sweetie? My sorority house was next door to his fraternity. I got my BA and my MRS degree in the same year." She laughed loudly again.

Dick grunted, still typing on his phone.

"Sounds charming." Sunny forced out the empty words.

Richard tried to speak up. "I think community college and trade programs are essen—"

"Barbie. Wine." Dick gestured to his empty glass.

With a flinch so brief Sunny would have missed it if she weren't looking right at him, Richard's face closed off even more than normal. Impossible to read, he looked around the room for an excuse to escape. Hopefully, she hadn't done anything wrong. She'd been on her best behavior as far as she knew, which was quite the accomplishment, considering she wanted to chuck her champagne glass at Barbie's head and kick Connor in the nuts. But controlling her facial expressions and knowing what to say had never been Sunny's strong suit; who knew if she was actually pulling off being polite? *Is it too soon to say alligator?*

"Oh, so sorry, dear." Barbie's fake grin grew even more forced as she called the server back, handing Dick a fresh glass. "So, do you two know each other through work or something?" Barbie's fake smile was grating on Sunny's nerves.

Richard answered. "Through Antonio. You met him when you visited me in New York. Gabe's friend from high school."

Barbie giggled. "Oh, the drag queen, right? I follow him on Instagram! Such a character! Is he still in New York?"

"No, he moved back just after I did. He's a choir teacher these days."

"They let people like him teach kids?" Dick interrupted, finally speaking.

Sunny froze just as her glass reached her lips. *I never knew someone could be worse than Lee's dad, but Dick is giving Mr. Jones a run for his money.*

"Yes, Dad. The gays are people now," Richard replied dryly.

"How is Miriam's boy doing?" Dick asked. "Such a shame you couldn't pin that one down. I heard he's back from New York, too. Tonight might be your chance."

Sunny couldn't keep her eyebrows from raising as she sipped her champagne. *Damn, Dicky, you weren't kidding. He really does want you to marry Gabe.*

"Dad!" Richard exclaimed, turning red. "The Coopers and I are very close friends without me trapping Gabe into marriage. Can we please have a more appropriate conversation in front of my girlfriend?"

Dick glared at Richard. "Elizabeth, don't throw away your value by marrying down. If you're such close friends with the Cooper boy, secure it with a fucking ring this time. I still can't believe you let that Stone girl steal him."

Richard exhaled a deep sigh as Dick looked at Sunny, finally acknowledging her existence. Sunny immediately missed when he pretended she wasn't there. She tried to keep the anger from her face, but the clicking as her jaw worked back and forth told her she was glaring at Richard's dad.

Dick looked her up and down, much like Connor had, before he said with condescension, "No offense, sweetie. She'll marry someone with more potential than an IT diversity hire without a degree. Nice tits or not, you won't last long once this lesbian phase is out of her system."

Fuming, Sunny turned to Richard, about to mouth "alligator" to him, when Connor opened his mouth. "Come see me when you get tired of my dyke sister. At least I have a cock. I know how needy you Thai girls are."

Sunny's soul flew from her body as rage blazed through her veins. Instead of the "alligator" careening around her brain, she heard herself say scathingly to the piece of trash that was somehow related to Richard, "I'm sure that's a *very* generous offer, but how about you blow *me?* I know how needy you farang boys are for girldick!"

Just as she lunged for Connor, Richard gripped her elbow and pulled her away. "We are so far past alligator." His arm covered the back of her head as shouts erupted behind them, and glass shattered at their feet.

Someone was gagging dramatically, probably Connor. She couldn't be bothered to care. Fury and hurt overtook her, and her arms, her breath, her body trembled. At least she finally got to witness what Richard had meant when he'd said his family was awful. *Mae's a fucking gem.* Sunny focused on Richard's hand on her elbow as he steered her out of the museum. His grip grounded her, kept her from going back in there and punching Dick in the face.

CHAPTER THIRTY-THREE

RICHARD

RICHARD LED THEM AWAY from the museum in silence, taking the quieter path along the riverwalk to get away from the noise of the street. The floodlights brightening the concrete path burned his eyes as tension built in his head, drying out his contacts past the point of irritation.

The surprise interaction with his parents had honestly gone better than usual, probably because they were in public. Only one broken glass, *and* he didn't have to clean it up? That had been the best family reunion in a decade. Yet Richard's nerves were raw. Any amount of time spent with his family made him feel flayed open, exposing all of the worst parts of him.

But the reminder of his rotten origins was nothing compared to the guilt steaming inside. It was one thing for him to sit through those conversations, but for them to treat Sunny that way had been heartbreaking. He'd never meant for her to suffer through that.

Stomach roiling, Richard clenched his jaw. He couldn't figure out what to say. How could he begin to apologize for the way his family had treated her? How could he explain why he hadn't stood up for her? Sunny had handled herself with grace and dignity in the face of classless elitism, racism, and scathing sexist remarks. Meanwhile, he'd sat there useless and panicking, waiting for Gabe or Miriam to rescue them. Sunny's family had been wonderfully hospitable, even with the rapid-fire questions and trial by chilis, and his family had treated her like a joke.

Richard wished could keep his cool around his family like Sunny had. His therapist had suggested that Dick had used Richard as a scapegoat, so his father wouldn't have to take accountability for his own actions. Logical, but it didn't keep Richard from freezing up. Reduced to the confused, hurt, scared kid he'd been, he reverted into someone unable to stand up for himself against the people whose approval he'd always craved and never received. He thought he'd moved past that; the cost of winning their approval would be a fate worse than death. Even now, after years of therapy, his father's disappointment still stung worse than the bruise forming on his shoulder, where the wine glass had struck him.

As they reached a footbridge that crossed the Mississippi, Sunny pulled her arm out of his grip. There were tears in her eyes that refused to meet his. "Bye, I guess."

"What?" Richard's chest tightened.

"I'm going home."

He'd rather debrief without Luna and Birdie's presence, but Sunny's comfort took priority right now. "Okay, let's go."

"No." Sunny shook her head firmly. "I just... I need to go home. You should too."

Every breath hurt. He swallowed hard. "You're going to walk home. After that. Alone."

Sunny nodded, her face clouded. "I need to think."

Richard's dread spiked. He had to say something. Anything. Her anger hurt, especially since he deserved it. Gaping helplessly, he floundered to find the right scripts in his head, something to earn her forgiveness. But everything he could come up with fell short. No words felt adequate enough.

Sunny turned on her heel to walk away from him, and all he could do was watch her leave. Mouth open, Richard was trapped, waiting for the right words that never came. The only sound was the clunking of her heels against the railroad ties that formed the footbridge, taking Sunny back to Eastside.

And wasn't that just like his whole life? Never being what people needed, because Richard's courage always failed when it mattered. Never enough for his dad, not his mom nor his brother, not any of his exes. He always paralyzed himself. Only Gabe and his parents, Antonio and his family, and Phineas had ever really seen his worth. As a man. As a person.

He'd been the problem from the moment he was born. Thirty years later, Dick still blamed him. He was intended to be Richard Carter V, the fifth generation of firstborn sons to take the name. Richard's anatomy had ruined the family legacy in his father's eyes—not that Richard had ever been thrilled about it, either. No matter what he did, no matter how much he tried to prove to his father that he was worthy, Richard could never make up for that deficiency. His original sin was so great that Dick had outright rejected giving his younger brother the name. The tradition had already been ruined, and it was "Elizabeth's" fault.

He had hoped that by changing his name to Richard when he'd transitioned, he might win Dick's favor. Instead Richard only received more vitriol. He'd changed it anyway, out of spite. He was born to be Richard Carter V, even if his body didn't cooperate. And once he'd begun to pretend Richard Carter IV didn't exist, he'd been relatively happy.

Barbie, unlike his dad, had believed the ultrasound. Pinning her dreams on the chance to relive her youth vicariously through a little princess, a clone of herself. Richard had disappointed her too, firmly confident in his gender identity even before he could understand his father's anger, or his mother's embarrassment. He had argued and pushed against her all his life, wearing the sparkly dresses only under threats of violence, and sabotaging the dance recitals with Sharpie mustaches. He didn't even like soccer, but Richard had thrown himself into it, forcing himself to excel to escape from pageants and modeling. As if that would stop Barbie from projecting all of her insecurities onto her embarrassing tomboy of a daughter. His mother would probably never be truly happy, but she wasn't constantly reminded of her failures as long as Richard stayed away.

And now Sunny, who'd seen him more deeply than anyone, was walking away after he'd failed to protect her from the filth he'd never intended her to see. After she'd witnessed the humiliation he'd never be truly able to escape, because that rot had made him. He'd tried to be the best version of himself for her. And he'd failed. Still never enough, and it gutted him because for her, he had *tried* to be enough. He *still* wanted to be.

With a heavy swallow and his nails pressed into his palm, he followed Sunny over the bridge. Keeping enough space to respect her desire to be alone, he stayed just close enough to keep her in view. Her apartment was three miles from here. She didn't have to acknowledge his presence, but he had to make sure she got home safely. It was the least he could do.

Besides, if Richard couldn't figure out what to do, there was someone else in Eastside who might help.

BLANCHE

"ALL RIGHT, ALL RIGHT! I'm coming!" Still damp from their hurried shower, Blanche tied their robe around themself as they went to see whoever was pounding at the door. Hopefully it wasn't a client. They were not in the mood and didn't have time. They had to get dressed. They had to do their hair. They had to plan what to say to the woman who'd been harassing them for months. And they had to figure out what to tell Tara.

Blanche exhaled as they unlocked the door; Tara was already pretending she wasn't crying in her bedroom over something she wouldn't open up about, but undoubtedly had something to do with Gabe. Who knew how she'd react when she found out he'd invited Blanche to some swanky party?

Richard stood on the other side of the threshold, blue eyes wide. "I need your help."

Blanche stepped back to let him in. "What happened?"

"Sunny's not talking to me, and I don't know how to fix it."

Oh, they were not in the mood for *this* drama on top of their own. Blanche sat on the couch, bending over to pull out a preroll and their lighter. "Well? What happened?"

Richard narrowed his eyes as they lit the joint. "I must be interrupting."

"Look, Dicky," Blanche exhaled. "I'm not in a great headspace right now. This?" They gestured with the joint in their fingers. "This will enable me to listen to your relationship drama and not spiral from anxiety. So unless you want to do my hair and listen to me vent first, don't judge me."

"Sorry." Richard perched on the couch. "I don't know what to do."

"So you've said. You still haven't told me what happened."

A door squeaked and Tara snuck in. Backpack slung over her shoulder, she mouthed an apology as she tiptoed quietly past the couch. "Oh. Hey, Richard. I heard voices and assumed it was a client."

Richard stood. "I can come back."

"Sit down, Dicky!" Blanche snapped, pointing at him. They stalked to the storage closet in the hallway, where they kept their evening wear. "Babes, perfect timing. Richard needs advice. Help him. I need to figure out what to wear."

Tara and Richard looked at each other, and back to Blanche. They both sat on the couch.

"Uh, the thing is, I don't know if I can get the advice I need from *Tara*." Richard gave Blanche a meaningful look.

Blanche rolled their eyes. "You can, and you will. Sunny's mad at him; that's as far as he's gotten. Tell Tara what happened. Maybe I'll listen."

"Aren't you and Sunny going to that fundraiser thing?" Tara asked. "Why are you here?"

That was today? Oh, shit, is that the party I'm going to? Blanche put the joint between their lips and inhaled deeply. They held the smoke in their lungs as long as they could stand, before slowly exhaling. They should have known Richard wouldn't come to them unless it was an emergency.

Richard gave Tara a pensive look. "She told you about us."

"Yeah." Tara shrugged. "I haven't told Lee, if that's what you're worried about."

"No, it's fine. I just didn't know," Richard said, running a hand through his hair. "I don't know how to make things right."

"And what happened was..." Blanche gestured for him to get on with it. They were already running late, but Gabe hadn't given them much notice.

"My family was there." Richard paused. "And they treated her like trash. I knew it wouldn't go well, but I didn't expect it to be that bad. And she went home instead of talking about it, and I can't figure out what to say to fix it."

"When you say they treated her like trash..." Tara trailed off. She grabbed the joint from Blanche while they tossed a garment bag on the couch, and took a drag on it herself.

His brow furrowed. "My mom asked her where she was *really* from, then called her fat and uneducated. My dad said she was a diversity hire with nice tits and a waste of my marriage potential, and my brother objectified her in the sleaziest way imaginable."

"No shit? What'd Sunny say?" Tara leaned forward, too eagerly for mere concern.

"She told my brother to blow her."

Tara and Blanche burst out laughing. "Classic."

"Tell me— I need— How do I fix this?" Richard sat on his hands.

Blanche turned their back and kept their robe on to be polite, shimmying the silk jumpsuit over their hips. It felt weird to change in front of Richard, but he was in their apartment, and neither Tara nor Blanche were shy about their bodies. "What'd you do?"

"I tried to redirect the conversation until I could find Gabe or his parents, but they all talked over me, like always. And when Sunny justifiably lost her temper, we left."

"And so you talked about it on the way home? Apologized?"

"I didn't know what to say. I figured we'd talk when we got home," Richard said, his normally steady voice soft and unsure. "But then she decided to walk to *her* home, without me. I followed to make sure she got back safely, and then came here."

Tara hummed. "She needs some space to figure out what she's feeling, but Sunny's resilient. She'll be back sooner than you think. Every time we argue, she makes us work it out before I've even had time to feel guilty."

"Her love language is quality time," Blanche offered gently, zipping the jumpsuit up their back as far as they could, so Richard wouldn't get an eyeful when they turned around. He looked so sad and pitiful, staring at his feet. They could spare a little emotional reserve for them. "When she's upset, she needs to process alone. And, like Tara said, she shows her love by showing up. Once she figures out what she's thinking, she'll be back."

"But what if she can't forgive me?"

Blanche and Tara's eyes met in bewilderment. Tara turned to Richard. "Are we talking about the same Sunny? I don't know if you've picked up on this, but all of us blame ourselves for everything. She probably thinks *you're* mad at *her*."

"I doubt that." Richard's sigh barely veiled his frustration. "She didn't do anything wrong. *I* brought her there. *I* didn't stop my parents from treating her like shit. And *I'm* the one who let her leave without apologizing first."

"Speaking of blaming ourselves," Blanche muttered, sitting back in their chair and swiping the joint from Tara. Gabe could wait until Richard wasn't in a crisis.

Richard rubbed his neck. "So how do I fix this? I've been trying hard to be good for her, but I've never cared this much about anyone before. I can't think of anyone who's had a similar situation. Gabe and Tonio's families are nice! I don't have a behavioral template for this."

"What the fuck is a behavioral template?" Tara shook her head in confusion.

Richard blinked, an equally puzzled look on his face. "A script with the optimal responses for different social situations?"

"That doesn't mean shit to me." Tara shook her head. "Fuck 'supposed to.' What do *you* want to do?"

Richard's brow furrowed. "I want to talk to her and apologize."

"Then do that." Tara shot Blanche a pleading look.

Blanche just handed her the joint with a shrug. This was the closest to an authentic Richard they'd seen.

"But what do I say?"

Tara exhaled sharply. "I don't know, Dicky! I don't know how I ended up giving *you* advice on this relationship I'm not supposed to know about. I don't do relationships, and I don't follow fucking behavioral templates and shit. I just start talking and words come out and sometimes it feels like I said the right thing." Tara shrugged and puffed on the joint in frustration. "Give her space. Validate her feelings. Ask how to support her. Listen to her?"

Richard's face twitched before he broke into a small smile. "You and Gabe will be good for each other once he gets his head out of his ass."

Her face fell. "I don't know what you're talking about."

Blanche fought a smile, even as their stomach twisted. "He'll be good for her, too."

"Nothing is happening with Gabe." Tara handed the joint back to Blanche.

"Those hickeys you left on him lasted five business days." Richard stood up. "But if Gabe asks, I know nothing. He hasn't opened up to me about it yet."

Tara froze. "There's nothing to open up about, *Dicky*."

Blanche laughed. "She winced every time she sat down for at least three days."

Tara's face was as red as her hair. "Again, nothing is happening!"

Richard smirked. "Look, fair is fair. You know about Sunny, so you should know I've observed things. Gabe *would* know about Sunny, but that'd require telling him about Antonio's stupid plan, and that should come from Antonio." Richard paused by the door as he put his shoes on. "Or if not Antonio, perhaps from *you*."

"He already knows," Tara muttered. "I told him. He and Antonio talked it out. I didn't tell him about you and Sunny, though."

Richard hummed. "Yes, that should come from me. For his sake."

"For someone who can't talk about your own feelings, you are certainly very considerate of his," Blanche muttered. "Maybe you should prioritize yourself as much as you do Gabe."

Richard snorted. "I'll take that into consideration. Thank you. Both of you. I'm going to go talk to Sunny, if she lets me. Sorry to interrupt your evening."

As soon as the door closed behind him, Blanche stubbed out the last of the joint into the ashtray. "Can you finish zipping me up? How's my hair, anyway? Can I get away with wearing it down?"

Tara dutifully zipped the jumpsuit up. "Maybe a hair comb to pull the flyaways back, but it's fine other than that. Where the fuck are you going, anyway?"

Blanche sighed and sat next to her. "Don't overthink this, but Gabe just texted me and asked if I wanted to go to the MAI fundraiser with him."

"Oh." Tara stiffened.

"Not like that. He saw that my patron and his fiancée were there, and asked me if I wanted to cause drama, and because he's anxious about being there by himself. Frankly, I want a chance to talk shit out with the future Mrs. Big Pharma with an audience, when that asshole isn't paying me to kiss his ass. So like I said, don't read into it. This is just as friends."

"Why would I care?" Tara smiled tightly. "Go and have fun. Tell me all about it later!"

For Tara's sake, and Gabe's as he was waiting for them, Blanche pretended they didn't see the waver of her chin. Pressing Tara on what had happened between them would only make her pretend she was fine even harder. So instead, Blanche pressed a kiss into her hair, slid their heels on, and left her alone to process. They fought to ignore the tightness in their chest as they closed the door behind them.

CHAPTER THIRTY-FOUR

BLANCHE

THE MUSEUM ATRIUM WAS practically empty as Blanche stepped out of their Uber. Only a few volunteers remained, tidying up the silent auction. Dinner must have already started. Their footsteps rang out in a lone arpeggio from the musical tiles as they headed for the exhibit hall.

"Excuse me," Blanche stopped a server on the edge of the dining area, passing by with a platter of half-eaten salad plates. "Can you tell me where the Coopers are sitting?"

Their optimism that they wouldn't need Gabe's mom's first name paid off as the server pointed to a table, front and center along the stage. Gabe's enviable curls rose above the crowd at a half-empty table.

Thanking the server, Blanche squared their shoulders as they passed through the sea of tables. Normally walking in alone, late, and while everyone else was seated, would make Blanche feel overwhelmingly exposed. But today, their obtrusiveness was perfect. They could feel all eyes on them. Their long hair cascaded between the bare skin of their shoulder blades, swept up artfully in some hair combs during the car ride. The satin of their wide-legged jumpsuit swished around their ankles as they strode past the sea of tables to join Gabe and his parents.

A loud clatter of silverware drew their eyes to their patron, his face draining of blood and jaw tightening.

Smirking, Blanche twitched their fingers in a graceful wave, the way Daisy always had when calling over a john to stop and chat. His fiancée looked positively murderous. Her knife scraped loudly as she cut her steak, glaring at Mr. Big Pharma. With a satisfied smile, Blanche swept past their table, touching Gabe lightly on the shoulder before pulling out the seat next to him.

"So sorry I'm late, darling." They smiled at the other two people at the table, the classy-looking couple they'd seen at the gala earlier that spring.

"I gave you almost no notice, so you're earlier than expected," Gabe said, greeting them with a side hug. "Blanche, these are my parents, John and Miriam."

Blanche nodded politely. "Pleasure to meet you."

"Likewise!" Miriam beamed. "It's so nice to meet a," she paused meaningfully, "*friend* of Gabey's."

Gabe sighed.

"Oh, 'friend' is *very* much the right word." Blanche laughed, then asked Gabe quietly, "What have you told them about me, and what can I tell them?"

"Almost nothing, and I promise they won't be shocked no matter what you say."

"Perfect!" Blanche grinned. "The short version is that I'm a friend of Lee's, and he and Antonio have been working very hard to make their friends be friends with each other. So Gabe is one of my newest friends."

Miriam beamed even harder, her brown eyes squinting with the force of her grin. "I always liked that Lee, even more now that he's broadening your stunted social life, Gabey."

"Thanks, Ma."

"If I can ask, is there a long version of the story?" John asked, in a voice as deep as his son's but calmer. Steadier than the anxious stutters and cutting sarcasm that sometimes twisted Gabe's.

"I'm so glad you asked!" Blanche's smile grew wider. "I'm a professional dominatrix. Gabe has heard me complain often enough about how much I hate my...sugar daddy, to use a conventional term, even though he is not that sweet nor is he a daddy. Anyway, he's right over there," Blanche waved again at their patron; the scum was glowering in their direction as his fiancée looked on the verge of tears. "And frankly, I wouldn't mind getting out of my contract, so Gabe here invited me to cause some drama, because he's a sweetheart when he's not around a certain—"

Gabe coughed, elbowing them.

"Oh!" Miriam raised her eyebrows, but true to Gabe's word, didn't clutch any pearls. Instead, she filled Blanche's wine glass with a heavy pour. "Well, happy to be a part of it. I love seeing entitled men taken down a peg."

Gabe looked around the room. "Richard said he was coming tonight, but I haven't seen him. He was apparently bringing a date, but wouldn't tell me who."

"You know, he might have left before we got here." Miriam took a sip of her wine. "I saw Dick and Barbie and their chode of a son getting escorted out by security when we walked in. Barbie tried to kiss my ass so I'd step in, but if I'd known that trash was on the guest list tonight, I would have had security block them in advance. If I had to guess, Richard probably saw them and turned right around. Have you texted him?"

Gabe nodded, brow furrowed. "He hasn't responded."

Stomach twisting at the worry on Gabe's face, Blanche opted not to say anything about Richard and Sunny's interaction with his parents. Gabe shouldn't hear about Richard's romantic life from them.

"Ahem."

Blanche twisted around; the future Mrs. Big Pharma was hovering behind them. Their patron remained in his seat, jaw tight as he watched.

So his fiancée had some power over him after all. Here Blanche thought she'd been coming after them because she couldn't get him to cooperate. Maybe they could get out of this contract sooner than later.

"A word, if you don't mind?" Their patron's fiancée shot a tight smile to the Coopers. "In private."

"They—" Gabe started to say, but Blanche silenced him with a hand on his arm.

"Lead the way, sweetheart." Blanche intentionally used the pet name their patron used for his fiancée. Grim satisfaction tugged their mouth into a smirk when she flinched. Blanche grabbed their wine glass as they rose, following her out of the great hall and onto a quiet balcony overlooking the river.

"I don't like you," the fiancée said, after a moment of silence. Meeting her like this—having a real conversation with her, instead of merely screenshotting the more threatening text messages to send to their patron to deal with—made the woman in front of Blanche all the more real. Yet Blanche couldn't bear to think of her by name. It was safer to keep her inhuman, like they did their patron and their other awful clients. Their nicer clients, the volunteers for their channel, could get names. But not the ones Blanche needed to keep at a distance.

Blanche shrugged. "I felt nothing but pity for you, until you started threatening me. Now, I don't like you either."

The fiancée squared her shoulders. "Wouldn't you do the same in my shoes? Wouldn't any woman?"

"Ah ah," Blanche mocked. "Not a woman."

"And somehow that makes it worse, doesn't it?"

"No need to be transphobic *and* a cunt, sweetheart. I'm not a threat to your marriage." Blanche looked over the riverwalk, keeping the woman in the corner of their eye. "Your fiancée does that well enough all on his own. I'm merely a bystander in all this."

"And yet, you won't leave."

"You know," Blanche turned to her, anger buzzing under their skin like static, "I *can't* leave. He can break our agreement any time he wants. I'm contractually obligated to humiliate and beat him until he decides to let me go, or I save up enough money to pay the fine for breaking the contract—which is an *obscene* amount of money for the record."

"Beat him?" Her head tilted in confusion, hesitation creeping into her voice.

Blanche paused. "Do you not know the nature of our arrangement? You never wondered about the bruises?"

"You're his mistress. I'd rather not know."

Blanche laughed. "I'm not his *mistress*, I'm his *domme*, sweetheart."

She flinched. "Don't call me that."

"Why not?" Blanche shrugged. "He does. I make him answer your calls. I've listened to your conversations on speakerphone. Sometimes it's me you're texting. Strange, how much power I have over him, and yet I'm still trapped." They scoffed and sipped their wine. "You don't need him, why are you marrying him?"

"I love him."

"Of course you do." Blanche rolled their eyes. "You love the man who treats you like shit and uses you? The man who cheats on you constantly, and I'm *not* just talking about me."

The fiancée didn't answer other than a hard swallow, her eyes shining but her chin set stubbornly high.

Blanche's heart went out to her. She was signing up for a life Blanche wouldn't wish on anyone. "You want him to be yours? Make him need you more than he needs me." They shook their head, voice softening.

"I want out of this as much as you want me gone. The only way that's going to happen is if you learn to dominate him. Or instead of me, it'll be someone else, and someone else, and someone else. And not everyone will be as discreet as me."

"You're *discreet*?" The fiancée laughed bitterly. "You're everywhere. Even at what was supposed to be a nice night just for us. Without arguments, without working, without drama. And then *you* waltzed in."

"And yet, you had no idea he was a masochist until tonight. I could end his career and put him away for a long time with one little tipoff from how much he's confessed to me." Blanche swirled their wine, tiring of this conversation. "You have no idea the emotional labor I've put in to make your relationship work. I absolve him of his guilt, so he can pretend he deserves you. Because in his own twisted way, he loves you, too. Just not more than himself."

Silence again from the peanut gallery.

Waiting for her to break, Blanche looked at the dark outline of the island across the river, where Daisy's ashes had been scattered into the Mississippi years ago.

Finally, she whispered, "Teach me what I need to know."

Blanche smiled into their wine glass. "Educational subscriptions start at fifty bucks a month on SubParty. I have a whole channel dedicated to tips and tricks for playing at home. I'll text you the link."

"Fuck you."

Blanche gloated. "You want to get rid of me? Become me, sweetheart. Study what I do. Buy my master class. I'll make a playlist just for you. Trust me, I want it as much as you do. But he's special, your future husband. He needs more than flogging and being called a bad boy. You won't learn it overnight, and I'm not risking the roof over my head in hopes that you're a quick study. Help me buy a new roof, and make him all yours."

The tears forming in her pretty eyes tugged at Real Blanche's heartstrings, but Work Blanche stood strong. They looked down at Mrs. Big Pharma until the woman turned on her heel and stormed off the balcony, leaving Blanche alone with their empty wine glass, adrenaline pumping through their veins, and a view of their past across the river. The past which had gotten them into this mess to begin with.

Blanche wasn't sure how much time had passed when Gabe leaned on the railing next to them. "You okay?"

They nodded.

"No emotional support dog today, but," he held out a silver case, flicking it open to reveal a neat row of prerolls, "Indica?"

With a relieved sigh, Blanche took one, pulling their lighter out of their bust to spark the joint between their lips. "Did you steal this from your mom?"

Gabe tucked the case into his jacket pocket. "She says to save her one."

"There's six more in here."

Gabe shrugged. "She smokes a lot."

"I like your mom," Blanche laughed, offering him the joint. "Thanks for this."

He took it, sucking in a light puff. "Your client was pacing in the hallway when I happened to walk by. If I didn't look the way I do, I think he might have tried something."

"Yeah, he's a coward. Feel free to beat the shit out of him."

"Not my style. I look tougher than I am." Gabe handed the joint back. "Good conversation with the fiancée?"

Blanche raised their eyebrows, leaning onto the railing on their elbows. "I'm getting in the way of her happily ever after, apparently."

"Isn't he doing that?"

"You'd think. But cognitive dissonance. It's easier to blame me." Blanche held the smoke in their lungs, letting it out slowly through their nostrils. "I'm surprised you didn't already have a date for this. Tara wasn't busy, you know. In fact, she seemed a little put out that you invited me and not her."

"I doubt that," Gabe muttered. "What's it going to take to let that go?"

"Understanding why you're in love with her, but still insist that you're just friends."

Gabe shook his head. "I'm not."

"Could have fooled me. No one says 'Kitten' like that platonically."

"I..." he sighed. "I love the idea of being in love with her. I don't know her."

Blanche raised an eyebrow. "You seemed to get pretty well acquainted on her birthday."

Gabe snorted. "One night isn't enough to truly know anyone."

"No, but it wasn't just one, was it?" Blanche couldn't fight their grin. "Her birthday, getting to know her over the past six months, your romp in the bathroom on New Year's. And the other one the birthday before. Seems like plenty of time to catch real feelings. Did I miss any?"

Gabe took the joint. "She told you about that?"

"Of course not." Blanche shook their head. "But I was at Confession that night, too. As were Lee and Sunny. But unlike them, I have eyes and a good memory."

Gabe sat silently for a moment, his jaw working back and forth, skin pale in the lights reflecting off the river. "I'm not ready for her. I... You were right, that she needs stability and support and everything good. And I can't give her any of that."

"Give yourself some credit—"

"No." Gabe shook his head. "I have too much baggage. Anything that might have happened between us is over, and we're on the same page about that."

Blanche waited, but Gabe sat silent. They sighed. "Relationships are complicated, aren't they? They leave scars that never quite heal."

Gabe snorted. "Head injuries don't heal easily, but I'm getting there. The emotional scars are somehow worse, but they're getting better too. I just gotta keep working at it."

"Head injury?" Blanche asked, understanding clicking into place. His confusion, his mood swings, the moments where he was lost for words—all symptoms similar to what Blanche had experienced for years after Daisy's client had put them in the hospital long ago.

Gabe raked a hand through his curls until he parted it. He bent over to reveal a bright white scar, running along his skull. "I fell. Apparently."

Their ears rang as rage coursed through Blanche. "What really happened?"

"I was in and out of—I'll call it subspace for lack of a better word—for most of that... Relationship is the wrong word, too. Arrangement? I have no idea what really happened." He shrugged, fluffing his hair. The scar was neat and flat, vanishing beneath his dense curls so easily Blanche never would have known it was there. "Last I heard, he dumped me unconscious outside of an ER and took off, so who knows?"

"Do you know where he is now?" Blanche asked coolly, wondering if the island would still be a decent spot to dispose of a body.

"No, but probably still in New York, along with the rest of my baggage." Gabe shook his head. "The worst side effects have gotten better because that was a decade ago. But I'm still dealing with mood swings and insomnia, mostly because I thought shitty relationships would heal me when I should have gone to therapy and PT. Love is a trap when you can't trust if your feelings are real or a symptom, and I felt everything so hard. The only people who wanted that intensity were toxic as hell. Hence, baggage. Limerence is a bitch."

Blanche let out a sardonic laugh. "Isn't she though?"

Gabe shot them a skeptical look. "What do you know about it? You're aloof as hell."

Blanche didn't answer. They fell into silence again, staring across the river at the island, until Blanche admitted, "The love of my life trafficked me."

Out of the corner of their eye, Gabe turned to them. "Whoa."

"I was thirteen when we met, and soon enough, I'd been used in every way scum might use an intersex teenager. Daisy was barely seventeen herself. She thought she was doing me a favor, because that was all she knew." Blanche's throat tightened, remembering how proud they had been to make Daisy happy every time they'd handed her their earnings, despite the shame crawling under their skin.

"And when I was eighteen and suggested we get out of the game, I was suddenly beaten half to death, and she got to act like the hero who saved me, instead of the one who set me up. She let me stop working the street, but before I was even out of the hospital, she'd found a dom to train me instead. I loved her so much, I worshiped her, so of course I stayed. Even though I knew she loved that she could control me more than she ever loved me." Blanche shook their head, their stomach twisting with guilt and relief to finally say that out loud.

They weren't supposed to be this open, but getting out the thoughts that had been poisoning them since their breakup with Sunny was cathartic. The mirror Sunny had unintentionally held up to their past had broken Blanche, and they had been stewing in the dissonance it had wrought for almost a year.

"And here I am, six years after she died, still caught up in the career I never wanted, contractually obligated to the piece of shit who pays my rent until I can pay him a small fortune, and the only money I do have is invested in Confession so Chas can keep majority ownership. I trapped myself." Blanche took a deep drag of the joint, holding the smoke in their lungs until it hurt. "And yet, I'd do it all over again just to hear that unhinged laugh one more time, to see her smile at me and tell me how happy I made her. If I could go back in time and die in her place, I would do it in a heartbeat.

"Funny how love works, isn't it? And that just keeps happening. I *let* it keep happening. I don't trust myself. It's safer to sign contacts with assholes who use me, because I know what I'm getting into. They control my life, but not *me*. If I let myself actually like someone, I'd get myself caught in that trap all over again, and I'd be fucking happy to do it." Their jaw hurt as Blanche snapped their mouth shut; they'd said far more than they'd meant to.

But that was the truth, wasn't it? Why they still dommed horrible people, when so many decent people wanted to play with them? Why they'd let Sunny push them into a relationship they'd known was a bad idea? Why they still were stuck in this awful arrangement with their patron?

Gabe pulled them into a hug, crushing them against his chest, and for a second, Blanche understood why Tara liked him. "I'm not equipped to help you the way you need, but I can recommend a couple of therapists. And a lawyer."

Blanche gripped his waist as they melted into the best hug of their life, even though that sour twist was back. "Sorry, I didn't mean to dump all that on you. I forget how bad it sounds to other people. I'm trying to say that I have my own past with shitty relationships if you want to talk about it, because it's hard to reconcile on your own."

Gabe's chest shook with a silent laugh. "We're friends, right?" At Blanche's nod, he said, "I don't want my friends to psychoanalyze me. And as much as I want to right now, I can't do that for you, either. I say this with love: you need professional guidance. Or at least, more than I can give. I support you and want what's best for you, but I can't do the thing where I think we can fix each other. Again."

"That wasn't my intention—"

"I know. But that's what would happen if I let it." Gabe shook his head and stepped away, plucking the joint from their fingers. "Part of the reason I have to stay away from Tara."

"But you're gonna stick around for her, right? As a friend?" Blanche asked warily.

Gabe's jaw worked back and forth, his mouth opening and closing.

Their stomach clenched. "How's this? You stick around for Tara, I'll follow your advice and...get therapized."

"Are you blackmailing me with your mental health?" Gabe laughed.

Blanche shrugged. "If it's not clear, I'd burn the world down for my ducklings. Seeing a therapist is the least toxic arrangement I've made yet."

"Your ducklings?"

"Tara, Lee, Sunny. Chas, Freddy and their family. Antonio, and maybe you and Richard, eventually." Blanche smirked. Richard was well on his way, and after this conversation, Gabe was already theirs, as was his dog. "I look out for the people I love, Gabe. And Tara's been through enough. As a friend, lover, or however it works out, just don't leave her."

With a sigh, he leaned on the railing next to them. "I don't think I could walk away from her if I wanted to." Gabe pointed a warning finger at them. "But you should still see a therapist. And a lawyer. So if you need me to pretend I'm blackmailing you, we can do that."

"Good." Blanche swiped the joint back from him. "In that case, I'll take your therapist's number."

"Oh, not *my* therapist." Gabe laughed. "It's weird enough sharing her with Tonio. I'll ask her for recommendations. The lawyer, though." He dug in his pocket. "Here, this is for my friend Phin, who is my lawyer. And Richard's. And Antonio and Lee's, kinda. He's an estate lawyer by practice, but he does whatever we need."

Blanche took the business card from him, tucking it into their bust without looking. "Could he get me out of this contract without risking Confession, or leaving me and Tara homeless?"

Gabe shrugged. "If anyone can, it's Phin. He's a mess of a person, but a surprisingly competent lawyer."

Good enough for them. When they'd signed that contract, they'd been desperate and grieving and lost. But everything was different now. Allowing Tara and Lee to help was turning out better than they'd imagined. Maybe Gabe and this Phin could help too. Perhaps they'd find a way out of this mess after all. As they passed the last of the joint to their friend, the tension in Blanche's shoulders loosened, and the sourness in their stomach finally began to ease.

Chapter Thirty-Five

RICHARD

THE FLUORESCENT LIGHTS IN the hallway of Sunny's apartment were like something out of a horror movie. The flickering did not do his building headache any favors as Richard stood in front of the Boonmee's door.

After leaving Blanche's, he'd found himself on a park bench on the island. Staring at the museum across the river, he'd debated if he should go home or back to Sunny's, and if he came back, what he should say. But when it came down to it, even if Sunny wasn't ready to talk, he should still apologize.

With a few deep breaths, Richard tried to steady his heart as he knocked on the door.

He banged harder than intended, jumping at the sound. He pressed his hand to his stomach to calm the anxiety roiling through his gut.

The door cracked open. Luna's head poked around the door. "What are *you* doing here?"

"I need to talk to Sunny," he blurted out. This was already going off-script, and he hadn't even seen Sunny yet. Luna answering the door was not how he'd planned this. Sunny was supposed to answer, and Richard was supposed to explain himself in the hallway, and if she forgave him, she would invite him in.

Or if she needed more time, he'd go home, and at least Richard could say he'd tried.

"Aren't you the reason she came home crying?" Luna raised her eyebrow and set her jaw, the way Sunny did when she knew she was right.

Richard couldn't begin to describe the dejected sound that came out of his mouth. "I need to apologize." Luna's expression softened briefly, but she narrowed her eyes again. "Can I talk to her? Please?"

Luna shook her head. "She's not here."

"She was here an hour ago!" Richard ran a hand through his hair.

"She's not now." Luna shrugged. "Don't shoot the messenger, bro!"

"Sorry," Richard sighed. This was supposed to go well. He was supposed to apologize to her, and she would invite him in, and everything would be fine, and Sunny would like him again. How was he supposed to make things right if he couldn't apologize? "Can you tell her I was here?"

Luna nodded. "Yeah, I'll tell her."

DEFEATED, RICHARD UNLOCKED HIS front door and turned to hang his keys on the hook.

Arms surrounded him from behind, a familiar citrus perfume igniting hope in his heart.

"I'm sorry," Sunny whispered into his neck. Her voice was thick with an emotion he couldn't name. "I ruined everything. I was trying to keep it together, and I lost my cool. They were just so awful to you."

To me? They were awful to you! Richard's mouth wasn't cooperating with his brain. Hot tears dripped onto his neck. He stiffened.

"Fuck. Shit. Sorry. I didn't warn you about the hug. Ugh, I knew I would fuck this up." Sunny wiped her eyes with her fist and stepped back, not meeting his gaze. Her dress was wrinkled like she'd been wringing the skirt in her hands. "I'll give you some space until you're ready to talk. *If* you want to talk to me again. I hope you can forgive me."

Tara had been right—Sunny thought *he* was mad at *her*. He had been silent as they walked along the river, and terse when he did speak. And just now, he didn't fucking hug her back when she was fucking crying. And she was about to leave before he could apologize. Leave looking so heartbroken and in tears, while she thought Richard was upset with her, when he was so incredibly sorry. *I'm such a fucking asshole.*

He grabbed her wrist as she stepped around him toward the door. "Don't leave."

Richard pulled her around to face him, slowly backing her against the door, bracketing her with his arms as if she might flee. She *had* to stay, to give him a chance to save this. Give him a chance to be better, to prove he could be the man, the boyfriend, the partner Sunny deserved.

"I'm sorry." Richard hoped Sunny could hear how much he'd packed into those two words as he searched her face earnestly. Her beautiful dark eyes were shiny, mascara smudged, but relief flooded him as she finally looked him in the eye. "My family is utter trash. I have to apologize for a thousand things, and I can't find the right words for any of them. *You* have nothing to be sorry for."

He stepped closer, burying his face in the crook of her neck to inhale her tangerine shampoo, arms falling from the door to cradle her waist. There was no time to second-guess if he was saying the right things. "You were amazing. Everything you said and did was perfect. I knew they'd be awful. They're always awful! I wanted to keep you safe from them. They're such terrible people, and they treated you like shit, and I was so angry I couldn't find the words to speak up. I feel like such an asshole for letting you down, and I hate it. I was trying so hard to be better than them, and then I fucking ruined it."

"Can I hug you?"

Richard nodded into her neck.

Her arms wrapped around his shoulders, tight and motionless around him. Sunny's hug was the best touch, even when she was squeezing the bruise blooming under his skin. "Why do you smell like weed?"

Richard laughed out a sob as he held her tight. "I thought I'd ruined everything, so I went to Blanche's because I didn't know what to do, and Tara gave me advice, and they were smoking. And then I went back to your house, and Luna wouldn't let me talk to you, so I thought that you didn't want to talk to me. I'm so glad you're here because I love you so much, and I was so scared you'd hate me after this. I have no excuse for allowing them to treat you like that. I hope you can forgive me."

He was crying now too, wetting the shoulder of her dress as Richard held onto her with everything he had. Telling her he loved her wasn't something he ever expected to come out of his mouth. If he'd been thinking clearly, he might have filtered it out. But he didn't regret it. Those words rang as true as the rest of the thoughts he'd just spilled out.

"Dicky?" She ran a hand through his hair, her nails scraping his scalp.

"Sunny."

Her grip on his hair tightened, pulling his head away from the safety of her shoulder. Relief washed over him at her smile, even as guilt ate away at him for causing the tears that brimmed in her eyes. He was supposed to make Sunny happy, not upset.

"You're such a confusing, infuriating human sometimes." Sunny pulled him closer and whispered against his lips, "I love you too."

With a shaky gasp, Richard poured his heart into the wettest and best kiss of his life. Their lips trembled against each other, salty with tears, saliva sharp with the tang of emotion and a non-zero amount of snot that he would prefer not to think about, because kissing her mattered more. He needed to show her everything he was terrible at expressing: his love for her, his admiration for her fire, her wit, and her passions, and his appreciation for her consideration and understanding. Sunny was everything that made Richard want to be a better person.

She broke the kiss first, murmuring, "Your family is so awful. Sure, you warned me that they'd treat me like shit, but you undersold how shitty they are to *you*." She hugged him tightly. "I don't know how you grew up in that and turned out as good as you are. I hope you'll forgive me for fucking up your relationship with them."

"What relationship?" Richard scoffed. "Trust me, nothing you did could fuck up my relationship with them worse than I did by being born." He pressed a kiss into her collarbone. "And here I had hoped they could be decent people in public, otherwise I would have dragged you out of there at a run."

Sunny laughed as she stroked his hair. Her nails scraping his ear sent shivers down his spine. "I mean, I have a newfound appreciation for Mae. But I trust you'll alligator us out of there next time."

"There will never be a next time if I can help it." Richard smiled against her neck, kissing the heartbeat fluttering below her jaw. He would never bring her around his family again. Hell, *he* might never see them again after that. "How can I make it up to you?"

"You don't need to make anything up to me." She moaned quietly, tilting her head back to allow him more access to her throat. "But if you uh...want to, then I just want to be close to you. Preferably naked. And I'm hungry."

Richard took her hand and pulled her away from the door, kicking his shoes off as they left the entryway. His feet throbbed after walking for miles around Bellamy in Oxfords. "I have everything to make up for after today. I'll order us dinner."

Sunny smiled, stepping out of her flats and pulling him to the bedroom. "Naked first. Then food. Girls my size do need empty carbs, but right now, I want you."

"God, why is my mom such a bitch?" Richard scoffed as he unzipped Sunny's dress. Digging through their toy drawer, he tossed an assortment of lube and toys on the bed that she'd appreciate if she wanted to be close.

"I probably would be too if I was married to your dad." She grinned over her shoulder as she unceremoniously pushed the dress from her shoulders. She was gorgeous, her curves revealed inch by inch as the dress fell away from Sunny's toned body into a satin puddle on the floor. She probably was trying to annoy him by leaving it there, but Richard wouldn't dream of caring. Not when she looked as good as she did, her beautiful hourglass figure shining gold in the sunset. Her pert ass looked positively smackable in her strappy red lingerie.

"Please don't talk about my dad when you look like that."

Sunny laughed. "I always look like this."

"Then let's never talk about him."

"Deal." Sunny laughed.

Richard had never met anyone who got him quite the way Sunny did. Even Gabe had encouraged him to leave communication with them on the table, unable to comprehend how devastating it was to be around them. But Sunny didn't need to understand. She just heard him, listened to what he wanted, and called him out for being an asshole when he deserved it. She respected his insecurities and unconventional boundaries like it was all completely normal.

Their relationship felt like relationships *should* feel. None of his exes had ever come close to making him feel like a regular person. Or maybe he'd never allowed himself to feel it, until Sunny came along.

He worked his end of Sunny's favorite strap into himself, fighting the urge to pull it out until his body adjusted to having something in it. Like always, once it was secured in place, his dysphoria eased, giving way to pleasure. Sunny lay back against the pillows, touching herself as she watched him get ready, teasing him with the scrap of lace around her hips. As pleasure jolted through his body with every movement, he climbed over Sunny on the bed, trailing kisses up her legs and stomach as her thighs parted around him.

For all their experimenting, the vanilla-est of missionary was their favorite, as long as he was topping her. They had tried it the other way and both were left with "the Ick," as Sunny called it. There was just something wholesome about fucking Sunny like this. Face to face. Intimate.

A big smile bloomed on her face as he laved her nipple through the lace. "Have I told you lately how wonderful you are, Richard?"

He blushed, sliding a hand around her back to unclasp her bra with a quick tug. "Please don't start." He hated compliments. Sunny's praise always left him nauseatingly vulnerable.

"No, I mean it." Sunny threw her bra across the room before pulling him close in a kiss, her lovely perfect tits falling into his waiting hands. "You are so considerate, generous, and handsome. And I love you."

"Love you, too," Richard whispered, his throat catching. He kissed her deeply, tweaking her nipples as he cupped her breasts. She arched into his hand, an adorable squeak flying from her mouth into his.

Richard worked his mouth down her neck, biting gently, licking and sucking. His torso pressed against her to give her friction, if she wanted it. Sunny bucked against him as he bit her clavicle hard, pushing the strap into him deeper and pulling a loud (and thankfully low-pitched) moan from him.

Sunny pulled his hair and bit his earlobe. He hissed, a wave of affection washing over him along with the pleasurable tension in his spine. Patting around the bed, he found the lube and warmed a generous amount on his fingers before pressing into her, working her open for him, licking and sucking as she whined underneath him. Richard loved her like this, spread out and desperate and begging for him.

Satisfied that she was ready, he stroked more lube onto the strap. It pressed delightfully against his nerves as he eased it slowly in and out of her, working deeper as she relaxed. Sunny bit her lower lip, her eyes screwed shut. Even after all this time, he couldn't tell when that was pleasure or pain or both, but now Richard wanted her to feel only bliss.

"This good?" he asked, voice hoarse.

Sunny nodded, exhaling sharply. "Absolutely stellar. No sarcasm."

Richard chuckled and cupped her clit as he bent down to kiss her, rolling his hips slowly. With an impatient cry, Sunny bucked against him as she kissed him back, sending thrills through his body. He set a slow pace, hand on her clit keeping rhythm, devouring her moans.

"Richard, can you turn it on?" Sunny asked. He hadn't even realized the vibrator was off. He was already so on edge just from wearing it.

"Are you trying to make me come?" he teased, blindly tapping around to find the button. The vibrations buzzed inside and around him. "Fuck, I'm not going to last long."

Sunny moaned loudly, arching her back as the vibrations hit her, too. "Yes, I love when you come when you're fucking me. Use me, let me see how much you love this."

Richard collapsed over her onto his elbows, burying his face in her neck as he thrust faster. His skin prickled as pleasure coiled within his muscles, forcing him to fight for control over his limbs. "Fuck, Sunny. I love you." He sucked her neck and earlobe sloppily, needing to put his mouth somewhere, anywhere. Fucking her hard and desperate, his lower back tightened like a spring.

Sunny hissed, her breath tickling his neck, her nails digging into his shoulders. "Fuck I'm close, please. Please!"

He didn't know what she was begging for, but Richard thrust harder anyway. Voice husky, he murmured her name. Told her how good she was, how much he loved her in all the ways that drove her wild. After all the practicing she'd made him do, making her react from his voice alone was a powerful thrill.

Biting down on the spot where her shoulder met her neck, Richard shuddered against her as his efforts brought him over the edge. Sunny let out a loud cry, arching against him as he twitched, the vibrator buzz turning unpleasant as he came down from his orgasm along with her.

He turned it off with an annoyed growl. "Did we..." he trailed off.

"Just come at the same time?" Sunny asked. "Hell yeah, we did! Up top!" She held a hand above her head. "We can add that to the Yes list."

Overwhelmed and confused, he high-fived her before they burst into laughter.

Richard pulled out as gently as he could and rolled onto his back. The bed shook as they laughed deliriously. Tears streamed down their faces from their shared delight after their tumultuous evening. His sides hurt, and his cheeks ached, but none of that mattered because Sunny's eyes were so beautiful as she laughed. He loved that he could be this open with her, laugh with her, have fun with her like this, even after everything they'd been through.

Breathing deep, Richard regained control of himself as he curled around her. "I'm sorry today didn't go well." He should write everything down so he could remember to say it out loud. Sunny deserved a proper apology, even if she had already forgiven him.

She kissed his cheek, still grinning widely. Her body was shaking from her giggles in his arms. "I thought it was fucking peachy."

"Sarcasm?" Richard asked, lips trailing along her shoulder.

Sunny ran her fingers through his hair, nails scratching his scalp as she smiled softly, dark eyes searching his face. "Only a little."

Saturday, June Twenty-Seventh

Chapter Thirty-Six

Blanche

Blanche and Tara climbed the staircase up to Confession's second-floor venue, decked out with giant posters of Antonio's album cover: a campy photo of Carlita Asada suggestively biting a sausage. Light shone around her wig like a halo, reflecting the sparkle in her eye. While they weren't late, the room was already packed with Confession's employees, regulars, people who resembled Antonio, and dozens of other faces. The crowd was bigger than Blanche had expected, but with Antonio's talent and charm, and Lee's knack for planning, they shouldn't be surprised.

"Oh, there's Lee!" Tara pointed through the buzzing crowd.

Lee, strikingly handsome in a dapper navy suit with his ever-growing hair in fresh twists, stood by a table full of CDs, stickers, and other Carlita-branded merchandise. Richard and Gabe sat behind the table.

A pang of inadequacy struck their heart. Blanche had been so caught up in their own shit that they hadn't even wondered if Lee and Antonio needed help. Even in Richard's time of need, Tara had been more helpful. But while Blanche had dropped the ball, everyone had been fine without them.

Somehow, the fact that they weren't needed hurt even worse.

Tara greeted Lee with an enthusiastic hug and a grin. "Congratulations! How's it feel to be done with your first ever album?"

Lee hugged her back. "Done? Oh, Buttercup, we're not done. Now we have to sell it. Luckily a few of Antonio's friends and the producer we've been working with in New York have been helping with some of that. We already got someone who wants to sample *Cake*."

"Where's the queen of the hour?" Blanche asked.

Lee pushed his glasses up. "Control room. Tonio told me to stay away from it, but *he* keeps going up there. You don't think he's up to something, is he?"

Blanche tried to exchange a confused look with Tara, but she was busy fussing with the merch. "I'm sure he's just double-checking last-minute details."

"Yeah, maybe. Anyway, I'm still gonna scope it out." Lee waved as he left to find Antonio, leaving Blanche with Gabe, Richard, and Tara. All of whom were completely silent.

Thankfully, Sunny joined them shortly. "Hey everyone!" she sang brightly as she waltzed behind the table and bent down so Richard could kiss her cheek. "Sorry, I'm late. My happy hour went long."

Gabe pulled a confused face—Blanche's favorite expression on him. The furrowed brows, the pursed lips that would open and close like a fish as he searched for the words to say, the rapid blinking as he took in new information. Though, Blanche was almost as surprised as he was that Sunny and Richard were so openly affectionate.

"You look nice. Did you wear that to work?" Richard asked, blatantly checking Sunny out in her floral sundress.

Sunny spun for him. "With a jacket, of course. I'm not giving my coworkers a show. Don't want to look— How did you say this dress looked? 'Immature and lazy?'"

Richard snorted. "Don't put words in my mouth. I said you looked youthful and carefree, though the combat boots don't exactly scream class."

"You don't like me classy, Dicky."

"As I said, you look very nice, Sunshine." He pressed a kiss to her hand.

Gabe frowned at Tara, crossing his arms. Tara's grin was smug as she mimed a drinking gesture. Mouthing "Sunshine" to her as he passed, he walked to the bar, the confused expression still on his face.

Sunny stole his seat. "What's his deal?"

Richard shrugged. "I still hadn't told him, but I didn't think he'd react *that* poorly."

"He's just a sore loser," Tara said with a shrug. "Yes, we were betting on you."

Gabe returned a moment later with a drink for Tara. She toasted him before taking a sip.

"Where's mine?" Blanche asked, teasing.

Gabe turned back to the bar without a word. Even after their weed-fueled heart-to-heart a couple of weeks ago, Blanche wasn't really sure where he and Tara stood. Tara was a bit closed off, but otherwise fine. Blanche kept an eye on her, a sense of unease prickling their skin.

Gabe returned a few minutes later with four more drinks, and a shadow behind his eyes.

Blanche felt a pang of guilt. "Gabe, I was just teasing, you know."

He nodded. "I know. I meant to buy everyone a round, but I was a little distracted."

"Everything okay?" Blanche touched his arm.

He nodded again with a smile that didn't reach his eyes, but he didn't shake off Blanche's touch. "Yeah, I started that new program at therapy this week. Feeling like a kicked puppy is all. But I'm still here."

The lights dimmed, and a smooth beat played an intro to cheers from the audience. Antonio strode on stage to applause, dazzling in a peach gown. Normally, Carlita was in full makeup and a wig, but tonight, Antonio was only Carlita Asada from the shoulders down. His brown hair fell neatly over his forehead in tight curls, his makeup minimal with eyeliner only.

Antonio's high tenor sang in Carlita's campy voice, crooning wistful verses with her characteristic raunch. Blanche knew as much about music as photography, but the notes sounded sensual. With a laugh, they swayed to the irresistible beat.

"I can see the way you're looking at me. Like you wanna taste me, touch me, fuck me. Does she know the way you're looking at me? How you wanna taste me, touch me, fuck me?"

To Blanche's surprise, Tara grabbed their hand to dance to the increasingly fast music. They knew Lee and Antonio's album would be fun, but knowing it and experiencing it was something else entirely. The beat was exhilarating enough that even Tara was dancing, albeit like an incredibly uncomfortable and awkward robot. But she moved with a complete lack of self-consciousness. Blanche grinned and danced harder to keep up.

"Let yourself go. Let's have some fun! Stop holding back. And make me come!"

Before they knew it, the song was over, and Antonio was thanking everyone for supporting their album, directing people to the merch table. As the next song started, Gabe joined them and Tara in their dancing, leaving Sunny and Richard at the merch table.

Blanche tried to step away so they wouldn't be the third wheel. But Gabe kept including them, dancing with Blanche as much as Tara. It was so awkward that Blanche couldn't listen to the lyrics other than the chorus; it was just the word "Cake!" repeated over and over again.

The sexual tension was still apparent between Tara and Gabe—Tara couldn't stop staring at his hips, and Gabe reached for her several times before pulling back—but for some reason, neither of them let Blanche slip quietly away. With a huff, Blanche resolved to stop letting their content schedule interfere with their friendships. They had to get to the bottom of this awkwardness and fix it. Get Gabe and Tara back on track— Blanche sighed. *Tara said no more meddling. I should let her handle it.*

"Where's Lee?" Antonio asked as the song faded, shielding his eyes from the stage lights as he looked through the window of the control room. "Leland Jones, get your ass up here! I told you to stay away from there! You're not working!"

Closing the control room door behind him, Lee shook his head with a laugh as he ambled toward the stage.

"Lee is my wonderful partner who helped make this album a reality, and he's easily embarrassed, so I want you all to cheer loud as hell when he gets on stage."

Blanche and Tara whooped and hollered as Lee climbed the steps. Tara took out her phone, propping her elbows onto a speaker to steady the video. Gabe snapped photos with a camera that Blanche hadn't noticed.

"Lee helped me write lyrics, made the beats, recorded, produced, and mixed the sound, and," Antonio laughed, "Really he did everything but the singing, and even then, he has a couple of ad-libs in a few tracks—which, ask me about *that* story later!"

"Do not ask about that story," Lee corrected into Antonio's earpiece.

Antonio grinned. "He deserves the limelight for this album even more than I do." Lee sheepishly covered his face with one hand, embarrassed by the attention. Beaming, Antonio took Lee's hand. "Lee has been my rock since the day we met at this very bar over a year ago." He turned toward Lee, kissing his knuckles. "I appreciate you every morning when I wake up beside you and every night when I go to sleep in your arms. My heart and my hole are yours, and yours are mine. I'm offering you my hand, and asking for yours, so we can keep it that way forever." Antonio knelt down amidst the gasps and titters from the crowd, his ball gown billowing out around him. "Leland Jones, Angel, love of my life? Will you marry me?"

Blanche's jaw dropped. They had not seen this coming, but they whooped along with the audience as Lee nodded with a smile. After all, why wouldn't Lee and Antonio get engaged? They were perfect for each other. And yet, Blanche's stomach twisted, a bitter resentment undermining their excitement. They scolded themself; they should be happy for Lee and Antonio. Their own confusing feelings could wait.

Lee wiped his eyes, allowing Antonio to slide an engagement ring over his finger before picking him up and spinning him around in a kiss. As the audience cheered, a sweet piano melody—strikingly simple after the immaculately produced house songs that had been playing—quieted the cheers into a lull.

"This song is called Lovingly," Antonio said before he began to sing.

Blanche's eyes burned, and Tara's hand found theirs. Antonio had written their story into a song. All traces of Carlita were absent from his voice as he sang it, just raw affection in Antonio's true singing voice. Lee wiped his eyes again as Antonio finished with a smile.

"Sorry everyone, that one isn't on the album." Antonio teased, pulling another ring from the necklace around his neck and sliding it on his finger. "Oh, and we've been secretly engaged for a hot minute, so I already have a ring. Sorry I didn't tell you, Mom."

As Antonio's mom and other family members called out jokes from the audience, Blanche looked over at Tara, who had stopped recording. She had a soft smile and tears in her eyes, until she made eye contact with Gabe. With a wince, Tara turned and walked away as the next song started.

Blanche started to follow her, but Gabe stopped them. "Don't worry about her. She's just a sore loser!"

Tara flicked him off, but returned minutes later, drink in hand for Gabe this time. She handed it to him, both careful that their fingers didn't touch. "You knew already."

Gabe nodded. "You also knew something." He gestured over his shoulder to where Sunny and Richard sat.

Tara shrugged. "Just took advantage of inside information."

Gabe scoffed. "Wow. More Moriarty than Sherlock, aren't you?"

They both laughed, visibly uncomfortable as they avoided eye contact. At a loss, Blanche stared between them. If they were friends, this was the most awkward friendship Blanche had ever seen, and they had just spent the past year trying to rebuild theirs with Sunny.

A second later, they were rescued from third-wheeling between Tara and Gabe by the most welcome presence, when Jazz appeared at their elbow. "Ah! Finally found you!"

"Jazzy, thank God! I didn't know you'd be here!" Blanche enveloped her in a hug. The awkward tension drained away as she squeezed back. Lee's little sister looked dazzling in a deep purple bodycon dress. Her hair, growing out from when she'd shaved it last year, was styled in a short afro.

"Lee snuck me in the back." Jazz's grin faded. "He won't get in trouble, will he?"

"No!" Blanche insisted. "And anyway, you're with me now. I could get away with murder here."

"Good. Dad thinks I'm doing a late-night study session. Can't imagine how he'd react if I got caught underage in a gay bar." She laughed the same big deep belly laugh as Lee. Blanche smiled fondly. They were so similar, but Jazz had a rebellious streak in her that Blanche could never imagine in Lee. "I can't wait to finally turn twenty-one next year, so I can hang out with you more often."

"Did you see the big moment?" Blanche nodded to the stage, where Antonio sang to a reggaeton beat. The song was, of course, about meat. Lee stayed with him, dancing along, looking surprisingly at ease as the center of attention.

"You mean, where I found out I'm getting a brother-in-law?" Jazz said, somewhat sarcastically, but Blanche sensed no bitterness in her tone. "I'm happy for them, but I had no idea they were that serious yet."

"Oh good, I'm not the only one who had no idea."

Antonio shouted a thank you to everyone for coming to their release party during the song, anticipation building with the beat until it dropped, and he sang, *"Don't want your fish! Don't want your peach! I go round the world to try that meat!"*

"Dance with me!" Jazz pulled them close, her hair tickling their temple.

Blanche obliged, much more comfortable dancing with Jazz than being the buffer between whatever was happening between Gabe and Tara. They were getting along, but there was a coldness between them that hadn't existed before. *They both need an emotional enema.*

"*Dónde está La Carlita Asada?*"

"Is this the Carmen Sandiego song?" Blanche laughed.

Jazz gave them a confused smile. "Who?"

Chapter Thirty-Seven

Lee

Hiding in the peaceful, dark, and quiet backstage, Lee admired the ring Antonio had picked out for him. It was a relief to have it back on his finger after that too-brief moment during their photo shoot. The white gold band with turquoise and opal inlays popped against his brown skin.

"There you are! I was looking for you." Heels clicking against the wood floors, Antonio joined Lee in leaning against a speaker.

Lee pulled him close, wishing for a second they were home and weren't hosting an after-party. A quiet moment with his fiancée before they went back out to the party was exactly what he needed. "I needed a minute away from it all."

"Me too." Antonio held his own hand up to his, the stones sparkling in the rose gold setting. "I finally get to wear this, instead of burning a hole in my chest. I was starting to feel like Frodo!"

Lee laughed, kissing the top of his head. "You were the one who waited so long to propose back."

"Maybe if someone hadn't insisted on a big flashy proposal, I could have," Antonio teased. Lee snorted; Antonio seemed to have forgotten that had been his idea. "Not that I'm complaining. I got to let the world know how much you mean to me." He twined their fingers together and kissed Lee's hand. "We can have a big wedding, right?"

"Of course babe," Lee replied. "Invite as many people as you want." Lee would only have his sister, Sunny, Tara, and Blanche there for him, but Antonio's family had adopted him into the fold. They would be his family now too.

Hopefully, he wasn't underestimating Antonio's family. Their wedding costs were already adding up. Blanche's bonus had been a godsend, even if he had practically shat himself when his account had several more zeros than normal. Their small wedding plans were quickly escalating into a big ceremony, but at least he'd paid Tara back.

"You ready to go back out there?"

Lee nudged his forehead against Antonio's. "Can we stay here? Or go to the Confessionals?" His thoughts, despite the long day, rested solely on the fact that he desperately wanted to be alone, preferably naked, with his fiancée. But they still had a couple of hours left of their release party, and then the after-party with their friends. He'd have to wait until after their guests were gone before he could finally show Antonio his feelings in private. "Seeing as my *hole* is yours? You not only totally plagiarized my whole proposal, but you had to talk about our assholes in front of your entire family and all of our coworkers?"

"Did I copy your proposal?" With a laugh, Antonio shrugged unapologetically. "I am who I am, shitty memory and raunchy humor and all, and you love me for it."

"I do." Lee kissed him, pleased that even if Antonio couldn't consciously remember the speech he'd worked so hard to perfect, the memory had still been stored somewhere in that wonderful, strange brain of his. "So, Confessionals though?"

Antonio smirked. "As lovely as *that* sounds, my dad sent me to find you. He and Oscar have shots waiting for you."

Lee sighed. "I guess I'll keep it in my pants a little longer. Why are we having an after-party again?"

"Because you're a type A Groomzilla who invited our wedding party over to ask them to stand up with us before I even proposed." Antonio's hazel eyes smiled up at him.

"Oh yeah. I did this to myself. What was I thinking?"

"That you love me so much that you can't wait to marry me?"

Lee grinned and kissed Antonio's forehead. "Sure, let's go with that."

FAR MORE THAN TWO shots had been pressed on Lee after they'd reemerged, and they were still getting bombarded with "congratulations!" from Antonio's family members and their coworkers from Confession. He forced a smile for every new person, but Lee was burning out. *I used to be an extrovert! What happened?*

"You okay, Angel?" Antonio asked, squeezing his hand. "Too much attention? Or maybe too much tequila?"

Lee shook his head. "I might need some water before too long, but I'm okay."

"I'll get you some." Before Lee could protest, Antonio was off, slipping through the surrounding crowd of his cousins and sisters. Lee wasn't alone, per se. But Antonio leaving, even for a moment, reminded him that he was only part of this wonderful, supportive family because Antonio had brought him into it. His bitterness toward his own parents always tasted more sour when in the company of the Floreses.

Luckily, Antonio returned soon after, two glasses of water in hand. And in tow, he'd brought Lee's family: Jazz, Sunny, Tara, and Blanche. Before he could get a word in, they had him surrounded him in a group hug.

"Congratulations, loser!" Jazz murmured in his ear as she squeezed him tight.

"Thanks, nerd." Lee hugged her back, grateful that he still had his little sister in his life, even if their parents may never know about it. Or about the way-too-grown outfits she wore out of the house.

"You're a hard man to find, Lee," Blanche teased. "We've been trying to find you all night."

Tara slipped her hand into his. Lee squeezed it, grateful for her comforting presence.

"Should have known you'd be in the middle of a crowd," Sunny added. "Why can't you be a wallflower like normal people?"

Lee just grinned, grateful for their teasing and the support he needed to keep going. He introduced them to Antonio's parents and siblings, grinning as Antonio's sisters and Lee's friends good-naturedly roasted both of them in turn.

"Lee, you've been holding out on me!" Paula, Antonio's mom, teased as she fawned over Jazz. "You have to bring everyone with you next time we have a get-together. Your sister is as lovely as you are!"

"Holy shit, can she be my mom, too?" Tara asked him quietly, watching the conversation half-hidden behind him.

"Be careful, she'll adopt you," Lee teased, pulling Tara into a side hug. "Even Richard hugs her voluntarily."

Tara snorted. "Yeah, well, from what he says about his parents, he probably needs a good mom hug."

"The fuck?" Lee shot her a look. "Since when do you talk to Richard about his parents?"

Tara shrugged. "We're kinda friends. Wasn't that the point of your stupid plan thing?"

"We're going downstairs to dance!" Sunny announced before he could tease Tara that his plan wasn't a total failure. "Lee, you coming?"

Lee shook his head, eyeing the dozens of people waiting to congratulate them. "I probably shouldn't bail at our own release party. Have fun, though!"

With one last hug, his family departed. Antonio sidled up to him again. "Better? You looked like you needed some Tara time."

"Thank you." Lee pressed a kiss into his hair.

"Well, isn't that cute?" Gabe teased as he approached, Richard and Phineas following close behind. He wrapped them both in a bear hug. "Congratulations!"

"Thanks, Gabey." Lee hugged him back.

"Congrats on the album!" Phineas grinned. "Don't forget me when you get famous."

Lee and Antonio exchanged an unsurprised smirk. "Is that all you want to congratulate us for?" Antonio asked pointedly.

Phineas gave them a blank smile.

"You just got here, didn't you?" Antonio rolled his eyes with a smile and waved his hand to show off his ring. "The *one* thing I invite you to, and you're so late you missed my proposal."

"Oh damn!" Phineas cried. "You two getting married? That's awesome! Congrats!"

"Thanks, Phin."

"No Signe today?" Lee asked. She'd been blatantly aiming for a threesome, but Phineas had seemed to genuinely like her, and frankly, a relationship might chill him out a bit.

Phineas's smile fell. "Nah, that's been over. I told you not to ruin it for me, man. One dinner with your eye candy ass, and suddenly I'm not enough for her. What else is new?"

"Sorry to hear that." Lee's heart went out to him at the forced cheer in his voice. For as awkward as Phineas could be, Lee liked him. Antonio may keep him at arm's length, but they both still cared about him.

"It is what it is, right?" Phineas shrugged. "You coming out tonight?"

Lee shook his head with a loud laugh. "No! I just got engaged. I'm going home!"

"Going out where?" Gabe asked, turning from his conversation with Richard and Antonio's stepdad.

"Gabe does *not* want to come," Lee said before Phineas could invite him. Hot Barber and Mo would probably look out for his most sensitive friend (assuming they were also going wherever Phineas would end up), but Gabe needed to come to their after-party so Antonio could ask him to be his best man.

Phineas seemed to think better of it. "Yeah, maybe it's best that he doesn't. Love you, Gabey, but that's not your scene these days."

"I thought you weren't going to meddle in Tara's love life anymore." Gabe teased, draping an arm around Lee's shoulders. "I'm pretty sure that counts as cockblocking."

Lee scoffed, holding Gabe's hand tight against his chest. "Please. That was for *your* own good. Tara's got nothing to do with it."

"Who's this Tara I keep hearing about?" Phineas asked.

A chorus of "none of your business" erupted. Lee was surprised Richard was as vehement as Gabe and Antonio.

Phineas's mouth hung open, hand pressed against his chest. "Et tu, Dicky?"

Richard's jaw clenched. "You'd be too good for each other in all the wrong ways. Trust me, you're welcome."

"Sounds hot." Phineas shrugged.

Lee bristled at the idea that Phineas would be too good for Tara in any capacity, but Richard had a point. Tara didn't need a workaholic who partied every weekend—she needed a boring homebody. *Damn, first Richard opens up to her about his parents, and now he can read her like that? My plan worked too well.*

RICHARD

FINALLY. RICHARD HURRIED DOWN the stairs in search of Sunny. He'd been worried Phineas would meet her without Richard there to run interference on his chronic flirting. But Phineas had come late and left early, as usual. Gabe and Tara were hauling boxes to Gabe's car. Antonio and Lee were caught up with Antonio's family. Hopefully, Blanche and Jazz wouldn't mind if Richard stole Sunny away.

He and Sunny planned on letting their friends in about their relationship, but they'd gotten as far as Gabe before the release party had turned into an engagement party. It was no longer an appropriate time to make any announcements of their own. Richard had spent a painful evening keeping his distance from her instead.

Rather than attend Antonio's after-party, Richard would strongly prefer to go home with Sunny, where it was quiet and the lights could be dimmed. Confession was not as overwhelming as Stormé's, but the loud music and flashing lights and press of people would be more tolerable after a few moments with her.

He spotted her on a barstool talking to a woman he didn't know, who was blatantly touching her arm as she leaned close to listen to Sunny. Her eyes were directed at Sunny's chest. Richard scoffed and shook his head.

Sunny spotted him and waved him over with a smile.

"Sunshine." He kissed her cheek as the woman leaned away with a disappointed look.

"There you are! I was just talking about my supply chain transparency app," Sunny greeted him cheerfully, oblivious to this woman's flirting as she always was. "This is my boyfriend, Richard."

The woman nodded, already looking around the room for someone else to flirt with.

"Pleasure." Richard did nothing to change the coldness of his expression. *Maybe it's a good thing I'm so bad at flirting. She would never have known I was interested if I'd managed to be subtle.* With a soft smile, he turned to Sunny. "Come and dance with me."

"Since when do you dance, Dicky?" Sunny asked skeptically. The woman was quickly forgotten as Sunny hopped off the barstool and held out her hand. "Or is this just an excuse to feel me up? Foreplay for another attempt at mild exhibitionism?"

"That wasn't my intention, but..." Richard shrugged as he led her to the dance floor. "For the record, I can dance. My mother had me in ballroom, ballet, and tap classes."

"So we're going to waltz to Britney?" Sunny teased, draping her arms over his shoulders.

"No, Sunshine, we are not going to waltz." He gripped her hips to pull her close, pressing his lips against her neck as they moved together to the beat. Richard lost himself breathing in her tangerine shampoo, the warm skin of her neck; Sunny was his favorite comfort zone.

"It was my intention."

"What?" Richard murmured against her neck, not understanding.

"Foreplay. Mild exhibitionism." Sunny reached into her bra and pressed a remote into his hand. "Take two."

Richard grinned, delighted at her squeak of surprise when he pressed the button. Muffling her gasp with a kiss, he led her toward the Confessionals. Just when he thought he had Sunny figured out, this woman kept surprising him. He never wanted her to stop.

Chapter Thirty-Eight

Blanche

"I still can't believe you've never heard of Carmen Sandiego!" Blanche teased, linking their arm with Jazz's as they left Confession via the alley. Jazz was worried the bouncers would see her and get in trouble, even though Blanche was sure they wouldn't care.

Jazz elbowed them. "Is this some '90s kid shit?"

"Ouch. You think I'm a '90s kid? Please, I'm an '80s baby through and through." Blanche laughed, accidentally letting out a snort.

Jazz's presence at their side all evening had brightened their mood. Even when things were awkward with Tara or Gabe, or when Antonio and Lee mooned over each other, or when Richard and Sunny made out on the dance floor, Blanche always had Jazz there, observing and teasing right along with them. Being Jazz's security blanket during her first foray into a gay bar had made the evening far more fun than it'd started out.

Jazz stopped in her tracks. "Did you hear that?"

Blanche listened. A rustle echoed from somewhere nearby. Slowly, they approached a dumpster in the mouth of the alley, waiting for another sound.

A meow, louder this time, echoed from inside the massive metal container.

Blanche opened the heavy lid and peered in, spotting a blanket-lined crate that didn't belong there. "Oh, you're in there, huh? Jazzy, give me a boost."

"You're going in the *dumpster*?!"

Blanche shrugged off their jacket. For the first time in months, that sour twist of their stomach eased. They had a purpose, someone who needed them. "Not the first time."

"That's so gross." Shaking her head, Jazz crouched down and wove her fingers together so Blanche could step into them. "I am not getting anywhere close to you tonight."

"Sometimes I forget how much you and your brother have in common. You pretend to be germaphobes, but you're really just snobby." Blanche laughed. "Maybe you should get in instead. It'll be good for your immune system."

"Not a chance in hell. You're *such* a good person, Blanche."

Blanche laughed at Jazz's shady tone as they climbed into the dumpster. Getting their footing on the garbage bags from Confession, they wobbled toward the back corner. With a click of their tongue, Blanche stuck a finger out over the crate.

Out climbed a scrawny orange kitten, maybe a couple of months old. It rubbed their dirty face against Blanche's finger. "Hello, precious kitten. Someone hoped you'd be found, huh? They should have put you *outside* the dumpster."

This filthy, underfed kitten had obviously been dumped there. Old enough to be away from Mama, but young enough to be innocent to the world. Just the kind of critter who tugged on Blanche's heart. Like Lee and Tara had been, when Blanche had found them in an alley not unlike this one.

"He's so cute!" Jazz said, peering over the edge of the dumpster.

"Did you just assume their gender?" Blanche teased, scooping up the kitten.

"Orange cats are usually male," Jazz declared. "At least according to the Internet."

"Well, if the Internet says so...*he's* coming to the after-party with us." Blanche teetered back across the garbage bags, kitten purring against their chest. "Come on, sweetie. Let's find you a home. If nothing else, I know an alley with lots of kibble until we find you some people."

They clambered out of the dumpster when their foot caught on the edge, and the lid slammed down on their ankle. Slipping from their foothold, Blanche curled protectively around the kitten as they tumbled out of the dumpster toward the concrete.

Jazz caught them around the waist before they hit the ground. "Shit, Blanche! You okay?"

Blanche nodded, heart racing from the fall. Jazz's brown eyes swam with worry as her arms encircled them. "I'm fine." They stood and brushed themself off, the kitten safely tucked under their arm. Ignoring the throb in their ankle, they smirked. "And you said you wouldn't get close to me."

Jazz smacked their arm. "It's a little different when you're about to smash your head on the pavement."

Draping their jacket over their shoulders, Blanche fell into step with her. "Thanks for saving me, Jazz."

Jazz linked her arm through theirs. "You're the one who crawled in the dumpster for a kitten. You're so...bold."

"I'm really not." Blanche snuggled the kitten against their chest. "I just... I need to be needed. And I think that's a problem."

"Is it?" Jazz asked with a teasing grin. "Uh oh."

Blanche nodded with a snort. "I... I have a consult with a therapist next month."

There. That was weird to say. It'd been one thing to email the contact that Gabe had texted them, to block the time out on their recording calendar that Tara was managing for them. It was another to voice it. Maybe they'd give it up right away, or maybe therapy would ruin the careful equilibrium they'd created for themself. But it was a step Blanche could no longer avoid.

"Oh, for real?" Her smile growing more serious, Jazz squeezed their hand. "That's great!"

"I hope it will be." They rested their head on her shoulder, ignoring the needle claws in their wrist as the kitten squirmed. It felt strange to admit that they might...need help. That they couldn't handle themself on their own. But frankly, Blanche had never handled anything on their own. They'd been stuck since long before Daisy's murder.

While they hadn't admitted that to anyone yet, not even Gabe, Blanche felt safe confiding in Jazz. Their ducklings would get their hopes up, and Blanche didn't want to disappoint them if they couldn't handle it. "It's terrifying, but I think it'll be good for me. I just... I make terrible decisions, and I need to be better."

"Blanche?"

"Yeah, Jazzy?"

"I love you, and I'm proud of you. But you smell like trash." Blanche laughed and stepped away, but Jazz caught their hand and tugged them closer. "Not that far away. Just not right in my nose."

Sunny

"So...when exactly did your arguments turn into a whole-ass relationship?" Gabe sat back in the armchair, staring at Richard's hand holding Sunny's on the love seat between them.

Sunny looked at Richard, curious how he'd answer the question. Or if he'd tell Gabe to stuff it with Lee and Antonio in the kitchen, having a quiet moment while they waited for Jazz and Blanche. Their apartment was decorated for the engagement party, with wedding bells and a Groom and Groom sign on the wall. With all of the decor from the album release party, their apartment looked ready to host dozens more than merely six friends.

"Please hold all questions for later," Richard muttered. "Antonio and Lee don't know yet, and their engagement party isn't the time to say anything."

Gabe shook his head in disbelief. "You're holding hands, dude. You hate touchy shit."

Glaring at Gabe, Richard squeezed Sunny's hand, as if worried she was about to pull away. "I don't mind touching people. I hate being touched, and you're *so* touchy. There's a difference."

A knock sounded on the door to the apartment. "You're late!" came Lee's voice seconds later. "Oh my god, what is that smell?"

"What happened to hello?" Blanche teased.

Jazz laughed. "Yeah, Lee, unclench! So what if Blanche smells like trash?"

A loud meow sounded from the kitchen. Sunny perked up, looking around to see who was watching a cat video. Instead, Blanche and Jazz entered, Lee and Antonio close behind them. Blanche wordlessly presented an orange kitten to her; Sunny squealed and brought it to her chest.

"A cat! Oh, what a sweetheart!" Sunny rubbed the top of his head with a finger. "Dicky, look, isn't he precious?"

Richard rubbed the kitten behind the ears. "How do you know it's a he?"

"Most orange cats are male," Sunny explained.

Jazz elbowed Blanche. "Told you."

Blanche elbowed her back. "I never doubted you."

"I wish I could keep him!" Sunny pouted. "Mae would never let me keep a cat."

"You could keep him at my place," Richard suggested.

"Are you serious?" Sunny whirled to face him, her jaw dropping in an exuberant smile.

Richard blushed as he noticed everyone in the room watching them. "I've been meaning to ask if you wanted to get a cat anyway. It's convenient timing."

"Dicky, you're so sweet!" Sunny kissed his cheek, taking care not to squish the kitten. She was so excited that crushing it was a real possibility.

"Hold on," Antonio cut in. "What is going on here? Are you two," he pointed between Richard and Sunny, "like fucking and shit?"

Sunny waved her hand as if it was old news. "Oh yeah, we've been 'fucking and shit' for ages now. We figured we'd let you keep going with your little plan until you caught us."

"And knowing you, you'd never catch on," Richard smirked.

"Babe, it worked!" Antonio turned to Lee, ignoring Richard's dig.

"Don't get too excited, we've been talking since before your little scheme began." Richard scowled. "We weren't trying to announce anything at your engagement party, but now there's a cat, you see. Priorities shifted."

"That long?" Gabe asked Richard, affronted. "And you never told me? But *she* found out before I did?" He jerked a thumb toward Tara. "Like I figured you were seeing someone, but you could have told me it was *Sunny!*"

"Like you're one to talk. You totally knew Lee and Tonio were engaged already." Tara shot back, crossing her arms.

Lee rolled his eyes. "Buttercup, you helped me buy the ring."

Gabe raised an eyebrow. "You helped buy the ring? And you pretended you didn't know?"

"Lee said to keep it a secret." Tara looked hard at the floor, avoiding everyone's gazes.

"Am I the only one who didn't know about the engagement?" Blanche asked, frustration palpable in their voice.

Sunny shrugged. "Richard told me ages ago."

"Dicky!" Antonio scolded.

Jazz patted Blanche's arm. "If it helps, I didn't know either."

Lee pushed his glasses up. "Sorry—"

Antonio cut Lee off. "Don't blame Lee for not telling you. It was supposed to stay secret until today. I'm just terrible at keeping my own secrets—which is why I usually don't have any. I didn't even tell my family."

"Oh, your whole family knew." Lee smiled sheepishly. "I asked for your parents' blessing before I proposed. And you know how your parents gossip."

"Angel!" Antonio covered his mouth with one hand. His hazel eyes watered as he rose up on his tiptoes to kiss Lee's cheek. "You're just...wonderful. Old-fashioned, but wonderful."

The kitten meowed, cutting through the hubbub.

"Why don't we get you cleaned up, huh, baby?" Sunny cooed. "Can we wash him in your bathroom? He's a little stinky."

"Yeah, just no fucking. Because that's something people do in our bathroom apparently." Antonio shot a look at Tara while he wiped his eyes. A blush crept on her cheeks as Tara stared at the floor. "Though I'm relieved we don't have to keep you from fighting anymore."

WHEN SUNNY AND RICHARD rejoined everyone in the living room, the damp and deeply annoyed kitten was wrapped in a towel. "So, we might have a weirdo kitten," Sunny said, interrupting the conversation as she dried off the kitten's head. It looked even cuter when it was angry and wet. "We just spent way too long looking up pictures of cat junk, but I'm pretty sure she's female."

"We have to bring her to the vet to check for a microchip." Richard scratched the kitten's chin.

With a grin, Sunny teased, "But you hope she doesn't have one because you love her."

"Absolutely. She's already ours." Richard nodded far too seriously.

"So, what should we name her?" Sunny handed Richard her phone.

"Well, in addition to cat genitalia, I researched names. Some of the suggestions were very serious human names, or the last food you had, or how you met them." Richard took a photo of Sunny holding the cat, snapping his fingers to get the kitten to look at the camera.

"Holy shit." Gabe wore a stunned look of disbelief. "You're an Instagram boyfriend. *Sunny's* Instagram boyfriend."

"So are we naming her Dumpster or Trash?" Sunny joked, ignoring him and everyone else in the room looking at them. She decided they were looking at the cat, instead of analyzing their relationship like Gabe was, proving why Richard hadn't wanted to tell them in the first place. They'd get used to it eventually, but until then, Sunny would have to distract them.

"Please name her Dumpster," Jazz laughed, sitting between Blanche and Lee on the couch. "That's hilarious!"

Richard sighed. "As much as I don't want to name her Dumpster, Jazz is correct. That is hilarious. What other options do we have? Pamplemousse La Croix? Duchess Ekaterina of Meowchester?"

"What is wrong with you, Dicky?" Sunny laughed. "The last thing you drank was a La Croix? We were just at a bar."

Richard smirked. "You apparently have not heard of responsible driving."

"You're so condescending." Sunny rubbed the kitten's chin. "Maybe Dumpster should be a nickname. What could we call her that starts with a D?"

"Richard Carter the Sixth," Richard said dryly. "Dicky Jr. My firstborn."

Sunny laughed again. "But what about your actual firstborn? Dumpster might live for twenty years, and then our kid would have the same name as our cat."

"What, are we going to name our future child Dumpster?" Richard teased.

Sunny pretended not to see Lee and Gabe's poorly hidden silent conversation of their shared shock that they were talking about kids. "You know what I mean, Dicky. Don't pretend you have a sense of humor."

Richard shook his head, determinedly ignoring everyone else in the room. "No, I've spent my whole life living up to the name I hoped would make my parents proud. I wouldn't put that on anyone, especially our kids. But I'm pretty sure this cat will be a better Richard Carter than any of the first five have been."

Sunny smiled at him softly before announcing proudly, "Richard Carter the Sixth it is. AKA Dumpster." She held the kitten out like Simba. The kitten meowed. "Although," she drew Dumpster back to her chest, "maybe don't tell your parents her full name."

Richard laughed. "Agreed. They couldn't handle *me* taking my name, let alone finding out I gave it to a cat. You just got a taste of how bad they can be."

"What the fuck? She met your parents?" Gabe asked. "Talking about kids is one thing, but you introduced her to Dick and Barbie?!"

"Not by choice." Richard shrugged. "They were at the MAI fundraiser. I had intended to introduce her to your parents. It was only fair after I met her family."

"Oh god, he met Birdie?" Lee groaned. "That must have been a disaster."

Sunny protested, "That was *not* fair, Dicky. My mom made you eat spicy food. Your dad called me a diversity hire with nice tits."

"Was that before or after you told his brother to blow you?" Tara jumped in with a teasing grin.

"You told her about that?" Sunny asked, shooting Richard a betrayed look. In hindsight, not her finest moment, but it was a pretty sick comeback. "You stole my thunder! I wanted to tell that story!"

Richard shrugged. "She asked."

"This is so weirdly reassuring," Lee said to no one in particular. "I knew I was right." At Tara's warning look, he added, "Not that it's an excuse! No more interference!"

Gabe shot Richard another confused look. "Since when do you and Tara talk?"

"Gabe, that's enough." Richard shot him a pointed look. "I'm sorry for hiding it from you, but please hold all questions and existential crises for later. Preferably not in front of everyone. We're not lab rats." He gestured at everyone else in the room. "That goes for all of you, too. Stop looking at us so hard. And you wonder why we kept this a secret, it's because you're so nosy."

"But his reaction is so validating," Blanche teased, more directed at Gabe than them, thankfully. "I might not have known about the damn engagement, but at least I'm in the loop about this."

"Speaking of the engagement, may I have your attention since Dicky doesn't want it?" Still in his gown, Antonio flounced into the room, gift bags hanging on his arms. He handed them out as he spoke. "Lee and I cordially invite you all to be in our wedding party! Our wedding is a year from now at Confession, of course."

Sunny pulled out a Save the Date with a photo of Lee and Antonio kissing, showing their rings to the camera, and a black satin sash that read Groomswoman. "How did you get these printed already, and your venue booked, when you literally just got engaged today?" she asked, waving the invite. The kitten in her lap tried to bite it.

"I like planning things, and we wanted to get the venue at Confession booked for the weekend after Pride before someone else got it." Lee bent down and pulled a three-ring binder from under the couch with *Wedding Plans* emblazoned on the front. He beamed in pride as he showed off the many vision boards and checklists. "Tara did all the work on the Save the Dates. A part of my soul died giving my ring back after the photo shoot, though."

"The boudoir shoot!" Gabe scoffed. "I should have known you knew!"

Tara grinned. "I am still surprised you fell for that, dude."

Grinning, Blanche held up a sash with Officiant printed on it. "You want me to marry you?"

Lee nodded. "Yes—if you want to, of course. Chas offered, but it wouldn't be the same without you doing it. She was pissed, but we asked her to emcee the reception as a compromise. Like, yeah, she introduced us, but she's not *you*."

"Freddy said there wasn't a dry eye in the house when you officiated his and Chas's wedding." Sliding his hands over Lee's shoulders, Antonio pressed a kiss to the top of his fiancé's head.

"Jesus, even Chas and Freddy knew before me?" Blanche pouted.

"Sorry. We had to tell Chas when we reserved the venue. And I'm assuming *someone* roped Freddy in on his proposal," Lee accused, but there was too much love in his eyes to have any heat. "That song wasn't on the setlist."

Antonio kissed his forehead. "Sorry, not sorry."

"Oh, I am going to tell so many great stories." Blanche's smile turned wicked.

"Does 'Best Man' mean I get to plan the bachelor party?" Gabe held his sash up.

"Maybe *one* of them." Tara held up her own "Best Man" sash. "It looks like I get to plan the other. And it's going to put *yours* to shame."

"You wish! I'm thinking—"

"Actually!" Antonio interrupted before they could argue. "You can plan our combined bachelor party together! Oh, and *please* help us plan the wedding itself. I have so many ideas, and I need you to tell me if I'm being too extra."

"And, I need my Buttercup to make executive decisions for me. So we need you to get along. Not a scheme to force you to spend time together or anything, we just both need our codependent friends. Is that going to be a problem?" Lee asked Tara.

"No, no problem at all. After all, we're friends, right?" Tara leaned over the arm of the couch to where Gabe sat in the chair nearby, her hand outstretched.

Gabe shook it. "Right. Friends. We can work together. No problem on my end." And kept shaking, their hands joined for far too long to be merely a friendly handshake.

Richard and Sunny exchanged a bemused look. She leaned against him, petting their new kitten, relieved that the spotlight had moved so quickly off of them. Their friends might find their relationship odd for a while, but they'd get used to it. A few months of prying eyes from their friends was nothing after they'd already won Mae over through sheer determination. Even if the Carters would never accept her, Richard was unofficially a Boonmee now, and no force on Earth could overcome that.

Saturday, July Eleventh

Epilogue

RICHARD

"Do the portions get bigger?" Sunny asked quietly, skeptically eyeing the minuscule servings of fried fish on her plate. Wearing a red dress that flattered her hourglass figure, she was gorgeous in the candlelight. The flickering glow danced across her visage. Shimmering with bronzer, Sunny had been sun-kissed to a deep gold after spending all afternoon walking around Lincoln Park and the Navy Pier, doing all the touristy things she'd insisted they do.

"No. It's a tasting menu," he murmured, fighting a smile as he sipped his wine. The sauvignon blanc was a little oaky for his tastes, but it paired well with the bite-sized cubes of trout that were supposed to be an artistic interpretation of fish sticks. The buttery wine played off the flaky moisture of the fish.

"But more food is coming, right?" Not bothering with a fork, Sunny popped the tiny piece of trout into her mouth. Her lips provided Richard with a distraction from staring at her cleavage in the off-shoulder neckline.

He nodded. The restaurant might have tiny portions of bougie foods, but there were over a dozen courses. "Yes. I promise you'll leave full. And if you don't, we'll stop wherever you want our way back to the hotel."

"I think this is my favorite pic from today." She showed him a selfie on her phone of the two of them in front of the Bean earlier; Richard had kissed her cheek because he hated how fake his smile looked in pictures.

He was about to agree when her phone buzzed and a message dipped across the screen. She grabbed it back before he could see it. With a grin, she typed a reply and put her phone away.

"Who was that?" Richard asked, wondering if she smiled like that when he texted her.

"Oh, that was my gamer friend wondering where I was. It's nice that he noticed I wasn't there. Black Hawk is usually the flaky one." She slid her hand into his, looking around to see if their next course was coming.

"Black Hawk?" Richard tensed, but it had nothing to do with her touch.

She cocked her head. "Yeah, my online BFF. We tell each other everything, basically."

"You told him what, that you were in Chicago?"

Sunny grinned. "I told him my boyfriend was taking me on a romantic getaway for the weekend. Why?"

Richard shrugged. "Safety reasons."

Sunny laughed. "Sure. Okay. Safety reasons. For the record, I have never told him where I live, my name, or any other personal information. He's the same way, even though we've been friends for almost a decade." She teasingly poked his hand. "I have some common sense."

"Well, that's reassuring," Richard murmured.

"Dicky, you're not jealous?" Sunny smirked.

"It's possible." He *had* been a little prickly until Sunny mentioned this friend's username, which couldn't be a mere coincidence. *It's probably better that I don't say anything. Lord knows what Sunny says about us. And it's good that Gabe is confiding in someone.* "I was annoyed that Dumpster let Luna cuddle her, when she barely lets me hold her."

The server set the next course on the table. It was technically a soup, but was merely a smear of tomato puree on a plate. An oversized crouton was set at an angle.

Sunny stifled her laugh as the server walked away. "Sometimes I forget how rich you are, Dicky. Dropping hundreds of dollars for *this* is next-level rich."

It was more like thousands. But she didn't need to know that. Most of it had gone to the nonprofit anyway. "I told you, you'll be full by the time we leave, but if you're not, we can go wherever you want. You deserve all of this and more. Especially after that disaster with my parents." Richard sipped his wine to wash the bitter memory away.

Sunny rolled her eyes. "Sure, I'm sure you tell that to everyone when you whisk them away on romantic weekend trips."

Richard shook his head. She really didn't get it. He must have done a terrible job explaining how special she was. "I've never brought anyone anywhere before. You're the first person I've ever cooked for or who has met my friends—or my parents, for that matter. The first I've said 'I love you' to."

Sunny was quiet. He searched for a reaction, noting only the brightness in her eyes. Finally, she smiled shyly. "Damn. You didn't even cook?"

Richard laughed. "Right. Red flags galore."

Sunny smirked. "Good thing red's my favorite color."

"I've been trying to be a better person for you." He paused, trying to remember what he'd rehearsed. "I wanted to apologize. For not speaking up when my parents were so cruel to you. For my brother harass—"

She held up a hand. "Dicky, you already apologized, and I already forgave you. I certainly don't need an itemized list. I was there," Sunny teased. "And I'm still here. Stop rehashing what went wrong because you're a perfectionist."

Richard sighed in frustration. He'd worked really hard to memorize his apology speech. But she was right. It wouldn't be productive and would probably be too rehearsed to be genuine. Actions would speak louder than words, so he reached into his pocket, pulling out a long jewelry box. He passed it to her across the table. "Fine. Even if you won't let me apologize, you should still have the gift that was supposed to go with the apology."

Sunny looked at him suspiciously.

"Don't worry. It's vintage," he deadpanned. "No one has been exploited in our lifetimes to make this. No promises about a few generations ago though."

Sunny made a face at him as she opened it. Inside were pearl earrings and a matching necklace. Her gaze flicked down to the pearls and back to him, the candlelight dancing in the reflection of her dark eyes.

"And she's speechless," Richard teased. "Should have started with the gift so I could say the apology."

She picked up her wine and downed it. Richard tensed before he caught himself; Sunny wouldn't throw it at him. He grounded himself with a hand on her knee under the table.

Her mouth opened and shut as if trying to find words.

"Is this a happy reaction?" Richard kept his tone teasing, but honestly, he'd never seen her like this. Her smile quivering, she nodded vehemently. "Good. It's not every day I give someone my grandmother's pearls." Richard took her hand across the table.

"Wait, this is a family heirloom?" Sunny finally got words out. "Are you sure you want to give this to *me*? That is much bigger than the bracelet!"

"It's not like I'm going to wear them," Richard said, before he admitted quietly, "I hope it's not too forward or presumptuous, but you're more important to me, more supportive of me, and more *everything* to me than anyone in the family I was born into." He paused. "That was part of my speech, by the way."

"Wow. Maybe I should have let you give the speech." Her smile was hesitant. "I don't know what to say, but I'm honored you think I'm worthy of a gift like this. Even if it means I have to be nice to Connor sometimes."

"I would *never* ask you to be nice to Connor. But I appreciate the sentiment." Richard let out a sigh of relief. After a lifetime of guarding everything he'd said, sharing things like that, even with Sunny, felt so vulnerable. "I would never want to come between you and your family either. Your mom and sister really care about you."

Sunny took out her gold hoop earrings. "And they care about you, too. Mae doesn't let many people in our circle, so you're stuck with us." She handed her earrings to him. "Now come on, take a good picture of me."

While Sunny adorned herself with the pearls his maternal grandmother had left him, Richard tucked her earrings into the jewelry box for safekeeping. Being a part of Sunny's family was an unexpected blessing. Birdie was hilarious, and Luna was a sweet kid; they were all obviously protective of each other. He already felt as much at home with Sunny's family as with Gabe and Antonio's. Certainly, more than he ever had with his own.

Richard politely snapped photos for her. He wasn't great at the whole "taking photos" thing. That was more of Gabe's skill than his. Even Antonio was better at it, even if he only took selfies. But Richard took photo after photo until Sunny was satisfied. She looked beautiful in every one, but she somehow always found a flaw that only she noticed.

"I want one for my desk at work," Richard said as he passed her back her phone.

Sunny smiled shyly. "You know, I'm starting to think all of that asshole talk was to just cover up the fact that you're a complete simp."

Richard merely smiled. She was right; he'd do anything for her.

Sunny

WHEN SUNNY STEPPED OUT of the bathroom, her breath caught in her throat. Richard was standing on the balcony of their hotel suite, framed by the open French doors. The streetlights reflecting off the river surrounded him with an ethereal glow. In his black suit with the champagne glass in hand, he looked like a model in a high fashion spread.

Somehow sensing her, he turned, giving her that adorable ghost of a smile that always made her heart skip a beat. Without a word between them, Sunny joined him on the balcony, tucking her hand into his as they stood looking at the river below. The cool breeze coming off the water made her shiver. The off-shoulder sleeves did nothing to warm her, even if the dress looked amazing.

"Cold, Sunshine?"

She nodded. "A little. Warm me up?" She'd let Richard be the perfect poised gentleman all evening. Dinner had been a dream; he'd been utterly charming and too sweet. It was time to mess his hair up.

Wrapping a warm hand around her elbow, he tugged her into the room, pressing Sunny against the French doors the second they clicked shut. Sunny sighed contentedly as Richard scraped his teeth down her neck and pinned her wrists together above her head with one hand. The glass chilled her bare arms.

"Wow, Dicky." Sunny gasped, trying to tease him for his eagerness. But she couldn't form words as he pinched her nipple through her dress. Pleasure made her brain short out.

Richard chuckled against her neck. "That's it? No quip? No snark? Is this dress cutting off the blood flow to your brain or something?"

"Yup," Sunny sighed. "Take it off."

Richard nipped her neck. "There's the sarcasm I was expecting."

"No sarcasm. Undress me." Sunny had been waiting for tonight since they'd arrived earlier that afternoon. She'd even prepared herself after dinner with a cute butt plug, leaving his favorite strap waiting on a towel in the bathroom. It wasn't the strap she liked, the one that always made him come when he fucked her, but it was Richard's favorite. He said it was because he could think clearly when he wore it, but it also happened to be the biggest one—not that she was complaining—and matched his skin tone perfectly. She was ready for him to fuck her within an inch of her life.

His hands gripping her hips, Richard turned her around, pressing her face first against French doors. Sunny couldn't keep the grin from her face as he unzipped her dress, kissing her neck. His lips traced down her back as the air cooled her exposed skin.

Tugging her bodice down, his hands cupped her tits as he sucked on her neck. Sunny groaned, arching against him. She relished in the press of him against her, the oud of his cologne, the firm chest and wiry shoulders holding her.

Richard sighed, his soft breath tickling her neck. "Don't make fun of me, but I'm going to hang up your dress before it wrinkles."

Sunny laughed. "Hang up your clothes too while you're at it. I don't want an interruption if you notice your pants are folded wrong later."

Richard snorted against her neck. "Don't move an inch, Sunshine."

"Wouldn't dream of it, Dicky." She let him undress her, stepping out of the dress and spreading her legs wide when he nudged them apart.

"Not an inch." He pinned her arms back up on the glass, leaving Sunny spread open and exposed. "That's cute." He tapped on the rose-shaped end of the plug between her cheeks. She bit her lip as it pressed inside her. "Is that for me?"

"No, it's for *us*."

He gave her ass a sharp slap before he walked away.

Naked but for the pearls he'd given her, the lace panties he'd bought for her, and the butt plug, Sunny waited. Hands pressed on the glass where he'd put them, she watched him move through the room in the reflection of the French doors. Her heartbeat thudded in her chest. His hair was still too neat; she'd have to fix that.

"Sunshine, what a lovely surprise," Richard said as he came out of the bathroom. She looked back over her shoulder. The sinew and muscles under his extensive tattoos were on full display. The strap hung heavy between his thighs, the harness emphasizing the muscles he worked so hard for. His square jaw softened into a crooked smile that made Sunny weak in the knees. "No wonder I couldn't find it when I was packing."

"I stole it," she teased as he massaged the globes of her ass. The thick strap nudged between them. She rolled her hips back against him, loving the attention he gave her.

Sunny turned around to make him feel good, too. Before she could touch him, however, his lips crashed against hers in hunger, pushing her back against the French doors with a clatter. Teeth sank into her lower lip before his tongue ran against it to soothe his bite.

A whine escaped her lips as she brought her hands into his hair, gripping it tightly to bring him closer to her, digging her nails into his scalp the way he liked. Kissing his soft lips was a dream.

She whined in frustration into Richard's mouth. Here he was, again, kissing the daylights out of her until she forgot how to breathe, when she was trying to get him off. Sunny broke the kiss and pushed against his chest, dropping to her knees in front of him.

"Sunshine." His voice had a warning edge to it.

She shivered. "Let me do this, Richard. I won't be able to focus until you've come at least once."

He didn't protest as she took him into her mouth, sucking the head of his strap as she looked up at those bright blue eyes of his. She ran her fingertips along the harness and between his legs to dip a finger into him, spreading the growing wetness there to his clit, rubbing slow circles in time with the bobbing of her head.

Richard bit his lip as she touched him, leaning on his elbow against the door, blue eyes staring down into hers. His hand tangled in her hair, pushing her farther down the strap. She took it as best she could, gagging a little around it, and pressing harder on his clit when she did. It only excited them both more.

"Fuck, Sunny." He bit his lip, his raspy voice ragged. "That's my girl. You're so fucking beautiful on your knees for me."

He must be close if he's talking like that. Richard could be so quiet, so stoic. Signs of his pleasure were hard to find. He might breathe harder, bite his lip, exhale sharply, his abs might flex. But hearing him say her name like that made Sunny whimper pitifully. She pressed a finger inside him as she choked and drooled on the strap, her thumb on his clit and the nails of her other hand scratching his hip and thigh.

Finally, his blue eyes wrenched shut as he shuddered, pulling her hair roughly as he barely caught himself from collapsing against the door.

The sting in her scalp was delicious. She gave him a moment to stop twitching before tentatively moving her thumb again.

"Stop, Sunshine." Richard was still leaning on his elbow against the door, eyes shut.

"I want to give you another one." Pouting, she pulled her hands away. The hand in her hair tugged her scalp until she rose. Sunny wiggled between him and the glass doors he still leaned against with his eyes closed. "Do you need a minute?" she teased, kissing his neck.

"Just committing that visual to memory," he replied. "No sarcasm."

She grinned as she nibbled on his earlobe. "Want to take this to the bed?"

He opened his eyes at that, smirking at her with his intense stare. "No. I want to fuck you against this door, tits against the glass where anyone could see us."

Sunny grinned at the idea that anyone might look into their room to see them, unlikely as it was based on the view of darkened office buildings from their balcony. "What happened to not sharing me?"

Richard smirked as he pinned her against the glass. "They can see you're mine." He kissed her neck, sucking hard enough that Sunny expected yet another hickey there the next time she looked in the mirror.

She loved the evidence his love left on her. When her throat was sore from deepthroating the strap. When her ass cheeks were red from him spanking her. When she had to wear foundation down her neck and chest to hide the teeth marks from how hard he loved her. "Richard, please."

Richard responded to her begging by roughly turning her around and pushing her against the door. Her nipples, already hard from desire, tightened further as he pressed her into the glass. His full lips sucked down her neck, followed by his teeth sinking into her shoulder.

Sunny closed her eyes, luxuriating in the exquisite sensations of his mouth on her skin, the strap nudging her ass, his hands gripping bruises into her hips, and his chest hot against her back. Pressed against the door, she rolled her hips back against him.

"Keep your hands there, Sunshine." Those words tickled as he whispered huskily against the shell of her ear.

She groaned as Richard cupped her clit. He knew exactly what she needed, where to press down, when to add pressure, almost as well as she did. The butt plug was eased out of her, replaced with the blunt tip of the strap, cold with lube. As he pushed slowly into her, Sunny couldn't help a happy sigh, delighting in the stretch, the fullness of him.

A squeak left her throat as he brushed against her prostate.

"You good, Sunshine?" That husky voice asked in her ear.

Madly in love, and ready for you to destroy me. "Fucking peachy. No sarcasm."

"Good girl."

She should probably find his "good girl" infantilizing, condescending. Any other time, she might have. But now? Sunny preened, proud of herself for being so prepared for him, for making him happy. She was so close already, and he was barely fucking her yet.

Rolling his hips, Richard worked up to a punishing pace, slamming into her hard and fast as she gasped and moaned against the doors. The fog from their breath misted on the glass as he fucked her roughly, the way she liked. Standing with her legs spread so wide, with this thicker, longer strap, made him hit spots on her Sunny didn't even know she had.

She wouldn't last long. Already, just a couple moments in, pleasure coiled in the base of her spine. Tension built in her legs, growing desperate as Richard massaged her clit. The strap was stroking her prostate with every thrust.

"I'm close," Sunny warned, her voice rising an octave as she tried to form words beyond his name. "You feel amazing."

"Don't come yet, Sunshine." Richard exhaled into her neck, fingernails digging in her hip. "Only come if you're going to scream."

Sunny huffed out a laugh. "You want a noise complaint? I've already been loud."

"Be louder."

Sunny smiled, teeth digging into her lip. She would be good and hold it in until she couldn't anymore. But being told not to come made it impossible not to, made her orgasm build painfully throughout her whole body. Her legs cramped, her back sore from the pleasure coiling within it. Her nipples ached against cold glass.

His teeth sank into the crux where her neck met her shoulder. The sharp pinch in such a sensitive spot tore a primal scream from her throat. She couldn't form words, not even his name, as he roughly fucked her, stroking oh so perfectly with every thrust. Hand pressed on her clit, teeth in her neck, white-hot pleasure erupted all over her body and out her mouth.

Richard caught her as she collapsed, holding her upright against the door. She shuddered uncontrollably in his arms until she caught her breath. His fingers twined through hers, gripping her hand firmly to pull them away from the glass to hug herself, surrounded by his arms. "Come to bed, Sunshine."

She wordlessly followed as he directed her to the soft bedding, where he'd already pulled back the duvet. In the wake of her orgasm, her brain had stopped working. She was a puddle. She couldn't speak. She couldn't think.

Richard kissed her as he pulled her panties off. "I'll be right back."

Before she could process where he might have gone, he was wiping her down with a warm damp washcloth. Starting at her neck, he tended to the bitemarks and hickeys, before working down to wipe the sticky lube away.

Sunny smiled as her brain slowly came back online. Richard always took such good care of her. Overcome with affection, she watched as he tidied up the evidence of their lovemaking around the room and got them both ready for bed.

Then he was tucking himself into bed around her. Handing her a glass of champagne, he clinked it against his own. "To you, Sunshine. Great scream."

Sunny laughed. "Couldn't have done it without you."

Behind his glasses, his blue eyes sparkled with warmth and love.

"You know you're a dream?" She ran a hand through his hair, pushing the blond forelock out of his eyes, only to muss it with her nails as she gently scratched his scalp. "I figured this would be over once my mom found us. Or after that disaster with your parents."

Richard smiled at her, blond hair ruffled adorably. "Sunshine, the only thing that could take me away from you is you telling me to go."

"And that's not happening." She sipped her champagne. Sunny believed him, now. After everything. This had never been a mere one-sided crush or an ill-fated fling; Richard saw her, understood her, loved her. More than she ever imagined possible. "Does this mean you've been a fucking simp this whole time? And I just never noticed?"

Richard pressed a kiss into her neck as he held her close. "I thought that was obvious."

Acknowledgements

Acknowledgements are so hard to write; I could probably list dozens of people who have shaped this book and still never reach everyone who deserves credit!

First, I want to thank the team of amazing people who helped make this book a reality: my editor, Mikko Lahna at Quick Fox Editors, for being such a huge cheerleader for Sunny and Richard's story. I'm so glad we had such a comforting story when the world went to shittier. Also my cover designer, Marta Susic, for going back and forth with me forever trying to get Richard's smirk exactly right. And all of the sensitivity readers who helped me ground this story and cast in reality.

Second, I want to thank the community of bookish friends I've made since starting this journey. Writing can be a very lonely hobby/career, but the writing, indie author, and queer romance communities makes me feel like I'm part of something bigger than just my writing desk. Keep being lovely, irrepressible, and sometimes dramatic!

Third, an undying shoutout to my friends: Kirsten, who was the first person to read this book and who went so feral for Richard, it gave me confidence to dig deeper to bring out the terse yet delightful awkwardness of him, and, Amanda and Katie who give me their two cents whenever I need some validation and an objective opinion.

And finally, a big thank you to my partner (and Richard's fellow January Capricorn) for giving me inspiration for all of Richard's snobbiest one-liners. I only wish I could have found a way to include "There's nothing worse than wearing Nike shoes with Adidas pants," because that is *totally* something Richard would say.

Also By Cozy

If you enjoyed this book (or if you didn't!), please kindly show your support by leaving a review and telling your friends about it. Honest reviews and word-of-mouth recommendations make it possible for indie authors to keep writing. Thank you!

Want to read more by Cozy? Check out their books at cozydubois.com

Confession Series
Book 1: _Loving Lee_
Book 2: _Love on the Sunny Side_
Book 3: _Tempting Tara_
Book 4: _Carte Blanche_
Epilogue: _Finally Phineas_ coming soon!

Standalone Novels
Earthly Ties

Summer Weddings in Solberg
Petty Roots
Familiar Faces

Long Nights and Bright Futures
Glimmer in the Dark
Dancing in the Snow coming November 2026

Sleighbell Springs
For Luck's Sake
Happy (Endings) for the Holidays coming December 2026
Searching for Starlight coming November 2027
More Happy (Endings) for the Holidays coming December 2027

Short Stories
"Dad, Are You..." — part of *Bi All Accounts: Volume 1.*

About the Author

Cozy DuBois (they/them) thought writing fiction was a long-lost hobby. A longtime lover of romance novels, Cozy has renewed their love for writing by telling stories for and about LGBTQ+ people. They hope to bring more books into the world that represent the complex and entangled relationships between friends, lovers, and chosen family found in the queer community they love.

Based in Minneapolis, they enjoy life with their partner, two hound dogs, a regal queen of a cat, dozens of houseplants, and a garden that has seen better days. Find them with a beverage in hand on a patio anytime the temp is above freezing or planning their next vacation when it's not.

Connect with Cozy on social media or via email updates at cozydubois.com for announcements about upcoming releases.